# THE CITY OF
# FADING LIGHT

D1495550

# JON CLEARY

THE CITY OF FADING LIGHT

A Critic's Choice paperback
from Lorevan Publishing, Inc.
New York, New York

Reprinted by arrangement with William Morrow & Co., Inc.

ISBN: 1-55547-271-0

First Critic's Choice edition: 1988

From LOREVAN PUBLISHING, INC.

Critic's Choice Paperbacks
31 E. 28th St.
New York, New York 10016

Manufactured in the United States of America

*To George Greenfield*

Life, as Mistinguett said, for once trying to take attention away from her famous legs, is a music-hall. And history, like truth, is a juggler's ball. It has been tossed this way and that by historians, politicians, generals and other assorted entertainers. Since this book is fiction, I have ventured to join the music-hall act.

The first major plot against Hitler took place in the summer of 1938; I have tossed it into the summer of 1939 and used my own characters.

By coincidence the missing sections of Dr Joseph Goebbels' published diaries are those covering the period of this story. I have supplied them from my own imagination, an illusionist's trick.

I can only hope that the reader in the stalls does not think my dexterity and deception is too clumsy. Please take your seat in the music-hall that was Berlin in August–September 1939 . . .

# CHAPTER ONE

## 1

'I am always puzzled,' said Dr Goebbels, 'which part of you is Irish and which is American. Are you sure there is no German in you? You speak our language so well.'

'Not really, Herr Reichsminister. But I grew up in Yorkville, the German section of Manhattan. I picked it up from the other kids. Then, since I've been working on this picture, I've had a dialogue coach.'

Cathleen O'Dea was a good actress: she disguised the fact that she was telling less than the truth.

'There is a very strong Bund in Yorkville. All good Germans.' Goebbels, too, could act: he made an expatriate group of Nazis sound like latter-day Pilgrims.

Cathleen had been at ease with most men ever since she had become aware of their interest in her; their admiration had never gone to her head but only into her bank of confidence. Joseph Goebbels, however, made her feel she was walking on thin ice, that beneath the veneer of casual conversation there was a deep black lake into which she had to avoid falling. He was smiling, his dark watchful eyes focused on her as if they were alone and not surrounded by his bodyguards and all the studio crew and executives. He had charm, of a sort, but she knew too much about him to be taken in by it. She had spent six years in Hollywood, where charm was a manufactured product; any girl who had been stroked, even if only on a film set, by Clark Gable and Robert Taylor was not about to fall on her back for a Nazi lecher. Her mother, an enemy of both Nazis and lechers, would not have approved.

The Reichsminister for Public Enlightenment and Propaganda was a notorious stud ram, the Ram of Babelsberg: there was no lying propaganda about that. Cathleen had been told, by someone who had professed to have the exact figures, that Dr Goebbels had bedded no less than 38 actresses from the UFA film studios at Neubabelsberg; there was no count on the number of actresses from the legitimate theatre whom he had serviced, though, being legitimate, they may have been harder to seduce. He was short, plain almost to the point of ugliness, and had a club foot: he was, in short, a most unlikely Don Juan. And now, Cathleen realized with queasy qualm, he was pursuing her.

'Do you like your role in the film?'

'It is a good part for an actress. I wouldn't like to have been her in real life.'

'Why not? Lola Montez had the world at her feet.' For a split moment he looked as if he wished he had chosen a better image; she noticed the almost imperceptible withdrawal of his right foot with its surgical boot. 'The Emperor Ludwig idolized her. Surely any woman would welcome an emperor who idolized her?'

She wondered if Hitler saw himself eventually as an emperor; if Goebbels wanted to be seen as the Crown Prince. Though people had told her that he would never be the Fuehrer's successor, that he would always be the outsider. 'Times have changed. There aren't any emperors any more.'

'King George of England is known as the Emperor of India.'

'I can't see Lola as being a piece on the side at Buckingham Palace.'

Goebbels laughed and his bodyguard and the UFA executives echoed him; Cathleen felt she had just uttered a Mae West witticism. But in the background she saw Melissa Hayes roll her eyes and behind her Helmut von Albern turned away in disgust at the cheap crack.

Shooting had stopped when the Reichsminister and his entourage had come on to the set. It was a set representing a wing in the Emperor's palace in 19th century Munich; Ludwig I, who had been the most flamboyant if not the maddest of Bavaria's monarchs, had built it in the style of Venice's Palazzo Pitti. The lath and plaster walls and ceilings towered

10

over everyone on the sound stage; carpenters rather than courtiers stood back in the shadows. Despite the workmen's overalls and the motley dress of the film crew, the set had a grandeur to it that impressed; the art director had let history go to his head. He had also been influenced by the fact that half an hour's drive away in Berlin similar monuments to a ruler's ego were being built. Though they, the boast went, were being built to last a thousand years and not, like this set, to be struck next week.

Goebbels lingered and Cathleen tried to keep up her part of the conversation. She knew it was banal, as bad as the dialogue she had been speaking for the past three months. *Lola und Ludwig* would never win an Oscar and she knew it would do nothing for her career; but she had not come to Germany to further her career. The picture was a big lavish production, sponsored by Goebbels himself as the minister responsible for films; it was the most expensive film so far produced in Germany, done in English and German, and aimed at the world market. Since the advent of the Nazi regime, German films had not done well in the foreign market and Goebbels, so rumour said, had taken it as a personal slight. He and Hitler were the two film enthusiasts amongst the Nazi hierarchy and both men considered themselves educated critics of what was good and bad in the cinema. It was no secret that Goebbels had great admiration for the Hollywood product, but the scriptwriters and the director on *Lola und Ludwig* had let him down badly, though so far he did not know that. It might have been better if they had forgotten Ludwig I and somehow linked Lola Montez with his mad grandson Ludwig II; that way some of the ludicrous dialogue might have sounded, if not believable, at least entertaining. Cathleen knew the picture was turning out to be a real turkey, a messy mix of second-rate Busby Berkeley and third-rate Ernst Lubitsch. What it needed, she had decided, was Laurel and Hardy: they might have succeeded in turning it into a comedy classic.

At last the Reichsminister decided he had to go. He had sensed that Cathleen was not flattered by his attention; his mouth had turned sullen and his dark eyes had lost their gleam of humour. He slapped his gloves against the palm of one hand, then pulled them on, despite the heat of the day; he was never seen in public without them and, though the image was ridiculous, he reminded Cathleen of the convent girls she had gone to school with; gloves had been an obligatory part of their uniform. Goebbels had once been a Catholic: if he had worn gloves as a schoolboy, that was all he had left of his religion.

'Goodbye, Fräulein O'Dea. We must meet again soon.'

The invitation was there, but she chose not to recognize it. He gave a curt little bow and was gone, his staff marching away after him like a pack of well-drilled guard dogs. They were all bigger than he and once he closed in behind him he was lost to view; he left no ghost of his presence. Small men should choose martial midgets as their entourage or, if they must have big men, be borne aloft on a ceremonial chair. But that, of course, would be too papal and, unlike Ludwig, he had no liking for things Italian. Except, of course, Machiavelli.

The studio executives breathed their collective sigh of relief and they, too, departed. Karl Braun, the director, came across to Cathleen. Plump, pink-faced and pretentious, given to gestures larger than his talents, he was everything that she despised in a director; it had taken all her control not to fight him from the very first day on the set. In Hollywood he might have held a job on the Republic or Monogram lots; here at UFA, which had once employed men such as Lubitsch and Lang, he was now one of the leading directors. Being a Nazi Party member of fifteen years' standing had its advantages.

'We may as well break for lunch, darling.' He always spoke English to her, in a thick guttural accent that made him sound as if he were speaking through a mouthful of porridge. 'The Minister, I think, has spoiled the mood for all of us.'

'Doesn't he always?' she said and walked away before Braun, a fawning Party man, could protest that he had meant something entirely different from what she had inferred.

She left the set, went out of the big dark stage into the bright hot sunlight and walked up towards the building that

12

housed the stars' and leading players' dressing-rooms. The UFA lot was the largest in Europe, but it did not match the size or the facilities of M-G-M in Culver City, where she had spent the last six years. Louis B. Mayer, who had sent for her and expressed his vitriolic disgust at her for wanting to go to Germany and had promised her that she would never work in Hollywood again, would have been pleased, if still not forgiving, to know that she missed all the advantages of the Culver City studios. For the first time she was a star, but she had done better as a contract supporting player on Mr Mayer's roster.

Fritz Till was setting out his lunch on a camera dolly as she passed him. He looked up and smiled at her, bowing a little without rising from his seat on the small wheeled platform; he always treated her with a courtesy that she found old-worldly and charming. He was the gaffer, the head electrician, and in terms of experience he was the oldest man on the lot. He had worked on *The Cabinet of Dr Caligari*, *Metropolis* and other classics of the German cinema and, a man of quiet but direct words, he had expressed to her his opinion of *Lola und Ludwig*. It tallied with her own.

'Fräulein O'Dea, we are fortunate to have so much sunshine. It has been a good summer.'

'Has it?' Always careful of what she said, she had occasionally discussed the international situation with him. 'What's the latest news?'

'The Italians are worried we are going to drag them into the war. Mussolini has sent Ciano up here again to talk to our leaders.' He had a harsh dry voice that he could use to sardonic effect. He was a big man with a big lugubrious face like that of an overfed bloodhound. The lunch he had laid out in front of him would have made three meals for Cathleen.

'No one here seems too worried.'

'The young ones don't know what the last war was like and the old ones have convenient memories – they don't want to lose their jobs. I spent three years on the Western Front and I remember every day of it.'

'Did you ever see Lewis Milestone's movie?' Back in

13

Hollywood she would have called it Lew Ayres' movie, but here one always called them directors' movies.

He nodded, looked more lugubrious, sounded more sardonic than ever. 'It was a film, that was all. Nothing like the real thing. Nothing ever could be.' He squinted up at the sun through fearsome eyebrows. 'Still, let's enjoy the sunshine while we have it. Maybe if our leaders keep talking, it'll soon be winter and then we'll be safe till next year.'

'You're a cynic, Fritz,' she said and was glad. Up ahead she saw Melissa, who was not a cynic but a new, untried friend and therefore less reliable. She left Fritz Till to his huge lunch of knackwurst, sauerkraut, potato salad, pumpernickel, two bottles of beer and several pieces of fruit. The inner man, if not the innermost, would be made happy.

Melissa held open the door for her and they went into the hallway off which the dressing-rooms were set. After the heat of the morning, first on an outdoor set, then on the brightly-lit indoor set, the air in here was cool but not refreshing. The smell of grease-paint, sweat-soaked costumes and exhausted bodies hung in the hallway and dressing-rooms and assaulted one like bad memories.

'That Goebbels man gives me the creeps,' said Melissa in a low voice. Doors were open along the hallway and one never knew whose ears were open for the wrong sort of opinions. 'I can't understand why you sucked up to him.'

'If you're going to make a career in pictures, honey, you better learn you can't thumb your nose at the boss.'

She had learned in Hollywood that men, and men only, ran the picture business. There was only one woman in Hollywood who had any power and she did not work in the business itself: she was Louella Parsons, the gossip columnist. There were, admittedly, Queens of the Silver Screen: Garbo, Shearer, Colbert; but their domains were only in the audiences' imagination. Men had the power in the real, matter-of-fact empires of the movie world: they controlled the money, owned the shares, owned, indeed, the cattle that were the queens and the stars and the contract players. Here in Germany the situation was the same; except that here, bigger than Mayer or Warner or Zanuck, there was a supreme emperor, kaiser, czar, call him what you liked. His name was Joseph Goebbels.

'In any case I wasn't sucking up to him. He knew it, even if you didn't.'

Cathleen led the way into her dressing-room. 'You want to have lunch with me? I can have it sent over from the commissary.'

Melissa hesitated, then nodded. 'That would be nice. I thought I was having lunch with Helmut, but he's gone off somewhere.'

'How's it coming along with him?' Cathleen took off her costume and put on a robe.

Melissa sighed, a sign that she had matured; she had not been a sigher when she had arrived in Germany four months ago. She had begun life as Alice Hayfield, but all through her adolescence she had lived in her own mind under a dozen *noms-de-théâtre*: she had been Claudette, Greta, Sybil, even Shirley; none of them, somehow, had seemed to go with Hayfield. At seventeen she had got a job with a provincial repertory company and a stage manager, with a flair for names and an eye for a nice piece of crumpet, had suggested Melissa Hayes; she had lost her given name and her virginity in the same week. For the next four years her new name had made little impression on anyone, not even the randy stage manager, who had moved on to another repertory company and other ambitious virgins. Then six months ago she had entered a competition run by an ultra-right-wing weekly that believed in Anglo-German friendship; first prize had been a contract with UFA and a part in *Lola und Ludwig*. She had won the contest and come to Germany determined to be the new Lilian Harvey, another English girl who had made good in German films. She had no politics, was naïve almost to the point of stupidity; she knew the Nazis were supposed to be nasty, but they had done nothing to her personally and she believed in live and let live. She had read the headlines of what Adolf Hitler was doing to Europe, but she had read nothing of the accompanying stories: too much education destroys illusion, though it was laziness and not cynical philosophy that had dictated her reading habits. She had only discovered the right-wing weekly and its contest because someone had told her it had an article on Repertory, the Breeding Ground for Stars. Lately she did not read even the headlines, since they were in German, but she had begun to listen to conversations, which are often more illuminating than newspaper talk, even if speculative. All she had listened to previously was gossip, but that is a notorious habit amongst actresses and is sometimes even educational.

'Sometimes I think Helmut doesn't give me a thought when he's not with me.' She looked in Cathleen's big mirror, as if to reassure herself of her own presence. She was pretty and would always be so; but she would never be beautiful, in the way that some pretty girls can become beautiful women in middle age. She was blonde, blue-eyed and wet-lipped and Helmut's camera liked her, even if he didn't. 'It's a terrible bore, being in love. I thought it would be thrilling, but it's boring.'

'Not when the man's in love with you, too.' Cathleen had been in love three times and each time the man had been in love with her; it had just been bad luck that the men had either been married or their careers had taken them away from her. She had been heartbroken for a week or two and philosophical ever since: one should not fall in love with actors, who can never give their undivided love. Not if they believe in themselves as actors, a faith that requires a good deal of self-love. 'Have you slept with him?'

'Four times.' She said it as if she would always keep count. Twenty times, thirty times: point scores in a game that she wanted to turn serious. 'But afterwards it's always as if he has something else on his mind.'

'That's the way it is with most men. They're never very interested or interesting once they've got the dirty water off their chest. Even the ones who truly love you.'

'How are things with you and your Aussie newspaperman? Does he sound as if he's in love with you?'

'Who knows? The only other Australian I ever knew was Errol Flynn and this one is nothing like him. I'm not sure whether he's a gentleman or just doesn't know how to approach a girl.' She did not really care how Sean Carmody

16

felt about her. She had not come to Germany looking for romance; it was the last thing she wanted, for it would only cause complications. But Sean was pleasant, if quiet, company, and having one regular man on hand kept the others at bay. It was not always true that there was safety in numbers. She smiled, put a hand on Melissa's. 'Don't get too upset about Helmut. If war breaks out, it'll be better for you to go home and fall in love with a nice Englishman.'

'Oh God, there can't be a war! Not now, when I've just got started!'

Cathleen was not put out by Melissa's tiny, selfish outlook. She remembered she had been just like that herself when she had first gone to Hollywood. Hitler had just been made Chancellor of Germany; Zangara, a fanatic, had tried to assassinate Roosevelt and instead had killed Mayor Cermak of Chicago; the Japanese were continuing their advance in Northern China: she had read the headlines but they had been only small print beside that on her M-G-M contract. Astigmatism and a sense of proportion just don't go together.

Then a waitress brought their lunch from the commissary, two snacks that Fritz Till probably would have overlooked as crumbs not worth picking up. When they had eaten, Melissa went along to her own dressing-room and Cathleen idly glanced at the mail on the dressing-table. All her personal mail, and there was not much of that, went to her apartment on Uhlandstrasse; fan mail, brought on by articles about her in the film magazines, was addressed to the studio and sent across by the studio's mail department. Some hate mail arrived, but she had learned to ignore that; even Hollywood had had its share of cranks. There was nothing cranky in today's dozen letters, except for one with no stamp or postmark: it had been delivered by hand.

She tore open the plain envelope on which her name had been written in block capitals. The note inside was written in the same block letters: WHAT DO YOU HAVE TO HIDE FROM THE ABWEHR? BE CAREFUL.

Her hand suddenly started shaking; the note fluttered to the floor. She felt a constriction in her chest, as if her heart had contracted; certainly her lungs did something, for she felt the breath hiss out of herself as from a balloon. She picked up the envelope: it was a German hand that had written her name on it. But of course: why should it be anyone else's? Because, she told herself no one in Germany knew who she really was. No one but her mother, and Mady Hoolahan had been missing for nine months.

She looked at herself in the big mirror, noticing at once that she had gone pale even under her screen make-up. She looked what she was supposed to be, a girl with an Irish father and an American mother: green eyes, dark red hair and, underneath the make-up, an alabaster complexion with just the faintest hint of freckles. Fan magazines had called her the Brooklyn Irish colleen, though she had set foot in Brooklyn no more than half a dozen times in her life. She had been considered a beauty even amongst the beauties of Hollywood; she had just lacked star quality and that had kept her down amongst the other contract players. She had been given the roles Maureen O'Sullivan had declined; or if Lionel Barrymore or Raymond Massey were to play an Irishman and needed a daughter, she got the part. She had played girls from Connemara, Cork, Boston and Brooklyn.

No one had ever known that she was half-Jewish, that Mady Hoolahan had been born in Berlin as Miriam Razman.

2

Sean Carmody came out of his apartment building on Ludwigstrasse, stood for a moment in the warm afternoon sunshine. This was a far different sun from that under which he had grown up; he had forgotten how that other sun could burn the hide off you if you were not careful. He welcomed any sort of sun; he knew he would never become accustomed to European winters. He had experienced three of them so far and he did not look forward to the prospect of another one. Yet he could not see himself going home to Australia, not while the world was falling apart on this side.

Over by the church of St Ludwig's, the *Leierkastenmann*, the hurdy-gurdy man, was playing another of his sad tunes. He had started coming by here early in the summer and his tunes then had been gay, the sort of music that brought people to their windows and children out into the street to drop pennies in the cup held out by his monkey. But now his music was sometimes dirge-like and though people still came to their windows it was to shake their heads and the children did not appear at all.

Carmody crossed the road to him, put some loose change in the monkey's cup; the monkey looked at him quizzically, as if expecting more. He did not like monkeys, their expressions too often were too human.

'Why do you not play something livelier?' Like most Australians he was not a good linguist; his German was stiff, almost stilted, and did not go with his easy-going manner. He had done a crash course with a teacher in the language when he had first gone to Vienna eighteen months ago; he could now carry on a conversation, but his drawl and his flat-vowelled accent played havoc with the language's portmanteau words. He could make *Magenschleimhautentzuendung* sound like a long low moan of pain. Which was close to onomatopoeia since it was the word for gastritis.

Kreisler, the hurdy-gurdy man, a small man with a lined face, grinned; he looked like a bigger brother of his monkey. 'Herr Carmody –' Carmody wondered how he knew his name, but didn't bother to ask. 'All our lively music sounds Bavarian and I'm afraid I am no longer a lover of Bavaria. Not that I ever really was. But our beloved leader seems to feel at home there.'

Since coming to Berlin Carmody had been surprised at the frankness of some of the natives. He knew they had always been considered, and considered themselves, as different from other Germans; with their sense of superiority, they had a liking for ridicule that all politicians, even back to Bismarck's day, had resented. Though the Nazis now controlled Berlin they had never won a majority in an election in the city. But elections, he had learned in Spain, Austria and Czechoslovakia, were not the only roads to power. Liberation had a new meaning: it was the alternative to democracy.

'Why don't you try some American music?' He tried to think of some gay Australian songs, but even *Waltzing Matilda* was about a suicide.

The grin widened, the lines increased in his face; even the monkey smiled. 'I'll bring some tomorrow.'

Now that he was on this side of the street, feeling that the church's steeple was leaning over him, either invitingly or threateningly, Carmody went into the church and said a prayer. He was only spasmodically religious, though he went to Mass every Sunday; but lately he had been praying regularly, for peace. Unlike most of his generation he had been in a war and had seen enough of it. War had made his name as a foreign correspondent, but he still did not like it.

He came out of the church, feeling pious if not hopeful, walked up to the Kurfürstendamm and caught a bus over to the Potsdamerplatz. His expense account ran to the luxury of taxis, but the habits of a poor boyhood remained and he did not believe in unnecessary extravagance. World Press, the American wire service that employed him, knew nothing of his concern for their finances and appreciated him less than he deserved.

He got out of the bus on the Potsdamerplatz and stood once again savouring the sunshine. He had heard Berliners boast that the city had its own quality of light and he had begun to believe them, though in memory's eye nothing equalled the light he had seen as a boy on the western plains of New South Wales. Here it was as if the energy of the people generated a reflection in the air that hung above the city: there was a glitter to it and the air itself sometimes felt as if it had been sprinkled with pepper. At night the city was the most brilliantly lit in all Europe.

He walked across the *Platz*, neatly dodging the traffic though he still had the slow ambling walk of a boy who had grown up in the bush, and stopped by one of the flower-sellers to buy a small bunch of carnations. Then he went on to the building where World Press rented two small rooms as the agency office and took the lift to the second floor. Fräulein Luxemburg was sorting the afternoon mail, but dropped the letters in a flurry as he handed her the flowers. It was a weekly ritual, one he had started after she had once casually re-marked that carnations were her favourite blooms, and though it gave them both pleasure it also embarrassed them. Neither the young man nor the plain middle-aged woman were accustomed to such a small social gesture.

'You are a gentleman, Herr Carmody.' Olga Luxemburg said the same thing every week, but meant it. Her English was good and she always spoke it in the office. She arranged the flowers in the vase that had been waiting for them, then took up the letters again. 'New York wants a thousand words on Count Ciano's visit to Herr Ribbentrop. They said to phone it through to London this evening on your six o'clock call and London can pass it on.'

'Is Ciano still down in Salzburg?' Fräulein Luxemburg nodded and Carmody swore under his breath. 'Doesn't New York ever look at the map? Salzburg is in Austria, it's not a suburb of Berlin.'

His secretary shook her faded blonde head at the ignorance of Americans. She had worked in this building for thirty years for a number of agencies and she was German enough to marvel at the shortcomings of foreigners. She knew Herr Carmody had many shortcomings, but she would never tell him so. She liked him too much and, in any event, she was sure that he was learning every day.

'Nothing's coming out of Salzburg. I'll go over and see what Dr Goebbels has to say. He's having a press conference this afternoon. A thousand words –' he muttered, shook his head just as Fräulein Luxemburg had done and went out of the office.

He walked over to the Leopold Palace, the headquarters of the Ministry of Propaganda. The Ministry was spread around town, occupying 22 houses it owned and another 23 that it rented: propaganda needed many voices. But the Minister's offices were in the Palace and if he was holding a press conference this afternoon that was where it would be held.

Carmody walked into the big ornate building, impressed as always; coming from a land where the only attempts at grandeur had been embarrassing imitations of mid-Victorian

21

Whitehall, he had to be stimulated by what he saw. Someone more sophisticated might have found the Palace a bad mixture of the past and the present. It had been built in 1737, converted once in the 1830s and converted again when the Nazis had come to power. The big reception rooms had been left untouched, but once beyond them and in the offices one was smack in the middle of today: all the heavy panelling and plush curtains had been removed and one might have been in a transatlantic liner, all art deco and bad taste. All that was missing was the movement of the ship.

As he crossed the main lobby Joe Begley, who worked for another wire service, fell in beside him. Begley, a balding thin man with bulging eyes and the longest chin Carmody had ever seen, was known as Trenchcoat Joe; summer and winter he always wore a rumpled trenchcoat, like Hollywood's idea of a foreign correspondent. But he was a good reporter and no one ever laughed at his despatches.

'The little guy is having his conference in his office today. He must be trying to impress us. You ever been in there?'

Carmody shook his head. 'I hope he's got something worthwhile to say. They've been far too cagey this past week.'

Another man joined them as they walked down the corridor behind the crowd of newspapermen being escorted to the Minister's office. Oliver Burberry, who should have worn a trenchcoat but instead always carried an umbrella, always unfurled as if ready for any sudden downpour, was the London *Times* man. Tall and heavily-built, handsome in a heavy way, he was not conceited yet carried an air of authoritative superiority about him. Some employers, like unwitting popes, can make bishops of those who work for them.

'My colleague in Moscow,' he said in his rich, port-wine voice; Carmody envied him his vowel sounds, 'writes me that rumours abound in the Kremlin.'

'Rumours always abound,' said Begley, who wrote a much flatter prose, 'but what the hell do they say?'

Burberry did not take offence; his episcopal air was partly self-mocking. 'That von der Schulenburg, the ambassador from this fair country, has been in and out of the Kremlin so

22

often in the past week that the guards no longer bother to check him. We –' he sometimes raised himself above episcopal rank into that of the royal plural '– we think our little friend inside may be making an announcement about it this afternoon.'

But they were to be disappointed. Goebbels, smiling broadly, a friend to the world's press, only wanted to make an announcement that the German film industry would be doubling its production schedule in the coming year. He hoped that would be further evidence that Germany was planning only for peace and not for war.

Carmody, against his will, once again found himself admiring the little man. He should have been lost in his huge office, made to look ridiculous by it; but he wasn't, he dominated the space and the trappings by sheer personality. There was an enormous desk, meticulously ordered and neat like the man himself; a portrait of Frederick the Great hung on a wall, an aesthetic eye looking almost benevolently at the commoner who now ran the arts of his country; tall windows let in sunlight between rich drapes. It all caught the eye on first entering the room, but in the end the eye had interest only in the man behind the desk.

'Herr Reichsminister,' said Burberry, 'would you care to comment on the events going on in Moscow at the moment?'

'What events are those, Herr Burberry?' Goebbels was undisturbed by the question. He drew back his sleeve, exposing another half-inch of cuff. The shirt, noted Carmody, a nondescript dresser himself, was the usual cream silk; Goebbels was known to change his shirts at least two or three times a day. He was said to have hundreds of suits and more pairs of gloves than a company of chauffeurs. A pair of gloves lay on the desk, looking out of place, almost untidy, in the ordered neatness of the wide top. '*The Times* is turning into a fantasy magazine.'

Only to accommodate your lies, thought Carmody; but left Burberry to answer the Minister. 'Is some sort of treaty to be arranged between Germany and Russia? A trade treaty perhaps?'

Bugger it! thought Carmody. Why give him an out? But it

had been *The Times'* habit to blow hot and cold over the Nazi government and Burberry had to play the game the way Printing House Square dictated.

Goebbels smiled again, though his eyes had no laughter in them. 'I think you should ask the Minister for Trade about that. Now isn't there someone who wants to ask me about our film plans?'

Carmody took a risk. He knew there was a file on him here in the Ministry and probably one with the Gestapo; it was no secret history that he had fought for the Loyalists in Spain and his despatches, once he had become a correspondent, had been frank and, he hoped, objective. 'Will you hope for the return of German stars from abroad? People like Marlene Dietrich and Conrad Veidt?'

It was difficult to imagine that a smile could disappear so quickly. But when Goebbels spoke there was no hint of anger. 'I doubt if there would be a place for them, Herr Carmody. We have our new stars. Fräulein Dietrich and Herr Veidt are *passé*, wouldn't you say?'

'They are still talented, Herr Reichsminister.' Why am I persisting with this? Carmody wondered. But the thought of Cathleen, out at Neubabelsberg, working for this smug little monster irritated him.

'Of course. If we have roles for older players that might suit them, I'm sure our producers will consider them. Next question, gentlemen?'

When the conference was over, Carmody was joined on his way out by Burberry. 'Why do you needle the little man so much, old chap? You spoiled it all for the rest of us.'

'I'm sorry, Oliver.' Burberry, a public school man, an old Etonian, always called him by his surname, but Carmody, brought up in the easy friendliness back home, thought it cold, formal and even a little rude. Oliver Burberry, on the other hand, had at first thought *him* far too friendly. 'I'm not naturally a trouble-maker. But he gets under my skin, he's such a hypocritical bloody liar.'

'You must learn, dear boy, that a thick skin is as necessary to us correspondents as it is to politicians. How else can we retain the objectivity our dear editors call for?'

'I'll try. I once had a thick skin, when I was a tar-boy in a shearing shed.'

'Don't tell me about it! It sounds obscene. A tar-boy!' He went off, opening his umbrella against the sun, striding along beneath it as under an episcopal baldachin.

Carmody went back to his office, wrote a thousand words that said nothing but which could be read as hopeful by the optimists and as despairing by pessimists, then phoned them through to London for cabling to New York. He had adopted this procedure over the past month to avoid any unofficial censorship at the cable office here in Berlin. It was remarkable the number of protectors of the Nazi good name who had appeared since talk of war had become so open. War, it seemed, was a decent subject only when it had broken out.

He left the office and, carrying his jacket over his arm, walked the couple of miles back to the Kurfürstendamm. The city had two main centres: that around the Unter den Linden and the Friedrichstrasse, with the government offices and foreign embassies on the Wilhelmstrasse and nearby; and that along the Kurfürstendamm, the bright mainstream of the newer Berlin, where the cafés and theatres flourished. He always enjoyed walking in the city: its citizens loved its trees and had preserved them, unlike the citizens of Sydney, the only big Australian city he had passed through. Everywhere one went in Berlin there was always a touch of green, like small reminders of the once-huge forests in which the Teutonic myths had begun. Berliners, the most cynical of Germans, still had inherited memories of gods who had dwelt in this land of great stands of trees.

Walking was his principal exercise. He occasionally went swimming and once a week he played tennis with Joe Begley and several other men; but he felt he was getting soft, he was no longer the hard-muscled youth he had been when shearing in the woolsheds with his father. Paddy Carmody, twenty-four years his senior and several inches shorter than him, could probably lick him in a couple of rounds and not even be short of breath. He grinned at the thought of his father who, with two beers under his belt, would have gone a round or two for a pound or two with the world.

He arrived on the Kurfürstendamm and turned into the Café Möhring, where he knew he would find Meg Arrowsmith. She was sitting at her usual table by one of the windows, lolling there with that quiet self-assurance, almost arrogance, that he had come to think of as the natural air of the English aristocracy. Though so far Lady Margaret Arrowsmith was the only aristocrat he had ever had tea with.

'Darling!'

She had a loud voice: another aristocratic habit, he presumed. She gave him her hand, as she always did, but he had none of the grace that, another presumption, her other admirers had; he did not kiss it but shook it and handed it back to her. He sat down opposite her, aware of the discreet stares of the others in the high-ceilinged restaurant. There were other more fashionable cafés, the Kranzler, the Romanische, the Trumpf, but Meg always came here for late tea before going on to whatever date she had for the evening. The Möhring's clientele was conservative, solidly-built men and women of solid money and position; Carmody sometimes wondered if she came here looking for an echo of what she had left behind in London. Though he had no idea what sort of life she had led in England or if the Marquis of Avalon, her father, was a solid man of wealth and position. He had read that some of the English aristocracy were as poor as church mice. Well, cathedral mice.

'Darling Sean –' She looked at him with affection. 'You are so unspoiled. Why didn't I meet you ten, fifteen years ago?'

At thirty-five she was seven years older than he and looked it; in another couple of years she would look ten or twelve years older than he. She was good-looking without being anywhere near beautiful; her main attraction was the liveliness of her small thin face. It was a face that showed the ravages of a hectic life; she had been a rebel all her life and now, too late, had come to realize she had rebelled against all the wrong things. Including the spirit of her own country. He felt sorry for her and that was part of her attraction; he had never been able to pass by a lame dog. He grinned, wondering what his mother, Ida, the drover's wife, would think of him if he fell in love with the daughter of an English marquis.

26

It would kill Paddy, his father, the Irish hater of all things Pommy.

'When are you going home, Meg?' His conversations with her often started so bluntly. It stopped her from the idle gossip that she loved and which bored him.

She looked out the window and for a moment he thought he saw her eyes glisten. 'Daddy telephoned this morning. He asked the same thing. You can both be so cruel.'

'That's not true.'

'Do your parents ever ask you why you don't come home?'

'They never understood why I came away in the first place.'

'Did politics take you to Spain?'

'I hadn't a clue what was going on there.' He marvelled now at his innocence of three years ago; he had been an ignorant newspaperman in those days, still blinkered by the parochialism of the country newspaper on which he had done his cadetship. 'I had wanderlust, something I'd inherited from my dad – he'd almost broken my mother's heart and I guess I did the same when I tossed up my job and went to the States. I spent a year there hobo-ing around. I washed dishes, sheared sheep in Nevada, wrote some pieces for the *Hobo News*. Then I caught a ship for Lisbon, walked up over the hills into Spain and there was a war just breaking out. I wrote some freelance pieces and some papers in London and back home picked them up. Then I joined the International Brigade – well, I sort of drifted into it. No,' he said reflectively, 'politics didn't take me to Spain. But politics brought me here to Germany.' He looked directly at her.

She looked away out of the window again. Politics had brought her here, too; but he saw her as naïve as he had once been. She truly believed that an alliance between Britain and Germany would be the saving of Europe, that nothing else could stem the tide of communism. She idolized Hitler, was on the fringe of his small social circle, had been one of Goebbels' many mistresses. She was intelligent and kind and gentle, except in her views about Jews, and she was a fascist through and through. Till he had come to Berlin he had never thought that he would be sitting down to friendly tea chats with someone who admired fascism so openly.

27

'I'll never be able to make you understand, will I?' She looked back at him.

He shook his head, waited till the waitress had placed in front of him a huge slice of strudel with a hillock of whipped cream and gone away. Cakes, not the persuasions of ideologies, would be his downfall; the Germans were getting at him through his stomach. He had put on seven pounds since coming to Berlin and he would have added more had he not done so much walking. War needed to break out to save him from his sweet tooth.

'I just hope you get out, Meg, before the roof falls in.'

'Darling, don't talk like that! Let's just talk of gay things –' Then she abruptly looked away again and said, softly and fiercely, 'War can't break out!'

He attacked his strudel, content to let the argument peter out. He would never convince her she was wrong: she had jumped off her cliff and there was no going back. But she did occasionally give him bits of gossip, some bitter, some sweeter even than the Möhring cakes. He had met her by accident four months ago in the Tiergarten, where she went every morning to walk her dog, and, recognizing her, he had cultivated her. It was only later he had come to like her and to feel sorry for her.

'General von Albern!'

She put up her hand and the tall elderly man, about to pass their table, stopped, bowed and kissed the hand. He was handsome, distinguished-looking and vaguely familiar to Carmody. He stood very straight, as if on a parade-ground, and the well-cut dark grey suit looked out of place on him: he should have been wearing a uniform.

Carmody stood up as Meg introduced him. He was of only medium height and von Albern topped him by five or six inches. The General looked down on him from an even greater height when Meg said he was a newspaperman.

'How interesting, Herr Carmody.' His English was good, if careful. 'You must find plenty to write about in Germany at the moment.'

'More than enough, Herr General.'

Von Albern nodded, kissed Meg's hand again, bowed his

head to Carmody and went on to a table at the rear of the big room, where a well-dressed woman waited for him.

'That's his mistress, Baroness von Sonntag. She's married unfortunately.' She did not like to see any hindrance, no matter how legal, stand in the way of love.

'Who's he? Somehow he looks familiar. Is he any relation to Helmut von Albern?' He had heard Cathleen O'Dea speak of her cameraman.

'His father. He was on the General Staff till about a year ago, then he suddenly retired, no reasons given, and went home to Hamburg. I gather he was not one of the Fuehrer's favourite generals.'

'Was the Fuehrer one of his favourites?'

She smiled. 'You don't trap me like that, darling. Finish your strudel and let's have no more argument.' She poured herself another cup of tea, Earl Grey's best: there were certain English things one could never turn one's back on. 'There are some whispers that Goering wants to fly to London to see if he can break the deadlock between us.'

'Can I write about them?' He always respected his sources' wishes: that way they remained his sources.

'Not yet, because nothing may come of it – he still has to get permission from the Fuehrer.' She never called him Hitler, always the Fuehrer. 'I'll let you know as soon as there's something definite.'

'Meg, what would happen to you if they knew you gave me all this information?'

She shrugged. 'I'd probably have a visit from the horrible Gestapo hoodlums.' She could be critical of some Nazi institutions. 'But I don't really care, darling. If I can do anything to prevent war between England and Germany, I'll do it. Would you care to come back to my flat and make love to me?'

She had often flirted with him, but had never been as direct as this before. For a moment he thought she was joking, then saw the lonely look in her eyes. He was embarrassed that he had to say no. 'I'm sorry, Meg. That would spoil our friendship.'

She rolled her eyes, laughed; but her eyes looked hurt. 'Oh

darling, you're so old-fashioned. But you're sweet – you'd never take advantage of a girl, would you? More's the pity.'

He felt inadequate and had a momentary urge to boast. There had been girls he had taken advantage of, as she put it: girls in Spain, in Vienna, here in Berlin. But they had all been girls who had come and gone in a night or two; and none of them had been a fascist, except in bed. Back home in Australia the one or two girls he had gone to bed with had been compliant, totally submissive; European women, or anyway the ones he had met, seemed to be different. He was losing his innocence abroad.

Meg appeared to have put him and his rebuff of her out of her mind. She was looking across the room at General von Albern and his companion. 'I wonder why he's come back to Berlin? He's supposed to have sworn he'd never set foot in the city again while the Fuehrer is still here.'

'Maybe the lure of the Baroness was too strong.'

She dismissed that with a wave of her hand. 'She doesn't live here. She's from Stuttgart. No, something else has brought him back.'

'Well, don't go telling your friends. Leave him and the Baroness in peace – they mightn't have much longer.'

She looked at him almost fiercely; then she shook her head, gathered up her handbag and gloves. She was always immaculately dressed, in the English style; she had told him, who knew nothing of such matters, that Berlin women were notoriously bad dressers and she hoped to set an example. 'Pay the bill, darling. And do leave a decent tip.'

When she had gone he sat a while carefully studying the General and the Baroness at their table in the rear of the room. He did not know how older lovers behaved when they met clandestinely; surely some of them must be more demonstrative than these two. They sat on opposite sides of the table, conversing with each other but not leaning forward as he would have expected lovers to do; there seemed no intimacy between them, just a constraint that might have been expected from an estranged husband and wife. Yet he was certain they had not quarrelled. Then he saw the General put a long arm across the table and take the Baroness' hand in his. They sat there in silence, staring at each other; but he was too far away to read the expressions in their faces. He had, however, seen enough faces in the past week to guess at what the General and the Baroness might be thinking. Many of the older Germans were afraid of another war.

He paid the bill, leaving a decent tip. His reputation as a poor tipper was spreading. Oliver Burberry, an expert in such matters, had told him that after women, who were the worst tippers of all, Australians came a close second. He would have to do something about improving the Australian image; but it would hurt. He hated giving money away for services that should have been paid for by the waitress' boss. He was still a union man, even if he no longer paid dues.

He went out into the street, started to walk towards Uhlandstrasse, where Cathleen had her apartment. It was a long ride out to the studio each morning but she preferred it to living in Neubabelsberg. As he walked along the Kurfür-stendamm he glanced at the passers-by. They did not look like people eager for war, even the younger ones; they were animated, but not excited. But what, he wondered, of the people in Munich, Frankfurt, Hamburg, Essen, Cologne? He was learning that Germany had more than one face, that it was a collection of leaderless palatinates, something Hitler had recognized.

3

*Extracts from the diaries of Dr Paul Joseph Goebbels:*

11 August 1939:
Goering is still persisting with his suggestion that he should fly secretly to England and confer with Chamberlain and his ministers. The Fuehrer is listening to him, but I hope reason will prevail. Would the English take the buffoon seriously? If anyone should be sent to negotiate peace, it should be I. Who else believes in the futility of war more than I do?

Out to Neubabelsberg today, where everything seems to be going well. I shall yet make our cinema the best in the world. We do not need the Jews and traitors who have fled to Hollywood.

Met Fräulein O'Dea 'again. Am attracted to her, much too much, I fear. She has legs that remind me of Lida's* – never thought I should see their equal. Never thought the Irish were noted for their legs. To be wrapped in Irish legs – what the English are missing!

A press conference, where I held sway as usual, despite the cheap remarks of the Australian, Carmody. What a pity he works for an American wire service, otherwise we could withdraw his permit. But we need every avenue to the American public, especially in these next few weeks. The news from Moscow is expected within the next week.

Then out to Schwanenwerder to see the children. How pleased I am to get them out of the city in the summer. What delight they give me! Spent an hour with them, the best hour of the day. Talked with Magda. Are all wives so difficult?

In the evening screened *Stagecoach*. The Americans do this sort of film so well: simple story, simple characters, simple-minded. I should screen it for Himmler and some of the others.

4

*Extracts from the memoirs of General Kurt von Albern:*

. . . I had gone with the Kaiser, as one of his junior aides, to the funeral in London of King Edward the Seventh. The Kaiser, as usual, was much too voluble, offering advice right, left and centre to anyone unfortunate enough to be within range. At the funeral

* Lida Baarova, Czech actress, with whom Goebbels had an affair in 1938.

service, however, the Kaiser was suitably quiet and suitably impressed. 'The English,' he said, 'do everything so well where pomp is necessary. Especially coronations and funerals.'

'They have had more experience,' said the Grand Duke of Mecklenburg-Strelitz.

'Of coronations perhaps,' said the Kaiser. 'But not of funerals.' Occasionally, though rarelv, he spoke sensibly.

. . . Few of us spoke, or even thought, sensibly in those days. But that, of course, is the hindsight of an old man. We believed, or said we did, in the divine right of kings; we believed in the efficacy of prayer; and, our biggest mistake, we believed in Bernhardi's theories of war.

I wonder now at the youthful mind that saw truth in Bernhardi's claim that 'war is a biological necessity', that nations must progress or decay and that, a natural progression from that latter thought, Germany must choose between world domination or its downfall. The duty to make war became almost a code of honour . . .

As I write this, the duty to make war is being sounded again, though in another hymn. The hymnmaster is mad, I am convinced of that . . .

It is foolish and self-defeating to long for a return to the past, but there were golden years, or so it seems, in my youth. Every summer my family would go down from Hamburg to Baden-Baden, but I preferred to stay in Berlin. That was before I had joined the staff of the Kaiser and was still with my regiment; one did not have to be so circumspect as later in palace circles, one did not have to feel as if one was in some sort of secular church. There in Berlin in those summers in the parks, in the cafés, at the dances in the grand houses, we young men drifted through a gentle storm of young girls. We dressed up, army blades in the splendid scabbards of our uniforms. We looked, I am sure, so much more splendid than the fat clown Goering in his musical comedy outfits; what enemy could be afraid of

33

a military man in powder blue! The girls, in memory, were all beautiful; the affairs discreet but satisfying; the future a golden road. But of course I was a career soldier and one dreamed of the glory of war, sometimes even in the arms of one of the lovely young girls . . .

. . . None of us was an intellectual. We did not read Fichte, Hegel, Nietzsche or Treitschke, who told us Germans that we were Supermen. If we read at all, we read Clausewitz and Schlieffen, but most of the time we exercised our minds not at all. Why is it that, with so many of us, wisdom comes too late?

How many of the Nazis will learn that lesson? . . .

# CHAPTER TWO

## 1

'Sean, there's nothing wrong with me, I tell you!' Cathleen knew she sounded shrill and she tried to compose herself. 'Please, honey – I'm just tired. I always am at the end of a picture –'

'How much longer have you to go?'

'Three weeks at the most, maybe less. I don't know. It's a lousy picture and I think the studio brass is getting worried Joe Goebbels might not like it. They may want to re-shoot some of the stuff.'

'Joe Goebbels, as you call him, has got other things on his mind – he's not going to be worried about a picture that's gone wrong.'

'You don't know him.'

'Do you?'

She smiled ruefully. 'No, but I think I'm going to. He's making a play for me.'

'Stone the crows!' He still had some of the expressions of his boyhood clinging to him like burrs. 'That's what's wrong with you. That would be enough to put anyone off their tucker.'

She smiled affectionately at him, thinking what a country boy he still was at heart. Yet she knew he had seen more and suffered more than she had so far; she knew, too, that he could be as shrewd in his opinions as his more sophisticated competitors amongst the newsmen gathered in Berlin. Europe might occasionally smile at him, but he, she guessed, might have the last laugh . . .

'. . . If there's anything left to laugh at.' Her thoughts, going off at a tangent, often broke into voice.

'What?'

'Nothing. You want your usual beer?'

35

She poured them both a drink at the glass-and-steel cabinet in a corner of the big room. The apartment belonged to a film director who was at present in South America and it reminded her of sets from early Joan Crawford movies, the Bauhaus gone Hollywood. There was glass and tubular steel and black leather everywhere; she never felt comfortable in it, surrounded by reflections of herself in the mirrored walls. Even an actress can have too much of herself.

She sipped her martini, found, too late to stop her tongue, that her mind had gone off at a tangent again. She would have to be careful in future. 'Do you have any contacts in the Abwehr?'

He choked into his beer. 'The *what*? Darl –' His mother and father had always called each other that, a diminution of *darling*; it was a measure of his feeling for Cathleen that he should call her the same. *Darling*, on his laconic tongue, would have been too effusive. 'Darl, what makes you think the German Secret Service would have anything to do with me?'

She said nothing, knowing the thought had been ludicrous. She flopped into a chair; the leather gasped beneath her like a flatulent old dog. She felt more depressed than at any time since arriving in Germany; and more afraid. She had got nowhere in her enquiries after her mother; inexperienced in such things, she had been afraid of being too open and had erred by being too cautious. But time was running out and she had become desperate.

'What's your interest in them?' said Carmody; then looked at her sharply, suddenly apprehensive. 'Or are they interested in you?'

'I don't know.' All at once she decided to take him into her confidence; her secret was eating away at her, weakening her. 'I got a note today at the studio, an anonymous one. It just asked what I had to hide from the Abwehr.'

'Do you have anything to hide?'

She took her time, gazing at him as if looking at him carefully for the first time. She had known him two months and up till now she had thought of him as no more than a pleasant companion, someone different from all the other men she had known. His looks were neither different nor outstanding; there was an ordinariness about him that she had found comforting. He was of medium height, had a solid build and broad shoulders; his features were even, though his jaw was a little long; his eyes were bright blue, but were already wrapped in a faint web of sun wrinkles. He had dark curly hair and beard shadow that showed dark late in the day. He had a relaxed air about him, but she had already learned that it was as imposed as much as natural: he did not believe there was anything to be gained by spontaneous excitement. She wondered if it was an Australian habit, a defence mechanism against the corruption of Europe. Whatever he was, a little gauche, a little suspicious of the world, a little afraid of women, he was not naïve nor untrustworthy. Most of all, if he was not the one, there was no one else to confide in.

'I'm here looking for my mother. She is Jewish, born right here in Berlin.'

He put down his glass. He did not like German beer compared to the brew back home; and he had not yet become a wine-lover. He showed no surprise at what she had told him; but that was a newspaperman's trick he had learned. He sat very still and for a moment she thought she had done the wrong thing: he did not want to be burdened with her worries.

Then he said quietly, 'If it'll help you to get it off your chest, tell me about it. I'm supposed to be a good listener.'

He was, she realized only now. He had listened to her gossip and her complaints about the studio without ever once looking bored, just sitting there quietly smiling and nodding as she had become excited about a particular item. He was not smiling now, but was serious and sympathetic.

'My real name is Miriam Hoolahan – I was named after my mother. My father was Irish – he was born in Galway, but was brought up in the States. He was an engineer and he came to Germany before the Great War to work in the shipyards at Kiel – he was on some sort of training course. He met my mother on a visit here to Berlin – her father was manager of a bank. They fell in love and were married a month after they met – my mother's parents were very much against it, but Mother was – is – a very strong-willed lady. She and Pop went back to the States and I was born there, in New York City.'

'Where's your father now?'

'He's dead. Pop went into business for himself after the war, but he lost everything in the Depression. He got drunk, he always could hit the bottle, and fell in the East River and was drowned. We never knew if it was suicide –' She stopped, drew a deep breath. She had loved Denis Hoolahan and even now, eight years after his death, she still missed him.

'My dad's Irish,' said Carmody.

'There's a melancholy streak in them when they're drunk.'

'I don't think my dad would ever commit suicide. If he did, he wouldn't choose any of the usual ways. He'd probably pick on a heavyweight Pom and hope to be pulped to death. He's only a little bloke and he hates England and the English.'

She smiled at the picture of his father; but she was in little mood for humour. 'After Pop died, Mother went to work in Gimbels – that's a department store,' she explained as he looked blank; even to her, New York now seemed a foreign city. She had lived too long in a make-believe world, first Hollywood and now Neubabelsberg. 'She wanted me to be a lawyer or a doctor – all Jewish mothers want their sons to be either of those, but Mother didn't have a son, so she nominated me. But she didn't complain – well, not much – when I said I wanted to go into the theatre. I started as a chorus girl – I've got good legs and I could dance a bit –' She drew up her skirt, showed him her legs. 'They were what got me to Hollywood, them and my red hair. I started out in a show called *George White's Scandals*, but I'd always had my eye on going to Hollywood. I'd changed my name – somehow Hoolahan didn't look right to be up in lights. I couldn't see people rushing to look at Clark Gable making love to Miriam Hoolahan. It was Mother who picked out my name. Cathleen O'Dea. Be Irish, she said, don't be half-and-half. And don't be Jewish. You want to go to Hollywood, you think they're looking for Jewish heroines out there?' She unconsciously imitated her mother's accent, was only aware of it when she

38

saw him smile. She returned his smile. 'Mother never lost her accent. Hollywood –' She mimicked the accent again. 'They want Jewish producers, Jewish directors, maybe even Jewish cameramen. But Jewish heroines? No, be Irish. So Irish I've been. Then an M-G-M talent scout spotted me and I went out to the Coast at a hundred and fifty bucks a week, a year's contract with an option. I thought I was made.'

'When was that?'

'Six years ago, 1933.'

Six years ago he had been working for four pounds, sixteen bucks, a week on the Coonabarabran *Chronicle* and thought he had had it made.

She shook her head at her dreams. 'I never really made it. There were dozens like me, contract players. Ruth Hussey, Mona Barrie, Rose Hobart – always in work but never in lights. My salary went up, but my name never did. Still, Mother and I had a good life out on the Coast. Then she started to worry about *her* mother here in Germany, when the Nazis started persecuting the Jews. She came back here in 1936 and tried to persuade Grandma to come to live with us in the States – Grandpa had died in 1932, before the Nazis came to power. But Grandma wouldn't move – she really believed the true Germans wouldn't tolerate the Nazis for long, that they would boot them out.' She shook her head at the naïveté of an old woman; but statesmen had believed the same. 'Mother kept writing to her, but Grandma wouldn't budge. Then early this year Mother came back again – Grandma was no longer answering our letters. Mother wrote to me to say that Grandma had disappeared – she'd been taken away one night and no one saw her again. Then I heard no more from Mother – I just kept getting my letters back marked *Address Unknown*.'

'Were you writing to her under your stage name? Maybe that's how the Abwehr got on to you?'

'Mother and I had worked out all that before she went. She addressed the letters to her own maiden name, Miriam Razman, and sent them to a box number in Santa Monica, one that belonged to a friend of hers. No, they couldn't have traced me that way.'

39

'What about your mother – have you traced her?'

She gestured dumbly, suddenly wanting to weep.

He reached across and took her hand. 'Have a good cry if you want to. No? Okay, where was she when you last heard of her?'

It took her a moment to recover, but she had held back the tears. She could be as emotional as any, but she had shed too many tears in the past months, she was almost dried out. 'She stayed at a hotel in Wilmersdorf, the Ernst. I rang there – I didn't dare go there – and they said she had checked out one morning, paid her bill, took her luggage and just went. That was the last week in January.'

'Where did your grandmother live?'

'In Wilmersdorf, not far from the Ernst. Kreugerstrasse, number 33 – she had an apartment there, a small one.'

He was still holding her hand, sitting awkwardly as he leaned forward; she leaned towards him, kissed him on the lips and pushed him back into his chair. All at once she was glad she had confided in him, knew he could be trusted and felt a little safer. He might not be able to help at all, but now she did not feel so alone in her search for her mother.

'What about the American embassy?' he said. 'Did you go there?'

'They were no help. I told them I was looking for my aunt, Mrs Mady Hoolahan – I didn't say she was my mother and I didn't say she was Jewish –'

'Why not?'

'I don't know. Once I arrived here, I couldn't bring myself to trust anyone, not even the Americans at the embassy – it was the atmosphere in Berlin, I guess. I told them my aunt was born here, that she wasn't naturalized, and then they seemed to lose interest. They made some routine enquiries or so they said, but they could have been looking for a lost dog or a suitcase. It was almost as if they didn't want to upset the Germans.'

'Some embassies are like that.'

'I've been here four months and I've learned nothing. I was too scared to go to the police – I just kept hoping I'd hear something by accident. I had the name of a man here – I got it from friends of Mother's in California, the same people who had the box number – this man, Wenck, helped Jews get out of Germany. I went to see him the second day I was here, but the neighbours said he'd gone away and left no word where he'd gone. Later I found out the Gestapo had taken him away, so I never went back.'

'There are still some Jews here in Berlin. I don't know how many or where they are, but Joe Begley tells me they're here.'

'So I believe, but if they know I'm looking for Mother, nobody has got in touch with me. Maybe they're too afraid for themselves.'

'You can't blame them –'

'I'm not!' Then she fell out of her chair at his feet, buried her face against his knees. 'I'm sorry, Sean – I didn't mean to snap like that –'

He stroked the beautiful dark red hair. 'Darl, I told you I'm a good listener – that includes listening to the snarly bits.' He pulled her head back gently, lifted her face and kissed the wet cheeks; it was the first time he had ever seen her weep and it touched him deeply. A slow smile spread across his face. 'I can't believe it. I'm in love with a film star.'

She had been afraid of this, afraid for him because she had not wanted to hurt him; but now she did not mind at all. There is a comfort to being loved so long as the lover is not a nuisance. He had not been that so far and she didn't think he would be one from now on. She felt suddenly comfortable with him, something she had never felt with any of her previous men, even those she had been in love with.

'Don't rush me, Sean. I like you – a lot – but I don't think I'm in the right frame of mind for coping with love –'

He was not certain that he could cope with it himself. He had deliberately avoided it when he had been working in Australia, always with his eye on more distant horizons than those around Coonabarabran. In America and here in Europe his life had been too full and peripatetic for any romances to blossom; there had been a girl in Vienna with whom he had been on the verge of falling in love, but he had moved on before the fatal step. Since coming here to Berlin he had been more settled; but it had been no more than a long

41

pause, the resignation of a man who knew that in spite of all that had gone before, the biggest storm of all was yet to break. Being in love might be a weakness and not a strength in facing what had to come. Especially now he had learned she could be in danger.

'Get changed and we'll go over to the Adlon for dinner.' A good meal sometimes settles the mind as well as the stomach.

'Don't throw your money around. You won't sleep.' She, too, knew his fear of extravagance. But she smiled, kissed him, lingeringly this time (gratitude or a promise? She wasn't sure herself) and went into the bedroom to change.

When they went downstairs the caretaker held out a box of red roses. 'These just came, Fräulein O'Dea, special messenger.' He was a little man with a little mind and a big eye, an ideal gossip. 'He was in a big Horch, a government car.'

Cathleen took the envelope from the box, but didn't open it. 'Take them up to my apartment, Herr Stumpf.'

In the taxi riding across town she said, 'He knows everyone's business in the building. He'd love to know who sent those roses.'

'So would I.' But he had already guessed and was uneasy.

She opened the envelope, took out the plain card. 'I am sure your performance will equal your beauty,' she read. 'It's signed J.G.'

'That's pretty gushing, isn't it?' But then he had never written a note or a card to a girl.

'No worse than some of the lines I've been saying in *Lola*. Or maybe Europeans are more poetic than you sheep-shearers from Down Under.'

It was a pity Banjo Paterson or Henry Lawson had never written love lyrics: The Man from Snowy River would never have got a girl into bed.

She was silent for the rest of the ride to the Adlon. When they got out of the taxi she crossed the pavement at once into the foyer of the hotel while he paid the taxi driver. Then he stood for a moment looking down the Unter den Linden. On the opposite side of the street men were working on the new IG Farben building, but even the construction work somehow did not jar in the general impression. The street fascin-

42

ated him, it had a glamour to it that no other street had for him, not even Fifth Avenue in New York or the Champs Élysées. The Nazis, for reasons of their own, had had some of the trees removed, but enough still remained to give the street its charm and character. Not all the trees were limes: there were maples, plane and chestnut trees as well; but they were all green balloons of summer, now catching the last light of day coming from behind the Brandenburg Gate. People promenaded up and down the broad path in the middle of the street, walking with the slow, almost measured tread of those who knew that, with time running out, an hour or two like this was to be retained and taken out of the memory as something to be treasured. And over it all, the street, the avenue of trees and the strolling, sober people was the marvellous Berlin light. There were lights in some of the windows and they only seemed to heighten the luminance in the sky. There was darkness on the underside of the trees, but the tops were touched with a green brilliance; it seemed to Carmody that he could almost count every leaf on the topmost branches. The light was lime-yellow, theatrical, and though he stood there for only a moment it seemed to him that it suddenly began to fade. More lights came on in the windows and as he turned into the Adlon he walked out of day into evening.

'You always do that,' said Cathleen, who realized only now that she had been observing him better than she knew. 'Stand and look up at the sky.'

'It's an old habit from back home. It usually tells you what tomorrow is going to be like.' But of course governments never took any notice of tomorrow unless it was an election day.

The dining room was full, but the hotel always kept a table or two marked with a *Reserved* sign to accommodate those whom it felt it could not refuse. Cathleen, being a film star, albeit a foreign one, was worthy of a table.

As they sat down she said, 'In a way we owe this table to Dr Goebbels.'

'How's that?'

'Emil Jannings told me that up till the Nazis came to power, movie people were ignored – we were on a par with jugglers

43

and vaudeville comics. When Jannings, and he was their biggest star, went to London or Paris, the embassies there would never think of inviting him to a reception. Goebbels changed all that. We're respectable now.'

'Bully for Goebbels.'

But he said it under his breath because a waiter, armoured in his stiff collar and his long formal coat, had come to take their order. With his quick eye Carmody had already noted that the dining room seemed unusually full this evening of top government officials. At a nearby table was Dr Mehlhorn, who administered the *Sicherheitsdienst*, the SS Security Service, under Reinhard Heydrich; with him were two young men, one of them with a broken nose which did nothing to soften the occasional arrogant looks he seemed to hurl around the room. The young man looked at Carmody then said something to Mehlhorn, who glanced at Carmody, tightened his lips, then replied to his broken-nosed junior. Carmody decided he wanted no messages carried from this table to that of the SD. All he wanted the waiter to take was their order.

When the waiter had gone away Cathleen said, 'I don't have a call till eleven tomorrow.' She looked around the glittering room, nodded to a few people who gave small stiff bows in reply, then she looked back at Carmody and said conversationally, 'I think I may encourage Dr Goebbels.'

He knew at once what she meant; she was not talking about being made respectable by the Minister in charge of film players. 'You want your head read if you do. How can you ask him about your –?'

'I'll have to think of a way. But if war breaks out, as all you newspapermen seem to think it will, I could be told to pack up and get out of Germany. And I might never find out what has happened to Mother.'

He knew time was running out for her; but he did not want her risking her neck by putting it in Goebbels' embrace. Besides, the thought made him uncomfortably jealous.

'Let me see what I can do, first. I can afford to take more risks than you.'

'Why should you?' She felt he should because he loved her;

but the duty troubled her. Then she put her hand across the table on to his. She had had only actors and directors as lovers and she had never expected anything of them. 'Sean, I think it would be best if you stayed out of this.'

Probably; but he would never say so. 'I'll go round to that hotel in Wilmersdorf tonight and start there. The night porter often talks more than the blokes on during the day. He gets less tips.' He would put it down to agency expenses.

The orchestra began to play: *Deep Purple* treacle came out of the saxophones and the strings were halfway between Vienna and Tin Pan Alley. The young man with the broken nose said something to Mehlhorn, then stood up and came across to bow stiffly to Cathleen.

'Fräulein O'Dea, I am a great admirer of yours – I have seen you in many American films. May I have the pleasure of dancing with you?'

'What a pity, Herr –?' But he didn't introduce himself, a most un-German thing. 'Herr Carmody has just asked me. Perhaps some other time.'

He didn't look at Carmody. He flushed, then bowed stiffly again and went back to his own table. 'So that means you have to dance with me,' said Cathleen. 'I hope you can.'

'You might have been better off with him,' said Carmody. 'I learned to dance with sheep. I was going steady with an old ewe.' She looked curiously at him and he grinned. 'An old shearers' joke.'

But he was light on his feet and had good rhythm, though not a wide variety of steps. 'How'm I doing?'

'Fred Astaire has nothing to worry about, but you're passable.'

'You may have something to worry about. I don't know who your bruiser friend is, but the older bloke at his table is Oberfuehrer Mehlhorn. I don't know what he's doing here – he and his SD men usually keep out of sight. They're worse than the Gestapo, if that's possible, because they pick on everyone, even good Party members.'

She looked back at the table where Mehlhorn and his two juniors were rising from their table. Mehlhorn was in uniform, but the younger men were in civilian clothes. As she and Carmody glided past, the broken-nosed man stared at them, but Mehlhorn and the other man ignored them. The three of them went out of the dining room and she noticed that if anyone recognized them at all it was with the barest politeness. Most diners studiedly looked at their food or their dinner companions. As the three SD men went out of the wide doors of the dining room, one of the saxophonists blew a sour note. A few of the dancers smiled, but those at the tables kept a straight face. No one was sure there was not another SD man in the room. Cathleen shuddered, suddenly pining for Hollywood, where informants might put you in dutch with the front office but where you were never jailed or beaten.

'Let's sit down,' said Carmody, feeling her shiver in his arms.

The waiter brought their first course as they sat down. Carmody was aware of people looking at them; earlier he had been proud of Cathleen's company when he had seen the admiring stares, but now it seemed the other diners were suspicious, even hostile. Carmody, who had grown up as xenophobic as most Australians, was once again feeling what it was like to be a foreigner. Most of the people in the big room would not have known who or what he was, but if he had incurred the displeasure of the SD they did not want to know. Foreigners were always expendable.

'Have you still got that crazy idea of encouraging Goebbels?'

'Yes.'

That spoiled the rest of his dinner. They did not dance again, though the music improved as the evening wore on; the orchestra played some jazz numbers, *Riverboat Shuffle* and others, one of the trumpeters rising to do solos that made even Carmody, preoccupied with Cathleen though he was, turn round. A couple on the floor had even begun to Charleston, laughing at their own efforts and causing merriment around them.

'That man on trumpet is an American,' said Cathleen. 'Fred Doe.'

'Is that really his name?'

'Probably not. But there are a lot of us like him –' Abruptly she gathered up her handbag. 'Let's go.'

'Steady on.' Carmody never allowed himself to be rushed. He looked around for the waiter and when the man came with the bill he carefully checked it before paying. Cathleen sat on the edge of her chair, fuming at his slowness. At last he stood up, took her arm. 'Don't whistle me and expect me to run, darl. You only do that with sheep dogs.'

It was their first disagreement and she knew she had been in the wrong. But she could not bring herself to apologize till they were out in the taxi. She had no more than the usual actress' vanity, but she had a stubborn ambition to be always in the right. Still, he loved her and he, too, was entitled to be stubborn.

'I'm sorry, darling.'

She took his hand and pressed it. He sat stiffly, unresponsive, and for a moment she was angry; he was acting like a goddam actor. But she tried again: with her other hand she turned his face towards hers and kissed him on the lips.

She was surprised at his reaction. He had kissed her before; now he seemed to want to devour her. His mouth covered hers like a boa constrictor's; she had been face to face with a tame one in a Tarzan movie. His hands were all over her like a plague of crabs; *Crab Island*, with Jon Hall. She wanted to laugh, she was being attacked by a junior class from Hollywood High; she was almost shocked at how gauche he was. But she didn't laugh, just bunched her fist and hit him in the crotch. He sat back with a gasp of pain, clasping the wounded parts. Men, she thought, never looked so ridiculous as when they were massaging their treasured possessions.

She straightened her dress, took out her compact and in the dim light of the taxi tried to straighten her face. 'If you're ever going to make love to me, you have a lot to learn. I can see now what you meant by going steady with an old ewe. Didn't she teach you *anything*?'

The pain had begun to subside, as had everything else. He shook his head, then managed a sick grin. 'You win. I'm willing to learn, if you're willing to teach me.'

She knew enough about men to know how much it had

taken for him to say that: men thought they had invented love-making. She patted the lower end of his lap, like a solicitous nurse. 'But not tonight. I'm going straight to bed. Alone.'

Then she wiped off the lipstick that smeared his face, kissed him on the cheek and they continued the rest of the way to Uhlandstrasse in silence, though she let him hold her hand.

When the taxi drew up outside her apartment building she said, 'No, don't get out. Call me tomorrow evening.'

He didn't press to get out; he had done enough awkward moving for the evening. Besides, he still felt sore. 'Stay away from the Doctor.'

She hesitated, then nodded. 'I'll be careful. I don't want the Gestapo knocking on my door in the middle of the night.'

But when she let herself in from the street the Gestapo, or a close relation, was waiting for her in the narrow entrance hall. With Herr Stumpf, the caretaker, was the broken-nosed young man.

## 2

Carmody leaned forward to speak to the taxi driver. 'Do you know the Hotel Ernst in Wilmersdorf?'

'Of course, sir.' The taxi driver was an old man with a tobacco-stained walrus moustache and a dislike for foreigners who hinted that he did not know his own city. He was a natural amongst his breed. He got in his dig: 'A good hotel if you want to save money.'

'That's me,' said Carmody.

Wilmersdorf was one of the better parts of town, its streets flanked by solid houses and apartment buildings, the houses and apartments occupied by solid citizens, solid Nazis amongst them; Carmody knew that several top Party officials lived here. The Hotel Ernst was in a side street, an ideal foxhole for someone who wanted to remain inconspicuous. He wondered how Cathleen's mother had discovered it.

48

He paid off the driver and went into the small lobby of the hotel. A night clerk rose up from behind his counter as if he were the subject of a levitation act, slowly and with no visible stretching of limbs. He was plump, young, bald and sunburned a bright pink; his head hung above the desk like a child's balloon. Teeth were painted on the balloon in a welcoming smile.

'I'm looking for an old friend who stayed here early this year. An American lady, Frau Hoolahan.' The name sounded like a joke.

The smile faded, the soft high voice became a harsh whisper. 'I wouldn't remember her, sir. So many people come and go . . .'

Carmody took five marks out of his wallet, saw the dead look in the clerk's eyes and made it ten. 'She is my mother's best friend –' He doubted if his mother Ida had ever said hello to a Jew; there were not many of them around the shearing sheds. 'She wrote my mother from this hotel, then we heard nothing more. She just disappeared. Did she check out at night, while you were on duty?'

The clerk hesitated, then took the money and leaned across the desk till his face was only inches from Carmody's; the latter imagined he could feel the heat from the sunburned flesh. The voice was still a whisper, but no longer harsh: 'They came for her about midnight – I was on duty –'

'They?'

The big head bobbed in a nod; or rather it seemed to float up and down in a nod. Carmody felt disconcerted by the man, felt he was listening to a blown-up puppet worked by invisible strings. 'Them. The Gestapo – you know what they're like –' Carmody didn't, but already he was beginning to feel that his knowledge of them was about to be expanded. 'They told me I was to mind my own business.'

'Have they taken anyone else away from here?'

'No one but Frau Hoolahan. This is a respectable hotel.' Not a whorehouse or a bookie's joint or a den for conspirators.

'How was Frau Hoolahan when they took her out?'

'Frightened.' How else? The clerk shrugged.

'She took all her luggage with her?'

'No. I believe they came back for that the next day.'

'So you told the hotel management what had happened that night?'

'Of course.'

'And they were like the Gestapo, they told you to mind your own business?'

The clerk didn't answer that one and Carmody knew the ten marks had run its course: there was going to be no more information. But the clerk wanted some information of his own, just in case: 'May I know your name, sir?'

It was on the tip of Carmody's tongue to say *it's none of your business*, but he contented himself with: 'I think it would be best if you didn't know.'

But he knew that if the clerk got in touch with the Gestapo they would have little difficulty in tracing him. The clerk might not recognize an Australian accent, but he would know it was different from an English or American one; there were very few Australians in Berlin and sooner or later the Gestapo would narrow down the field to himself. He was not worried for himself, the worst they would do would be to take away his accreditation and have him deported; but he was worried that they might connect him with Cathleen. He abruptly said goodnight and hurried out of the hotel lobby, hoping the clerk might have difficulty in remembering what he looked like. He had always thought of himself as average-looking and that could be an advantage now.

He stopped at the corner of the street and pondered whether he should go to Kreugerstrasse and try to find out something about the disappearance of Cathleen's grandmother. Then he looked at his watch and decided it was too late. A knock on the door of No. 33 at this hour could only cause apprehension, even terror, for those inside. If the Gestapo had called there once, there was always the chance that they would call again.

He walked back to his apartment, glad to breathe the cooler night air. He passed a bar, Rosse's, and all at once felt like having a beer; but when he pushed open the door and saw the other customers his thirst and taste abruptly disappeared.

The bar seemed full of uniforms, including too many black uniforms of the SS. Before anyone could turn to scrutinize this newcomer, he had closed the door and walked on.

When he turned the corner into his own street he saw the two men coming out of the front door of his apartment building. He pulled up, as alert now as any scout stalking through Nationalist territory in Spain; he had not been as tense as this since the night patrols amongst the ilex and eucalypts (smelling like home) in the Casa de Campo outside Madrid. He saw the two men pause for a moment under a street lamp and he guessed at once who they were.

They were as type-cast by their dress as gangsters in a film about Chicago; he was reminded of plain-clothes policemen back home who all seemed to wear pork-pie hats. The Gestapo had its own wardrobe: suits that were too tight and always worn buttoned-up and hats that looked as if they could be used to smother their owners' victims. The men walked on, turned round beyond the church and were gone.

Carmody waited a minute or two, letting the tension seep out of him, then he went on to his front door and quickly let himself into the building. There was no one in the dimly-lit entrance hall, no janitor or curious other tenant, and he went quickly up the stairs to his first-floor apartment. His door had not been forced; it was still locked. But as soon as he opened it and entered he knew someone had been in the apartment.

He could smell the cigarette smoke; he did not smoke. He found the butt in a saucer on the table in the kitchen: they had left a calling card and, he was sure, not by accident.

3

'I have come to pay my compliments, Fräulein O'Dea.' Back at the Adlon she had not noticed that the broken-nosed young man had had too much to drink.

Cathleen looked at the caretaker. 'Did you let this man in, Herr Stumpf?'

51

'I could not stop him, Fraulein. He pushed his way in –' Stumpf was a mixture of curiosity and fear. His eyes were lottery balls, anything might come up.

'I think you had better give me your name, Herr –?'

The young man looked cunning; one eye seemed to look speculatively in on his bent nose. 'Why should I do that? Don't you care for anonymous admirers?'

'No more than for anonymous critics.' She did not sound as uneasy as she felt: she was acting, doing what came naturally on the surface. 'Thank you for your compliments, whatever they are, and now, please, I'd like to go upstairs.'

He had moved to the bottom of the stairs; drink and temper were making him sway a little. 'I want to come up with you and discuss the social significance of your film *Lola und Ludwig*.'

She laughed at that, but made it sound inoffensive. 'There's no social significance – it's just pure entertainment.' Which wasn't true: it was the clumsy attempt to put propaganda into a musical comedy that had turned the picture into the dog it was going to be. 'You've got the wrong girl if you're looking for socially significant conversation. Try Leni Riefenstahl.'

'You don't admire Fräulein Riefenstahl?' He leaned forward belligerently, just managing to keep his balance.

*My big mouth.* She was aware of Stumpf watching all this with bulging eyes, but he would be no help to her in getting rid of this lout. 'I don't know Fräulein Riefenstahl, only her pictures. Now please get out of my way or I shall have to get Herr Stumpf to call the police.'

Stumpf almost fainted at that and the broken-nosed man giggled. 'Do that, Fräulein. See which of us is arrested – you, me or him.' Her jerked a contemptuous thumb at Stumpf and the caretaker shut his eyes in pain.

Cathleen was at a loss for a moment. They had been speaking quietly, but she knew their voices would have been floating up from the tile-floored hall through the stairwell to the landings above. No faces had appeared at the balustrades on the landings, but she was certain she had heard a door or two open. She hardly knew any of the other tenants in the

52

building, but those she had met on the stairs had appeared friendly. But they were not going to rush to her assistance in getting rid of an obnoxious SD man.

'It might be me who is arrested, but I am sure Dr Goebbels would see I was released immediately. And whoever ordered the arrest would be in trouble.' She had taken a risk in naming Goebbels, but if she was going to have an admirer let him be a genuine one, not a drunk like this.

'Ah, Goebbels!' There was no mistaking the contempt in his voice; but for the first time he looked unsure of himself. He hesitated, then stepped aside, clicked his heels and bowed unsteadily. 'Goodnight, Fräulein O'Dea. I should not have expected anything more from Hollywood. You sleep with anything!'

She was about to hit him with her handbag, but restrained herself just in time. But she knew she had won, if only for now. 'Get out!'

He glared at her, then, going out of his way to get close to Stumpf, he pushed the caretaker aside and went out of the front door, slamming it behind him. Instantly, faces appeared hung above the balustrades on the landings, popping out like the heads of prairie dogs she had seen in the Mojave Desert; the hollow column of the stairwell hissed with whispers. She looked up, smiling at her neighbours.

'I'm sorry you have been disturbed. It was just a fan being a nuisance. It won't happen again,' she said, trying to convince herself more than them.

Cathleen said goodnight to Stumpf, who just nodded, already building tomorrow's gossip in his head. Then she slowly climbed the stairs, all at once feeling more like Lola Montez than she had at any time on the lot out at Neubabelsberg. Lola had spent the last four months of her life ministering to the inmates of a Magdalen asylum near New York. Germany was turning into a mental asylum, but she couldn't see herself staying here to do good works. She had to find her mother and get out before the madmen tried to take over the world.

Further across the city, in his small flat overlooking the Landwehr Canal, Helmut von Albern lay in his bed with Melissa Hayes in his arms. They had made love and, as always afterwards, he felt a heavy guilt. He was only half in love with her and that was not enough return for a girl who held nothing back from him. His mother had been a famous beauty and had had scores of admirers besides his father; his parents' marriage had been a true love match, but he knew his father had not been her only lover, though she had never told him so directly. But, as with most mothers with an only child, she had given him advice that other mothers, more fecundly blessed, might have given only to their daughters. She had told him of the vulnerability of women, which is a terrible thing to lay on any man with a conscience.

But guilt about Melissa was not von Albern's main concern right now; she was asleep, so he put his conscience to sleep beside her. He was more concerned for his father, the man he loved more than any in the world and more than he did Melissa. The general had come to Berlin, something he had sworn to his son and others that he would never do again, and he had not told Helmut he was here. The latter had found out by accident, from an uncle who had let slip that Kurt von Albern had come to Berlin from the family estate outside Hamburg. It was not like his father to try to avoid him; they were too close for that sort of manoeuvre. Something was wrong and Helmut was worried.

He eased his arm out from beneath Melissa's head and got out of bed without waking her. She was so violent in their love-making that she wore herself out; she always slept like the dead for an hour or so afterwards, though there was a sly smile on her face that no corpse would ever wear, except perhaps one that had died while making love.

He slipped on a robe and went out to the living room,

closing the bedroom door behind him. He switched on a desk lamp; even its limited illumination was enough to show the untidiness of the room. Though he came of a family with a long military tradition, he had done no more than the compulsory training service and it had done nothing to teach him how to take care of himself domestically. At home there had always been more than enough servants to keep his rooms neat and tidy; he had never had to worry about getting meals or seeing they were served at the right time. The flat was not squalid, but it was a description that might have come to the mind of his father had he ever visited the flat. This week's dirty clothing and last week's laundry, still un-ironed, were at opposite ends of a couch; the dishes from what looked like a week's meals were on a table in the centre of the room; books, newspapers and set sketches littered the floor and occupied all but one of the four chairs. But he never saw any of it: the upper class have a talent for the blind eye. It has helped them survive in worse surroundings than a slum.

He picked up the phone, dialled a number. He waited, realizing only as he heard its insistent ringing that the hour might be too late; elderly men might retire early. Then a grumpy voice said, 'Count von Albern's residence.'

'Vogel? This is Helmut. May I speak to my uncle?'

The old butler's tone softened: Helmut had always been one of his favourites. 'He is in bed, sir. Perhaps in the morning –?'

'*Now*, Vogel. It is important.'

It was a minute or two before Wulf von Albern came on the phone. He sounded even grumpier than his butler: 'Yes, what is it?'

Helmut apologized for disturbing his uncle, then said, 'I want to get in touch with Father.'

There was a moment's silence at the other end of the line. Then: 'It is not possible. I don't know where he is.'

'*Uncle –*' Helmut was a favourite nephew, but he could not tell his uncle outright that he was lying.

Again there was the silence. Helmut could see his uncle struggling with his loyalties. Wulf and Kurt were the only children of Helmut's grandparents; Wulf was the elder by ten years and had always been his brother's protector. Helmut knew he had no sympathy for the Nazis, but he had retired from public life five years ago on the death of his wife and disliked anything that disrupted his routine as a retired gentleman. He would go to the horse races at the Hoppegarten, to tea at the Adlon and to the opera or concerts. Occasionally he entertained women friends, but Helmut had no idea whether he had affairs with them. His money, like the family's, came from the land and from shipping, but he left the management of it, like a good aristocrat, to managers he trusted. He involved himself in nothing but his own quiet enjoyment of what remained of his life.

'Helmut, dear boy –' He had gone to Oxford as a young man and still had some English speech mannerisms. 'It would be better if you left your father alone for the time being –'

'Uncle, the fact that you say that only convinces me I should know why he is in Berlin. Now please tell me where he is.'

Again the silence, then a heavy sigh: 'All right, but explain to him that I tried to dissuade you. Try –' He gave a number.

Helmut thanked him and hung up. He looked at his wrist, then remembered his watch was on his bedside table; making love with one's watch on was too much like a sporting event. There was a clock somewhere in this room, but it was lost amongst the riotous disorder. As if on cue the bedroom door opened and Melissa, wearing Helmut's discarded shirt, appeared.

'Telephoning? At this hour?'

'What time is it?'

She looked at her watch. Women, Helmut had noted, rarely took off their watches in bed; but then, he had also noted, they usually closed their eyes when making love. Except, of course, the professionals and they needed to keep an eye on the clock. 'It's 11.30.'

Automatically she began to clean up the room. He was amused by her passion for being neat and tidy; on Judgement Day she would be tidying up, leaving her world as she had found it. He did not bear to think of her as a wife: neatness and tidiness should be taken only in small doses. He put down

56

the phone: he would call his father first thing in the morning before he left for the studio. Kurt von Albern, still a good soldier, was an early riser.

'Sweetheart – are you mixed up with the Nazis?' She was picking up last week's laundry, sorting it out so that Helmut's cleaning woman could take it away for ironing.

He looked at her in astonishment. 'Mixed up – what do you mean?'

'You've had something on your mind all evening.' She was rolling his socks into balls; playfully she tossed one at him and he caught it gingerly, as if it were a grenade. 'You can tell me, if you want someone to confide in. It often helps. So they tell me,' she added less than confidently. She had been confiding in people all her life and where had it got her?

'I thought you weren't interested in politics?'

'I'm not.' They always spoke in English because her German was virtually non-existent; her voice was being dubbed in the German version of the film. 'But I'm interested in you. I worry for you.'

He was touched. He loved her, but he wished sometimes he could fall in love with her; he would hate to hurt her when the time came for them to part. 'Darling, I'm like you – I'm outside politics –'

'No, you're not. Not like me. I'm stupid about politics, but you aren't. I've watched you – I saw how you looked today when Dr Goebbels was smoodging up to Cathleen.'

Love was not always blind: sometimes it kept too close an eye on you. 'Smoodging up? Was that what the Reichsminister was doing?'

'He's a dirty little man, you know that. He'd be smoodging up to me if I was the star instead of Cathleen. You hate him, don't you?'

'If I hated him, why do you think I'd be mixed up with the Nazis then?'

She began to fold a sheet, pondered a moment. 'I don't know, I suppose that's contradictory, isn't it?' She knew nothing of the rivalries and jealousies amongst the Nazis. Then she added stubbornly, belting a crease into the sheet, 'But something *is* worrying you.'

He took the sheet from her, put his hands under his shirt, felt the smoothness of her, still warm from the bed. 'I'm worried about whether war will come, that's all.'

'And you get out of bed with me at this hour to talk with someone about *that*?' She was not entirely without shrewdness; or, he wondered, was it a woman's vanity?

'The war will be bigger than both of us.' He wanted to laugh at his reply: it sounded like a bad line of dialogue from a Hollywood film. He was surprised and relieved when she, too, laughed.

'Let's go back to bed,' she said, slipped off his shirt, added it neatly to the pile of this week's wash and led him back into the bedroom.

During the night he heard air raid sirens in his sleep. He woke with a start, sweating, certain that he had not been dreaming; but there was no sound in the night other than Melissa's steady breathing beside him and, somewhere over to the south, the thin scream of a train whistle. He was shocked that he should have been so afraid, even if in sleep: it smacked of cowardice. He lay on his back and prayed for peace; though peace, officially, was still the atmosphere in Europe.

He rose early and, while Melissa prepared coffee and toast, he phoned his father at the number he had been given. A man's voice answered that it was the Hotel London: he had never heard of it, but it was certainly not the Adlon, where his father had always stayed in the past.

'General von Albern.'

When his father came on the line he knew he had not woken him: the voice was crisp, wide awake. 'Helmut! At this hour?'

'I have to leave for the studio in a few minutes –'

'How did you find me?' It seemed that his father sounded more worried than irritated.

'Uncle Wulf – I pestered him till he told me where you were. Father, why are you here in Berlin?' Melissa was out in the small kitchen; he lowered his voice. 'Why didn't you tell me you were coming?'

'Helmut –' The voice lost its crispness, sounded unnaturally hesitant. 'Helmut, please don't ask such questions –'

'Does Uncle know why you're here?'

'No. You are not to bother him again.' It was an order; the voice was crisp again.

'When are you going back to The Pines?' That was the family estate outside Hamburg, not its official name but the one by which all the family referred to it. He often thought of it with nostalgia, but it belonged to another age, his boyhood.

'I don't know. Please, Helmut, no more questions –'

'Father, I must see you –'

The General sighed, then said reluctantly, 'Helmut, Romy is here with me –'

'Oh.' He was embarrassed, out wondered why; he was a grown man, so why should he feel awkward about his father's affair with a married woman? 'I'm sorry, Father . . . Call me when you are going back to The Pines.'

'Of course. And Helmut – don't worry.'

But he was already worrying as he hung up the phone. Why would his father and Romy von Sonntag have their rendezvous in Berlin? Why not some city or town where they were not known? He was infected with suspicion, he could no longer accept things at their face value, not even a reassurance from his father. Germany, since the last war, had become a country of conspiracies and now he was suspecting his father (and Romy?) of being a conspirator of some sort. With war imminent, had his father decided he must somehow get back on to the General Staff?

Melissa came to the kitchen door, wiping her hands. He knew she would have cleaned up the kitchen before she prepared breakfast. 'How's your father?'

So she had heard some of the conversation. She had never met his father and he had no plans to introduce her. 'He is well. We'd better hurry – my call is for eight o'clock . . .'

Going out to Neubabelsberg in his small Opel, they were passed by a convoy of seven Mercedes. The cars went by with klaxons screaming and ahead of them the traffic peeled away as if a giant wind were splitting it. Sitting in the rear seat of the middle car of the convoy, clearly visible with the hood down but with the bullet-proof windows up, was the Fuehrer. He was staring straight ahead, seemingly oblivious to the aides in his car and of the pedestrians jumping out of the way of the convoy, some of them still managing to fling up their arms in a mixture of balancing act and *Sieg Heil!*

'Was that Hitler?' Melissa said.

He nodded. He had seen this same convoy before, knew, from what his father had told him, the make-up of it. The twenty SD men who travelled in it, each carrying two 9 mm pistols; the submachine-guns and the light machine-gun in the support cars; the 4500 rounds of ammunition – 'Enough to start a small war,' as his father had said. And the Fuehrer, in his armour-plated Mercedes 770K, sitting there stiff-necked under his special officer's cap with its reinforced steel band that weighed 1½ kilos. All that for a beloved leader.

'Where's he going?' said Melissa.

'To Hell, I hope.'

# CHAPTER THREE

## 1

Things were not going well. So far there had been seven takes on this particular scene; Cathleen and her co-star, Willy Heffer, were like strangers who had just met that morning. This was their last scene together in the script and Lola and Ludwig might have been Mary Magdalene and one of the Pharisees. Right from the start of the film Cathleen had felt there was little chemistry between her and Heffer; like Braun, the director, he bowed his knee to the Party, but on top of that he was totally mis-cast as Ludwig. Like Cathleen, however, he was a professional and they had managed to get through their scenes smoothly and on schedule. This morning they were not doing even that.

'Cut!' Braun sat back in his canvas chair, fanned himself with a mauve handkerchief. He was never invited to parties by Goebbels, who could not stand homosexuals, but he was always a welcome guest of Goering. One could not hope to be everyone's favourite and life, up till now, had been fun. But he was afraid of the possibility of war, knew when it came all the fun would be over, and his pessimism had spread to his handling of this film. He no longer had control of the way it should go. 'Let's all take a break, darlings. We must hope inspiration strikes us while we're having coffee.'

'Not amongst the dregs, I hope,' said Cathleen, and Braun gave her a weak smile.

She sat down in the shade of a large umbrella and looked at Helmut von Albern, who dropped into a chair beside her. He was a handsome man, reminding her of a less stern Conrad Veidt (all her comparisons of men were with actors but so far she had found no comparison for Sean. He was not to be compared with Errol Flynn). She had looked at him with interest their first day on the set, when they had had lighting tests, but he had shown no interest in her other than professionally. He was unfailingly polite, in contrast to some cameramen she had known in Hollywood, but there was a certain arrogance to him that occasionally unsettled her. She had not been surprised to learn that he came of a family that could trace its lineage back five hundred years. There was a difference between the arrogance of a true aristocrat and that of the Hollywood aristocracy which went back only one generation.

'What's the matter with us this morning? Does it look as bad through the camera as I feel it is?'

'It's pretty bad.'

'It's been pretty bad all along. Why did you come on this picture?'

She knew his record. She had not been a star, at least not till this picture and even now she felt no sense of stardom, but she had known the thoroughness of some stars and she had followed the pattern. She had wanted to know all about the chief technicians on the picture and she had been impressed by those who had been engaged. Helmut von Albern had started work as a clapper boy on one of Luis Trenker's famed 'mountain' films; he had worked his way up the ladder, through focusing to operating the camera and finally to being the lighting cameraman or director of photography. He had worked for Pabst, Trenker, Hartl and Sierck and she wondered why he had agreed to work for such a hack as Braun.

'I had no choice.'

She knew what he meant. There had been the same sort of authoritarian discipline at M-G-M.

They were some distance from any of the other actors or crew and she dropped her voice. 'Helmut, are there any spies in this unit?'

He raised an eyebrow. 'Spies?'

'You know what I mean. All pictures have them, jerks who spy for the front office.'

'Has someone been spying on you?'

'I think so.' But she dared not mention the warning about the Abwehr. She was certain that he was not a Nazi, but one could not be certain of anything in Germany. But if he knew of some front office spy, she might have a lead to where to start looking for whoever had sent her the anonymous warning. She looked across at the crew, at the assistant directors and the assistant supervisor and the continuity girl, at the score or more of people working on the picture; altogether, including those not needed today, there would have been over a hundred on *Lola und Ludwig*, not counting the extras brought in when needed. 'I'm a foreigner, so I'm a marked woman with some of them.'

'You haven't put a foot wrong – politically, I mean. Why should anyone report you to the front office? Or are you afraid of the Gestapo?' He laughed softly. 'Cathleen, our beloved Reichsminister wouldn't allow the Gestapo to pester one of his stars. Don't you know he and Herr Himmler hate each other's guts?'

She was not reassured. 'I'd heard about it . . . I'll just be glad when the picture is finished.'

He looked at her carefully then. 'What happens then? Will the Americans let you go back to Hollywood? There's talk they won't.'

'I'll have to face that when the time comes.' Suddenly she wanted to weep, knew that this morning's poor chemistry was entirely due to her. She was drained, had nothing to give; it was a pity there was no dying scene in the picture. She conjured up an actress' smile. 'Maybe they'll give me a job as technical adviser on all those anti-Nazi pictures they're making.'

'Maybe. In the meantime I'd be careful.'

He rose abruptly and walked away, leaving the words *be careful* ringing in her ears. She stared after him, waiting for him to look back and give her some hint that it was he who had written her the warning note. But all he gave her was his lean back as he disappeared round the fake wall of the Feldherranhalle, Munich's Hall of Generals.

'Fräulein O'Dea?' A uniformed chauffeur had appeared from nowhere, was saluting and holding out an envelope.

Cathleen took it, opened it: there was a note from Goebbels asking her to have supper with him that evening at 9 o'clock. She hesitated, hearing the echo of the warning: *Be careful*. But she had not been careful in sacrificing her career in Hollywood, in coming here to Germany: she could not afford to be careful in these last few steps, not now with time running out. She took a pen out of her handbag, scrawled an acceptance on the bottom of the note and handed it back to the chauffeur.

'Tell the Reichsminister I should like to be picked up at my apartment at 8.45.'

The chauffeur saluted and disappeared as swiftly as he had come. Then Braun came back, still fanning himself with his handkerchief. He was wearing a wide-brimmed straw hat, swept up at the side in the same way as Goering wore his hats; he often imitated his idols, but so far had not grown a Hitler moustache; there were limits to flattery. Besides, a toothbrush moustache was lost in a washbowl face. He flopped into the chair beside her, almost breaking it beneath him.

'The Reichsminister's personal chauffeur?' He knew everyone and everyone's servants. Cathleen revised her opinion of him: he would not have been working at Republic or Monogram but would have been working for Louella Parsons. He searched among his chins for one to prop on his plump hand. 'We're his latest favourite, are we? He's taken a long time to get round to you, darling.'

'Don't be jealous, Karl. I'll put in a good word for you. Now, can we go back to work?'

'Of course, darling. And this time be a little more of a bitch – that is what Lola is at this point in her career.'

She smiled sweetly. 'It'll come naturally. But Willy would be better in the part.'

'Is my name being taken in vain?' Willy Heffer had come back with the crew.

'Who would ever be vain about your name, honey?' said Cathleen, then retreated behind the make-up girl's powder puff.

They got through the rest of the day without too many extra takes, but when Cathleen at last left the lot she was exhausted. She sat in the back of the car on the drive back to

Berlin and wondered if she should call up Dr Goebbels and postpone their supper date. She would be in no condition for dealing with him if he became amorous; if she had been fresh and on her mettle she was confident she could have handled him; isolated from their office, all men trying to get their trousers off were the same. Unless they were bent on rape and she was sure that Dr Goebbels was too proud of his record to attempt that.

But when she had bathed and had had a martini she changed her mind about postponing the date. He might not ask her again and the opportunity, faint though it was, would be lost. She had no idea how she would approach him about her search for her mother ('a friend's aunt') and she would have to play it by ear as the evening progressed. She dressed, not provocatively but still with some allure, and looked at herself in the mirror. The green silk dress contrasted with her deep red hair and showed off her smooth alabaster shoulders and arms (thank God, she had no freckles there): she had put on a little weight around the bosom since coming to Germany, but that was no handicap in this country of stout-bosomed women. She had heard that the Doctor was a man for legs, so she had put on a pair of dark-green silk stockings and a pair of fragile court shoes that showed off her instep. She nodded with satisfaction at her reflection, put a pair of small scissors in her evening bag, just in case extraordinary defence was needed, and was ready when the car called.

Herr Stumpf opened the front door for her, bowed her out with a deferential smile and one big eye on the limousine parked at the kerb. He knew a top official's car when he saw one: he wondered whose it was.

'Have a pleasant evening, Fräulein O'Dea.'

*If only you knew . . .* At least the drive through the summer evening was pleasant; Berlin had more charm, though it might be a bit heavy, than Los Angeles. The car took her to the Reichsminister's official residence on Hermann Goering-strasse; she did not know that he hated the thought of living on a street named after one of his most detested co-ministers. But that was where the former Palace of the Marshals of the

Prussian Court was, standing in its own grounds bordering on the Chancellery park, and Goebbels, who appreciated irony, occasionally smiled sourly at the joke, though never in front of others.

The car pulled up before the front door, where a butler was waiting for Cathleen. He took her into the big house, through an interior that reminded her of a museum (she did not know that it was furnished with pieces 'borrowed' from museums) and up to the first floor. She was shown into a large room that looked out on to the garden. Her host for the evening was silhouetted against the light coming through deep windows: he looked taller, bigger, against the light. Nature plays no favourites, it flatters the evil as well as the good.

He stepped down off the window step, instantly diminishing himself. He came towards her smiling, both hands held out as if greeting an old friend (or lover). He had no gloves this time; it was the first time she had seen him without them. He was impeccably dressed, as usual; no man clad as immaculately as this was going to commit rape; by the time he had taken his clothes off, careful not to crease them, any swift-legged girl would be gone. She gave him her hand, then turned, an actress' practised movement, while he took the wrap from her shoulders. She waited for him to kiss the back of her neck, but he was too short to do that without effort: he was not going to make a fool of himself.

The apartment was furnished and decorated in the same style as downstairs and she dismissed it with a quick glance around. Music was coming from a large cabinet gramophone, large enough to be a museum piece, in one corner and Goebbels must have thought she had moved her body to it.

'You like Mozart?'

'I prefer Gershwin.' Her knowledge of classical music was almost nil. You couldn't tap dance to it and you never heard it in *George White's Scandals*. Then she saw the look on Goebbels' thin bony face. 'What's the matter?'

'Have you come here to defend the Jews?'

'The Jews?' Then she laughed, but nervously; she had certainly got off on the wrong foot. She almost said that, then remembered his club foot. 'Honestly, Herr Doctor, the thought never crossed my mind. I'd forgotten George Gershwin was Jewish. Okay, no more talk about Jews.'

His face remained stern and dark for a moment, then it broke into a pleasant smile. He took her hand in his long-fingered one and led her to the small table set for supper. The anger went out of his voice, deep for such a small man, and it became almost sensual. She began to understand why some women might have found him attractive. Not all the 38 UFA actresses had gone to bed with him solely out of career ambition or Party loyalty. She refused to believe there were that many whores out at Neubabelsberg.

'The Fuehrer has a passion for Wagner, but I don't think Wagner is the proper background for a tête-à-tête.'

'I once had a tête-à-tête with a background of a 90-piece brass band. We were making a circus picture and the producer thought he'd teach me a few tricks.'

He laughed, sat down opposite her. 'And did he?'

'Herr Doctor, I learned every trick there was while I was in the chorus on Broadway. And every counter-trick.'

The butler brought in smoked salmon, thin slices of pumpernickel and toast. He poured wine into the cut glass goblets, then retired. Cathleen wondered how many other servants were here in the big house, all privy to their master's little tête-à-têtes. She wondered, too, where his wife and six kids were, but a girl never asked a question like that. That was one of the tricks she had learned.

'You're not hungry?' She noticed he had hardly glanced at the food on his plate.

'Food and wine don't interest me. I eat enough to keep up my energy, that's all.'

'Are you a vegetarian? I believe the Fuehrer is.'

'He is always trying to convert me –' He suddenly looked bored at the small talk. Food was not food for thought nor conversation; especially what the Fuehrer ate. Hitler would be beside himself with rage if he could see this intimate little supper, and not at what was on the table. Fortunately he was down in Berchtesgaden and no one in this house ever carried gossip as far as that. It was a boon to a philanderer to have trustworthy servants. 'How is the film going?'

She sipped her wine, took a chance: 'Do you want me to be frank or polite?'

'Be frank. Women usually are.' Magda always was, and what a pain she could be. Yet in the first years of their marriage, that was what had been so appealing about her.

'It's not going very well. I think we've missed out.'

'What is wrong with it?' He showed no concern.

'Well, I'm probably saying the wrong thing . . . The propaganda is getting in the way of the story. Every time I open my mouth to say a line of dialogue, I feel I should be up on one of those big posters you have all over the country.'

'You don't like our propaganda?'

'I don't care one way or the other –' Which wasn't true; but one could be too frank, dangerously so. 'Sam Goldwyn once said something – "If I want to send a message, I'll call Western Union." Have you heard of Sam Goldwyn?'

'Of course.' He was not smiling and his face seemed to have turned to stone.

'What I'm saying is that if you want to sell this to American audiences, then you've got the wrong script. Americans don't buy tickets to listen to messages. They get enough of those free from President Roosevelt.'

Then he did smile. Any joke against the Jew-lover Roosevelt was a good joke. 'Why didn't you say all this before? We have almost finished the film.'

'Who would have listened to me, some Hollywood dame trying to tell Germans how to make pictures? I better shut up. I've said too much already.'

'I don't think you are a Hollywood dame, Fräulein O'Dea. You have too much of what I believe Americans call class.'

His flattery was smooth; done, she thought, with class. But she had to hold him at bay: 'How many Hollywood dames have you met?'

He smiled again. 'None, I believe. But I am an expert on American films, I recognize the various types. You have always had class – I shall show you later what I mean. I don't understand why M-G-M never made you a star.'

'You don't understand the system, Herr Doctor. Contract

players like me were the alternatives, the threats to the stars. If they refused a role, they were told they'd be suspended and one of us would get it. It almost never happened, but it kept us and the stars in our places.'

The butler brought in the second course, pork chops baked in cream: just the dish for a half-Jewish girl trying to keep her figure. She thanked her stars that her mother had not run a kosher home, and tucked into the dish. Goebbels watched her indulgently while he just picked at his own plate.

'You enjoy your food, don't you?'

'It's no good for the figure.'

She was glad when he didn't make the obvious compliment. Despite herself she was finding his company – well, not enjoyable: she would feel guilty if that were so. No, interesting: yes, that was it. It excused her coming. Which, she added ruefully and with her usual self-candour, only added hers to the excuses of the 38 other actresses of UFA.

The conversation was a mixture of oblique banter and probing for information on both sides; she found he had a sense of humour but sensed he would and could not laugh at himself. Mozart was replaced on the gramophone by Strauss: a selection from *Der Rosenkavalier*.

'I'm a romantic,' said Goebbels.

'Who is not?' she said, who had stood within two feet of Jeanette MacDonald singing something like this and had her ears blasted.

Dessert was a Sachertorte with whipped cream. She drooled at the sight of it and looked across the table at him. 'How did you know this was my favourite?'

'You'd be surprised how much I know about you, Cathleen.' He had been calling her by her first name for the past twenty minutes, but hadn't yet invited her to call him anything but Herr Doctor. Still, that was a little less formal than Herr Reichsminister. There are limits to the status gap at a tête-à-tête.

His reply unnerved her. How much did he know? Suddenly the evening became dangerous; she realized how foolish she had been in thinking she might use him to help find her mother. She dug into the Torte, but it tasted like sawdust from the Vienna Woods; the cream turned sour in her mouth. She was glad of the coffee when it was poured.

'Beautiful coffee,' she said, feeling she had been suspiciously quiet for too long.

'There are still some stocks of the best coffee available.' But only for the select few, though he did not add that. The masses were having to put up with coffee bastardized with chicory and other substitutes. 'I shall send you some. I understand Americans don't know how to make coffee.'

'Where did you hear that?'

'I have my sources in America.' He smiled, and again she felt uneasy. Was she imagining it or was there no smile in those dark eyes?

'Let's go downstairs,' he said, rising abruptly. 'I have something to show you.'

He took her arm and led her downstairs into a room that she saw at once was a combination drawing room and small theatre. A screen had been let down against one wall; in the opposite wall she could see the apertures for a projector. She and Goebbels sank into deep, silk-covered chairs. Without thinking she crossed her ankles in that sinuous way that some women, those with slim legs, have of showing off the curve of their instep; she caught his appreciative glance and wished she had been more modest. The lights went out and the familiar trade mark of Leo the Lion came up on the screen. Then the titles came up and she gasped with surprise. It was her first picture.

'How on earth did you get a print of *that*?'

'I told you – I have my sources.'

She shrank down in her seat, embarrassed at herself up there moving so awkwardly through Cedric Gibbons' sets, playing a little rich girl and looking like someone who had come straight in from a relief line. She was Norma Shearer's sister, always running into scenes like a heifer into a china shop; the only good performance was given by her legs and then only when she was standing still. The film lasted 84 minutes and she was on screen for about a quarter of that time, every second mortifying agony. Occasionally she glanced at Goebbels, but he seemed to be fascinated by the

70

film. She had expected him, once the lights went down, to take her hand or go even further: picture theatres all over the world were dens of seduction. But he was a model of correct behaviour, a gentleman in the dark.

Only when the lights went up did he take her hand. He patted it in congratulation. 'Even then you had something.'

'Sure. A talent for tripping over myself. I remember Norma telling me not to come within a yard of her for fear I knocked her out of shot.'

He shook his head. 'It was to be expected in your first film. No, you had promise. But you looked so innocent then.'

'And I don't now?' He was still holding her hand.

The smile changed, looked sensual: here it comes, she thought. 'I don't place much value on innocence.'

Her tongue once again got away from her: 'What about your children's?'

He dropped her hand as if it had suddenly become leprous. 'That's damned impertinent!'

She was torn between being abjectly apologetic and fiercely independent. But she had never been able to crawl: 'It wasn't meant to be. I'd have thought you'd be concerned for your children.'

'I am!' He stood up in a rage; she was shocked and frightened to see that he was actually trembling. 'You had better go. Goodnight!'

He went swiftly out of the room, hobbling in his haste, leaving her alone in the big room. She looked towards the wall behind which the projection booth was hidden; the apertures stared at her like square unseeing eyes. But she knew that there were eyes behind those eyes that had seen what had gone on; the projectionist may not have heard what had been said, but he knew she had been dismissed like a cheap whore. Then the butler appeared in the doorway carrying her wrap.

'This way, Fräulein.' There was no mistaking the contempt in his voice; he sounded like a German version of Eric Blore in the Astaire–Rogers pictures. She remembered something an English actor, who specialized in such roles, had once told her: the two biggest snobs in the world are butlers and

71

floor-walkers. They see so much of the error of other people's ways, while wishing for the same opportunities.

She went home, disappointed and afraid.

## 2

*Extracts from the diaries of Dr Paul Joseph Goebbels:*

13 August 1939:
Reports from Obersalzberg. Ciano is now there with the Fuehrer after two days at Fuschl with Ribbentrop. What a meeting of minds that would have been – it is difficult to believe that the future of Europe could lie in the hands of those two. No wonder some of our enemies do not take us seriously. But Ciano is now with the Fuehrer, who has told him that Germany will go to war if our demands over Danzig are not met. Ciano, I understand, protested that war over Danzig would spread into a general war throughout Europe, something Mussolini is evidently afraid of. I fear the same, but cannot say so. The Fuehrer will listen to me only when I agree with him. The others are taking over . . .

Out to Schwanenwerder again this afternoon. Took the children out for a boat ride on the Havel. How fortunate they are! I often want to compare their childhood with mine, but resist the temptation. Let them keep their innocence . . .

A subject that came up tonight when I entertained Fräulein O'Dea. I lost my temper, something I should not do, especially in front of a foreigner. But the children must be protected . . . Still, I wish the evening had ended on a better note. I am becoming bewitched by her. Perhaps those legs of hers remind me too much of Lida . . .

But she did tell me some disquieting news about *Lola und Ludwig*. The script, she says, is full of clumsy propaganda. Clumsy? There is no one better than we at propaganda. I shall have some heads out at Neubabelsberg . . .

To bed, alone, at 2 a.m. A mountain of work; but I don't mind. This study is like a womb. All red: the chairs, the carpet, the curtains . . .


# 3


'How many concentration camps are there, Oliver?' said Carmody.

They were sitting on the terrace of the Kranzler Café on the Kurfürstendamm having tea. Strong, with milk and plenty of sugar for Carmody, a real shearer's brew; weak, with lemon for Burberry, an Oxford aesthete's choice. Carmody was hoeing into a thick slice of apple cake and Burberry was munching delicately on English biscuits.

'My dear boy, that is a subject left well alone –'

'Oliver, dear boy –' Carmody grinned when he said it. 'You've given me a lot of good advice since I came to Berlin. But I'm a big boy now and I want to write my own stuff. Now how many camps do you know of?'

Burberry sighed, wiped a biscuit crumb from his lips. On the wide pavement beside the terrace people hurried by, some glancing enviously at those who had the time to sit in the sun and take tea. Further along the street the gold ring of the clock-face on Kaiser Wilhelm Memorial Church showed exactly four o'clock; he heard the chimes even as he looked at the church tower. Four o'clock: time for tea in any civilized country. Except that here civilization was crumbling like the biscuit in his hand.

'I really don't know how many camps there are. When I first came here in 1936 there were already 50 or more. I believe they've closed a lot of the smaller ones and larger ones have been built. Why do you want to write about them now when we're trying to cool down Hitler over Danzig?'

'Appease him again, you mean.'

Burberry shook his head. 'I don't think London will stand for any more appeasement. There are too many voices against it.' He looked about him, at the passers-by on the pavement, at the loungers at the tables sipping their coffee or tea and tucking into their strudel and cake and sundaes. The inner man must be appeased, he thought. Then he looked up at the sky, at the burnished blue air through which soft clouds floated like scraps of dreams only vaguely remembered. 'How could war break out on a day like this?'

'War is a summer sport, isn't it?'

'Ah, dear boy, you have been with us decadents too long. That sounds like European cynicism.' He called for the bill, paid it and rose. He picked up his umbrella, looked up at the sun and decided he could stand a little more of it. There was a slight tan to his pink face and bald head and he looked marvellously healthy, ready for war or any disaster. He swung the umbrella, narrowly missing the head of a woman sitting at the next table. 'I must be off. Be patient – there may be bigger things to write than what you have in mind.'

He went striding off along the Kurfürstendamm; Carmody, looking after him, felt he should have been wearing a flag. He envied the English their self-confidence: the sun might be setting on their Empire, but they were looking the other way.

He sat for a while luxuriating in the warm sun, relishing the sweat he could feel on his chest and in his armpits. The sun had been one of the few pleasures of Spain; he ached still from some of the bitter memories of the war there. He had been here in Berlin when Hitler had reviewed 14,000 members of the Condor Legion who had fought in Spain; it had taken all his self control not to hurl abuse at them as they marched by. When he saw Sperrle, the architect of the bombing of Guernica, he had turned away, sickened by the memory of what the man had done. But the war in Spain was over now, all the battles had been in vain, and now the sun was shining on what, he was certain, would prove to be the biggest battlefield ever. He wondered if some of the sweat under his shirt was the sweat of fear.

He left the terrace, carrying his jacket over his arm, and

walked leisurely back to his apartment. Kreisler, the hurdy-gurdy man, was playing outside his front door.

'Still playing dirges, Herr Kreisler?'

The man smiled his gap-toothed smile and the monkey, also gap-toothed, reflected it. 'I'm thinking of playing some hymns. But the priests in the church –' he nodded at St Ludgwig's '– might object. They don't like competition, especially from an atheist.'

Carmody had a sudden idea. 'Is your monkey house-trained?'

'Like a good bureaucrat.'

Carmody wondered if he talked like that only to a foreigner. 'Come upstairs. I'll give you a drink. What's your preference?'

'Scotch whisky, if you have it,' said the organ-grinder, elbows out of his jacket, boots looking as if they had walked thousands of miles: a connoisseur of Scotch whisky if ever I've seen one, thought Carmody.

'And the monkey's?'

'A little schnapps. It brings tears to his eyes, but then he looks even more human.'

Carmody took them upstairs, glad of his idea, a story on the unknown musicians of Berlin; tonight he would go looking for Fred Doe, the trumpet man from the Adlon. There would be half a dozen more to choose from: a bass drum man from one of the bands which played in the park, a violinist from one of the cafés: he hoped they would all prove as cynical and observant as Herr Kreisler promised to be.

Kreisler parked his hurdy-gurdy, tied the monkey to a hallstand, took off his battered hat and looked admiringly round the apartment. 'You live well, Herr Carmody. As you deserve to.'

'Thank you,' said Carmody, but forebore to ask why Kreisler thought he deserved so much.

The apartment had been inherited from the man he had succeeded at World Press. Before that it had belonged to a Jewish doctor, who had fled to Australia one jump ahead of the Gestapo; Carmody liked to think of him and the doctor changing places, he comfortable here in this city apartment, the Jewish doctor sweating somewhere in a shearing shed, unable to practise because the AMA would not recognize his qualifications. The exchange would be grossly unfair and Carmody sometimes had pangs of guilt.

The furniture and furnishings were heavy, but the best Gothic: Carmody sometimes felt he was trapped in the Middle Ages. The cabinet from which he served the drinks had been made by Leistler; he felt he should be serving a witches' brew or some potion handed down by Woden or one of the other gods. The monkey gulped down his schnapps and instantly fell over. Kreisler took no notice of him, but sipped his own drink appreciatively.

'Where did you get your taste for Scotch?'

'In Edinburgh. I went there for a conference of International Socialists. It was my downfall. I discovered a passion for the good things of life, especially liquor.'

'You gave up socialism? Or were you a communist?'

'Oh, a communist through and through. Or so I thought. I discovered that if you want the good things in life, you need money to buy them. I turned to forgery. That was another thing I discovered – that I had a very fine talent for forging.'

Carmody felt his story was rushing at him. 'Forging money or signatures?'

'Oh, both.' He looked at his glass, savoured another mouthful of Scotch. 'This is a beautiful whisky. I haven't tasted anything like this in years. Not since they sent me to a concentration camp back in 1934. I had a farewell drink the night before the Gestapo picked me up.'

Carmody began to feel suspicious that Kreisler was feeding him fiction, buying his drink with what he thought Carmody wanted to hear. 'What camp did they send you to?'

'Sachsenhausen.'

'For forgery or for being a communist?'

'Oh, I was never arrested for forgery, though they suspected I'd been at the game. No, I was a communist and that was bad enough.'

'When did they release you? I thought all the communists were still locked up.'

'They are. But I recanted.' He finished his drink, looked at his empty glass. Carmody took the hint and gave him a refill. Kreisler went on as if there had been no pause: 'I discovered the merits of National Socialism as opposed to Marxist socialism.'

'What are the merits?'

'They get you released from concentration camps – if you're lucky.' He smiled, but he was watching Carmody shrewdly. 'Why are you entertaining me, Herr Carmody?'

Carmody had another idea, wide of his original one: 'I thought you might be spying on me for the Gestapo.'

Kreisler looked shocked; the monkey stood up, then fell over again. 'The Gestapo watch *me*, Herr Carmody. I give you my word – I am not a stool pigeon.'

'I apologize. No, originally all I wanted was to do a story on you.' He explained his idea. 'Maybe I'm looking for a theme in the music that's being played in Berlin today.'

Kreisler shook his head. 'Leave me out of it, please. I'm sorry you wasted your whisky on me.' He stood up, reached down and picked up the monkey, chucked it under the chin. 'Your schnapps must be strong. FDR usually can take his liquor.'

'FDR?'

'There are no American tourists now, at least not many. It makes the locals smile when I call him FDR. At least some of them. The Gestapo, for instance. Their sense of humour is very simple.'

'I think you're still something of a forger, Herr Kreisler. You've made a forgery of yourself.'

'Of course.' He was stroking the monkey's head; it was dozing off, looking like a hundred human drunks Carmody had seen. 'The world is full of us. Especially Germany. But don't quote me, as you journalists say.'

Carmody nodded, though reluctantly. Then he said, 'How much do you know about the concentration camps?'

Kreisler had relaxed, but now his face set again. 'I wouldn't want to talk about Sachsenhausen.'

'It was as bad as that?'

'The point is I still have friends in there.'

'Are there any women there?'

'There weren't when I was there, but there may be some now. Most of the women were sent to Ravensbrueck, in Mecklenburg. Why do you ask?' The monkey seemed to be peering at Carmody from half-closed eyes. 'Are you looking for some sort of music theme in the camps? I assure you, Herr Carmody, it is very sad music.'

'No. I'm looking for the aunt of a friend of mine.'

'A Jewess?'

Carmody hardly hesitated. 'I don't believe so. No, we're not sure if she wasn't involved in some political thing.'

'I couldn't help you.' The monkey had gone to sleep now. Kreisler put on his hat, slung his hurdy-gurdy over his shoulder by its strap. 'I'll try to think of some gay tunes for tomorrow, Herr Carmody. Thank you for your hospitality.'

He touched the brim of his hat, opened the door and was gone before Carmody could show him out. The latter stood for a moment, wondering if he should run out on to the landing and shout down to the hurdy-gurdy man that he would write his story anyway. But he was not that sort of newspaperman. He might write a story that would send a man to jail (though so far he never had), but he could not write one that would return a man to a concentration camp.


4


Admiral Wilhelm Canaris was weary; not tired, which was a different state. He always saw to it that he got plenty of sleep, even to an hour's nap on the couch here in his office at Abwehr headquarters. It was an office that one would not have expected of a career naval officer: shabby, the desk cluttered with papers, two dachshunds dozing in their baskets, their blankets lying in crumpled heaps beside them on the faded carpet. A model of the light cruiser *Dresden*, undusted, stood on a side table. On the mantelpiece were three Japanese bronze monkeys, dumb symbols of the three cardinal virtues of any spy organization: See all, hear all, say nothing. There was the obligatory photograph of Hitler and also, a strange icon for the chief of the German secret service, a photograph of General Franco. Both photos were fly-speckled.

Canaris was weary of his battle to fight off a dozen ailments, all of which were imaginary, and the battle to fight off all those who tried to encroach on his domain. There were pills to help in the suppression of his ills; the drawers of his desk rattled with bottles. There were no pills to stave off invaders like Himmler and Heydrich, unless one resorted to cyanide. But that was not a naval man's way, though he knew cyanide was on the Abwehr's requisition list for emergency use by its operatives.

There was a knock on the door and Colonel von Gaffrin came in. Hans von Gaffrin was the fashion-plate of the service, an elegant cavalryman who was everything his chief was not: handsome, witty, athletic. He was also tall, which made the Admiral, who was only five-three, dislike him intensely. If he could have had his way he would have staffed the Abwehr with men shorter than himself. Which, eventually, would have made them highly identifiable spies.

Canaris retreated behind his desk and sat down, the only high ground for a short man. 'Yes?'

Gaffrin had one thing in common with Canaris: he was a monarchist and, like the Admiral, occasionally dreamed of the old, better days. 'Our beloved leader is at it again. More threats over the Danzig question. Something is brewing. I've just learned that the SS has put in a requisition for 150 Polish uniforms. Why? Is Goering putting on another one of his fancy dress balls?'

Canaris thought his senior aide sometimes went too far; but he was too weary today to argue. 'I have to go down to Obersalzberg next week, the Fuehrer wants to see all his senior officers. Perhaps I'll learn something then.'

'Not about those Polish uniforms, I'll bet. Do you want me to put someone on to it, find out why they're wanted?'

'If you wish.' He picked up a file on his desk. 'You live a very social life, Hans. Have you had any experience of the American actress Cathleen O'Dea?'

'Experience?' Gaffrin raised an eyebrow, an expression he had been practising all his life; everything about him was practised and practice, he was certain, had made him perfect. 'Not in that sense.'

Canaris looked irritable; he was prudish and he did not like even veiled hints about sex. 'Please, Hans, for once try and not be witty. Have you met her at dinners or parties?'

Gaffrin showed no reaction to his chief's reprimand; he practised urbanity, too. 'Several times. Do we have something on her? I'm told that Goebbels has his eye on her, poor girl.'

'I heard the same. We'll keep an eye on her, too.'

A few matters of business, then Gaffrin left. As soon as he was gone from the room Canaris stood up, felt taller. He carried the file on Cathleen O'Dea over to a window, stood there looking out on Tirpitzufer. It was another beautiful day, but he hardly saw it. He ran a slow hand over his white hair and his long rectangular face seemed to lengthen. His thick brows came down over his blue eyes as they always did when he slid into deep thought. What to do with the information in the file on Fräulein O'Dea, especially now that Goebbels was courting her?

The information had come in from New York only last week. The agent there had done his work well, though it had taken him several months. Cathleen O'Dea was half-Jewish, was here in Germany not just to appear in a film but to look for her mother Mady Hoolahan, born Miriam Razman. Should the head of the Abwehr do the right thing and pass the information on to Himmler, head of the SS and the Gestapo? The two organizations were supposed to co-operate and frequently did, though the relations between the two had grown strained in the past year as Himmler had tried to expand his own empire. Or should he pass the information direct to Goebbels? But no: why should he do a favour for such a champion adulterer?

He had no time for any of the senior Nazis. Once he had believed that National Socialism might be the only way to revive what he had always believed in, 'the eternal Germany'. But disillusion had set in, like a slowly growing disease, and there had been no pills or panaceas for that. The Nazi hierarchy, given to excesses, blinded by their own hunger for power, warped by their prejudices, were not the men who would lead Germany back to its entitled pinnacle.

He walked slowly back to his desk, put the file in a drawer and locked it. He sat down, looked at his dachshunds and whistled softly to them. They got up and waddled across to him. He bent down, his long-nosed face close to theirs, and patted their heads. An astigmatic visitor, coming suddenly into the room, might have thought there was a distinct family resemblance. The Admiral would not have been offended by the thought. He always thought of these animals as more his family than the wife and two daughters who bore his name. It amused him to think that until Germans had become the British royal family, the English had ill-treated their dogs.

*Meanwhile elsewhere:*

# SHIFT IN THANKSGIVING DATE AROUSES WHOLE COUNTRY

## Merchants Hail Roosevelt Plan
## Football Coaches Decry It

. . . Senator Bridges (Republican – NH), commenting on President Roosevelt's plan to change the date of Thanksgiving, suggested that the President might also abolish winter while he was at it . . .

## *ROGERS PEET'S END OF SUMMER SALE*

### Palm Beach Suits – $15.50

. . . Negotiations by followers of Father Divine for the purchase of Mrs James Lauren Van Alen's 700-acre estate adjoining President Roosevelt's home at Hyde Park, NY, have reached an impasse.

Father Divine, whose followers worship him as God, said, however, 'The earth is the Lord's and the fullness thereof. Anything my followers desire, they can have.'

Mrs Van Alen, said to be an Episcopalian, was not available for comment.

*Little Sir Echo, how do you do?*
*Hell-o, hell-o . . .*

## ROOSEVELT SAILS ON IN FOG-RIDDEN SEAS

. . . President Roosevelt, on the sixth day of his vacation cruise aboard the USS Tuscaloosa, once again found the weather against him . . .

---

**THE TRIP OF A LIFETIME**

Leaving Sydney, March 1940.
See Britain, France, Italy, Germany . . .

**£358/15/-**

---

. . . The Professor of Education at Melbourne University suggested today that parents should send their children to good talking pictures if they wanted them to speak correctly. Questioned as to whether that included Wallace Beery films, he said he was not familiar with Mr Beery . . .

. . . An elaborate ceremony is being planned for the unveiling in Planetta Square, Vienna, of a bust to Otto Planetta, murderer of Dr Dollfuss, the former Austrian Chancellor . . .

. . . A monument commemorating the first shot fired by the British Expeditionary Forces in the Great War is to be unveiled this week at Casteau, near Mons. The shot was fired by Corporal E. Thomas, 4th Royal Irish Dragoon Guards, on August 22, 1914 . . .

*When the deep purple falls*
*Over sleepy garden walls . . .*

# CHAPTER FOUR

## 1

'I used to think actors were interested in what I was saying to them,' said the man from the *Manchester Guardian*, 'till I realized they were only looking at the reflection of themselves in my glasses.'

'I once saw a motion picture,' said the *Christian Science Monitor* and left it at that.

'German films,' said *Le Matin*, 'are like knackwurst in celluloid skins. Very heavy.'

The foreign press had been invited out to Neubabelsberg to see some of the shooting on *Lola und Ludwig* and to talk to the stars. Welcoming a break from the dreary, unproductive government press conferences of the past week, the foreign correspondents had come out to the studio in force. But, with one or two exceptions, they were not film fans and they were not going to lower their dignity by appearing impressed by whom and what they saw. Foreign correspondents, like ambassadors, hate to write despatches beneath themselves. Snobbery has to be aspired to.

Carmody, no snob and a film fan ever since he had seen *Intolerance* in an outback bush town when he was six years old, was enjoying himself. Tables had been set up in one of the sound stages for luncheon and Cathleen, using her pre-rogative as a star, had insisted he should sit beside her. On his right was Melissa and beyond her was Oliver Burberry; on Cathleen's left was Lindwall, of the *New York Times*, who had suddenly found that, if no film fan, he was at least an admirer of actresses, especially one from New York. The other correspondents were spread amongst the other players, the director and his senior assistants and those of the studio brass who didn't think it was beneath their dignity to consort with foreign newspapermen. The atmosphere took everyone's attention away from the food which, like *Lola und Ludwig*, was badly cooked and lay heavy on the chest. Only the wine and beer were good.

'I had supper with our friend the other night,' said Cathleen, looking sideways at Carmody with that way women have of throwing stones into still pools.

He showed no ripples. 'Did you learn anything?'

'Only that I say the wrong thing too often. No –' She shook her head when she saw his sudden look of concern. 'I didn't get around to asking him about *her*. I left early, you'll be pleased to know.'

'Good,' he said; the ripples were showing. 'What's Colonel von Gaffrin doing here?'

'Where?' Then she saw the tall elegant figure in uniform sitting next to Helmut von Albern. She felt suddenly afraid, stared at the Abwehr officer and was still staring at him when he looked towards her, half-rose from his chair and bowed stiffly. She recovered, gave him a star's smile and dropped her eyes to her plate. 'Yes, what *is* he doing here?'

'Do you know him?'

'I've met him a couple of times at parties.' She was watching Gaffrin and Helmut: they were deep in conversation, the conversation of intimates.

'Just act naturally.'

'God, you sound just like Karl Braun!'

'Pardon?' said Lindwall on her left. He was a squarely built man with a square face and a thick military moustache; he had a slow Alabama drawl which made his German worse to listen to than Carmody's. He would have felt more at home covering events leading up to the War between the States.

'We were just wondering why Colonel von Gaffrin should be out here for lunch. Is he keeping an eye on some of you correspondents?' She had learned enough not to call a foreign correspondent a reporter to his face; newspapers, too, had their star ladders.

'The Gestapo do enough of that. What do you know about Colonel von Gaffrin?'

She wondered if she had said too much; but decided to go

further. 'Only that he's in the Secret Service.'

Lindwall glanced past her at Carmody. 'Did Sean tell you that? Well, I guess it's no secret. That's one of the unsubtle things about the Abwehr – it's really not such a secret service. We foreign newspapermen all seem to know who runs it.'

'Colonel von Gaffrin is very senior?'

'Number two, I'd guess. Or pretty close to it.'

'Then why is he out here?'

'Maybe he just likes actresses. There are so many pretty ones out here and I believe they are very popular with some of the top men.'

'You've been listening to gossip, Mr Lindwall.'

He smiled. 'It's a handicap you lovely ladies have to bear, Miss O'Dea.'

'You're just an old Southern gentleman, Colonel Lindwall.' She gave him the accent she had used in *Mansion in Memphis*.

'I wish I were,' he said soberly. 'Life in Alabama would be pleasanter than here in Germany, even for the nigras.'

She knew nothing about the nigras in Alabama; it was enough being half-Jewish. At least there were no concentration camps in Alabama, none that she knew of.

When lunch was finished she rose and went across to Helmut and Colonel von Gaffrin. She was testing the high dive platform again; but this time she would not dive in with her mouth open. She was aware of Carmody staring after her, was sure he was silently shouting a warning to her to be careful, but she did not look back at him.

'Colonel von Gaffrin –' She gave him her hand, something she had learned since coming to Berlin, and he clicked his heels, bowed and kissed it. The gesture always pleased her; it was so much better than the Hollywood kiss on the cheek. 'I didn't know you and Helmut were such friends.'

'I served under General von Albern – I have known Helmut since he was a boy.'

Helmut said nothing, just stood rather stiffly and very quietly, as if telling her he would rather not have had his conversation with Gaffrin interrupted.

'You have never been out here before,' Cathleen said. 'Are you to be a technical adviser on some picture?'

'Something like that.' He gave a thin, practised smile.

'A cavalry picture?' She knew he still posed as a cavalry officer, though Carmody had told her most people knew his true posting.

The smile broadened, was warmer. 'We should make something like those films about the US cavalry. We have no Indians to attack, unfortunately.'

Helmut said quietly, 'One would have thought there were plenty of other targets.'

'Ah, but we are talking about the past, Helmut, when we used horses. You are a photographer. Which would you rather photograph attacking Fort Apache – horses or tanks?'

There is something between these two, Cathleen thought; there was a tension that was almost visible. She waited for Helmut to give Gaffrin an answer, but he just shrugged.

'Did you ever play in a cavalry film, Fräulein O'Dea?'

'No, Herr Colonel. Hollywood never saw me as the old-fashioned type.'

'This is an old-fashioned film, is it not?'

'Yes. But Lola Montez was years ahead of her time. I think she may have even been at home in Germany today.'

'You must tell me more about her some time. But I must go –'

He bowed, kissed her hand again, said goodbye to Helmut and went striding away across the sound stage, looking handsome and theatrical enough to have been one of the studio's stars. Willy Heffer, running to fat these days, no longer the matinée idol he had once been, was one who was glad to see him go. There is nothing worse for the professional than to be outshone by an amateur.

'So you're friends with the Abwehr?' said Cathleen, diving off the high board into what she hoped would be deep water.

'Don't be ridiculous,' said Helmut, keeping his voice low as a hint for her to do the same. 'He is just a friend of the family. You have spies on the brain.'

'Maybe you're right. But you're not a foreigner.'

'What makes you think things are easy for all Germans? I have seen a dozen Jews disappear from this studio since I first came here.' His tone softened, he put a hand on her arm: the first time he had ever touched her. It was not something she would have expected from him, someone from an aristocratic family. She was used to being pawed, but this was a gentle, warning touch. 'Cathleen, I assure you – the Colonel was not out here to spy on anyone, least of all you. He came to see me and I invited him to the luncheon.'

'What did you do when they took the Jews away?' The water might get deeper.

'Nothing. I wasn't proud of doing nothing, but there was nothing one could do.'

'That sounds a bit mixed up.'

'Everything is mixed up.'

She dived deeper: 'Helmut, did you leave me a note telling me to be careful, that the Abwehr was interested in me?'

The luncheon group was breaking up, the correspondents getting ready for the drive back to Berlin, smart, superior phrases already forming under their hats. It had been a mistake inviting this particular lot and Cathleen, her mind only half on them as she smiled goodbyes, wondered who had blundered. She was sure Dr Goebbels would have chosen better.

Helmut waited till they were alone again. 'Why should I do that? Am I your guardian angel?'

'You should have said, "Am I my sister's keeper?" We're brother and sister in this trade, Helmut, we should be looking after each other. From what I've heard, all of us in the arts –'

'The arts? There hasn't been any art in films for years.'

'You know what I mean. Entertainment – movies, theatre, music, the opera, books. Nobody knows when he or she is going to put a foot wrong.'

'You're always likely to do that, Cathleen,' he said almost kindly and abruptly walked away from her. She remarked that he had not answered her question.

'Are you working this afternoon?' Carmody stood beside her.

She came up out of water that had proved shallower than she had hoped. She blinked, as if clearing her eyes of water, and looked at him. 'What? No, I'm not working. They're all Willy's scenes this afternoon.'

'Can I ride back with you?'

She gave him her hand and a big warm smile. He was reliable, he answered questions when put to him. 'Do you think Helmut might be working for the Abwehr?'

'Darl, you're becoming paranoic.' It was a fashionable word with correspondents, it was just the description needed for Hitler and his actions.

Well, that's a direct enough answer, she thought; and immediately resented it. 'You mean you think I've got a persecution complex. Well, so would you have if you were in my position –'

'Darl, I'm sorry –' He would hate to be in her position, looking for his mother in a country like this. He had left home and come to the other side of the world, but he loved Ida, his mother, as much as Cathleen must love hers. He just doubted that he would ever be able to explain that to her. He doubted very much that he would be able to explain it in so many words to his mother. He was one of those Australians who became inarticulate when it came to sentiment. 'Let's go home.'

'That would be a good idea.' But she was thinking of another home, not the apartment on Uhlandstrasse.

Driving back in the studio car, with the studio driver up front and no glass partition to cut him off, they said very little to each other. They passed a long army convoy heading east, but they just looked at each other and made no comment. Carmody knew there had been a lot of troop movement in the past week, but he had not been able to keep up with all of it.

Once in her apartment there was a moment's hesitation between them, then he took her in his arms. She was glad of their comfort; but she hesitated another moment before she gave him her lips. She had been kissing men for as long as she could remember and now all at once she was afraid of what it might mean.

His kiss wasn't fierce, but he took his time about it. Then he let her go. 'Your heart's not in it.'

She stared at him, then suddenly she grabbed him and kissed him almost ferociously, threatening to swallow him: it was the sort of kiss she gave in bed. When she let him go he put his hand up to the back of his neck and it came away streaked with blood.

'Oh God!' She looked at her nails, saw the blood under them.

He grinned. 'Well, the old ewe never did that to me.'

Suddenly she loved him; though was not yet in love. 'When this is all over –'

'What?'

'Nothing.' When what was all over? The search for her mother might never be over. 'Take your shirt off and come into the bathroom while I put some antiseptic on that.'

In the bathroom, when he had taken off his shirt, she was surprised at the muscles in his arms and shoulders. In the mirrored walls he saw her looking at him. 'I got those shoulders from my dad. And working in the sheds. Shearing builds your muscles but breaks your back. That's why I gave the game away. I always wanted to see the world, anyway.'

She looked at him in the big mirror, shaking her head. 'How did you get here?'

'It's been a long road,' he said, looking at himself and her, wondering how much further there was to go. 'A lot of roads, actually.'

He had been born on the road, in a tent outside Wilcannia in western New South Wales. A whole atlas of roads had followed: the droving tracks of eastern Australia, the highways across America, Fifth Avenue, the road out of Portugal up into Spain, the Extremadura Road into Madrid, the Brenner Pass and the road that led to Vienna and back to Prague, and now the Unter den Linden, maybe the end of the road.

'Are you tired?'

He knew what she meant. 'No, I'm too young for that. Maybe in another ten years or so. When I'm as old as Joe Begley or Oliver Burberry.'

'Do you think they are tired?' She dabbed at the scratches with cottonwool, was pleased when he didn't flinch at the bite of the antiseptic.

'Not tired, maybe. Disillusioned.'

'Are you disillusioned?' All at once she wanted him not to be.

'Not yet. But it's happening. I'd never read much history till I came to Europe. I'd always thought of Europeans as being truly civilized, much more than we Aussies. But the skulduggery that goes on here –' He smiled at her in the mirror. 'I guess you have to be civilized to get up to what they do. Back home we just carve up each other, bosses and unions. Here they carve up nations.'

She gazed at him in the mirror, looking at herself as well as him: a pair of innocents. She bent and kissed his back between the shoulder-blades; she suddenly wanted to take him to bed. Then she straightened and went quickly out of the bathroom, calling back to him to get them both a drink. He sat on the stool in the bathroom a few moments, staring at himself, seeing the ghost of her there beside him and the look that had been on her face before she had bent and kissed his back. Then he smiled at himself, not smugly but with the expression of a man who was learning about women. Who was, in other words, becoming civilized.

He put on his shirt and tie, went out into the living room and made her a martini and poured himself a beer. He stayed another half-hour, but she remained out of his reach and he didn't pursue her. Each of them knew a corner had been turned in their relationship; there was no going back, but neither was there any rushing ahead. They enjoyed each other in the mirrored walls and left it at that for the moment.

He told her about his visit to the Hotel Ernst. 'The cove I saw, the night clerk, I'm sure he's an informer for the Gestapo.'

She spilled some of her drink. 'They'll trace you!'

'Maybe. But it's not me I'm worried about, it's you. You can bet they have someone on the day staff who's in their pay. He'd have told them about you going there.'

She shook her head. 'I wore a wig and glasses. It was a

pretty lousy disguise, but I think it was enough. It was a cold day and I was rugged up in a thick coat.'

'They'd have still spotted you for an American.'

'Maybe, but I don't think so. I spoke German – I pretended I had a bad cold, so they wouldn't pick my accent –' She was pleased when he nodded reluctant admiration. 'I'm an actress – it's one thing I know how to do –'

'I just wish you'd be careful.'

'I could say the same to you. If the Gestapo pick you up –'

'They're not going to throw me into any concentration camp –'

'They wouldn't dare do that to me, not after bringing me over for the picture –'

'No, probably not. But if they traced you to your mother, they might make it even tougher for her, wherever she is.'

'I wonder –' She looked pensively into her drink. 'I wonder what would happen if I came out in the open – I could have given that press conference today out at the studio something that would have made them sit up – Dr Goebbels wouldn't want that sort of publicity for a picture he's trying to sell on the world market –'

'It might work – and it might not. I don't know whether it's worth the risk – these bloody Nazis are so unpredictable. Goebbels might want your mother released, if –'

'If what?' She had picked up his momentary hesitation.

He had almost said, *if she's still alive.* He recovered adeptly: he was becoming an actor. 'If Himmler said no, where would that leave you? He and Goebbels can't stand each other. He might deny the Gestapo knew anything about your mother. You can't play these blokes against each other, darl. It's too dangerous.'

She saw his point, realized he knew more about the skulduggery amongst the top Nazis than she ever would. When it came time for him to leave to go to his office to file his day's copy, she kissed him goodbye at the door, a sisterly kiss.

He grinned as her hand pressed against his chest, keeping him at a distance. 'If my editor wasn't hanging on the phone –'

She smiled, liking him immensely. 'I have another late call tomorrow. Come back and take me to dinner.'

He nodded. 'Then we'll go to the Sportspalast, it's the last night of the six-day bike races. There are some Aussies and Yanks racing.'

'Sean, I'm really not in the mood –'

Her hand was still on his chest; he put his own over it. 'Darl, I know how you feel, but I think it's better if you don't mope around. Or do you want to come back here after dinner and we'll go to bed?'

She was surprised at his directness, it was so unlike his approach up till now; it was the sort of approach one got in Hollywood. Her hand stiffened and she pushed him out the door. 'We'll go to the bike races.'

He was grinning when he got out into the street. Going against the grain of his pocket, he caught a taxi across to the Potsdamerplatz; he would have enjoyed the long walk thinking about his love, but there were a thousand words to be written, none of them about love. He paid off the driver, surprising himself more than the man with his tip, and, whistling, went into the agency building and up to the World Press office.

He opened the outer door and Olga Luxemburg said, 'These two gentlemen wish to see you, Herr Carmody.'

He didn't need the note of fear in her voice to tell him who they were.

2

It was too warm for them to be wearing the black leather coat that had become almost the obligatory uniform for them. They held their hats in their hands, but they were the sort of hats he would have expected them to be wearing. Their suits, too, were as he expected, buttoned up like serge safes holding secrets. He was surprised to see that they looked more puritanical than brutal.

'Good afternoon, Herr Carmody.' The one who spoke had a round pink face and ginger hair that, brilliantined, lay on his head like a coating of orange jelly. He had sad benign eyes and might have been a failed priest, one who had chosen the wrong religion. 'May we see you in your office?'

Carmody nodded and gestured for the two of them to go ahead of him into the inner office.

Fräulein Luxemburg sniffed at the backs of the Gestapo men. 'Can I get you anything, Herr Carmody?' A cup of coffee, a lifebelt, a regiment of tanks?

'Thank you, Fräulein Luxemburg, I'll be okay.' He went into his office and closed the door. 'Who are you gentlemen?'

The ginger-haired man said, 'I am Inspector Lutze and this is Sergeant Decker.'

'From the Gestapo?'

Lutze made a face, as if Carmody had said a dirty word. 'The Secret State Police.'

Carmody knew how much some State Police officers hated the word *Gestapo*. He had once done a piece on how it originated. The German name for the department was *Geheimes Staatspolizeiamt* and some anonymous postal clerk, told to come up with a postal cancellation stamp, had coined the word *Gestapa*. It had soon turned into Gestapo, a name that came to mean more than just the cancellation of mail. Out of such accidents history picks its villains and heroes.

'You have some questions you want to ask me?'

Lutze looked at Decker, who opened the safe of his suit and took out a thick black notebook. He was a tall thin man who looked slightly mouldy, as if summer had failed to dry him out. He had a voice to match, coated with fuzz.

'You have been enquiring for the whereabouts of a woman named Mady Hoolahan?'

The ten marks hadn't gone far enough with the night clerk at the Hotel Ernst: there had been a higher bidder, or bigger threats. 'Yes.'

'What is your interest in this woman?'

'I was asked by my New York office to see if I could find her.' He sounded convincing, at least in his own ears.

'Would you have a copy of that request?'

'No. It came through London, by phone.'

Lutze chimed in, nodding his head understandingly. 'Of course.'

'Did they say why they wanted you to find her?'

'I gather she came to Germany from America earlier this year and then just disappeared.'

'What exactly do you mean by *disappeared*?' said Lutze, looking puzzled. Or doing a very good impersonation of it.

'She left the Hotel Ernst one night with her luggage and hasn't been seen since. I think that's what I mean by *disappeared*.'

'You haven't told us why World Press should be interested in her,' said Decker.

'You haven't given me a chance to answer,' said Carmody a little testily.

'Of course not,' said Lutze, giving absolution. 'Take your time, Herr Carmody.'

'She is the aunt by marriage of one of our stringers in Kansas City. He was concerned about her.' I'm a bloody awful liar, he thought. Fiction had never been his strong point; which made him such a good objective reporter. 'It was just a personal thing, not an official agency enquiry.'

'What is a stringer?' Lutze was puzzled again, this time by a word he had never heard before.

Carmody himself had only just invented it, knocking together his own portmanteau: *Schnurkorrespondent*. 'A part-time correspondent.'

'What is this man's name?' said Decker, pencil poised above the notebook.

Carmody grabbed a name out of the shearing sheds back home. 'Venneker, Rupert Venneker.' He hoped to God there was no Venneker in Kansas City; he hoped even more fervently there was no Gestapo stringer in that town. 'I've never met him.'

'Of course not,' said Lutze, again nodding understandingly. His sympathetic agreement had begun to annoy Carmody. Why wasn't the bugger playing true to type?

Even Decker seemed only mildly interested in the questions he was asking. 'So Frau Hoolahan means nothing to you personally?'

She did mean very much to him, since she was Cathleen's mother: she was beginning to assume the importance of someone on whom his own happiness might depend. 'I am just doing a favour for someone. Maybe you could help find her?'

'How do you think we could do that, Herr Carmody?' said Lutze.

'Perhaps some of your colleagues in the Secret Police have picked her up.' That was a mistake and he knew it as soon as he said it.

'Why do you think they would have done that?'

'I'm sure they have their reasons for everything they do, but I've never been able to find out why. After all you are the *Secret* State Police.'

Lutze nodded again, this time approvingly. He took out a handkerchief and wiped his face, which had got pinker in the warmth of the room. The windows faced west and the afternoon sun was pushing against the glass like a physical force, threatening to crack it. Carmody felt comfortable in it, but it was proving too much for Lutze. Decker, on the other hand, looked as if he might be losing some of his mould. He was warming to his questioning.

'You are an acquaintance of Lady Margaret Arrowsmith?'

'As a newspaperman I'm an acquaintance of a lot of people.'

'Of Fräulein Cathleen O'Dea, the film star?'

'I've been doing a story on her, that's all.'

'Have you written stories on Lady Arrowsmith?'

They had been watching him more closely than he had imagined. 'No. I just like her as a person.'

'She is a great admirer of the Fuehrer.'

'So I understand. But we never discuss politics.'

Lutze said, 'A foreign correspondent, and you don't discuss politics?'

'Not with women. I think the Fuehrer would agree with me. How many women does he have in his Ministries?'

The heat was too much for Lutze; the brilliantine had

95

started to glisten in little beads, the orange jelly looked ready to run. He gave up, though reluctantly. 'We must talk again some time, Herr Carmody. It has been very interesting.'

He ran his handkerchief over his head and it came away streaked with grease. Decker, looking disappointed, put away his notebook and buttoned up the blue serge safe. Then they both put on their hats, like a vaudeville duo about to make an exit off-stage. Only for that moment did they look ludicrous, but Carmody knew he had nothing to laugh about.

But he threw out a line: if they were going to continue watching him, he must try to gain something from them: 'Will you let me know if you hear anything of Frau Hoolahan?'

'Of course,' said Lutze. 'We mustn't forget why we came.'

When they had gone Carmody took off his jacket and found his shirt soaked with sweat. He flopped down in his chair and looked up as Olga Luxemburg put a worried face inside the door.

'What did *they* want?' Her tongue was almost in a knot with contempt.

'Just routine.'

'Nuts,' said Fräulein Luxemburg, who might have been vulgar if her life had been different. Carmody often wondered what had kept her a spinster with no visible male in her life, but he would never have dared ask her. 'You don't usually get hot and bothered like that.'

'Am I hot and bothered?' Indeed he was. He got up and pushed both windows high, letting in the noise of the Potsdamerplatz. 'Do you think you could send down for a nice cold beer? Two.'

'Thank you,' she said, though he hadn't meant the second one for her.

She went out and he turned to his typewriter. He glanced at the tapes and clippings on his desk. Von der Schulenburg, the German ambassador to Moscow, was still seeing Foreign Minister Molotov; Hitler and Ribbentrop, the German Foreign Minister, were still down at the Berghof in Obersalzberg. Europe was coming to the boil, the most unlikely of partners looked as if they might finish up in the same pot, and New York was waiting on another two thousand words of conjecture. He began his two-fingered pecking at the keys. He wondered if, when the end of the world came, there would be final editions of newspapers on the day after.

## 3

'I tell you, mate, it's a bugger of a way to make a living. Round and round the bloody track night after night, riding up your own arse. This week Berlin, last week Cologne, the week before that Amsterdam. Still, I tell you, mate, I'd never make this sort of money doing anything else.'

'How do you get on with the German riders?'

'Great, except when there are big-wigs up in the boxes. Then they all have to start proving they're good Nazis.'

'How do you feel about that?'

'Don't mean a bugger to me, mate. They get rough, me and me mate and the Yanks we get rough, too. It's all good dirty fun.'

He reminded Carmody of shearers he had known: tough, sinewy, his body worn to the bone by the rigours of his trade. He had the used, lived-in face that is impossible to name for age: he could have been anywhere between 25 and 45. He came from Sydney, had been on the world six-day track for ten years and sounded as if he might welcome a world war as an excuse to go home. Carmody had come down into the middle of the track to talk to him and one of the American riders, hoping to get something that would lighten the stories he had been filing for the past two weeks. The American had been just as bluntly expressive and Carmody, feeling pleased with what he had, wished the Australian cyclist good luck and went back up to join Cathleen.

'It's a hard way of making a living,' she said, watching the twelve cyclists on the track as they whirred by, the wheels beneath them flickering silver circles, all their backs bent over in matching curves like a ballet line of symmetrical hunchbacks.

97

'That's what they both told me. Like boxing.'

He looked up and about him at the Sportspalast. The huge arena was packed, but he had seen it filled to denser capacity. This was where Hitler came to preach to the faithful; then the bicycle track was removed and the centre of the arena became a seething mass of acclamation for the Fuehrer. This was Berlin's indoor equivalent of the huge outdoor stadium at Nuremberg, where Hitler wielded his magic, where *Sieg Heil!* became a terrifying chorus that came out of the throat of Hell and the impartial observer feared for the rest of the world. He had seen Hitler address 15,000 Nazi Party officers in this Sportspalast, with hundreds of swastika flags fluttering high above them like a storm of red, black and white clouds, and the booming shouts of the crowd another storm in the body of the huge arena and he had gone away convinced that war in Europe was inevitable, that passionate ambition such as he had seen could not be contained.

Tonight was different; but the memory of that other night clouded his mind. Lights blazed on the track; the cyclists went round and round in their whispering pursuit of each other; the crowd murmured and chattered and occasionally shouted as some cyclist tried to make a break on the main bunch, but there was no hysterical frightening din. Yet Carmody kept waiting for the atmosphere to change, for the bike-riders to turn into charging lancers, the crowd to rise to its feet and start chanting and for that modest figure in the brown Party uniform suddenly to appear, raise an arm and turn the night into another terrifying threat.

A hand touched him on the shoulder and he jumped, still deep in the misery of his imagination. Or was he expecting a summons from the Gestapo? He turned and almost laughed with relief when he saw Meg Arrowsmith. She had just sat down behind him. 'Darling, are you a bicycle fan?'

'No,' said Cathleen, turning round, 'he's a fan of mine.'

Oh crumbs, thought Carmody, who knew nothing of women's rivalry. He introduced them to each other and saw at once that women were not natural friends; knowing the other's reputation, each looked at the other with a suspicious eye. They were smiling, but their eyes had the same metallic glitter as the whirring wheels out on the track. Carmody wondered what he would have made of the encounter if he had been a gossip columnist. His pen, as yet, was not sharp enough to be malicious.

Meg introduced her escort, a young bull who knew he would be of service tonight; he kept looking at Meg as if he were already beside her, or on top of her, in bed. 'Herr Krebs is with the Ministry of Sport.'

He would be, thought Carmody.

'I'd never have guessed it,' said Cathleen, giving the muscular young man a smile that made him wonder for the moment if he had chosen the wrong woman for the night. 'You look more the Ministry of Culture type, Herr Krebs.'

Lay off, said Carmody silently and pressed her knee. She gave him the same dazzling smile. 'Don't you think so, Sean?'

Carmody was saved from an opinion on Herr Krebs by a spectacular spill on the track. Three cyclists at the rear of the field went down in a wild tangle of arms, legs and bikes. Attendants rushed to their aid; the crowd stood up hoping for some serious injury, then, breeding overcoming instinct, sighed with relief when they saw the three riders get groggily to their feet; excitement simmered down and the race went on as the injured riders' partners came on to take their place. By then Krebs had his arm in Meg's and his thoughts a couple of hours ahead.

'Shall we ask them to have supper with us?' Cathleen whispered.

'No,' said Carmody.

'I'd like to know her better.'

'I can tell you all you want to know.'

'I'll bet.'

There was a sexual bantering to her voice that had never been there before, at least not with him. He was encouraged by it, but not enough to agree with her to having supper with Meg Arrowsmith. 'Why are you so keen to know her better?'

'I'd like to know what sort of woman hangs around Hitler, especially an Englishwoman.'

'From what I hear, she's out of favour with Hitler at the

99

moment. She thinks he and Chamberlain should get together instead of sparring with each other.'

'Then let's ask them for supper.' They were still whispering, heads together like lovers. He wondered what Meg, sitting immediately behind him, was thinking.

He sought a distraction, looked out at the track, then up at the galleries and found one: 'Look, there's Himmler! In the main box —'

He was the man he did not want to see; the head of the SS, the *Schutzstaffel*, also controlled the Gestapo. Carmody had no illusions about his own importance; he was small fry, Himmler would not even know he had been interrogated by Gestapo junior officers. But he had become sensitive about whom he was with: sitting beside him was Cathleen, favoured by Goebbels, and right behind was Meg Arrowsmith, once favoured by Hitler. He was sure that the information had already been conveyed to Himmler. Even as he looked up at the box, at the Reichsfuehrer SS and his bodyguard of uniformed toughs, Himmler looked down at him through binoculars. Then the binoculars were handed back to an aide and the SS chief went back to watching the track and the circling cyclists.

'What's he doing here?'

He shrugged; but he had a shrewd guess. For the past ten days, while tension had grown over the question of the Danzig Corridor, which Hitler claimed was German territory and should be returned by Poland, ministers and other top officials had been appearing at the opera, concerts and other public functions, as if to reassure the nervous Berliners, and by extension other Germans, that the current international crisis was under control. That Himmler, the ex-chicken farmer who looked like a fussy schoolmaster but who ran concentration camps instead of schools, who fostered the idea that he was an elitist mystic, should come to the bike races to suggest that everything was normal, struck him as a bad joke. Berlin was noted for its wicked wit, but Himmler was not a Berliner.

He felt another tap on his shoulder. Meg said, 'Would you and Miss O'Dea care to have supper with us at the Adlon?'

'We'd love to,' said Cathleen before Carmody could think of an excuse to decline. 'Now or later?'

'Why not now?' said Meg. 'Men on bicycles don't excite me.'

'Me, neither,' said Cathleen.

Carmody and Krebs, neither of them on a bike, rose reluctantly. Carmody wanted to keep Cathleen away from Meg; Krebs wanted Meg for himself. But in the social game, women are rulers: both men followed Cathleen and Meg obediently. As he went down towards the exit Carmody looked back and up at the boxes. One of Himmler's aides had the binoculars focused on the departing party.

Meg had hung back to wait for him. 'Did you see Himmler?'

He fired a random arrow: 'He had the glasses on you.'

'Not me, darling. You and Miss O'Dea.'

'No.' He shook his head emphatically. 'What have you been up to?'

But she wasn't taken in by his fake attack. 'Darling, my life is an open book to the Gestapo. What have *you* been up to?'

Cathleen, with Krebs adrift beside her, was waiting for them at the bottom of the steps. 'What's been going on behind my back?'

'I was just giving him some sisterly warning,' said Meg. 'We Empire types must stick together.'

'What empire was that?' said Cathleen.

On a raft of splintered smiles they all floated out to find a taxi. The two men were stiff and cagey, but the two women were completely at ease, foes on common ground. Contempt had bred familiarity.

Krebs was out of place at the Adlon; he was a beerhall diner. But he kept his mouth shut except when eating and his eyes never stopped moving; after a while they began to remind Carmody of the spinning wheels of the six-day bike riders. For his own part Carmody, too, kept quiet, leaving the two women to provide most of the conversation. Which they did willingly.

'Is it true you were one of Dr Goebbels' mistresses?' said Cathleen, plunging into the deep end again.

101

Carmody, jaws locked on smoked salmon, waited for Meg to erupt. But she just smiled, a blade of white steel between her lips. 'What sort of question is that to ask an English maiden?'

'If I knew an English maiden I shouldn't ask it,' Cathleen's smile was a reflection of Meg's. Carmody resumed chewing, knowing the battle was going to be deadly but civilized. Krebs' eyes stopped swivelling for a moment; then he gave up and sank out of his depth. Carmody, the boy from the bush, all at once felt terribly sophisticated alongside him.

'No, I wasn't.' Meg was not a good liar; she had to avoid Carmody's eye. 'Though he tried. But I'm very un-English in some ways – I don't like being in a queue. Do you?'

That stung Cathleen, but she didn't show it. She went off on another of her tangents: 'Do you think there will be war?'

'How should I know?' But doubt and worry suddenly showed: the evening was turning serious, something Meg always tried to avoid. Days were the time for serious discussion, evenings were for fun. Lately, Carmody had discovered, she had taken to avoiding people during the day.

'From the circles you move in. You know all the men who count. Hitler, for instance.'

Meg laughed; it sounded just a little hysterical. Krebs' eyes came back from their tour of the dining room, focused on her: the conversation was on a level he could understand, at least for the moment. 'I haven't seen the Fuehrer in weeks.'

'I thought you were one of his favourites?'

'Gossip, darling. You should know what it's like – gossip is food and drink to film people, isn't it? Aren't you supposed to have had countless lovers?'

'No, that was Mae West. I always counted mine.'

The band began to play *I'm in the Mood for Love* and people in the big room became misty-eyed, including even some senior SS officers. Carmody waited for Fred Doe on trumpet to blow a sour satirical note, but tonight Doe wasn't misbehaving, just playing straight. There were too many uniforms at the Adlon this evening.

When the number was finished and the band left its stand to take a break, Carmody excused himself from the table and went round to see Fred Doe. He introduced himself and explained what he had in mind, his story on the musicians of Berlin.

'Sure, pal.' Doe was no more than thirty-five, but looked at least ten years older. He had thick grey hair, a thin moustache and a long lined face whose summer tan looked yellow. He had dark short-sighted eyes that had never looked past tomorrow and never would, a husky voice and a horn blower's callus on his bottom lip. 'But nothing political, okay? I saw who you're with tonight, that Lady Arrowsmith dame.'

'I'm with Cathleen O'Dea,' said Carmody and couldn't help the note of pride in his voice; he was like a schoolboy going out with the prettiest girl in town for the first time. 'Lady Arrowsmith is just a source.'

'Well, good luck with your source, pal. And good luck with the O'Dea dame. I know who'd be the less poison.'

Carmody resented the jazz man's opinion, but said nothing. He made an appointment for the next day and went back to his table. Krebs was still eating, still swivelling his eyes, and Cathleen and Meg were still sparring, neither showing any visible wounds. Meg, indeed, was offering advice.

'When your film is finished darling, take your money and run. You asked me if there is going to be war –' she paused, decided the evening was not going to be all fun after all, and went on, 'Yes, I think so. I think it is stupid and will be terrible and the only winners will be the Russians.'

'That's one theory I haven't heard,' said Carmody, aware that Krebs had come back into their orbit again. 'Who told you that?'

'Ah, darling, do you give away your sources of information?'

'Germany will be the only winner,' said Krebs.

'Yes, darling,' said Meg, patting his hand as she might have that of a stupid child. 'Let's go home, everyone's getting too serious. Don't worry about the bill, Sean. It's on my account. Goodnight, Cathleen darling. Do take care of yourself. There must be so many temptations in your business.'

'And in yours,' said Cathleen, 'darling.'

Meg kissed Carmody on the cheek, took Krebs in tow and led him out of the dining room, smiling and waving to people as she went. She might have nowhere to go, thought Carmody, but she knows how to make an exit.

'She knows how to make an exit,' said Cathleen. 'What are you smiling at?'

'My mother used to say that when two people thought the same thing at once, they'd finally reached the stage of being truly married.'

'Are you proposing to me?' Her smile was wicked. Then she relented. 'I'd never put you over a barrel like that, not in times like these.'

'What times?'

'Let's go home,' she said abruptly.

She led him out of the room, making her own exit. It seemed to Carmody that it was a less successful one than Meg's. In times like these, he thought, actresses are less important than courtesans. Then he smiled again. Meg would be amused to hear herself described as a courtesan, especially at the court of a leader who was said to be asexual.

When they got out of the taxi outside Cathleen's apartment building, Carmody's first instinct was to look up and down the Uhlandstrasse.

'What's the matter?'

For the first time he told her of the visit from the Gestapo that afternoon. 'I don't want them calling on you.'

She, too, looked up and down the street. 'I can't see anyone. Are they usually obvious when they're watching you?'

'I don't know.'

They went up to her apartment. He opened the door with her key, took her in his arms and kissed her. It was a lingering kiss; she didn't push him away. It seemed the proper end to the evening and it was all he expected. Then she undid two buttons of his shirt and her hand was caressing his chest.

'I should be doing that,' he said.

She took his hand and put it inside his shirt. 'Go ahead, be my guest.'

They went into the apartment on a laugh that seemed to

104

come out of the same mouth, so closely were they locked. Laughter is a good thing to take to bed; tears have toppled an erection but never laughter. They made love surrounded by themselves in the German director's mirrors. It was like being in the best brothel in Berlin, but it was free and the love-making, as well as the love, was sincere. He couldn't have been happier. She, being an actress, wasn't sure.

## 4

*Extracts from the memoirs of General Kurt von Albern:*

. . . I was in love in the last weeks of peace in 1914, with my wife and my young son Helmut. I had been married eight years and was settled down; I was a major, the youngest in my regiment, and life, it seemed, could not have offered more. But then it did: it offered war . . .

We were afraid of the Russians. (How history repeats itself!) But the Kaiser was looking for excuses for war to break out; now, answering to conscience, rather than patriotism, I think we all were. I came of a class bred for war, like cavalry horses. My father had fought against France in 1870 (another war in search of excuses); my great-grandfather, who would go anywhere for a war, fought at Waterloo in Field Marshal Blücher's army. I had the family appetite, much to my wife's distress. There is no such thing as a proper soldier's wife; women are much too sensible about violence, though they too often cause it. But they never long for war, even if their husbands are generals, which I was not then . . .

I took her to Kranzler's, where we had gone when courting. It was where the Guards officers congregated; the café was thronged with them that evening. Usually the talk was of horses or dogs, occasionally of women; that evening the talk was of war. The sundaes turned sour in front of us, the street musicians outside were playing military marches, the officers strutted between the tables like turkey cocks. I saw the sadness (it might even have been disgust; I have never been very good at reading women's expressions) in my wife's eyes and I knew I had just seen the first casualty of the war, though it had not yet begun . . .

Now, with Eva dead, I was once more back in Berlin preparing for a war based on excuses. This time I was with Romy, a woman who understood what we were about and was prepared to help. I loved her, but no more than I did Eva . . .

I had to see Helmut. I had hoped to avoid him, but he was too devoted to me; and I to him. I should have to tell him . . . He, unfortunately, was so much like his mother . . .

# CHAPTER FIVE

## 1

Helmut von Albern turned off the autobahn and on to one of the side roads that led into the Grunewald, the Green Forest of Berlin. He had not been surprised that his father should suggest they meet there rather than in some hotel or café in the city; it was consistent with his father's strange behaviour over the past few days. He parked the Opel, got out and walked into the woods, following a path that, though he had not followed it in years, was still familiar. Nothing, he thought, changed in the Grunewald; it looked as manicured as ever, not a pine cone or broken branch littering the floor of the woods; the firewood gatherers had done their scavenging. He caught glimpses of horses and their riders through the trees; he had ridden that same path as a boy with his father. At the weekend the woods would be alive with picnicking families, but in the early evening of this weekday there were few people around.

He found his father waiting for him at the spot he had named; he was surprised to find Romy von Sonntag with him. What was going on? Were they going to elope?

He shook his father's hand and kissed Romy's. It was all very formal, so different from meetings at the studio, but it had been like that all his life. The strange thing was that there was more warmth and true affection between himself and his father than anything he had experienced with those he had met in the easy camaraderie of the film business.

'Shall we walk?' said his father. 'We'll look less conspicuous than standing about like street-corner conspirators.'

Helmut looked at Romy, who smiled at him. She was in her early forties, blonde and slim, as beautiful as any woman he had ever photographed, an aristocrat whose only fault was that she had married for money. She came of an old Saxony family that had lost its holdings years before she was born; she had married Harald von Sonntag, whose family had made their money in the Kaiser's day and had come very late, by her own family's standards, to the *von* in their name. She was not the first nor would she be the last woman who had chosen money ahead of love; she was not the first nor would she be the last who had discovered their mistake too late. Silk sheets are a luxury but they don't always make the happiest bed.

'What are you two up to?'

Romy was walking between the two men; she took Helmut's hand rather than the General's, a gesture Helmut noticed. 'Your father hasn't slept for two nights, wondering whether he should tell you. We are planning to kidnap Hitler. Or kill him, if needs be.'

He could hear birds singing in the trees above him, the hum of cars on the distant autobahn, the soft tattoo of a cantering horse; yet it seemed his head had gone hollow, that the sounds he heard were not really sounds at all but only memories, as in a dream. Even what Romy had said was something out of a dream, a nightmare.

His father looked past Romy at him. 'It had to come, Helmut. We could not let him go on.'

'We?' He stopped dead, letting go of Romy's hand. 'You and Romy?'

The General and Romy had pulled up, were turned to face him. He saw for the first time the strain in their faces. There was no fierce light in their eyes: these two were not fanatics. He realized, because he knew how his father's mind worked, that what they planned was a course of duty. He remembered something his father had once quoted to him from an essay by Prince Friedrich Karl of Prussia, written some time last century: Honour alone was a Prussian officer's task-master; conscience was his judge and his reward. There would be no politics, at least not on his father's part, in the plot to kill Hitler.

'There are others involved,' said the General. 'I can't tell you their names.'

108

'They are people like us,' said Romy. 'Who care for Germany and its future.'

'I care for it!' He hadn't meant to sound so fierce. 'But to kill him?'

'If that is necessary, yes. But we hope to stop him by kidnapping him. He will have us at war within a week or two. We're not ready for war, not yet.'

They walked on again, walking slowly. It was cooler here in the forest after the heat he had experienced all day on the set at Neubabelsberg, but Helmut felt more than cool; he was chilled. Romy had taken his hand again and he noticed her hand was as cold as his own.

'Hitler has surrounded himself with yes-men on the General Staff,' said the General. 'Not all of them, but too many of them. Keitel, for example. They call him Ja-Ja – he's never been known to say no to Hitler. They'll lead us to disaster.'

'Are the English involved in this with you?'

It seemed he could not have insulted his father more; the General stopped in his tracks, absolutely rigid. Romy said sharply, snatching her hand out of Helmut's, 'How dare you suggest such a thing to your father!'

'I'm sorry.' It had been a grievous mistake; he should have known it would have been impossible to countenance such a conspiracy. His father was not anti-British, indeed he retained some of the old German aristocracy's pre-1914 admiration for things British; but he would never have accepted foreign help in a plot to save his own country. Germany was a German's concern and only his. 'One hears so many rumours.'

'Not at the film studios, I hope,' said his father, still stiff and affronted. 'Nothing that will help Germany has ever come out of there.'

There was no answer to that: the General had only contempt for the film business. 'No, not there, Father. Colonel von Gaffrin was telling me about them.'

The General and Romy looked at each other worriedly, then back at him. 'Hans? Have you been to see him?'

'He came to see me.'

'Why?'

Helmut hesitated, then said, 'He wanted me to give a warning to someone working on our film. The Abwehr has a file on her.'

'Her?' Romy was quicker than the General. 'Is it the American actress or your friend, the British one?'

'How did you know about her? Melissa, I mean.'

'We, too, hear rumours.'

'From Hans? Damn, why doesn't he mind his own business!'

'Perhaps you are his business,' said the General, his stiffness lessening. 'He always looked on you as a nephew.'

Helmut nodded, chastened. 'I know. But I don't want to be caught up in anything . . .'

'Is your friend caught up in anything?'

'Melissa?' He almost laughed at the idea. 'No, of course not.'

'Then it's the American girl,' said Romy. 'Has Hans got something on her?'

'Not Hans. But Admiral Canaris has something. I don't know what it is, but Hans felt she should be warned.'

'Did you warn her?'

'I left her an anonymous note. She suspects there is something between Hans and me. Why were you so concerned about his coming to see me?'

Again the look passed between the General and Romy. The General looked around, as if he suddenly were looking for spies amongst the trees. There was a pale dusk down here on the floor of the forest, but the sun still struck obliquely through the upper branches, so that the three of them stood beneath a green-gold ceiling. The birds seemed to have gone; the horse riders had cantered away; all that could be heard was the faint hum of the autobahn traffic. The General decided that a forest was the ideal place for sharing a secret.

Nonetheless he lowered his voice even more; Helmut had to lean forward to catch what he said: 'Hans is in the plot with us. He has been our main contact here in Berlin.'

Helmut leaned back, shaking his head at the reckless foolishness of the older generation. 'You'll all be found out! God, don't you know Berlin, more than anywhere else, is rotten with spies? No one, not even the top Nazis, trust each other.'

'That's our safeguard. They are so busy watching each other, they don't have time for us.'

'They must know you're in town.'

His father nodded. 'I'm sure they do. That's why Romy is with me. They know she is my mistress –' He smiled at her, a lover's smile. 'Do you mind my calling you that?'

'It's the nicest compliment. At my age –' There is something about the smile of a woman in love that a man can never equal. Helmut had seen the same smile on his mother's face. God, he thought, how lucky Father has been! It did not occur to him that he had been blind to the expression on Melissa's face.

'They think we are having a stolen week together.'

'Is that all you're having?'

'No,' said Romy. 'I am helping them with their plan.'

'How, for God's sake?' He felt so much older and wiser than they. He had turned the years round: his father had spoken to him like this when he had first broached the subject of going into films.

'We are drawing up a map of every Gestapo station in Berlin. Romy is going to drive me around at night while I mark the stations on the map. They will be surrounded by troops, loyal troops, as soon as Hitler is taken.'

'Take him? What are you going to do when you kidnap him?'

'We shall announce we have taken him into custody for his own safety, that Himmler and others plan to overthrow him. Then our troops will move.'

'Where do you get these troops? Loyal to whom? Father, you're dreaming. And letting Romy drive you around! In that big Horch of hers? Why not in a bus with a big sign on the side?'

The General was a rare one: he admitted his mistakes. 'You're right. We must get a less conspicuous car . . . You have an Opel, haven't you? Everyone has one of those, haven't they?'

'Father, you never did have the common touch –'

'For which I thank my stars.' But he had the grace to smile; and so did Romy. 'You mean the working-class is not as well off as Hitler leads us to believe?'

'If you mean do they all have cars, Opels, no, they don't. But yes, an Opel is less conspicuous than a Horch or a Mercedes.'

'Would you lend us yours?' said Romy. 'You can drive the Horch.'

They're drawing me in, Helmut thought, even if that's not their intention. He looked at his father, afraid for him. The General was not *old*: he could not think of him as an old man. But he belonged to the past, to the dreams of the 'eternal Germany', of a wise monarchy and an intelligent elite that knew what was best for its country. Helmut himself was no socialist, National or Marxist, but he knew and believed that the days of elitism were gone forever. It was tragic and sad for Germany that the Nazis preached their own form of elitism.

'What if Himmler moves first? Goering? The Luftwaffe is loyal to him.'

'The country would never follow them the way they have Hitler.'

'Do you think it will follow Hitler into war?'

'Of course. Have any people ever rebelled against their leaders at the beginning of a war? At the end when they've lost the war, yes. But never at the beginning.'

'You would know more about that than I,' said Helmut, but did not mean to be unkind, though his father appeared to flinch.

'Please, Helmut –' Romy put a hand on his arm. 'We are committed to what we have to do. Please don't let us argue about it. Will you lend us your car? I shall use it only at night –'

He sighed inwardly. He was an amateur in any sort of conspiracy, a complete maiden in a kidnap or assassination attempt; but he was a student of film, he had learned how a plot was constructed; out of fiction he would try to show his father and Romy some lessons in fact. 'I'll come with you, be your driver.'

It was Romy who protested, not his father. The General

112

put out a hand, clutched his son's shoulder. 'Helmut, we'll fight him together –'

'Yes, Father,' said Helmut, though that had not been his intention. 'But don't ask me to pull any trigger.'

## 2

'Fräulein O'Dea?' said the orange-haired man in the buttoned-up shirt.

'Yes.' Cathleen had finished shooting for the day, was in her dressing-room removing her make-up. Her dresser had taken away her gown to Wardrobe for repairs and she was alone, peering into her mirror, when there was a knock on the open door and the two men appeared. 'What is it? How did you get in here?'

'I am Inspector Lutze and this is Sergeant Decker. We are from the State Police.' He didn't explain how he and his colleague had managed to get past the studio security guards and in here unannounced. The inference was that the Gestapo could go anywhere it wished.

Cathleen was in her underwear, a state of undress that wouldn't have worried her if some studio personnel had knocked on her door. But these men from the Gestapo were a different kettle of pop-eyed fish. She reached for a robe and slipped it on before Decker's eyes fell out of his face.

'We understand you are a companion of the Australian journalist, Herr Carmody?' said Lutze.

'Companion? What do you mean by that?' She was fluttering inside and her mind was trying to fly off in all directions; but her voice was under control, had a hard edge to it.

She had not asked Lutze and Decker to sit down; they still stood in the doorway, pressed awkwardly against each other. It struck her that she might have an advantage, that they looked a little unsure of themselves. Behind her on the dressing-table lay the note that had just arrived from Goebbels, but they couldn't have seen that nor known about it. But perhaps they knew of the visit to his apartment the other evening. Hating the thought of where her advantage might lie, she decided she would use it if she had to.

'Friend, then,' said Lutze.

'In the movie business, it pays to be friends with journalists. We need the publicity.'

'Of course. But it also pays to be careful of one's company. Has he spoken to you about a Frau Hoolahan, an American woman?'

It is difficult not to respond to one's own name; it is like a dog responding to its master's whistle. It seemed to her that her ears pricked; she was thankful that Lola Montez's hair style hid them. She made a pretence of looking amused.

'Hoolahan? That's a joke name, surely.'

'We are not joking,' said Decker, opening his mouth for the first time.

But Lutze smiled. 'It is an Irish name, no? The Irish are all jokers, so I am told.'

'I'm Irish – or anyway, Irish-American. We never joke about ourselves – we leave that to other people.'

The phone rang on the dressing-table and she picked it up. It was Sean, but she had enough control of her tongue not to say his name. 'No, I can't tonight. I have a date.'

'I've got something to tell you –'

'Not now.'

'Who's your date with.'

She wanted to say, *Don't be like that*. He sounded like all her other lovers: you went to bed with them and they hung their label on you. She lied to him, something she hated to do: 'Someone from the studio. I'll tell you about it tomorrow.'

'Have you got him there with you? You sound sort of – tight.'

She was facing the mirror, could see Lutze and Decker behind her taking in every word she was saying, doing their best to guess what was being said to her. 'No. It's just been another bad day on the set. Call me tomorrow.'

She said goodbye, knowing she sounded abrupt and discouraging, and hung up. She turned round and Lutze said, 'Was that your friend Herr Carmody?'

'No. I don't think you have any right to ask that question.'

'We have the right to ask any questions we wish,' said Decker.

'Perhaps Fräulein O'Dea is correct.' Lutze looked pained at his partner's blunt approach; the big stick was evidently not the inspector's favourite weapon. 'After all, she is an American citizen.'

'And I'd like you not to forget it,' said Cathleen, sensing she had the advantage again, if only for the moment.

There were footsteps in the corridor outside and Melissa said from behind the barricade of Gestapo meat in the doorway, 'Cathleen? Is there some trouble?'

Lutze and Decker stood apart and Melissa squeezed in between them. She looked worried and Cathleen was touched by her concern. 'No, there's no trouble. The gentlemen are just leaving.'

It was a ploy she doubted that few Germans would attempt, to show the Gestapo the door; in her case it worked. Sometimes it pays to be a foreigner, though it is best to come from a foreign country that, besides being neutral, is also powerful. Foreigners from San Marino or Andorra have rarely had their own way.

'It was a pleasure meeting you, Fräulein O'Dea,' said Lutze. 'This young lady is Fräulein Hayes?'

They probably have a file on everyone in the picture, Cathleen thought. 'Yes. Totally innocent. Like me.'

'Of course.' Lutze smiled, gave a little bow of his head and went out of the dressing-room. Decker was less polite: he looked both women up and down as if to suggest they had their price, then he jammed his hat on his head and followed Lutze.

'Who were they?' Melissa looked relieved, as if glad her arrival had despatched the two intruders so easily; a supporting player, she was not accustomed to playing heroines. 'Fritz Till asked me to come in. He said he didn't want to come in himself . . . Were they Gestapo?'

Cathleen nodded, did not blame Fritz Till for sending in Melissa. The file on him was probably larger than anyone else's. 'I suppose we're lucky they haven't been to see us before.'

'I don't know about you, but why should they want to see me?' She had an innocence about her that, for other people, is harder to bear than guilt.

'They don't need any reasons, honey.' Cathleen took off her robe, went into the bathroom and began to run a bath. Melissa stood in the doorway, watched her as she stripped and slid down into the bath. 'I don't know why they wanted to see me. Unless it was because of my date this evening.'

'Sean Carmody?'

'No, Joe Goebbels.'

Melissa didn't look surprised, just disgusted. 'I heard about that – you going to supper with him the other evening. Fat Karl told everyone. How can you do it?'

Cathleen suddenly wished she had the other girl's respect; but only the truth, which she couldn't afford, would bring her that. 'Melissa honey, I spent six years in Hollywood going out with monsters, guys who wanted no more out of me than the Doctor does. They didn't get it and neither will he. I'm going out with him for your sake and Fat Karl's and Willy's as much as for my own. His is the hand that feeds us and I'm not going to bite it.' She felt virtuous and self-sacrificing as she said it, Joan of Arc in a foam bath.

'Nuts,' said Melissa, who was losing some of her innocence, though it was not evident yet. 'You can bite his head off, for all I care. Where is he taking you?'

'Out on his boat on the Havel.'

'Watch out he doesn't run out of petrol. Or is it a sail-boat?'

'I haven't the foggiest. It will probably have a crew of twenty and half the German Navy as escort.'

'Well, don't suck up to him for me.'

The end of the picture was in sight and it had come to her in the past couple of days, as a sudden jolt, that, for her at least, everything else in Germany was coming to an end. UFA had made no offer to renew her contract and Helmut, it seemed, would also kiss her goodbye when the picture was ended. Her dreams were down around her feet, she was already beginning to contemplate the awful prospect of going back to repertory in England, eight shows a week in some dreary town in the provinces, a pay cheque of four pounds a week if

116

she was lucky and, worst of all, no Helmut. She was a dreamer but not an optimist, a contradiction she didn't herself understand.

She left, to go home to a lonely night in her flat in Neubabelsberg, and Cathleen lay in the bath a few minutes longer, wondering if she would be doing the sensible thing by accepting Goebbels' second invitation. She knew from gossip on the set that he had an estate at Schwanenwerder overlooking the broad expanse of the Havel River. His wife and their six children stayed there during the summer and she wondered if she was going to be introduced to Magda Goebbels. It seemed likely and she did not relish the prospect.

She dried herself, put on clean underwear and, an afterthought, added a piece of defensive equipment. The invitation note had arrived only two hours ago. There was no time for her to go back to Berlin to change, so she would have to wear what she had worn to the studio this morning. It would suffice for a boat ride: a cream silk shirt and cream slacks and a cashmere cardigan; Mr Mayer had been adamant that none of his contract players dressed like bums and she was glad now that she had fallen into the habit of being presentably dressed. She took extra care with her hair and make-up; the Reichsminister's wife would have a sharper eye than he. She looked at herself in the mirror, wished herself luck and went out to the car that had been sent for her.

As she came out into the warmth of the early evening Fritz Till was waiting for her. 'Did our Gestapo friends make trouble for you, Fräulein?'

'No, Fritz. But thank you for sending in the cavalry.'

For a moment he looked puzzled, then he laughed, his chins shaking like ferrets trying to get out of the big bag of his face. 'Oh, Fräulein Hayes? I couldn't come in myself. They know me.'

'Have you ever been in trouble with them?'

He nodded, no longer laughing. 'In the early days. But I'm too old now to be a hero. Besides,' he patted his stomach, 'I don't have the figure for it.'

As she walked on he called after her, 'Be careful!'

117

She stopped and looked back at him. But he just nodded at the waiting car and she knew he had guessed whose it was: he, too, had heard the gossip. She made a reassuring gesture, went on to the car and got in. The chauffeur was the same man who had driven her the other night: he looked at her as at an old friend. Or at least he looked friendly.

Goebbels was waiting impatiently for her when the car deposited her at the dock. 'You're late.'

'I was held up. I'll explain on board.' Three sailors were on the dock ready to cast off the ropes and she was not going to let them know she had been visited by the Gestapo.

Goebbels said nothing, just nodded irritably. He was dressed all in white, with a white peaked cap; he looked like the admiral of a fleet of ice cream vans. The boat, a motor cruiser, was large enough to require a crew of two; they remained at the stern while Goebbels and Cathleen sat in the forward well, he at the wheel. He had all the studied nonchalance of a weekend sailor who knew he had two experienced men right behind him.

'Our family boat is larger than this,' he said. 'But I thought you would enjoy this more.'

'I thought I might be meeting your family.' She hadn't had an opportunity to see the house on the estate; she had just caught glimpses of it through the trees as the car had skirted it. 'I was looking forward to it.'

They were playing a game; he smiled, his irritableness suddenly gone. 'You shall meet them, but not this evening. They have gone to our other place on the Bogensee.'

He spoke with the pride of a man still not accustomed to owning more than one home. Cathleen had heard of the Schloss Lanke, which had been given to its *Gauleiter* by the city of Berlin, though Fritz Till had told her that the citizens of the city had had little or no say in the gifting. It had been furnished by the film industry 'in recognition of his services to the industry', though here again, Till had said, *he* had never been asked to vote for the recognition. But then, he had further said, if the true recognition of leaders were left to the general populace, who would keep the scroll-makers in work?

'You should not wear trousers. They hide your beautiful legs.'

'They are common dress in Hollywood. Marlene Dietrich made them popular and she has better legs than I have.' It was a small shot but dangerous. She was determined not to make the evening a gift for him. He had performed no services for her, not yet.

But he dodged the shot; or it had been a dud. He took the boat past a yacht tacking against the evening breeze, waved a gloved graceful hand in response to the polite waving of the people on the yacht. They were out on the broad expanse of the Wannsee now; Cathleen could see people on the public beaches, staying till the very last of the sun; small sail-boats, with the pouter-pigeon breasts of their spinnakers ballooning before them, were engaging in an impromptu race. Backing it all was the Grunewald, bright green in the low sun. The water itself caught the slanting light, slicing it into silver bars that came and went like fool's currency. It was hard to believe what Sean had told her was the truth: guns were being drawn up behind the façade of these peaceful days.

'Will there be war?' she said out of the blue of a sudden mood.

He looked at her sharply. 'Don't let us spoil our evening. I have champagne back at the house. It will have gone flat if it has heard you.'

She smiled, throwing off her mood, though it was like tossing an anchor overboard. 'Who writes your dialogue?'

He laughed, stroked her hand with his gloved one. The glove was doe-skin: it was like having a chihuahua rub itself against her. 'You have a delicious sense of humour, you Americans. So dry. I am a great admirer of Mark Twain.'

She hadn't read Twain since she had left school. 'Me, too. Did you ever work on the riverboats on the Rhine?'

He had turned the motor-boat round; two sail-boats scooted out of his way, recognizing him and who really had the right of way. 'No, I was at university when I was a young man. My only interests were philosophy and politics.'

'No girls?'

'Ah, yes, there were girls.' He spoke with a certain wistful-

119

ness, like a man who remembered one or two girls in particular. Then he said, 'We must go back. It is getting cool.'

The evening had lost none of its warmth, but she didn't argue with him. Perhaps the memory of the girls of his youth had cooled the evening for him. He turned the boat over to the two crewmen and when they had docked it, he led her, not up to the main house, but to a small villa, little more than a lodge, hidden amongst the trees. She recognized it for what it was, one of his 'forts', the houses he had on his estates where he entertained women he did not want his family to meet. Cathleen had been told about them and suddenly, as they reached the front door of the small villa, she felt dirty, a whore being sneaked in the back door. The evening did feel cool, even cold.

He led the way into a small sitting room where a table had been set up for supper; silver serving-dishes stood on a side table and a bottle of champagne lolled in a silver ice-bucket. There was no sign of any servants. She was about to play Lola again, but her suitor this time was no Ludwig.

He put a record on the gramophone in one corner: Mozart again. The menu was the same as she had had in the residence in Berlin; he wasted no intellect on trying to win her heart through her stomach. Though, she told herself, he was not really interested in her heart: he had his eye, like most men, on something lower down and more basic.

As he poured her a second glass of champagne, he put his hand on hers; he had taken off his gloves, which was an improvement. 'Why were you late? Are you having trouble with someone at the studio? I can fix that.'

She sipped her champagne, taking her time, letting him still hold her hand. 'Can you fix the Gestapo?'

He let go her hand, sat back. '*They* came to see you? What did they want? Did they ask you about me?'

'Relax, Herr Doctor.' She felt safe, at least for the moment; she was surprised he should think the Gestapo had been enquiring after him. 'They said it was just routine.'

'They have no right to question you without my permission!' He put down his glass so heavily that the champagne spilled over; he licked his hand like a schoolboy, recovered, picked up his napkin and did a more decorous job. 'What was this routine questioning?'

She put down her own glass, carefully. 'They asked me about an American woman named Frau Hoolahan.'

'Hoolahan? Who is she?'

Would he go as far as having the two Gestapo men brought before him to be questioned, when the true nature of their questioning of her would be brought out? She had to take a risk: 'She is the aunt of a girl I knew in Los Angeles. She came to Germany earlier this year and she has disappeared.'

'Is that all?' He appeared uninterested; women disappeared all the time. 'Did they say what she had done? Was she a communist?'

'Not as far as I know.' Mady's only crime was being Jewish. 'Maybe you could find out what happened to her.' There, it was done: more casually than she had expected.

'My dear woman –' He shook his head in mock wonder. 'I am a senior Reichsminister. Why should I bother about some missing American woman who has got herself lost?'

'In America one goes to a politician for help.'

'So I understand.' He did not consider himself a politician, not any longer; there would be no need from now on for politicking, for campaigning. That was for those who believed in democracy, a mish-mash that had proven it could not work because it was based on hypocrisy and myths. 'But they demand payment, don't they? They never help those who vote for the opposition.'

'Are you asking me to vote for you?' She had stopped calling him Doctor, but had not yet got round to calling him Joseph.

'I don't need votes, not any more.' But he smiled, feeling the evening was going well. 'I'll have someone look into the woman, if you really want me to. What's her name?'

'Hoolahan. Frau Mady Hoolahan.' She could feel an excitement trembling in her, but she managed to remain looking calm and relaxed.

'I can do nothing if the Gestapo won't respond. Reichsfuehrer Himmler and I are not the best of friends.' He smiled again, letting her in on a secret, being intimate. Producers had tried the same game with her, letting her in on the secrets of studio politics. 'Let's sit over there to have our coffee.'

*Over there* was a two-seater couch, an elegant piece that made her feel safe: it was too narrow and delicate for any gymnastics. She poured the coffee and he sat back waiting to be served; they could have been a happily married couple. She asked him how things were at the office; he asked her what was happening at the studio. It was all a game, one that they had both played before, though not with each other.

Then, as if to say *let's get on with it*, he put down his cup and moved closer to put his arm round her. He smelled nice, her nose was glad to tell her; but all her other senses were suddenly affronted. Up close he was indeed ugly; at a distance ugliness can sometimes have a charm, but not close up. She stiffened inwardly as his arm tightened about her; then his mouth closed on hers. She had been kissed before by men who had no appeal for her, including several actors; she had learned to fake reaction, but this was much harder. Those other men had had only their personality and their physical unattractiveness working against them; this little man in the white suit, still decorous with his jacket on, was a master of political evil, a man who hated Jews. He was more repellent than any of the others she could remember, yet she did not push him away at once. Mady, the Jewish mother, was pushing her towards him.

Passion was taking hold of him; she was surprised that the hand that squeezed her breast was trembling. She didn't brush his hand away; she even opened her mouth a little under his kiss. This was one of the Perils of Pauline; but she knew something the villain didn't know. His hand went down to her belly and that was when she said, 'That's far enough, Joseph.'

He drew his face away from hers. 'Why?'

'I have my period.'

'I don't believe it!' He slid his hand down between her legs, felt the pad there and drew his hand away in disgust. 'Why did you come if you were like that?'

The pad had been the piece of safety equipment she had installed; her period was two weeks away, but he was not to know that unless he stripped her. Goebbels was an experienced seducer, but there were limits beyond which he would not go. He was so fastidiously clean she would not have been surprised if he had worn surgical gloves to make love. It was his fastidiousness on which she had relied. She was an experienced seducee.

'I came because I enjoy your company,' she said; flattery is the best salve for a wounded lover. 'Women are always fascinated by powerful men. Haven't you been told that before?'

He was half-mollified, half-angry; his ego was at odds with his genitals. 'I had planned we would do more than just talk. There are other ways of enjoying my company.'

*Oh God, the ego of men!* She wanted to laugh at him, at his way of putting things; but there was still a long way to go, her mother was still missing. 'Joseph –' She put everything she had ever learned into the way she said his name; the M-G-M dialogue coach would have been proud of her. 'I am not a whore. If I spend an evening – or a night – with a man it's because I like him for himself, not just for sex –'

He had gone to stand in front of the tall narrow fireplace, something he should not have done: it made him look shorter. He knew enough not to stand with his hands behind his back, the natural pose of men in front of fireplaces; that pose only narrowed his already narrow shoulders. His hands were stuck jauntily in his pockets, he was a rake in virginal white. She was glad he did not stand with arms akimbo and legs apart, the stance of so many German men these days.

His humour had improved. 'We should have had supper months ago. By now –'

*By now we'd be in bed*: she gave him the sly smile he expected. Her nerves were becoming frayed; she was nowhere near as composed as she looked. He had given her a glimmer of hope that he would trace her mother; she could not let that glimmer be put out by throwing cold water on him. She was playing the scene as she would play it on the set: make-believe gave her a grip on reality.

'You were the one who was slow – *I* couldn't ask *you* to supper.'

He nodded, his good humour completely returned. 'We don't have long to make up for lost time.'

*Is war going to break out?* But she couldn't ask him that. 'You mean, the picture will soon be finished? You could offer me a new contract.'

'I'd have to talk to the studio about that.'

That, she knew, would only be a formality, certainly not a necessity. When her agent had told her that UFA was looking for an American actress to star in *Lola und Ludwig*, a casual remark over lunch, he had been surprised when she had told him to do everything he could to get her the job. She had not told him why she wanted to go to Germany, except to say she was fed up with her progress at M-G-M; she had seen it as a heaven-sent opportunity to go looking for her mother. Advising her against the move, he had reluctantly done as she told him; he had come back to her to say that the evil little son-of-a-bitch Goebbels was personally choosing the actress who would get the contract. There had been a dozen actresses who had applied for the part; she had said Catholic prayers for her Jewish mother and she had won the role. She had been welcomed by Goebbels at a reception on her arrival, but he had made no instant play for her. He had, however, given her the strongest hint who was her boss: himself.

'I'd be willing to stay, if the right picture came up.' She had to keep him on the string.

'Even if there is war?'

'I don't believe Germans want war.'

'Who told you that?' But then his voice softened; he was not going to play the Gestapo with her. 'Of course nobody wants it. Why should they?'

'Then if you find the right picture . . .'

'I should like to do that.' He allowed himself a little make-believe; he knew she would be gone as soon as the current picture was finished. 'I have two favourite women's films – *Anna Karenina* and *The Blue Angel*. I should like to re-make them. Which would you prefer?'

Despite herself, she jumped with interest; there will be actresses willing to play the Devil's mistress on Judgement

Day, so long as they get equal billing. 'Garbo and Dietrich? I could never be as good as them.'

'Perhaps not as good as Garbo.' The best, most intriguing of them all; he had run the film at least a dozen times. 'But Dietrich? All she has are her legs. Yours are as good.'

'Who would play the Professor in *The Blue Angel*? You?'

He laughed aloud, like a schoolboy; indeed, for a moment he looked like a schoolboy in his all-white uniform. 'Do you think I could play a man besotted by a woman?'

'If the woman was the right one.' She knew how besotted he had been with Lida Baarova. But she smiled, keeping the focus on herself: 'That would depend how I played the part, wouldn't it?'

He stopped laughing, his eyes grew darker. Damn it, he thought, she knows that I think of her as more than just a night's entertainment. Why did he fall for actresses? None of them was intellectual, certainly not this one; nor had Lida been. Their beauty attracted him, of course; and their sexuality, less hidden than that of women in government and business circles. Perhaps it was their glamour, however one defined that. Or was it that their world was one of make-believe, where, no matter what fantasies he had, they would always respond without question? He did not recognize the fact, but fantasy had taken him over under the guise of power. But that was in his *persona* as Reichsminister; now he was the lover. He stared at her, looking at the future and knowing even then any affair they might have would be doomed. The Fuehrer would see to that.

'No,' he said, 'I could never play the Professor. I could never be made a fool of by a woman.' *Forgive me, Lida.*

'Well, try me for Anna Karenina –' She stood up, picked up her cardigan and threw it round her shoulders. 'I must go.'

'To throw yourself under a train?'

'Like Anna?' She shook her head. They were smiling at each other, but there was an underlying air of seriousness. He was afraid of his infatuation with her; she was afraid of it, too. But both would play the dangerous game for their own ends: 'I hope you'll invite me again. Oh, and will you try and find out something about Frau Hoolahan for me, please?'

He kissed her hand, something he had learned from the Fuehrer, the Austrian; Hitler had always kissed a woman's hand, even in the days before he had risen to power. Steeling herself, Cathleen leaned forward and kissed him lightly on the lips. Down payments have to be made.

'Next time . . .'

## 3

Carmody was annoyed and jealous that Cathleen was spending the evening with another man. He was even more upset that the man might be Goebbels; he had not believed her story that it was someone from the studio; she had sounded too nervous for such an innocent date. She was creeping out on a limb that might fall off beneath her at any moment; he wondered if she appreciated the danger she was in. He wished she had listened to what he had to tell her, that there might be no need to try to enlist Goebbels' help in tracing her mother.

He had met Fred Doe, as arranged, at the Kranzler at two o'clock that afternoon. Doe, a night worker, had ordered breakfast; Carmody had settled for coffee and a sandwich. They were at a table on the terrace, hemmed in on either side by other occupied tables. Carmody, still a bush boy at heart, did not like to be so close to strangers; Doe, it seemed, wanted to be in someone else's pocket and conversation. He kept turning his head as he picked up scraps of conversation around him.

'You ever listen to the man in the street?'

'All the time,' said Carmody, who had begun to doubt if the man in the street, especially in countries where the Gestapo operated, had anything worthwhile to say.

'That's the guy I wanted to play music for. Once upon a time . . .' He grinned sourly above his ham and eggs. 'Now I play in a joint where the man in the street couldn't afford a cup of coffee.'

'How did you finish up here in Berlin?'

'Finish up? An undiplomatic phrase, pal. But you're right. This is the finishing line. If war breaks out, I gotta go back to the starting gate.'

'Where was that?'

'Charleston, South Carolina.' There was just the faintest trace of Southern accent in the husky, rotted voice. 'I started playing there when I was a kid, seventeen, eighteen. I was gonna be the greatest cornet man since Kid Ory, King Oliver, those guys. The first great white guy on trumpet. Then I heard about a guy up north, Bix Beiderbecke, from Iowa, some place in the cornbelt. Everyone said how good he was. So I went up to hear him. He was with a band called the Wolverines, they were playing a date at Indiana University. Bix stood up, played a chorus of *Panama* and that was it – I knew I was never gonna be the greatest man on cornet. You gotta hear the greatest to know how mediocre you are.'

'You're better than mediocre,' said Carmody truthfully, though he was no authority on jazz, just had an ear for it.

'Maybe.' Doe was unflattered; he had his own standards. The tables next to them were empty now; it was the slack hour between lunch and afternoon tea. With no surrounding conversation to distract him, he seemed to have turned in on himself. He was talking to himself as much as to Carmody, the eggs congealing on his plate as he forgot them: 'I went on up to New York, got a job there, but I kept hearing those notes from Bix's horn. So I took a job on a liner, the *Berengaria*. Maybe going to work on the *Berengaria* was an omen where I'd finish up. She was originally a German ship, the *Imperator* – the British grabbed her as part of the reparations after the Great War. I did four crossings, but every time I went back to New York it was like I could still hear Bix. So I went to London, then to Paris.'

'Why did you leave Paris?'

'I fell out with a guy I was living with, so I skipped town.' He looked at Carmody, who looked blankly back at him. 'You know what I mean?'

'No.'

'I'm a homo, for Christ's sake. I'm queer, as you'd describe it.'

'I'd never have known.' He felt suddenly ill at ease, as he always did. He had met more homosexuals since coming to Europe than he had believed existed in the whole wide world. His innocence, he sometimes thought, was a world in itself. Mateship between men was all right; but love, sex? Australia had taught him nothing.

'We don't all waltz around with limp wrists and falsetto voices. I make you uncomfortable?'

'No.'

'Don't bullshit me, pal. Relax, I'm not gonna rape you.'

'Why did you come to Berlin?' Carmody changed the subject; or thought he did.

'This is the homo capital of the world. Or it used to be. It's mostly underground now, like the Jews. Goering would let it come out into the open again, but Hitler's too goddam strait-laced. I think he's like you, pal.'

Carmody managed to smile. 'Thanks for the comparison. When did you come here?'

'1931. That was the year Bix died. But I still couldn't go home . . . Crazy, isn't it? Running away from a guy's music. But you dunno, pal, how much I wanted to be the greatest,' he said wistfully. 'To be remembered.'

'Are there any good jazz men here in Berlin?' Carmody tactfully made no effort to console Doe.

'One or two, but they don't really understand what it's all about. It's improvisation and that don't fit the German mind. They like their music organized, like everything else. There was one little guy, a Jew, he understood it. But he had to drop out.' He looked at Carmody and the latter raised his eyebrows in an unspoken query. 'No, the Gestapo didn't get him. He survived a lot longer than most of 'em, up till a year ago, but then he knew it was time to go. I gave him some names in New York and he went. I dunno how he's doing, I told him not to write me, just in case.'

'How did he get out? Just bought a boat ticket and went?'

Doe waved to a waiter to take away his plate and ordered more coffee. He lit a cigarette, took it out of his mouth and looked at it. 'They're killing me, them and the grog. But if you don't die one way, you die another. Right, pal?' Then he looked carefully through the cigarette smoke at Carmody. 'You want a story on me or the little Jew-boy?'

'Both,' said Carmody, wondering where the second story would lead.

'You careful about what you write? About the people who give you your information? That dame Lady Arrowsmith, you ever mention her in your stories?'

'Never,' said Carmody, and hoped, for Meg's sake, he would never have to.

The waiter came back with the coffee and when he had gone again Doe said quietly, 'There are still Jews here in Berlin. Some of them are like the pale nigras down home, I guess – they pass for white. They got Benny out. I dunno how they do it, but they've done it with some other Jews, too. They are a sorta – what did they call it in Spain?'

'A fifth column.' Carmody could not see any Jewish organization operating in Berlin as the Nationalist Fifth Column had done in Madrid. There was no army at the gates of the city as there had been in those days. At best the Jews could run only a rescue effort . . . 'Do these Jews keep track of people who disappear?'

'What do you mean?'

'If someone is taken away by the Gestapo, do they try to find out where he's been taken?'

'I wouldn't know, pal. Why?'

Carmody took a chance: 'I'm trying to trace someone, an American woman.'

'Jewish?'

He took another chance: 'Yes. She came over from the States earlier this year and her family haven't heard from her since. Could you put me in touch with your Jewish friends?'

'They ain't my friends, pal, they were Benny's. Benny was *my* friend. You understand?'

Carmody was not so slow this time. He nodded, all at once sad for the lonely man.

'Okay, I'll ask them if they'll see you. But you'll keep your mouth shut?'

'I told you – I never disclose a source.'

'What about your story on me?' Then Doe grinned, waved

a hand. 'Don't worry, pal. Nothing you could write could rescue me from obscurity. I don't care any more. If I went home, became top horn with Artie Shaw, any of them big bands, it still wouldn't matter. I'd still be hearing Bix playing better than me. I got that sorta ear, it itches with memories.'

*Thank God Shakespeare doesn't affect me that way: I'd never write another word.* 'When can I meet these people?'

'You in a hurry? Sure, why shouldn't you be? War's gonna break out any day.' He said it as if it would not concern him in the least; he could be expecting an outbreak of influenza. He was a true neutralist, much more so than the isolationists back home: he was close enough to make a considered choice. 'I'll try them soon's I leave you. If they say okay, how about tomorrow?'

'Any time they say, anywhere.'

When they shook hands on parting Carmody said, 'I'd go back home and try your luck. You sound great to me and I'm sure a lot of other people would think the same. There's room for someone besides Louis Armstrong.'

'Sure, pal. I'll think about it.' But one knew he had already given up, that he would be forever haunted by music from the past. His resignation, Carmody guessed, was a form of integrity.

So now Carmody, sitting in his apartment, surrounded by the furniture of the Jewish doctor who had got away, itched to tell Cathleen that at last he might be on to a lead that would tell them where her mother was.

4

*Extracts from the diaries of Dr Paul Joseph Goebbels:*

18 August 1939:

I spoke by telephone today with the Fuehrer. He is still down at the Berghof at Obersalzberg, waiting to hear what transpires in Moscow. Why is Stalin stalling? (I do not mean that as a pun – one leaves that sort of humour to the English.) Cannot he see the advantages of a pact with us? Or is he as devious, as unscrupulous, as we have been led to believe? Is the Fuehrer taking too big a gamble with him?

The Fuehrer told me of his military conference four days ago, when he told the generals he was ready for war. He pointed out to them the military and economic weaknesses of the English and the French. Neither of those countries, he said, will come to the aid of Poland. They cannot afford a major war. The generals, not even Goering, questioned the Fuehrer's plans. He is indeed a great leader! How fortunate I was to recognize this so early in the piece!

Magda and the children are at Lanke; I shall drive out tomorrow to see them. I miss the children every day I do not see them; but not Magda. She was in another of her moods when she left for Lanke. She said it was her time of the month, but I doubt it. Women use that excuse far too much . . .

Cathleen O'Dea used it tonight; though I did believe her. She is an intriguing woman, so down to earth. Not intellectual nor very well educated; one can't discuss music or books or philosophy with her. But then women who can do those things bore me. I am becoming more and more infatuated with her. Or is it because I have not yet made love to her? Is it more satisfying to anticipate than to achieve?

She has asked me to trace some American woman who has disappeared. They always ask something for their favours. A fur coat, a case of champagne, always something. All except Lida, who gave and never asked. And Magda . . . Though she has asked for enough in the past year. And got it.

. . . A speech to prepare for the national conference of teachers. Speech-making comes so easily to me now. No more of the rehearsing in front of mirrors; though that was where I learned to be so good. Lida once told me I was a better orator than the Fuehrer. I agreed with her . . .

# CHAPTER SIX

## 1

It took Fred Doe three days to arrange the meeting with the Jews who might be able to help Carmody and Cathleen. He did not explain the delay, but Carmody guessed they might be checking on him before they agreed to a meeting.

Sunday morning Doe phoned him. 'They'll see you tonight. The Green Man beer-garden in Mariendorf. Eight-thirty.'

'What's their name? How will I know them?'

'They'll know you,' said Doe and rang off. He sounded tired and irritable, as if he resented having to wake so early in the day to do someone a favour.

Carmody looked at his watch: ten o'clock, a time when everyone should have been up for hours. No matter what time he went to bed, he was always wide awake by seven at the latest; the habits of his boyhood still clung. He dialled Cathleen's number and she, a girl from the bush of Yorkville, sleepily bit his head off.

'I should have let you stay the night – at least then you might have appreciated how tired a working girl can be at the end of the week. What do you want?'

He told her of the call from Fred Doe. 'It's going to be a long day, waiting around for tonight. I thought we'd go out to Wannsee, have a picnic and a swim.'

'I could sleep all day –' But, awake now, she knew she could not contain her impatience for tonight by trying to go back to sleep. 'All right, pick me up at noon. I'll have Hilde make us some lunch.'

Hilde was the plump motherly woman the studio had engaged for her as a daily housemaid. She did not live in, because Cathleen, hopeful right from the beginning that she would find her mother, had not wanted someone spying on her if, through whatever circumstances, her mother had to be smuggled into the apartment. She now trusted Hilde, but she had let the arrangement stand and Hilde had been agreeable, since it gave her every evening free. She came in every day, including Sundays when she worked only in the morning. She was always freshly starched and ironed, like a great billowing hospital sheet, and she believed everyone should eat more than he or she thought sensible. The picnic lunch she prepared for Cathleen and Carmody, whom she had not yet met, would have satisfied a gang of road-workers.

Carmody went round to a local garage and hired a car; the garage owner knew him and had rented cars to Carmody whenever the latter had had to go out of town on a story. The cars were always modest, mostly Opels, and the rental was modest, too. Even in love Carmody had an asbestos pocket: money was not going to burn a hole in it to impress his beloved.

'I was hoping for a Mercedes tourer,' said Cathleen. 'It's such a lovely day.'

'You'd only get sunburnt. You're always telling me you have to keep that Irish colleen complexion. Anyhow, I think it's better we're not too conspicuous. Wear your hat – that red hair of yours stands out.'

She put on her wide-brimmed straw hat and dark glasses. 'You and I will never be compatible. You're too tight with a penny.'

'Pennies I spend. It's the quids I hang on to.' He was not offended by the jokes about his reluctance to spend. Unlike most people, he was never unhappy in the bargain basement.

They drove out to the Wannsee, parked the car and found a reasonably uncrowded spot on a small quiet beach. Cathleen declined to go in the water, but sat, under her hat and behind her dark glasses, in the shade of the trees. Carmody, who had worn his bathing trunks under his outer clothing, stripped off and went down to the water. Offshore the lake was crowded with sail-boats; they brought back a memory of billabongs crowded at morning light with herons and cranes and pelicans. He had begun to think a lot of home this past week, as if

133

his mind were seeking a hole to run to when the worst happened.

The water was cold, but he enjoyed it. He was a powerful swimmer, with his shearer's shoulders and arms, and he had a lazy Australian crawl stroke that set him apart from the other swimmers, most of whom floated along on a breast stroke. He turned over on his back, gazed up at the burning sky and tried to imagine it full of bombers. But the thought was beyond him. He rolled back on to his front and swam slowly and gracefully back through the crowd, wondering how many of them had looked at the sky and tried to test their imagination as he had done. None of them, it seemed. If Germany was holding its breath it was not apparent here in the shouts and screams of laughter of the Berliners on Sunday.

'You're a beautiful swimmer,' said Cathleen as Carmody dried himself off. 'You're also beautiful with your clothes off.'

'Cut it out.' He was not accustomed to women complimenting him on his looks. Besides, *beautiful* was not a word you applied to a bloke. He sat down, changed the subject slightly: 'Is your mother beautiful?'

'Yes, I think so. Different than me, though. She's smaller, more – *vital*, I guess. She's dark, too. She'd never get sunburnt, freckled like me.'

'How did you get on with her?'

'Pretty well. We didn't live together in California and I think that helped. She was a typical Jewish mother and she'd have run my life if I'd let her – they love you to death. She was always trying to pick my boyfriends for me –' She looked at him, gave him a lovely smile under the dark glasses. 'She'd have picked you, a nice solid boy sensible about money. She'd have preferred you to be Jewish, but if she couldn't have that she'd settle for Irish.'

'You love her a lot, don't you?' he said perceptively.

She nodded, not saying anything; behind the dark glasses tears formed in her eyes. He put a sympathetic hand on hers, squeezed it, then turned and opened the picnic basket. There was ham, sausage, sauerkraut, sliced cucumbers in sour cream, potato salad, tomatoes, two sorts of bread, an apple tart and a bottle of white wine wrapped in a wet cloth. It was enough to lift the spirit while weighing down the stomach.

Half an hour later, both of them full but the basket only half-empty, they lay back on the rug they had brought and looked up through the trees. Most of the swimmers had come out of the water and were having lunch; a murmur of chatter had replaced the shouts. There were several families seated close by and Carmody and Cathleen now spoke to each other in low voices. There was no point in speaking German; they knew they had been recognized as foreigners. Cathleen was not afraid of being recognized as herself; she had received a good deal of publicity, but she was far from being a Lilian Harvey or a Renate Müller, who would be known at once in any crowd.

She had worked late Saturday and he had seen her only for a couple of hours last night. She had been tired and he had not pressed her with questions about Goebbels; it was easier to put the man out of his mind. She had been excited when he had told her of Doe's trying to arrange a meeting with the Jews who might be able to help; but he, ever the Celt, had told her not to build her hopes too high. They had spent the evening like two old lovers content to do no more than hold each other and listen to the radio. The programme had featured the Berlin Philharmonic, under Furtwängler, defender of Bach, Beethoven and Brahms. But they were not experts in classical music, knew nothing of the political battles behind the composers, and just enjoyed the sounds for what they were. She had sent him home rather than let him sleep with her and he had not protested. He felt certain there would be other nights when he would be asked to stay.

They left the beach before the city-bound traffic began to thicken. He dropped her at her apartment. 'I won't pick you up here. Take a taxi to the Hohenzollernplatz U-Bahn and I'll be there. Eight o'clock.'

'Are you afraid we'll be followed?'

'Maybe. Just keep an eye out when you're in the taxi. The bloody Gestapo are still interested in us, I'll bet.'

'Sean, you don't have to do this –'

'You're wrong, darl. I do have to do it.' He kissed her. 'Take care.'

She was already waiting outside the underground station when he arrived in the Opel. He didn't recognize her at first, not till she had opened the car door and got in beside him. She was wearing a dark wig and pale horn-rimmed glasses. 'You look like a schoolmistress.'

'Nobody followed me.' Inwardly she was trembling with anticipation, but she was trying to maintain a calm exterior; she did not want to put too much hope in what might prove to be another dead end. But she could not help putting a hand on his arm and saying, 'Say a prayer this may lead somewhere.'

'I went to evening Mass. All the angels and saints are on our side.' But he did not feel as hopeful and light-hearted as he sounded.

He drove south to Mariendorf, found the Green Man beer-garden not far from the Underground terminus. The warm evening had brought out the drinkers; the families with children had gone home. Whether the hot day had tired them or dusk had brought a reflective mood, the drinkers were much more subdued than those Carmody had seen in beergardens earlier in the summer. Many of them seemed to be staring into their beer glasses as if they were amber-coloured crystal balls; Carmody had seen the same preoccupation in bush pubs back home. Then the band struck up, *oompah oompah*, and everyone looked up, suddenly brighter, and Carmody wondered if it was not his own vision that had become sombre.

He and Cathleen found a small table in a corner, ordered two beers and looked around, not knowing whom or even how many people to look for. Would it be a single person or a committee? The garden seemed to be full of a cross-section of the accepted idea of Germans, as if a club of cartoonists had invited all their models to a party. There was a preponderance of stout drinkers, some of the men with *en brosse* haircuts and waxed moustaches looking as if they had been left over from Great War cartoons; the women were blonde,

136

big-breasted and hearty. But then a second, longer look saw thinner, dark-haired drinkers, like shadows, amongst the weighty, fair-haired ones. They all, blonde and dark, stout and thin, seemed to be looking at the two strangers in the corner. Carmody realized that this beer-garden, like pubs back home, was the haunt of locals and any newcomers were instantly spotted. He wondered why the Jews had chosen it.

A plane roared overhead, going down to Tempelhof airdrome nearby, and Carmody looked up, his imagination caught again by the thought of bombers. Tempelhof had been a parade-ground in the Kaiser's day; it would be only a progression of military history if it should become a parade-ground for Goering's Luftwaffe. We progress through arms, someone had once said: probably an arms dealer.

When Carmody looked down again two people had slid into the seats on the opposite side of the table.

'Do you mind if we sit here?' He was a tall man, handsome, with a deep pleasant voice that could be heard without effort despite the noise in the garden. 'Our name is Schmidt.'

'A common name.' The woman was small, with bright dark eyes and a wide friendly smile that spread her mouth right across her thin face.

'My name is Carmody. This is Fräulein McCool.' It was his mother's maiden name and he dragged it out of the air on the moment. He and Cathleen had completely overlooked the precaution of giving her another name; she had disguised her appearance, but they had almost shouted her real name. We are going to have to learn, thought Carmody.

'We were expecting only you, Herr Carmody.' Schmidt had sat back and was speaking casually. 'Act as if we have only just met, the way people do in places like this.'

'My husband always wanted to be an actor,' said Frau Schmidt and looked affectionately at her husband.

He returned her smile, then ordered drinks for them: beer, with a schnapps chaser for him, lemonade for her. 'What connection does Fräulein McCool have with you?'

'She works for me.'

Schmidt shook his head, 'No, she doesn't. Fräulein Luxemburg works for you. You are going to have to be more honest with us, Herr Carmody, if you want our help.'

Carmody looked at Cathleen, who nodded. 'Tell them the truth.'

Which Carmody did, sitting back in his chair, trying to look relaxed as if he were swapping trivialities with strangers he had just met. The band up on its platform, red-faced and sweaty, galloped its way through a piece that was vaguely familiar; it was halfway through the second chorus before he recognized it as *The Music Goes Round and Round*. He finished Cathleen and Mady Hoolahan's story as the band, looking as if it were about to blow itself apart, blasted out the last phrase of *The Music*.

'Frau Hoolahan may have been picked up under her maiden name, Miriam Razman.'

'What was your grandmother's name?' Schmidt asked Cathleen. He seemed unimpressed that she was a film star, but his wife had sharpened her scrutiny, as if trying to see beneath the dark wig and the horn-rimmed glasses. Women, sensibly, never take other women at face value.

'Frau Rose Razman.' Cathleen gave her grandmother's address. 'Can you help us? I'll pay anything –'

'Money is not important, Fräulein McCool. We'll continue to call you that, just as a precaution. If you wish to make a contribution to our funds, that will be welcome – there are always expenses. But we don't place a price on people's lives.'

'I'm sorry. I didn't mean to imply you were mercenary –'

'I'm sure you didn't,' said Frau Schmidt, but her smile was not so wide this time. 'Where you come from, nothing is done for free, is it?'

'America or Hollywood?' Cathleen's voice was suddenly stiff.

Carmody thought it was time he stepped in again; he had the male's suspicion of women trying to do business. But he noted that Schmidt looked mildly amused. 'How soon do you think you could get us some information?'

Schmidt shrugged. 'If Frau Hoolahan – or indeed both women – are in a concentration camp, we should be able to get you their whereabouts within a week.'

'That long?' said Cathleen, suddenly desperately impatient.

'Fräulein, we have our sources – that's what costs us money. But we don't have immediate access to all the records. Would you care for another drink?'

'My shout,' said Carmody and hailed a passing waiter, gave their order and waited till the man had gone away. Then he said carefully, putting his hand on Cathleen's: 'What if they're not in a camp?'

'You mean if they're dead?' Schmidt saw Cathleen's hand turn over and clutch at Carmody's. 'I'm sorry to be so blunt, Fräulein, but that, unfortunately, is the way life is in Germany these days . . . Rudi! Dorothea! Going home so soon?'

A couple had stopped by the table: middle-aged, middle-class, healthy and happy-looking. The man had all the cheerfulness of one of the beer-garden's waiters, except that his was not an act; his wife might have been a transvestite mirror image for him. They were friends to the world, especially to any friends of Heinz and Inge Lang.

Schmidt didn't bat an eyelid at being revealed as Lang (if even that is his real name, thought Carmody). He introduced Carmody and Cathleen. 'Herr and Fräulein McCool are on their way home to America. They say they have been having a last look at our wonderful country.'

Rudi Heck feigned amazement; he was a bad actor and looked ridiculous. But his wife, his travelling audience, laughed heartily at his performance. 'A last look, Herr McCool? You think Germany is going to sink out of sight?'

'I'm afraid of war, Herr Heck. Aren't you?'

Heck laughed; behind him the band, less energetic now, had begun to play a Schubert love song. 'There will be no war, Herr McCool. I have it on the highest authority.'

'Whose?' Schmidt/Lang was also laughing.

'Hers,' said Heck, slapped his wife on her broad rump and dragged her off, both of them laughing heartily, between the tables.

The laugh abruptly died on Lang's face; he picked up his glass and gulped the beer down as if it were a suicide draught. His wife patted his arm, looked at Carmody and Cathleen.

'Heinz has to put up with that oaf every day. They work together.'

'Where?' said Carmody.

'A government department,' said Lang quickly, taking his face out of his glass. He looked severely at his wife. 'It is better they do not know too much. You understand, Herr Carmody?'

Carmody nodded. 'I always protect my sources, Herr Lang. It is part of a newspaperman's code.'

'Not in Germany,' said Lang. 'I think you had better go now. Say goodbye as if we are no more than casual sharers of this table. I'll be in touch with you at your office.'

'What if we want to get in touch with you, if there's an emergency?'

'Herr Doe will contact me. Goodnight, Fräulein. I hope we can get some news for you.'

'I must see your film when it is released,' said Inge Lang, her smile once more unrestrained.


2


Carmody and Cathleen were in bed, their love-making done. It was Monday night and both of them had had a busy day, their minds too occupied by the demands of their trades for them to devote much thought to the meeting with the Langs on Sunday night. *Lola und Ludwig* had gone badly again; Willy Heffer had, belatedly, begun to realize that the film would do his reputation no good whatsoever; Cathleen, nerves on edge, had had a shouting match with him and Karl Braun. Carmody, for his part, had spent the day running between the Foreign Ministry and the Propaganda Ministry; when he went back to the office there was a query from head office in New York as to why he couldn't supply more 'hard' news. By the time he and Cathleen met for dinner, they were both ready to fall into each other's arms.

When they had returned to her apartment there had been no argument or even discussion as to whether he should stay the night. She needed sustenance to get her through the night and though it might not be the first choice of nutritionists, sex can sustain. They made love to music, with the radio turned down and the programme, as if designed for lovers about to have their last exercise before settling down for the night, supplied appropriate music, *scherzo* for the livelier moments, *andante* for the afterplay. Ready for sleep, Carmody reached across to turn off the radio when the music suddenly stopped in mid-bar.

'We have an important announcement,' said a voice that sounded almost breathless with excitement (or disbelief? Carmody later wondered). 'The Reich government and the Soviet government have agreed to conclude a pact of non-aggression with each other. The Reich Minister for Foreign Affairs will arrive in Moscow on Wednesday, 23 August, for the conclusion of the negotiations.'

Carmody lay waiting for further comment, but after a few moments the music resumed where it had been interrupted. Still music for bedtime lovers; was the radio station manager ringing up the Ministry of Propaganda for advice on whether some Russian music should be played? Perhaps the *1812 Overture*? But Carmody knew very little Russian music and this was no time for cynical musing. He sat up, turned the radio even lower but kept it going in case there should be a further announcement, and switched on the bedside lamp.

Cathleen had been on the verge of sleep, but now she turned over on her back. 'What's the matter?'

'I think war's just got that much closer. Didn't you hear that announcement?' He explained what the non-aggression pact meant, that it would leave Hitler free to pursue his aims towards Danzig or anywhere else in Europe where he had designs to expand. 'I'll call London. Then I'll have to go to the office.'

He put on his underpants, then dialled the London bureau of World Press. He had never met the London night editor, but the latter had a prissy public school accent that suggested he might work in the daytime as the headmaster of some

141

church school. You did not phone him naked with a naked girl lying in the bed beside you.

Carmody wasted no time once the Berlin operator had connected him. 'I know no more than that bare announcement.'

The night editor swore obscenely, dispelling the church school headmaster image. 'We'll put it out as is – it'll make the Stop Press in the nationals. When can you give us more?'

'Christ knows. I'm on my way to the office now – I'll see if I can dig up someone at the Foreign Press Office. Give me a couple of hours. At least we should catch the New York morning editions. And the Australian afternoon editions,' he added nationalistically.

'Of course,' said the night editor sarcastically, a true imperialist. 'Mustn't forget the Colonies. Ring me when you have something.'

Carmody hung up, then looked at Cathleen, who was now wide awake. 'It looks bad, darl.'

'For me? You mean finding Mother?'

He didn't blame her for her selfish viewpoint: when war came, most of those caught up in it would be concerned only with their own survival. He had gone into the war in Spain to fight for a cause, but soon had been concerned only for Carmody.

'No, darl, for everyone. I wouldn't mind betting Hitler is already calling his generals together.'

He stood up, went into the bathroom, had a quick wash, came back into the bedroom and started to dress. After the warm evening and the love-making he felt like a shower, but there was no time for that; feeling clean wasn't going to make him feel any better. A door was about to be opened, one through which he had entered once before. This time, though, it would open on a wider and more terrible scene. It would be the biggest story he would ever cover, but he felt none of the usual newspaperman's excitement. All at once he wished he were back home, safe in the sheds or the paddocks, where the only wars were the brawls between drunken shearers on Saturday nights, where the only dictator might be a station boss who could be brought to his senses by the shearing team going on strike. He had covered those sort of stories as a cadet and been proud and excited when one of the Sydney papers would run a couple of column inches of what he had written. Those innocent days, however, were gone forever. He had a sense of foreboding, as if someone had just turned the first sod of his grave.

He kissed Cathleen. 'Go back to sleep. I'll be working all night, probably all tomorrow, too. I'll ring you when you get home from the studio.'

She held his hand. 'Thanks, darling.' He looked puzzled, his mind already elsewhere, chasing contacts in the Foreign Press Office. She explained patiently: 'For everything. Getting in touch with the Langs, for being so kind, for this –' She patted the bed. 'I think I'm in love with you.'

'What a time to tell me.' He grinned, kissed her again. 'If all this turns out to be a false alarm, I'll be back.'

But he knew it would not be a false alarm. Already in his head he could hear the bombs falling.

He let himself out of the apartment, went quietly down the stairs. As he reached the hallway the front door opened and a man and a woman came in, laughing softly. They said good evening to him, didn't give him a second glance but went up the stairs with an arm round each other, still laughing. They hadn't heard the news, they still had the whole night in which to enjoy each other.

He went out into the street, walked up towards the Kurfürstendamm looking for a taxi. As he crossed the road he saw a man step out of a doorway and walk hurriedly away. There was no mistaking who it was: Decker.

3

Helmut, sleeping alone, was sound asleep when his father called him.

'It has just come over the wireless. A non-aggression pact with the Russians, with that monster Stalin. They have done

143

their best over the years to kill off all the communists in Germany and now they make this treaty with the worst of them! Is there no end to our madman's perfidy?'

Despite the news, Helmut smiled: only his father's generation and class would say *Treulosigkeit*, perfidy. But it was a situation that perhaps only operatic words could describe: 'It is hard to believe, Father –'

'Is that all you have to say?' Helmut had never heard his father so wrought up; he sounded like a junior officer who had just learned his troops had run away from him. 'Hitler can do what he likes now! He will have us at war within a week!'

'Father –' Helmut sounded like a patient parent trying to calm an over-excited son; he could remember reverse situations in his own boyhood. 'There is nothing we can do immediately. I have to work tomorrow, but as soon as I've finished I'll come to your hotel. Is Romy still with you?'

'She went back to Stuttgart for the weekend. She'll be back here tomorrow afternoon.'

'Did she go by car?'

'No, the Horch is still here. But you'll be bringing your car, won't you?' The General was once more his calm, cool self: he was making plans, a general's task. 'We'll go ahead as planned. We *must*.'

'I'll be there, Father.' He no longer thought his father's plan was mad; dangerous and foolhardy perhaps, but not mad. The more he had thought about the kidnapping or assassination of Hitler, the more he had come to appreciate that it was necessary. His father had told him that the generals, the sensible professionals, not Hitler's sycophants, believed that Germany could not win a war if it was started immediately; such a course would only result in another defeat, a return to a situation as bad as that of the years right after the Great War. Hitler, somehow, had to be removed.

He slept fitfully the rest of the night, rose early and drove out to Neubabelsberg. He was surprised at the amount of troop movement; it seemed that the number of convoys had trebled since last week. It did not surprise him that they were heading west; cynically he assumed that the troops were already in place on the Polish frontier; within twelve hours the west-bound troops would be facing France's Maginot Line. He drove behind the last truck of a convoy, staring ahead at the glum faces staring back at him from the truck. They did not have the look of heroes eager for war.

He was in the reserves and he knew his call-up might come any day now. Then would come the dilemma: whether to respond to the call-up and stay and fight for Germany or flee to another country, one like Sweden which would remain neutral or to France or England, which would surely go to war. He could not see himself sitting out the war in Sweden, being so close a witness to the destruction of his fatherland; neither could he see himself joining some force in England or France that would fight against his own countrymen. For all his liberalism he was still an Albern, his father's son. Commoners can forget their past, aristocrats never: or so his father, a man with a sense of the aristocracy's brittle present, had often told him.

At the studio everyone was talking about the news in this morning's papers. Helmut picked up one newspaper, Dr Goebbels' own *Angriff*, read only one line – 'a long and traditional friendship produced a foundation for a common understanding' – and threw the paper away in disgust. Fritz Till picked it up, looked at it and said, 'Is communism now respectable? I must dig up some old friends, tell them they can come back from the grave.'

Helmut's action in throwing away the paper had been hasty; he was not entirely foolhardy. 'Keep it down, Fritz. Don't let's start any war here on the lot.'

Till laughed, a ton of mirth. 'You think anyone here wants to be in a war? Even our esteemed director, who wears his Party badge to bed, will be looking for a nice comfy job somewhere a long way behind the front.'

'I'd still be careful, Fritz. We don't want to lose you to the Gestapo. At least not before the film is finished.' He smiled, but he was deadly serious.

Till, too, was serious; he suddenly stopped laughing, looked around the set in which they stood, the dining hall in Ludwig's palace. When he looked back at Helmut there were tears in his eyes. 'Why do we produce so many madmen? This is a wonderful country. What is wrong with us?'

But Helmut had no answer. He turned away, avoiding Till's next question: 'What does your father think?'

Karl Braun came waltzing on to the set: he would fight the war with vivacity: 'Let's forget all that stuff in the newspapers! We have our film to finish. Where's our darling star?'

'If you mean me,' said Cathleen, coming in with her hairdresser and make-up girl, 'I'm right here.'

As Helmut set up his lights he noticed that Cathleen looked wan and tired. He called for the lights to be switched off and moved in beside Cathleen. 'Are you all right? You don't look well.'

'That's what this scene calls for, isn't it? Ludwig is kicking me out.'

He was not taken in; her smile was too bright and forced. 'Nobody else is going to kick you out.'

They were in the centre of everything, but too much was going on for any notice to be taken of them. Electricians were calling for lamps to be moved; carpenters were making last-minute repairs to a wall of the set; an argument was brewing between Braun and the film's supervisor, Leander, who had just come down from the front office; the assistant director was running about looking for a target for his authority. It was the sort of chaos that everyone cherished, since it made them look important to any spectators wandering in from outside. It was the only way to combat the importance of the stars.

For a moment she looked less wan; she looked interested, curious. 'What do you mean by that?'

He hedged. 'You're worried there might be war, aren't you?'

She nodded. 'Aren't you?'

'Of course, but not with America.' Perhaps he could go there, join all the others who had gone, Lubitsch, Sternberg, Lang. Hollywood suddenly looked far enough away to be Heaven, of a sort. 'As soon as the film is finished, you can leave.'

'Have you seen Colonel von Gaffrin?' Her face suddenly looked pinched, driving in behind her blunt remark.

'No. Why?'

'Ask him why the Abwehr is interested in me.'

The lamps had come on again; they moved out of range while Cathleen's stand-in stepped forward to take the discomfort of the lights; every trade has its slaves. Helmut stood beside a lamp, his face partly shadowed. He owed her more than evasions now; everything was coming to a head. 'He hasn't told me –'

'Did you leave me the note telling me to be careful?'

'Yes,' he said reluctantly. Now was not the time to be linked to a minor conspiracy, not with the huge conspiracy right on the family doorstep.

'Then find out why they're interested in me. Please!'

Then Braun, face flushed from his argument with the supervisor, appeared beside them. 'The things they expect! Two weeks from finishing and suddenly they want everything more pointed! They want to turn it into a propaganda film!'

'I thought that was what we were making,' said Helmut and walked away, escaping from both of them.

He avoided Cathleen for the rest of the day. In the afternoon Melissa came out to the studio for a late call; her part in the film was almost done. The call this afternoon was for retakes of reaction shots, close-ups that had not satisfied Braun. As he set the lamps to light her face, Helmut could feel her eyes following him. When he looked at her through the view-finder she stared back at him almost accusingly. There was pain in her face and, for the first time, with the eye of a professional, he saw beauty there and not mere prettiness.

'That's what we want, darling!' Braun gasped; he was at the end of his tether. It had been a *dreadful* day. 'If only you'd given me that last time!'

Melissa said nothing, didn't alter her expression; sometimes the best acting is no acting at all, though she had arrived at it by accident. Helmut gave the signal to the camera operator, looked at Braun and nodded. The camera began to roll and Melissa began to look like a star, just as her contract

147

was about to end. It was too late, Helmut knew: she had done nothing in this film that would get her a contract back in England. Or rather she had done something that would assure her of *not* getting a contract in England: she had appeared in one of Dr Goebbels' German propaganda films.

'Cut!' said Braun and sat back, fanning himself with another of his crêpe-de-chine handkerchiefs. 'Darling, you were marvellous! What a pity you will be leaving us!'

'Yes, isn't it?' Even her voice seemed to have changed, there was no longer that light girlish note, that false voice she had learned in the theatre; there was some of the roughness of where she had come from, the outskirts of Bradford. She had never been in danger of having to work in the woollen mills, but her father was an accountant in the woollen trade and nobody in that trade talked 'naice'. Something had happened to her and she had reverted to her true self, the self that had been born and raised in Bradford, the self she had tried to deny with her dreams even as a child. 'A bloody pity!'

Braun raised his eyebrows, looked at Helmut, shrugged and waddled off. The operator and his assistant wheeled the camera away, the gaffers picked up their lamps and went looking for another face to light, more corners to illuminate, and Helmut and Melissa were left alone.

'What's the matter?' He was surrounded by disturbed women today. 'Are you worried there might be war?'

'No. Yes!' She was twisting a handkerchief round and round her hand, a theatrical trick to portray anguish. He was tired of actresses, one never knew when their emotion was genuine. But he could see that she was truly upset and all at once he felt very protective towards her. 'I'm pregnant!'

'Oh God.' He said it wearily, though he didn't mean to; it is a way men have of sounding when confronted by a woman's problem over which they have no control.

'Don't sound like that!' She had never been in this situation before, but she had a woman's instinctive ear. Men are selfish, her mother had warned her; and driven her father back to his profit and loss columns. 'I didn't want it to happen any more than you did!'

'Are you sure?' It was a man's question, as if a woman's biological functions was something a woman wouldn't understand.

'Of course I'm bloody sure!' It came out rough and coarse, Bradford thick on her tongue. 'I've just come from the doctor. I've missed two of my periods. I've missed before, I tend to be that way, so I wasn't too worried when I missed the first time.'

He said nothing, because he could think of nothing to say. He had been fortunate in all his previous affairs; none of his girls had missed their periods, or if they had they had not told him so. His first reaction was selfish: why hadn't Melissa been more careful? He did not want to be a father, not yet; not while he had the responsibility of his own father, who had to be protected as much as a young mother-to-be. She said, 'Haven't you anything to say?'

'What do you want me to say?' It was the sort of dialogue he had heard in bad scripts, where the writers had not known how to get over a weak spot in the story. Padding, it was called. But padding was the last thing Melissa would want now.

'Take your time.' She got up from the stool on which she had been sitting for the close-ups. 'But we'll have to talk. Soon.'

'Tomorrow night?'

'Why not tonight?'

'I can't – I have to meet my father. Family business.' Making plans to kill the Fuehrer.

'Helmut –' Her tone softened, she sounded afraid. 'I don't want to have an abortion.'

More family business: killing a foetus. 'Are you a Catholic?' She shook her head. 'Do you want the baby?'

'I don't know. Yes, I think I might.' The handkerchief was just a handful of shreds now. 'Oh, I don't know!'

He put his arms round her and she began to sob. The set was dark now, but he could see some of the crew looking at them from the other end of the sound stage. Karl Braun was pacing up and down and he knew that in a moment the shrill petulant call would come. It did: 'Helmut, do you *mind*?

149

We'll call off the rest of the day's shooting if it's important to you and little Fräulein Hayes –'

Helmut waved that he was coming, kissed Melissa on top of her head. 'I should be home by eleven. Here's a second key to my flat. Let yourself in and wait for me.'

'Helmut –' She made the mistake of a woman truly in love with a man she isn't sure of: 'I'll do anything you say. If you don't want me to have the baby –'

'We'll talk about it tonight.'

He got through the rest of the day only because he was a professional; there are bonuses besides money to knowing one's trade. When he left the studio at six-thirty he felt like a man who hadn't slept for 48 hours or more. He was not unaccustomed to responsibilities; he had worked as chief cameraman on too many films to have dodged those. But he had had no personal responsibilities; it occurred to him only now that he had led a charmed life. Everything had been so easy: the only child of a rich, distinguished father; a smooth, almost too-smooth career in films; girls who had been in love with him but never troublesome . . . He drove back to the city in what seemed to him a deeper light than yesterday's. He remembered the poet Goethe's death-bed last words, 'More light!' It was the cry of desperate cameramen; or anyway of this one. He smiled, but anyone riding in the Opel with him might have mistaken it for a grimace of pain.

An hour later he picked up his father and Romy at their rendezvous, outside the Café Möhring. They got into the back seat, sat well back. The General was wearing his hat brim turned down all round, not his usual style, and Romy had on a broad-brimmed hat. They looked like conspirators chosen by the UFA casting director.

'We made sure we weren't followed from the hotel. It would be comical to have the Gestapo following us while we were mapping all their stations.' The General was gravely excited, a schoolboy about to murder the headmaster. He was back in harness, though this time the killing was to be more personal, something not usually done by generals.

'Where do we go first?' Helmut asked.

Romy had spread out a large map on her lap. 'We'll start at

their headquarters on Prinz Albrechtstrasse and work east.'

'We have planned our reconnaissance on a grid system,' said the General.

'Where did you get these addresses?' The lights were coming on along the Kurfürstendamm as Helmut drove along it. *More light!* But Goethe had been dying, not spying.

In the driving mirror he saw his father and Romy exchange glances. Then his father said, 'We must take him into our confidence – we owe him that much.'

'Of course,' said Romy and looked at Helmut in the mirror. 'The head of one of our biggest insurance firms is on our side. Or rather his wife is. She gave me the list.'

'You mean the Gestapo has insured all its stations? What against?'

'The usual, I suppose,' said Romy, who, being married to an industrialist, was more commercial-minded than the General, who, being a soldier, had never concerned himself with the cost of replacement of anything. 'Fire, theft, riots –'

'Theft?' Helmut laughed; and all at once the two in the back seat also laughed. They were suddenly all more relaxed, at least with each other if not with their situation.

Helmut drove them around for two hours while Romy, like a good aide-de-camp, made marks on the map and the General sat beside her, nodding appreciatively at the staff he had assembled. He complimented Helmut on knowing the city so well.

'It comes of being a worker, Father,' he said good-humouredly. 'You just never got around to the right places.'

The General nodded, also in good humour. 'It's too late now . . . No, perhaps it isn't. When this is all over and everything is settled down again, you must show me the real Berlin.'

'And me, too,' said Romy.

Helmut looked at them in the mirror; their optimism was almost naïve. 'It's a promise,' he said and tried to sound truthful.

He dropped them outside the Café Möhring. 'Will you be staying on in Berlin?'

'Of course. We must act within the next few days. *He –*' no names must be mentioned, not even amidst the traffic noise of the Kurfürstendamm '– will be coming back here any day now. There is to be a review of troops.'

'We must have dinner together when it's all over,' said Romy; she loved the social side of life. 'Bring a nice girl. You do have one?'

'Yes,' he said and drove on home to the waiting Melissa.


# 4


*Extracts from the diaries of Dr Paul Joseph Goebbels:*

22 August 1939:

The announcement of the Pact with the Russians has created a world sensation. The Allies have been left stunned; it has been a master-stroke on the part of the Fuehrer. How I wish I had been more involved in it! It stabs me deeply that so much credit is being given to the champagne salesman Ribbentrop. But he cannot sell it to the German people. That task has been left to me. I started today with a story in *Angriff*. Most convincing, I think, considering how I must explain our about-face. Perhaps there was a grain of truth in what was written – 'a natural partnership'. After all, I was a communist all those long years ago. History is full of ironies . . .

The Fuehrer called all the military leaders to Obersalzberg today. So far I have not heard how the meeting went. I do not trust most of them. Like all military men they do not understand the needs of their own country. Though I do agree with them – we are not yet fully prepared for war.

I spoke to the Fuehrer on the telephone this morning before the generals arrived. He said he spent a sleepless night on Sunday waiting on word from Moscow – the Russians dragged everything out till the last minute. I wondered where Germany would have gone if the Russians had said no to our proposals. But I did not ask such a question of the Fuehrer. I have too much respect for his feelings. I always have too much respect for other people's feelings. It is a weakness.

. . . How I wish war were not so imminent! I should have more time to concentrate on Cathleen. I think of her constantly. I, like the Fuehrer, have sleepless nights – but for a different reason. I should love to telephone her, hear her voice, talk to her as I used to talk to Lida. Erotic talk. But I fear my telephone may still be tapped, as it was when I was with Lida. Why cannot we trust each other? I must bring up the subject with the Fuehrer when we are next alone. But these days we are so rarely alone. It will be worse in the coming days. He is surrounding himself with the military, none of them true Nazis. Just arse-kissers like Keitel . . .

Spoke on the telephone with Magda and the children. How sweet they all are! Magda says the Bogensee house is coming along too slowly, the workmen are still there finishing it off. What has happened to the German workman? He does not work as hard as he once did. Have we made life too easy for them? I shall have to see there is a piece in *Angriff* telling them we need more effort. If war comes everyone will be expected to work as hard as he ever has in his life . . .

Magda asks me if war is now inevitable. She is concerned for the children. Does she think I am not? I tell her she should be concerned for the English and French children. They will be the ones to suffer. Theirs will be the countries which will lose the war . . . I hope I am right . . .

*Meanwhile elsewhere:*

# JAPANESE OCCUPY HONG KONG BORDER

## BOOK NOW FOR CONTINENTAL SKI HOLIDAYS

. . . Six hundred desperate and homeless Czech Jews who embarked in the Panama vessel *Parita* at Constanta, the Roumanian Black Sea port, are reported to have mutinied at Smyrna, Turkey. For weeks the ship has been seeking a port at which the passengers could be landed . . .

Letter to *The Times*:

Sir, – I wonder if you can help us in Clements Lane to find our lost apostrophe?

. . . Unwanted artificial teeth gratefully received. Send all donations to the Ivory Cross Dental Aid Fund . . .

. . . 134 East 70th Street, New York: 3½-room Apartment, large terrace **$110 per month**

# LOU AMBERS REGAINS LIGHTWEIGHT TITLE

## Beats Henry Armstrong in Savage Fight

### FOULS GALORE

. . . EAST KENT – Gun required to complete congenial party. Bag 4,000 pheasants, 1200 partridges. Reduced subscription accepted due current situation. Marvellous opportunity for practice . . .

. . . An estimated 10,000 people queued yesterday at Radio City for the opening performance of the new M-G-M movie, 'The Wizard of Oz' . . .

. . . An estimated 10,000,000 people are still unemployed in the US . . .

. . . Dividends for August from US companies are expected to top $315,000,000, the highest disbursed since 1937. Business leaders are optimistic. War industries, in particular, are buoyant . . .

*Somewhere over the rainbow . . .*

### J.P. MORGAN'S PICNIC MENU FOR ROYALTY KEPT SECRET

. . . King George and Queen Elizabeth enjoyed another outdoor picnic lunch in Scotland with an American host . . .

## GERMAN LINERS CALLING AT SOUTHAMPTON

. . . The German liner *Bremen* called at Southampton today and landed holiday-makers, students and others from Bremerhaven . . .

# CHAPTER SEVEN

## 1

Admiral Canaris had flown down to the Obersalzberg that morning. There had been others on the plane: Admirals Raeder and Boehm, Generals Witzleben and Thomas; but Canaris, true to form, had sat alone at the back of the plane. As they had been driven up to the top of Hitler's private mountain he had looked out at the domain Martin Bormann had created here for the Fuehrer. Farms had been bought up and their buildings demolished, wide tracts of state forest confiscated, roads laid; the fence round the inner area was two miles long, that round the outer area nine miles long. Bormann, a man with no respect for nature, had turned paths through the forests into paved walks. Nature, it seemed, could not be trusted. Bormann, an untrusting and untrustworthy man, had run true to his own nature.

The winding precipitous road, which always made Canaris queasy, ended abruptly beneath the rock on which the Berghof was built. Canaris got out of the staff car, took a pill from among the dozen or so in his pill-box, followed the others across to the elevator built into the rock, and hoped his stomach would have settled before the Fuehrer got down to one of his interminable harangues.

The Berghof was not one of Canaris' favourite houses; he always thought of it as a mountain asylum designed by one of the inmates. He knew that Speer, the Reich's principal architect, abhorred it but hadn't had the courage to say so; it had been based on an impromptu design by the Fuehrer himself and furnished by Bormann, Hitler's administrator. Neither expense nor bad taste had been spared; Canaris felt depressed every time he entered the house. The servants were all members of the SS, a fact which did nothing to

155

lighten his mood. The only item about the whole estate that pleased him was its huge debt, something known only to a self-selected few. There are malicious joys in being a spy that only spies know . . .

Hitler was waiting for them as they all entered the main salon. Bormann stood just behind him, looking what he was: a peasant who had made good cultivating a different field. Hitler appeared to trust him completely and the man's arrogance towards everyone but the Fuehrer reflected the knowledge of that trust. He stood there in the background, burly as a bull, face as insentient as a fist. Canaris, like most of the other military men, ignored him, but the snubs seemed to have no effect on Bormann. He knew who was the court favourite, the court jester who had no jokes but had more tricks than a zoo of monkeys.

'Gentlemen!' Hitler was moving up and down on the balls of his feet; he seemed ready to bounce. Occasionally he gave his characteristic peculiar kick back with his right leg. Canaris had never seen him so bubbling with excitement, and groaned inwardly: they were in for another long harangue. He took out another pill, surreptitiously popped it in his mouth, wishing it were a sleeping pill. 'What did you think of our coup?'

Everyone left it to General Keitel, the yes-man, to answer for them. He had a rosy-cheeked, soft face with a fair moustache that looked like a complement to the Fuehrer's dark one; he always struck Canaris that he would not argue the state of the weather unless he had a battery of howitzers behind him. 'A master stroke, Fuehrer! It is a pity we could not have seen the looks on the faces of Chamberlain and Daladier when they got the news.'

'Yes! Yes!'

Canaris smiled to himself. The roles had been reversed: Hitler was playing yes-man to Ja-Ja.

There was a stir at the back of the large group and Goering came into the big room. He was adjusting his trousers under his blue double-breasted tunic. 'My apologies, Fuehrer. A call from nature . . .'

Hitler laughed, turned round and walked with his jerky

156

stride round to stand behind a large table on which were spread out some maps. It seemed that nothing could dent his ebullient mood, not even the rude late entrance of his second-in-command. Then, as Canaris had seen so often before, in public and in private, his mood abruptly changed.

'I have called you together to give you a picture of the political situation in order that you may have some insight into the individual factors on which I have based my irrevocable decision to act and in order to strengthen your confidence . . .'

Though he was not sneering openly there was no mistaking the fact that he considered them all political novices. None of them, except Goering, had fought in the streets: the streets were for parades, not political battles. They sat there, none of them below senior staff rank, like cadets in a military academy being lectured by a veteran field commander. The corporal from the Great War had realized the ambition of all non-commissioned officers: he was giving the brass the rough end of the grenade.

'. . . Essentially, all depends on me, on my existence, because of my political talents. Furthermore, the fact that probably no one will ever again have the confidence of the whole German people as I have. There will probably never again in the future be a man with more authority than I have. My existence is therefore a factor of great value . . .'

Such conceit, thought Canaris. How wonderful it must be not to be burdened by modesty. Unburdened, the Fuehrer took off on wings of rhetoric; his listeners, those with musical imagination and an ear for flat notes, could hear Wagner rising and falling in the background. Canaris, sitting by the huge, wound-down picture window, overcome by the smell of petrol fumes coming up from the vast underground garage and the constant din of the Fuehrer's voice, felt himself falling into a queasy doze. He straightened up in his chair and then, bent over like a white-haired, hunch-backed monkey, began to creep away from the window.

Hitler stopped in mid-harangue: 'Where are you going, Admiral Canaris?'

'I am getting closer, Fuehrer,' said Canaris, still bent over but changing direction, 'to hear you the better.'

He heard the faint snigger of those closest to him and, completely out of character, he winked at them and slid embarrassedly onto a vacant chair. Hitler went on, picking up as if he had no more than stopped to brush away a fly. At times like this he lived in a world of his own voice.

The meeting, or rather the monologue, droned on. Then abruptly the Fuehrer said, 'Now we shall have lunch,' and instantly his mood changed again. He smiled, became the quietly modest host. Bormann, the major-domo, took charge and ushered everyone, like a sullen, nasty dog herding sheep, into the huge dining room.

Lunch was as Canaris' stomach liked it: simple. There was soup, a roast and vegetables, an apple tart with cream; to drink there was mineral water, bottled beer from Berlin, not Munich, and a cheap wine that most of those who had ordered it left in their glasses. Canaris, partly as a gesture, partly because of his upset stomach, which he was sure now was the beginning of cancer, ordered the same vegetarian dish as Hitler. The Fuehrer, looking down the long table at him, gave him a gentle smile. The way to his heart was through a vegetable patch . . .

After lunch there was a break. Canaris was standing out on the wide terrace admiring the view across to the Untersberg on the other side of the valley, when Goering came out and stood beside him. He could smell the Reichsmarschall's perfume and his quick eye caught the gleam of the painted fingernails; but, this being a working day, there was no rouge on the plump cheeks.

'Did you enjoy your vegetable hash, Canaris? Every time I come here I promise myself that next time I'll bring my own picnic basket. Something substantial, with some good wine instead of that sweet piss. Well, what do you think of our chances?'

'Of getting good wine here or going to war in Poland?' He did not like this vain fat man, but at least one could talk to him without being harangued. He had also been a good flier, in the last war, a good officer, not a corporal.

'We'll walk into Poland – there'll be no opposition there. No, what do your agents tell you about England and France?'

'Nobody there wants war.' *Nobody here but the fools wants war, either.* 'They aren't prepared. Especially the English. The Luftwaffe should have no opposition at all.'

'Now all the waiting is over, I'm actually looking forward to it.' He didn't say *the war*, but Canaris knew what he meant. The Reichsmarschall was staring out across the valley, as if he could see the sky filled with his beloved air force. 'I just wish I were young enough to fly again. And slim enough.' He laughed and patted his belly beneath the tunic. 'It's a pity we have to age, Canaris. Do you ever pine to go back to sea?'

'Not really. I don't think I have the stomach for it any more.'

He had not meant to make a joke, but Goering threw back his head and laughed. He patted the tiny man on the shoulder and, still shaking with laughter, said, 'I don't think you have much of anything, old man.'

Canaris smiled weakly, hating the gross Reichsmarschall, and turned away with relief as Bormann came out on to the terrace and announced that the Fuehrer was ready to resume his meeting.

Hitler took up where he had left off. He rambled on, piling lie upon lie like straw bricks; Canaris recognized them for lies and waited for someone senior to himself to query them, but no one did. The Fuehrer began to work himself up, fury steaming through his words: he was addressing the world at large, not just this room full of his own generals and admirals. Canaris, bored by the repetition, let his mind wander back to work that lay on his desk in Berlin. Then he thought of the thin file locked in an office drawer and, his mind taking off on a flight of fancy as it sometimes does when trying to avoid falling asleep, wondered what Goebbels was doing at this very moment. Was he sending more flowers to the Jewish actress, did he know or care where the mother was? Should I go to him? Canaris wondered; and pictured the scene. Two small men facing each other like bantams . . .

159

He came back to the Berghof with a start. He heard Hitler, calmed down again, say, 'The order to march will be given later. It will most probably be next Saturday, the 26th.'

Goering stood up, began applauding. Everyone else in the room got to his feet, some quickly, some slowly, as if they could not quite believe what they had heard. The applause spread round the room, gathering volume like that of hail on the roof of an empty house. Canaris put his hands together, but they felt like two sheets of paper being flapped against each other.

This is how we greeted the news of the coming of war, he thought, with the clapping of hands. As if we were applauding a show we hadn't enjoyed.

## 2

Carmody had received a letter from his mother. It was like a despatch from a never-never land in a never-never time . . . 'It has been a mild winter so far, just a few frosts,' Ida wrote. 'Your father had a droving job last month, taking a mob of 1200 sheep, mostly wethers, out to Cawndilla. I went along with him. It was just like old times. I kept looking behind me to see if you were straggling along behind us with Cobber and the other dogs. Dad and I went to a hop in Cawndilla and had a good time. He is still light on his feet but I'm not as spry as I used to be. I hope you are having a good time in Berlin. I don't like the sound of that Hitler . . .'

The letter was eight weeks old and there was no mention of war. He all at once felt a longing to see his parents again and wondered how much they had changed in the three years since he had left home. *It was just like old times* . . . He could smell the dust and the sheep, feel the smooth coat of the crossbred dog rubbing against his bare leg, taste the rabbit grilled on the end of a stick over a camp fire, see the mulberry cloud coming up behind a lone tree on a distant hill. The crisp morning bit into him, but gently, like the love-bite of Nature;

the afternoon sun warmed him, like the dimly remembered comfort of his mother's arms when he had been quite small. And the stars at night, identified for him by Rupe Venneker, the English remittance man, the sailor who had roamed the world, the man who had started his education . . .

He was not a man for tears, but suddenly he wanted to weep.

He put the letter away with all the others his parents had written and went out to work. Since Monday night it seemed that he had hardly slept. New York and London, where the editors worked in shifts and not round the clock, had been constantly phoning him, asking him for more copy. They were calling for hard news, for background, for profiles: the world had to know all about those who were going to end it.

He went to an early supper at La Trattoria, the Italian restaurant just off the Potsdamerplatz. It was run by a tall thin Tyrolean from the Brenner Pass and his stout but timid Polish wife; it had become a gathering place for most of the foreign correspondents and some of the senior Berlin newspapermen. Gossip was served as garnish with the *pollo alla Romana*; malicious comment took the sweetness out of the spumante. He did not go there regularly, because he was not naturally gregarious and he soon grew weary of crowd conversation; but in times of crisis, like the present, it was the place to pick up items that he had missed on his rounds of government offices. Official press handouts were like marriage certificates: they were no guarantee that anything would or ever had been consummated.

He took a seat at a table opposite Joe Begley. Tinkler, the owner, brought him a plate of spaghetti *bolognese*. He looked up at the thin dark face, more mournful-looking than ever. 'What's the trouble, Luis?'

'The wife.' Tinkler had once been an actor; he had a beautiful deep voice. 'She's Polish, as you know. If we go to war over Danzig, where does that put her?'

'Pack up and take her to the States,' said Begley; then grinned at his own recipe. 'America, the answer to everything.'

161

He had taken off his trenchcoat and looked naked without it, a turtle without its shell.

'How long has she lived in Germany?' said Carmody.

'Twenty years,' said Tinkler. 'But you think that will matter? I had Jewish friends who had lived here for two hundred years – or anyway their family had. You think it saved them?'

'Why don't you go back to Austria?'

'The Austrians have worse Nazis there than we have here.'

'No,' said Begley, pausing to wipe some ravioli from his chin, 'the worst one of the lot is here.'

'He's an Austrian, isn't he?' said Tinkler and went away, stooped over as if already grieving.

It was Frau Tinkler who brought them fruit and cheese. She was almost as tall as her husband and must have outweighed him by at least 30 pounds; but she had a bird-like timidity about her, as if afraid the weight of the world would crush her. Her voice was so soft one felt like burrowing in her stoutness to wrench it out of her. Her eyes were perpetually downcast, which made it difficult for customers signalling for service.

'Do you have family in Poland, Frau Tinkler?' said Begley.

She nodded and whispered something neither man caught. 'Pardon?'

'Danzig.' Her voice was still little more than a whisper, but she glanced up and about her as if she had involuntarily shouted an obscenity.

'Do you hear from them?' said Carmody. 'What do they think about the situation there?'

'They are frightened. They are Poles, not Germans.' It was the longest speech either of them had ever heard her make. She ducked her head, folded her face into her chins as if ashamed at being so voluble.

Then Tinkler, coming away from serving another table, stopped by her. 'All her mother's letters to us have been opened. She never gets ours.'

'If Herr Carmody or I have to go to Danzig, would you like us to take them a message?'

Frau Tinkler lifted her head, her big round face lit up.

'Would you? Perhaps you could take something for my mother – a small gift?'

'Sure.' Carmody had no plans for going to Danzig, he had been there only two weeks ago; but he could not deflate the woman, she seemed to have ballooned with gratitude. You had better go to Danzig, he silently told Begley, you had no right making such a promise. 'We'll let you know when one of us is going.'

The Tinklers thanked them and went away, Tinkler saying as he went, 'We'd never want to leave Berlin. It is the best city in the world, don't you think?'

'Naturally,' said Begley, who came from Chicago, the next best.

'If you say so,' said Carmody, who had never seen a city till he was eighteen years old and those he had seen since had been under siege of one form or another. 'We're lucky. Being outsiders, I mean.'

Begley nodded. 'You think I don't know it? When I see what's going on here, I sometimes have sympathy for the isolationists back home. Who in his right senses wants to get mixed up in all this? But then I have a conscience, something my first city editor told me to get rid of when he sent me out on my first story. I've been trying to get rid of it ever since, but it sticks to me like shit to a blanket.'

That had been a favourite expression of Paddy Carmody's, though never about his conscience. Carmody suddenly felt nostalgic for the sound of his father's voice.

'Are you coming to Goebbels' press conference this evening?' Begley said.

'It'll be worth it to hear how he justifies the pact with the Russians.'

Outside the restaurant Carmody bumped into the Australian cyclist he had interviewed, getting out of a taxi. In a suit he looked older, a lean bone of a man ready for burying. He and his partner had come second in the six-day event, losing out to a German pair. The Germans seemed to be winning everything this summer.

'Did you write that piece on me?'

'Yes,' lied Carmody, who had had too many other pieces to

163

write in the past week. 'Where do you go next? Paris? Munich?'

The cyclist shook his head. 'I'm going home, mate. Things are starting to look crook here in Europe. Any message you want me to give Australia?'

'Just tell it to stay where it is.'

'Bloody good advice, mate. Well, hooroo. Keep your head down.'

He went into the restaurant, bandy-legged and bow-backed, and Begley, once more wrapped in his trenchcoat, said, 'Who was that?'

'An Aussie philosopher. We breed 'em by the hundreds.'

They took the bike rider's taxi and rode over to the Propaganda Ministry. Everyone was there, from Tass to the *Christian Science Monitor* and all beliefs and persuasions in between. Carmody had never seen such a crowded conference; it was a scrimmage with everyone pushing and shoving for a vantage point. The fountain pens were loaded, ready to fire the first shots of war.

Oliver Burberry stood leaning against a side wall; Carmody and Begley propped themselves up beside him. 'I had hoped for a front seat, out of respect for *The Times*. But Tass has my chair, as you will notice.'

'Never mind,' said Carmody. 'It's more decent back here amongst the Colonies.'

'You better get used to it,' said Begley, wrestling himself out of his trenchcoat again. 'We're in the Jim Crow seats from now on.'

Then Goebbels made his entrance. This evening, Carmody noticed, he was wearing uniform, complete with gloves; for the past month more and more ministers had been wearing uniform every day. There was no doubt the well-cut tunic lent more authority to the slight figure. 'He looks like my old Scouts master,' said Burberry. 'Perhaps I should salute.'

It was the first time Carmody had seen Goebbels since Cathleen had had supper with him. He felt jealousy gnawing at him; or rather hatred. He had always had contempt for the Minister: he was a liar, a womanizer and a Jew-hater; he was

164

also an opportunist and Carmody knew that breed could never be trusted.

'He will now stand on his head,' said Burberry.

Which the Propaganda Minister proceeded to do, at least verbally and philosophically. 'The Fuehrer, ever mindful of the German people's, indeed the whole world's, desire for peace has once again shown his remarkable talent for diplomacy and statesmanship. . . Our two great countries, Germany and Russia, have had a long tradition of friendship. More recently we have had the greatest respect for each other's system. There have been differences, of course, but they were in the nature of different circumstances in our respective countries . . . You have a question, Herr Burberry?'

'Yes, Herr Reichsminister. Will both countries now allow free elections, with all parties free to participate?'

'Our elections are free, Herr Burberry. At the moment, however, we are not planning any.' Goebbels smiled and all the correspondents in the front row smiled back at him, even those who were not German or Russian; a smile was cheap admission, if it meant you got a front row seat at future conferences. 'Yes, Herr Carmody?'

'In view of the long tradition of friendship, how does the Minister reconcile that with the fact that Germans and Russians fought on opposite sides in the recent Spanish civil war?'

'They were all volunteers, Herr Carmody. You must know that – I understand you were there. Germans are free to go anywhere they wish to fight for their beliefs.'

'Like the German Jews,' said Begley under his breath.

The conference went on, but the questions now were bland; the more cynical correspondents had given up. Goebbels spread his answers like butter, was always in command, never lost his patience. As he stood up to close the conference there came the sound of church bells through the open windows. It seemed an incongruous sound for the circumstances and the incongruity of it silenced the room for a moment. It was the moment when Burberry chose to say, 'There is the death-knell for the British Empire.'

Everyone turned to look at him, including Goebbels.

Carmody, suddenly alert, saw the Minister's eyes light up and his mouth open in a wide smile.

'May I quote you, Herr Burberry?'

Burberry looked ready to bite his tongue off at the root. He sighed, smiled weakly. 'A slip of rhetoric, Herr Reichsminister. I've been hearing it for years.'

Goebbels nodded, smiled again and made his exit. But Carmody and Burberry and everyone in the room knew the remark would be quoted to the Fuehrer, if to no one else. A good opportunist would never let an opportunity like that slip by.

Carmody felt sorry for Burberry. 'Bad luck, Oliver.'

Burberry looked at his umbrella point, as if contemplating stabbing himself with it. 'I've always hated church bells. They disturb one's sleep on a Sunday morning. The bell-ringers have just had their revenge.'

Carmody left him and Begley, went to his office and filed his piece on the press conference. Olga Luxemburg looked at him worriedly. 'You should go home and get some sleep, Herr Carmody.'

He stood at the window looking out on the Potsdamerplatz. Was it imagination or were more customers going into the chemist's shop on the corner opposite? Were they after headache powders, some anodyne against the future? 'What are you going to do, if I have to leave?'

She came and stood beside him. He glanced at her and saw that she was not looking down at the *Platz* but straight out across the city. There was still light in the sky, a pale yellow that turned to lemon as he looked at it. The far skyline was etched against it, the domes and steeples of churches dominating the frieze: it was the profile of Berlin of the past, of Bismarck, with all the Nazi banners lost in the shadows. 'I shall stay on here, Herr Carmody. There is nowhere else to go – I am a Berliner.'

'Will you find it hard to get a job, having worked for foreigners for so long?'

'Perhaps.'

'I'll see that you get a good pension,' he promised rashly, 'if we have to close down the office.'

'How will I be paid? If war comes, how will the money be allowed in?' She was a practical woman, more practical than he: 'I don't think they'll close the office, at least not till America declares war on us. But you may have to go, you will be thought of as English.'

He smiled: that would kill his father, the Pommy-hater. 'I'll cultivate an American accent.'

'I don't think that will help. I was not going to tell you – I didn't want you to worry –' She turned and looked at him and he saw something in her eyes that he had never noticed before. It shocked him, because he was a modest man: he recognized it as love. 'Those two men, the Gestapo, came back again this morning. They interrogated me, wanted me to tell them all about you, what you wrote, whom you knew in the Ministries . . .'

'I'm sorry. You shouldn't be drawn into this –' He wanted to put a hand on her arm, but now he was afraid. 'What did you tell them?'

'As little as possible. I was polite –' She would always be that, even to her executioner, should she meet him. She was as plain as a woman could be, but now he saw the beauty in her, something that had nothing to do with her features. He had the blinkered look of most men, especially the young: he had always looked for the more obvious attributes of a woman. Courage, devotion, would never win beauty contests; but now they began to win him. He felt suddenly humble and still afraid. Because he would never be able to repay what she was offering him. 'So were they. Or at least Inspector Lutze was. Not that other one, that Decker.'

'Were they satisfied with what you told them?'

'I don't think so, but how can one tell? At least they didn't take me away. But you must be careful –' There was anguish in her pale blue eyes and it hurt him to see it.

'I'll try. You be careful, too. They probably have our phones tapped.'

She tried to smile, but it was difficult for her. 'Only my mother calls me. I don't think even the Gestapo would consider her subversive. She does not like the Fuehrer, but

Reichsmarschall Goering is her pin-up. She likes him even more than the film stars.'

*Everyone to their taste*. 'Well, still be careful. You don't have to shove your neck out for World Press.'

'I have never before shoved my neck out –' She had a little difficulty with the phrase. 'Perhaps it would be a change.'

No, he thought, it's too late now for the revolution. You and all the Germans like you should have shoved your necks out when you realized the truth about Hitler. But then, fair-minded as ever, a weakness the Nazis would have despised, he wondered if his own countrymen or the British or the French or the Americans, given the same circumstances, would have rebelled. In the past, yes; but now? Revolutions now were led by generals, as in Spain. There were no generals in Australia or any of the Allied countries who could fire the citizens into rebellion. There were German generals who would have led a rising against Hitler, but the German people no longer trusted their military leaders.

He said goodnight to her, told her to lock up the office and go home (to her mother, the admirer of Goering) and went out into the Potsdamerplatz and began the long walk home to his own apartment. Occasionally he looked over his shoulder to see if he could catch sight of Lutze or Decker or anyone else who might be following him, but all he saw was the sauntering crowd, carefree and unthreatening. Or so the crowd seemed on the surface: but behind those smiling faces, beneath those sober suits, he saw the grim-faced, uniformed soldiers of tomorrow. He walked on, utterly depressed.

His spirits lifted for a moment when Cathleen got out of a waiting taxi as he came to his front door. 'I've been waiting half an hour. I didn't want to come to your office –' She paid off the driver, giving him a tip that sent him away humming, put her arm in Carmody's and pushed him inside the building and up the stairs to his apartment. 'I had a phone call from Frau Schmidt. Lang.'

'Where? At your flat?'

'No, at the studio. Don't worry, we were both so discreet. She probably thought it safer to call me there – the phones to the dressing-rooms aren't tapped.'

'How do you know?' He offered her a drink, but she shook her head. He poured himself a beer, sat down beside her on the big leather couch. 'What did she have to say?'

'They have a lead, but she wouldn't say what. I think she was only ringing to encourage me. I haven't been able to sleep – I'm excited one minute, depressed the next . . . She probably understands how I feel. A woman would.'

'Some men would, too,' he said, feeling wiser by the hour.

She pressed his hand. 'You would, I know. Can I sleep here tonight?'

'Sleep or make love?'

'Both. I have no call tomorrow. Willy Heffer has the 'flu, so they are shooting around us tomorrow. I'll be glad of the rest.'

'You may not get the picture finished in time.'

'You mean war? I don't care, not about the picture. I only came here to find Mother – that's all I care about now. I don't want to collapse just when I look like finding her.'

They went to bed, but Carmody first set his alarm clock. 'I have to phone New York at one o'clock. They'll want to know if there's any late news for the morning editions.'

Editors were like wives: they hated the thought that their men might be doing nothing while they themselves were slaving. Or so he had been told by married newspapermen.

They made love, gently and violently, the best way; then fell asleep. It seemed only minutes later when the alarm went off. He sat up, switched on the bedside lamp and looked at Cathleen's face on the pillow beside his. She was frowning and even as he watched her she twitched sharply, devils running dagger-toed through her sleep. He smoothed the dark red hair, darker still with sweat, away from her brow, wished, like all true lovers, that he could protect her from all suffering and threats. Then he got out of bed and went into the living room to phone his editor in New York, another threat.

'What the hell's happening over there?'

*I've just been making love to my girl.* 'Nothing. Everybody's marking time.'

169

'They're doing what? This is a bad line.' Carmody had never met this editor, but he had the reputation of believing the world was against him. Tonight it was the Atlantic Ocean sitting too heavily on his conversation. 'Why aren't you in Danzig?'

'I was there two weeks ago. This is where things are going to happen, if they happen.'

'The first shots are gonna be fired in Danzig. Get over there for a coupla days.'

'And get shot?'

'What you say? I told you, this is a goddam awful line.'

'Yeah, isn't it?' said Carmody and hung up. When he turned round he saw Cathleen, nude, standing in the doorway. 'That doorway suits you. I should buy it as a frame.'

'I didn't know you were poetic.'

'Neither did I,' he said, admiring her, still marvelling at his luck. The boy from the bush sleeping with a beautiful film star . . . Then he said, coming back to earth, 'I have to go to Danzig.'

'For how long?' She looked frightened, as if she did not want to be left alone.

'A couple of days. There's a morning train at eight. Let's go back to bed.'

She shook her head. 'No, let's go out somewhere. A nightclub, anywhere. I can't sleep.'

He imagined he could see her nerve-ends, frayed as old rope. He was shocked at how suddenly she seemed to have gone to pieces; it had happened since Sunday night, when they had met the Langs. Hope, it seemed, had unravelled her.

'Righto. Let's have a bath first. I'll pack a bag and bring it with me.'

It was two o'clock when they went out. In the deserted street he looked for someone spying on them; but there was no one, or if there was they were doing their job perfectly, not letting him know. They walked to a night club on the Kurfürstendamm, where most of the customers were drunk or half-asleep by now, where the chorus girls danced behind tired smiles and the resident comedian told tired jokes; after

170

half an hour Cathleen wanted to move on and Carmody, glad to get out of the place, gladly followed her.

They went to another nightclub but Cathleen also grew bored there. They caught a taxi over to Friedrichstrasse, found a bar which turned out to be a haunt for transvestites. Carmody had ordered drinks before he became aware of the stares of the other clients; at first he thought he and Cathleen had fallen into a suppertime canteen for prostitutes. Then he saw the muscular legs of some of the 'women', the blue jaws showing through the make-up of some of them, and he suddenly realized where they were. This was not the notorious Eldorado, on the Motzstrasse, but its clients were possibly the younger brothers (the sons, too?) of those who had gone there in its heyday. Berlin was not the wide open sin city it had been in the Twenties, but it was still a magnet for deviates.

'What's the matter?' said Cathleen.

'I think I'm the odd man out in here. And you're the odd girl.'

Cathleen looked around. The bar-room was decorated in Art Deco style; the walls were hung with posters and cartoons that had survived from the Twenties. There were only two or three men present, none in uniform, and the only swastika in sight was on a small flag hung behind the bar. Then she looked again at the women in the room and realization dawned. But unlike Carmody, she was not embarrassed. She smiled at four 'girls' at the next table; the four looked at each other, then smiled back. Cathleen turned back to Carmody. 'If it pleases them, what's the harm? At least they're not out molesting kids.'

'I'd dong 'em if they tried to molest me.' He knew he sounded unsophisticated and narrow-minded, but growing up in a shearing shed hadn't prepared him for the switches in sex he had met since coming to Europe. The waiter, a man (or was he a girl dressed as a man? Carmody wasn't sure), came back with their drinks.

'My friend would like to buy drinks for the four ladies at the next table,' said Cathleen. 'Will you take their orders?'

Carmody swore under his breath; and swore again when

171

the four 'ladies' ordered champagne. Cathleen turned her chair, faced the next table and said pleasantly, 'I like your outfits. Where do you buy them?'

'Anywhere that catches our eye,' said a big blond with a false bust and a false voice. 'Where do you get yours? That's a beautiful dress, so chic.'

'American,' said Cathleen, standing up and showing off her dress. 'I got it in New York, Bergdorf Goodman's.'

'I've heard of it,' said a tall thin brown-haired one with bangs and a 1920s shingle cut. 'It's a Jewish store, isn't it?'

'I believe it is,' said Cathleen, sitting down, crossing her legs and showing them off. Carmody noticed that the four pairs of legs at the other table seemed to creep back out of sight. 'But they always have the nicest stuff, don't you think? I believe Kohner used to be the best couturier in Berlin, wasn't he?'

'We could never afford his creations,' said the blond, then laughed, showing teeth like those of a guard dog. He played with one of his dangling ear-rings. 'He never made my size.'

The conversation went on and Carmody, not asked to join in, sat silent and bemused. His embarrassment had faded away, but was revived when one of the transvestites, petit and with a gold-chestnut curly wig, leaned across and put a slim hand on his knee.

'When you came in with that bag –' he nodded at Carmody's small overnight bag '– we thought you were going into the loo to change. You'd look good in slacks and jacket. Those shoulders – like Marlene Dietrich's.'

It was Cathleen who lifted the slim hand from Carmody's knee. 'He's mine, sweetheart. He gets nervous when strange girls touch him.'

The curly-wigged one smiled, sat back. 'Half your luck, darling.'

Carmody gave him a weak smile for the compliment. Then he said, 'What happens when you girls get your call-up?'

They fluttered their hands in exaggerated gestures, rolled their eyes; all except the big blond, who said in his true voice, a rough baritone, 'What business is it of yours? Why don't you foreigners go home?'

Carmody stood up. 'I think we might do that. Anywhere would be better than here.'

Cathleen, too, stood up. She had been recklessly gay all night, had got into conversation with the transvestites out of a perverse mood that she herself didn't understand; it was as if her nerves were prodding her on, daring her to create situations the outcome of which she couldn't guess. But now she saw this was a situation of which she had lost control. The men, one in male clothes, the others in their dresses, suddenly were at odds. It struck her that, deep down, how the five men were dressed had nothing to do with the antagonism that had suddenly flared.

The blond stood up, but the tall thin brown-haired one grabbed him and tried to pull him down into his chair again. 'Don't, Karl! You'll only get into trouble!'

The curly-wigged one all at once grabbed Carmody and Cathleen by the elbows and pushed them ahead of him towards the steps leading up to the street. Carmody allowed himself to be pushed, surprised at the strength in the slim hands and wrists. 'Get out quickly and don't come back! He is an SS lieutenant. Go – quickly!'

Carmody looked back, saw the SS officer still on his feet, glaring after him with an angry hatred that the distance between them did nothing to dissipate. He had snatched off his wig, exposing a nearly-bald head that shone with sweat; something had happened to his bust, perhaps a strap had snapped as his muscles had swelled, and his bright red dress hung on him like a limp banner. He looked ridiculous and Carmody had to check himself from laughing. Instead, he turned and pushed Cathleen ahead of him up into the street.

'Christ Almighty!'

'I'm sorry, darling –'

'Don't you ever get me into a spot like that again!' He would not have believed he could be so angry with her; but he was. He was taking deep breaths, trying to control himself. He was alarmed at how he felt: he wanted to strike her. Not because she had got him into danger, but because she had endangered herself. 'If there'd been a fight, you'd have got hurt, too. At the very least we'd both probably have finished up in jail. Christ, can't you understand we have to stay out of trouble? Now, especially, when we could get word about your mother –'

'I said I'm sorry. I am, really. But you shouldn't have asked them about their call-up – that must have got under that SS man's skin –'

He was cooling down. 'I couldn't help that. I didn't mean to needle them – I was just curious. How often do I talk to blokes like that?'

She looked at him in the yellow glow of the street-lamps. Sometimes she thought of him as remarkably young; but perhaps she herself was innocent, she had mistaken decency for immaturity. She had lived too long in a world where decency was only something dreamed up by the Hays Office, the film industry's guardian of the morals of everybody but its own. All at once he looked older, he knew more about the real world, of the quick and the dead, than she possibly ever would.

He was standing with his back to a *Litfasssäule*, one of the thick pillars that stood like a robot sentry on almost every street corner dressed in advertisements and official placards. Immediately behind his head was a poster advertising a recent gathering at the Sportspalast: Hitler glared at her over Carmody's shoulder, the hypnotic eyes seeming to blaze out of the poster. A police car went by, followed by one of the green police wagons; she started as the klaxons began to blare. She leaned forward and put her head against Carmody's chest and he put his arms round her.

'Come on,' he said gently, 'I'll take you to the Adlon for breakfast, then you can put me on the train.'

They began to walk up towards the Unter den Linden, turned into it and walked beneath the trees towards the hotel, their arms round each other; happy lovers, one might have thought, after a full and happy night. Then abruptly she giggled.

'What's funny?'

'You and your shoulders like Dietrich's. I can just see you dressed like her. I'll buy you a beret to go with the slacks and jacket.'

'Do me a favour – don't ever mention tonight in front of the other fellers. Joe Begley would split his trenchcoat.'

But he was laughing with her as they went into the lobby of the Adlon. Then he stopped laughing as he saw who had entered just ahead of them. He looked around for a place to hide, wanted to duck behind one of the square clouded-yellow marble pillars. But Meg Arrowsmith had already turned round and seen him.

'Darling!' She was in evening dress, a black silk shawl slung over one shoulder; she looked the worse for wear, as if she might have been in the same dress, unchanged, for two or three evenings; she was setting no example this early morning for the badly dressed Berlin women. The man with her, however, looked as if he had just been freshly laundered and pressed, an elegant bear. 'And the darling Miss O'Dea, too!'

Carmody waited for Cathleen to bare her teeth and her wit; but she looked at him and he knew she was leaving the approach to him. 'Hello, Meg. You're up late. Or early. Whichever it is.'

'Late, darling. We haven't been to bed yet. We've been to the most marvellous party – oh, you don't know Nicky Klatt, do you?'

Klatt was bald, beefily handsome, with bright blue eyes that one knew would always be wide awake to an opportunity to make either a woman or a profit. Carmody knew of him, if he didn't know him: he was one of the industrialists who had backed the Nazis and the bet had paid off in millions. Part of his fortune had been made by buying up plants, at bargain prices, from Jews who had been ordered to dispose of their properties. He looked fit and muscular enough to wrestle a bull, thought Carmody, and probably could. Yet he might find a match for him in Meg, when he finally got her to bed.

'We're about to have breakfast in the bar –' He had a booming hoarse voice that bounced off the marble pillars. 'Do have it with us!'

Cathleen smiled, but remained mute, leaving the decision to Carmody. He wanted to escape, to take her somewhere quiet for their last couple of hours together before he caught the train for Danzig; but his tongue was stumbling, he was tired and he could not think of an excuse on the spur of the moment. Too, his newspaperman's instinct was too strong: so far, in the months he had been in Berlin, he had never had an opportunity to sit down and study one of the rich men backing Hitler. Wars could not be fought without money and he might learn something by listening to one of the sources.

'Thank you,' he said, and felt Cathleen squeeze his arm. But wasn't sure whether she was pleased or disappointed in him.

They went into the bar, sat at a table and ordered bacon and eggs. 'And I'd like a steak with mine,' said Carmody.

'A man with an appetite!' Klatt boomed; he sounded like a battery of guns on a wet morning. 'At this hour, too!'

'He's travelling,' said Cathleen, speaking for the first time. Meg had been looking sideways at her, obviously wondering why she was so quiet. Women suspect silence in another woman; they are just annoyed by it in a man. 'He's catching the eight o'clock train for Danzig.'

'Darling!' Meg put her hand on Carmody's, caught Cathleen's eyes, smiled and took her hand away. Carmody, despite himself, felt flattered: women and transvestites were at odds over him. 'Why go to that dreary place? Nothing's going to happen there.'

'I can vouch for that,' said Klatt, lowering his voice to the boom of a mortar bomb. Why do I keep thinking of him in arms terms? Carmody wondered. Klatt was not an armaments manufacturer, he built roads and government buildings. 'The Poles won't fight, not now with the Russians sitting right behind them.'

'What will happen?'

'It will be settled by plebiscite. There are 400,000 Germans in Danzig – they have a right to belong to the Reich. But don't let's talk about politics at this hour – that's for students. I have seen your American films, Fräulein O'Dea. Very entertaining.'

Cathleen, being an actress, accepted a review from any source; still, she showed her surprise. 'I was never a star, Herr Klatt. How would you have noticed me?'

'Dr Goebbels pointed you out to me – I have been to his private screenings. We have adjoining houses out at Schwanenwerder. You must come out there!'

Cathleen looked at Carmody, who said nothing. It was Meg who spoke up: 'Can't you see, Nicky, Fräulein O'Dea goes nowhere without Herr Carmody? You must invite both of them. And me, too.'

'Why not?' He smiled, showing a mouthful of the most expensive teeth, and putting a muscular paw over Meg's bird-like hand. 'You won't mind meeting my wife?'

'Of course not, darling. I've been meeting men's wives ever since I left Cheltenham Ladies' College.'

Klatt let out a laugh that made Carmody want to duck. 'Sunday then? Will you be back from Danzig by Sunday, Herr Carmody?'

'War permitting, yes,' said Carmody.

For just a moment the bright blue eyes hardened; then they were merry again. He had too much energy to be morose; he had more than enough to be angry, but he was not going to expend any of it on an argument with a foreign newspaper-man over bacon and eggs (and steak) at five o'clock in the morning. Dealing with Nazi officials had given him a sense of perspective and priorities. There was no profit in political argument.

'Do you play tennis?'

'He is a champion,' said Meg, holding the Empire together. 'Aren't all Australians?'

'Good! We'll play half a dozen sets!'

I'll bet the bastard would, thought Carmody. Klatt had that characteristic that so many self-made men had, of having to prove themselves in everything they attempted. Carmody's experience of them was limited, but they all seemed to be the same. It pained him, a democratic republican, to find himself preferring the relaxed air of the aristocrats with inherited wealth. They might be arrogant bastards, but they did not challenge you to six sets of tennis at five o'clock in the morning.

'I'll get in some practice in Danzig,' he said.

Again there was the momentary hardening of the brilliant

blue eyes, then the instant smile. 'Good, good! You can tell me how the Poles play.'

The two women had been uncharacteristically quiet, watching the two men duel with each other. They did not take sides, since the men were not duelling over them. Breakfast arrived and the two men attacked their plates; the women toyed with theirs. Cathleen was pleased to see that Carmody had not lost his appetite; she had feared that the night had been such a disastrous one that he might have gone off his food. She did not want him going off to Danzig feeling totally empty. It was enough to be depressed without also being hungry. He looked up at her from his plate and smiled and she felt a warmth run through her that was like a sedative on her nerves. I'm in love, she thought, and could hardly believe it.

She was relieved when, as soon as Klatt had finished his bacon and eggs and drunk his coffee, Meg Arrowsmith rose from her chair. 'I'm for bed. It's been a long night. Be careful in Danzig, darling.'

'All the time,' said Carmody. He shook her hand and Klatt's, felt the intimacy of hers and the challenge of his. 'See you Sunday.'

'Do you play tennis, Fräulein O'Dea?' said Klatt. 'I forgot to ask.'

'I'm just a little ol' novice,' Cathleen gave him one of her sweetest smiles. 'I just pat the balls back and forth.'

'Ball, darling,' said Meg. 'Not balls.'

'You'd know,' said Cathleen. 'Sleep tight.'

Meg gave her an acknowledging smile and Klatt boomed a laugh that woke up the dozing bartender. They went out arm-in-arm and Cathleen said, 'What does she see in him? He's an oaf.'

'He's probably a champion in bed.'

'So are you. Has she made a play for you?'

He grinned modestly. 'Once. I declined.'

'Why?'

'I feel sorry for her, but I don't feel sexy about her '

'Why do you feel sorry for her?'

'She's in no-man's-land –'

'A bed is no-man's-land?'

'I don't mean that. I mean politically – well, no, nationally. She's a Nazi, but she'll never be a German – she's too English for that. But she can never go back to England, be English again. They'd never accept her.'

Cathleen pondered, then shrugged. Women, having had more practice than men at making beds, have less sympathy for other women who make their beds badly and then have to lie in them. 'I say serves her right.'

'I thought you might.' He ate his second piece of toast with English marmalade, drank his second cup of coffee and sat back. He was a little more prepared now for Danzig. 'I wish you could come with me.'

'So do I.' She squeezed his hand, loving him and still amazed at her feeling. 'Like she said, do be careful, darling. Don't go picking fights with any SS officers, in drag or out of it.'

'I'll ring you to let you know I'm okay.' Then, his thought processes going off at an angle as obliquely as hers, he suddenly stood up. 'Excuse me a minute. I have to ring someone.'

He went to the bar phone, looked up the number of La Trattoria and dialled it. Tinkler's voice, deeper than usual with sleep, answered. 'Who is it, for God's sake?'

'Sorry to call you so early, Herr Tinkler. It's Sean Carmody. I'm going to Danzig this morning. Have you any message for your wife's family?'

'Yes, yes!' Tinkler was instantly wide awake. He turned his head away from the phone; Carmody could hear hurried murmurs in the background. Then Tinkler was back on the phone. 'Would you take a parcel for us, Herr Carmody? A small gift for Anna's mother. We'll bring it to the station.'

'Sure. The train goes at eight.'

He went back to Cathleen and she said, 'What was that about?'

'I'm doing someone a favour.'

'You always are,' she said gently.

She went with him to the station and while they waited for the train they walked up and down in the huge, smoke-grimed cavern. Engines blew steam like witches' mist, whistles shrilled like dying souls and pigeons fluttered under the glass-domed roof like vampire bats; the sun came up through a haze of smoke and they walked through a beam of hellish red light. There came the sound of clumping boots and onto a neighbouring platform marched a contingent of pack-laden troops. A voice roared *Halt!* and boots thudded to a stop; the sound had the impact of a blow against the eardrum. Cathleen looked across the tracks at the soldiers, young men bound for God knew what, and suddenly her nerves began jangling again. She clutched Carmody's arm so tightly that he looked at her in concern.

'It's all right. They're not interested in us.'

'They're going east.' Her voice was low, almost fierce; all at once she wanted him not to go. 'There must be war!'

He tried to calm her, but he had the same fear. 'Troops have been going east for the past month.' But the station seemed to be filling up with troops; everywhere he looked there were uniforms. A cloud of steam evaporated and disclosed a squad of SS men; they broke off and melted away like black devils. NCOs whistles were shriller, fainter echoes of the engines' whistles; the pigeons beat silently against the glass roof, trying to escape the noise; out beyond the platforms the tracks suddenly were bright in the sun, like silver entrails. 'Relax,' he said, but could feel the tension in himself.

Then Tinkler and his wife arrived, hurrying on to the platform with awkward runs, he leaning forward as if he were running ahead of his long thin legs, she leaning back as if afraid her weight would pitch her forward on to her face. They were carrying a large basket with a cloth hiding whatever it contained.

'Food, wine,' Tinkler gasped. 'We don't know if they have rationing in Danzig – Anna's mother loves her food –'

Anna laughed nervously, the first time Carmody had ever seen her laugh at all. 'You have only to look at me . . . Thank you, Herr Carmody. Tell her to write – to give you a letter for me –'

Then the train conductor blew his whistle, yet another in the chorus of whistles, and a moment later the train began to move. Carmody had only time to hug Cathleen to him, to kiss

180

her, then he jumped aboard. He leaned out of the doorway, waving to her and to the Tinklers, tempted to jump off and go back to her and them. He looked across at the opposite platform, saw the soldiers there coming to attention again, beginning to move towards the train that had just drawn in on the other side of the platform. An engine's whistle shrieked, seeming to go on and on as the Danzig train pulled out of the station into the bright glare of the summer's day. When he looked back into the shadow of the station he could see nothing.

## 3

*Extracts from the memoirs of General Kurt von Albern:*

. . . When Colonel Hans von Gaffrin told me that Hitler had set the date for the invasion of Poland as Saturday, 26 August, I felt as much relief as excitement. Relief that at last we should have to move and quickly, that the doubters amongst us could no longer advocate caution. History shows that there are always those in a conspiracy who hope that events will over-run plans, that God or destiny or pure accident will accomplish the deed they have planned for and they will have their lives and their consciences left intact. Conspiracy is abhorrent to me, it is utterly foreign to any code that was bred into me. If, however, there was no other way to save Germany from destruction, then there had to be a conspiracy. Only a madman tries to save the world on his own.

We called a meeting. Our telephone calls were guarded, couched in mundane terms – 'Your uniform, sir, will be ready for a fitting tomorrow morning at 10.' Of course we did not meet at 10 in the morning; we were all too well-known to converge on the one spot in daylight. The meeting was for 10 p.m. and the place was the home of General Werner von Heller.

His home, incongruously, was just off the Gendarmenmarkt, the centre of the financial district. It had been in his family for over a hundred years and stubbornly his family had refused to move as the money-men moved in about them. The house, solid-looking as a bank, was surrounded by banks; it did not look out of place in itself, but only because of who resided there. Heller was out of place for another reason: his family no longer had any money.

He was tall, thin, always red-eyed as if he had just been poking a smoky fire, and a charming host. He was a widower and lived alone with two servants, an ex-corporal from the Uhlans and his wife. I was the first to arrive, probably because I was the most enthusiastic of us all, and saw the calm, hospitable way in which he received the rest of us as we came in, at five-minute intervals, through the front door. There were five others: Mueller, Nagel, Gussing, Rein and Gaffrin. All seven of us were entitled to *von*: we were, if you wish, a conspiracy of aristocrats. We came from the Foreign Ministry, the Army, the Navy and from industry. Only the Luftwaffe, that den of Nazis under Goering, was unrepresented.

Heller, the most senior, called the meeting to order . . . I shall not describe it in detail: we were planning a military operation and for outsiders military operations are often boring. Suffice to say, we had thought of everything; or thought we had. How many battles have been lost for lack of a proper map co-ordinate?

'Unfortunately,' said Hans von Gaffrin, 'I have not yet been able to learn if and when Hitler is returning to Berlin.'

'We cannot reach him if he remains at the Berghof.' Mueller was an ex-ambassador to Washington and now held a senior post in the Foreign Ministry. He was a tiny man with a sharp face and sleek brown hair; he always reminded me of a sparrow with pince-nez spectacles. 'Unless one of us volunteers to go there and sacrifice himself.'

'Out of the question.' Walter von Gussing was

second-in-command of the Northern Fleet, a merry man in most circumstances but not this evening. He looked the sort of man who should have been playing Saint Nicholas to his grandchildren at Christmas time; he was, he had told us, in our conspiracy for the sake of his grandchildren. 'Sending only one man to commit the deed would only lessen the chances of success.'

'Better to send a fleet,' said General Rein, but smiled to show he agreed with Gussing. He was my best friend amongst those present and all these years later I can still remember his handsomeness, enhanced by the duelling scar down his left cheek, and his graceful movements. His particular *bête noire* was Himmler and I knew that he had been practising pistol shooting in the hope that, somehow, somewhere, he could challenge the SS leader to a duel. 'No, we just have to pray that he comes back to Berlin before Saturday.'

'He has begun to isolate himself down there at the Berghof.' Theodore von Nagel was the industrialist. He owned steelworks in the Ruhr and one would have thought would have more to gain from war; but he was a peaceful man and wanted his steel used to build peace. He was a pillar of steel himself, grey in hair and face, despite the summer we had had, always dressed in grey, hard-edged and uncompromising in his attitude.

'He is terrified of assassination,' said Gaffrin. 'As soon as he leaves Obersalzberg, we have to act. He may fly direct from there to somewhere close to the Eastern Front – if there is an Eastern Front. We must get to him before he boards his plane.'

Heller had been quiet up till now. He had been Deputy Chief of Staff up till the previous year; he had resigned at the same time as myself. He was a man of few words, but those were always spoken in a soft, almost kindly way. There was no man I respected more and had he been agreeable, which I knew he would not be, I should have nominated him as President of the new Republic we had planned.

'We seem to be forgetting the gist of our plan,' he said quietly. 'I thought we had decided at our last meeting that there should be no assassination? That we were to take Hitler and Goering into custody for their own protection after we had announced that Himmler and the SS were planning a rising against Hitler. Have we doubts now about our support in the Wehrmacht and the Navy?'

'No, Herr General,' said Gaffrin. 'But he has caught us on the wrong foot with the date he has set for going into Poland. If you remember, we had not expected it to be for at least two weeks – he is still hoping that the English and the French will back down. Admiral Canaris told me that General Halder and all the other officers at Tuesday's conference at the Berghof were shocked at the earlier date.'

'Did they protest?'

'No, sir.'

Heller sighed at the spinelessness of those who now surrounded Hitler. He and I had resigned because we would not stand for our military arguments being shouted down by an Austrian ex-corporal, who saw himself as a combination of Clausewitz, Schlieffen and Bernhardi. He turned his red-rimmed eyes on me and it seemed that they looked more tired and sadder than usual.

'Have you finished your mapping of the Gestapo posts, Kurt?'

I nodded. 'Copies of the map are now being run off for distribution. The posts can be taken over and those in charge arrested as soon as the command is given.'

Heller looked at Gussing. 'What about the Navy, Walter?'

'I have officers who are ready to take over the radio installations. Orders will be broadcast for ships to remain at stations.'

'What about Admiral Raeder?' Grand Admiral Erich Raeder was Commander-in-Chief of the Navy and had always been willing to be led by the ex-corporal.

'He will be taken into custody,' said Gussing and

gave his huge Saint Nicholas smile. 'For his own good.'

'So all that remains is for Hitler to come up from Obersalzberg and into our trap.' Heller looked round us all. 'I am a religious man. I shall go to Mass in the morning and pray that God delivers him to us.'

'God, they say, is an Englishman,' said Alfred Rein. 'Would it not be ironic if God did deliver him to us?'

. . . I was never a religious man. Perhaps I should have been. Our prayers, had there been more of them and more fervent, might then have been answered. The world, till now, has not known how close we came to saving it from war . . .

4

'Do you want me to go home?'

'Home? You are home.'

'I mean to England. When the film is finished.'

Helmut had come to Melissa's flat in Neubabelsberg, the first time he had done so. It was a gesture of conscience on his part, a way of showing he did not expect her always to be running after him. He was still off-balance at her pregnancy; he had woken that day with his own morning sickness. His thoughts did not go as far as to whether he cared for children or not; it had only just occurred to him that he knew none, except some of the brats who appeared occasionally in films, and no one could care for them. Melissa's baby, so far, was an abstract, another shadow in a life that had, it seemed, become invaded with shadows in the past few months. What disturbed him about the pregnancy was that it made him responsible for *her*.

They had talked last night in his flat, but they might have been strangers discussing someone else's adopting a baby. She had realized it before he did and she had gone home, refusing to let him drive her but slamming out into the night and, her only stroke of good fortune for the past few days, finding a taxi whose driver, for a ransom price, drove her home to Neubabelsberg. Helmut had gone out looking for her and, not finding her, had come back to a sleepless bed. It was then that his conscience, the only thing of his that had never before been stirred by a woman, had begun to itch.

'It would be best,' he said. 'Going home to England, I mean.'

'Why?' It was not an innocent, naïve question; she had matured, was more composed than he now. She had, for the moment at least, accepted her pregnancy; she had decided, most strongly, against abortion and there were another seven months to go before birth. She had decided to be fatalistic, which is to say she had given up depending on him.

He looked at her, as much surprised by her composure as by her question. 'There is going to be *war*. You can't stay on in Germany, not to have a child.'

'If there's a war, there'll be war in England, too.' She lost her composure for a moment at that thought, though she did not show it. She could not imagine war in the Yorkshire Dales, could not see Bradford or London bombed: war happened in other countries.

'I doubt it.' But his father had told him of Luftwaffe officers who were rumoured to be boasting of what they would do to London when they were let loose with their bombers. 'Anyhow, if you remained here you would be an enemy alien, you would be interned.'

'Not if I were married to a German.' She had never been so composed; or acted better. He wasn't sure which.

'Which German did you have in mind?' He had once been witty, but he felt no wit this evening. Then he saw, just for an instant, the quiver of her lips and once again conscience bit him, like a pet squirrel he had neglected too long. 'I'm sorry. *This* German.'

'Are you proposing?' Her lips were firm once again, she had recovered.

'I don't know. Am I? Do I love you, Melissa?'

'That's for you to decide. I don't honestly think you do, or you wouldn't be asking me. But I wish you did, Helmut. Oh crumbs, I wish you did!' Her lips did quiver then, her composure broke and she wept. He tried to put his arm about her, but she brusquely brushed it away, got up from the couch on which they were sitting and flung herself into a chair opposite.

He sat helpless, looking at her, trying to fall in love, just to please her. But weeping women upset him; he looked away from her, around the room. His cameraman's eye took in every detail: the flat, though rented, had her mark on it. It was as neat and orderly as his father's house, which had five servants to run it. The prints on the walls were of German castles and cathedrals; a print of St Paul's in London was an alien note. There was a studio photo of herself, back-lighted and with every small imperfection air-brushed out; and a photo of her parents, a middle-aged pleasant-looking couple who seemed to be miles apart even while in the 12 × 8 frame. We'd be the same if we married, he thought, and looked back at Melissa.

She had dried her eyes, was blowing her nose. Men, he thought, can blow their noses and still look presentable; women should never blow their noses, it is one trick they have never mastered. He was looking at her through a deep-focus lens, something no lover, or would-be lover, should ever do. It is a trick for cads looking for an excuse for their own decisions.

'Melissa –' He leaned forward across the space between them, managed to take her hand. 'I'm not thinking straight. I have another problem – one with my father –' *That* was caddish, bringing his father into it. But it was true: his father *was* a problem. The hours spent in the Opel last night, driving around listening to his father and Romy, had convinced him that the two of them, without realizing it, were embarked on a suicide pact. He had to prevent it, and soon. It was something that was going to happen this week, not in seven months' time.

'Can I help?'

*Yes, take them back to England with you.* But he knew they would not go. 'Melissa – be patient with me. I'll stand by you –' Was he reciting dialogue he had heard from some film

187

or were the words always as banal as this in situations like this? Perhaps the B-film scriptwriters had a truer ear than one gave them credit for. 'I don't know why, I just never even thought it could happen to us –'

'What? That we might fall in love or that I'd get pregnant?'

Both; but he didn't say that. He stepped off a cliff: 'Do you want to get married?'

'Oh Helmut –' But she didn't burst into tears; she sounded so much older and wiser than he in affairs of the heart. She even sounded *motherly*. 'If you have to ask it like that, you don't want to marry me. I'm disappointed – some day I may even hate you –'

He shook his head. 'No, don't ever do that. Give me a little more time to think –' *To fall in love*: but he didn't say that, either. He had the best intentions in the world towards her; he just hadn't expected such commitment to her, not so soon. He suddenly felt callow, like a boy with his first girl. 'I really am caught up in something else with my father – I can't turn my back on him, not now –'

'Is your father a Nazi?'

'No!' He hadn't meant to sound so sharp. He suddenly wished he had taken her to meet his father some time; perhaps his father could have given him some advice. 'No, he's anything but that. It's just – well, like everyone else he's afraid of war.'

'Even though he's a general?'

'They know more about it than we do. At least the winning or losing of it. But he's no longer on the active list – he's retired.'

'I'd like to meet him. I haven't said that before – I've always had the feeling you didn't want me to –'

'You will meet him. When –' But he couldn't say when. Then he thought of someone who might give him advice: 'He has a friend, Baroness Sonntag, I'd like you to meet her, too.'

She had brightened, looked vulnerable again. 'When?'

'I don't know – Friday, Saturday. No, Sunday.'

When the problem of his father would be solved one way or another.

She rose from her chair, came back and sat beside him on

the couch. She put her arms round his neck and kissed him gently on the lips. 'Helmut, don't *worry*. If it doesn't work out between us, I'm still going to have the baby. That part of it doesn't frighten me at all. What I am afraid of is that if war breaks out and I'm back in England, I shan't know what's happened to you.'

He had never wanted to shed tears before because of a woman, but they were close to the surface now. He put his arms round her and wondered if he was in love and hadn't recognized it.

# CHAPTER EIGHT

## 1

'I love you,' said Ludwig, 'but you must go, for your own safety. My subjects are forcing me to abdicate.'

'I'll stay,' said Lola. 'They love you – they know you were right in all you've done. It is the foreigners with all their propaganda –'

'Cut!' called Karl Braun, and Willy Heffer and Cathleen fell out of their embrace with mutual relief. 'That was terrible, darlings. You sounded like a couple of bureaucrats making love after office hours.'

'I think this script was written by a couple of bureaucrats,' said Cathleen. 'Or was it five or six?'

Two of the writers were on the set and they slunk away, knowing they had no defence; writers were always blamed for all the shortcomings on a film, they told each other. Braun called for the lunch break and Cathleen headed for her dressing-room. She knew the morning's poor takes were not entirely the writers' fault, though the script was ludicrous; she had not been concentrating, had done nothing to lift the lines out of their banality. Willy Heffer, for reasons of his own, had given up the battle and was just working out his time, ready, like King Ludwig, to abdicate.

As she went down the corridor to her dressing-room she passed Melissa's room. The door was half-open and she saw Melissa sitting in front of her mirror, staring at herself in the unlit glass. No lights were on and the only illumination came through the window set high in one wall. Cathleen knocked lightly and pushed open the door.

'Something wrong?'

Melissa looked at her in the mirror and then Cathleen saw the tears on the English girl's cheeks. 'Tomorrow is my last day, some re-takes. Then I'm going home.'

'It may be the best place to be. You want to have lunch with me?'

Melissa dried her eyes, stood up, came and kissed Cathleen on the cheek. It was the first time she had ever done it; they had never exchanged the usual actresses' hypocritical pecks. But she did it naturally now and Cathleen knew it said more than she put into words. She took Melissa's hand and squeezed it.

'How does Helmut feel about you going home?'

Melissa just shook her head, her eyes filling with tears again, and Cathleen knew she had said the wrong thing at the wrong moment. Still holding the other girl's hand, she led her along the corridor to her own dressing-room. She slipped out of her costume, gave it to her dresser to take away for pressing, put on a robe and sat down opposite Melissa.

'Do you want a big lunch?'

Without thinking Melissa said, 'Cathleen, I'm pregnant!'

'Then you want a big lunch.' She picked up the phone, ordered two big lunches from the commissary, then sat back. 'I'm not pregnant, I just feel empty today. So . . .' She looked sympathetically at Melissa. 'Does Helmut know? Is it his? Sorry, I shouldn't have said that.'

Melissa had regained her composure. 'He knows. It's – sort of floored him.'

'Did it floor you?'

'No. I'm – I'm sort of glad, in a way.'

'Is he going to marry you?'

'I don't know. He offered to, sort of.'

'Sort of. Everything seems to be sort of. Is he going to marry you or not?'

'I think he will if I insist. He's very honourable.'

'Melissa honey, any marriage that's based on the honour of the groom is going to be a mess of horseshit, if you'll forgive my Hollywood French. He marries you because he loves you or he doesn't marry you. Period. Or maybe period is the wrong word, since that's what you haven't got. Does he love you or not? And I don't mean sort of.'

Melissa was silent for a moment. She had never expected to

191

weigh love on scales, but love, she supposed was a commodity, since it seemed to have its price. Whores had known that for centuries, but she, being a romantic, had thought of it as a give-away. 'I think he does love me. He just won't admit it, even to himself.'

Cathleen sighed. Though a woman, she was continually amazed at the blind faith of women. She was not a cynic, just someone who had learned from her experiences. 'Honey, men will rarely admit anything to themselves about women, except to abuse us. They're afraid of us, most of them. Even the ones who belt the hell out of us. Especially them.'

'He'd never do that, I know.'

'I'm not saying he would. He's a gentleman, I know. He'd be more of a gentleman if he was honest with you –' There was a knock on the door. 'Come in. You were quick –'

But it wasn't the waitress with their lunch; it was Helmut. He pulled up sharply when he saw Melissa. 'I'm sorry – I wanted to see you, Cathleen, about changing your dress –'

'What's the matter with it?'

'I'd like a lighter colour. It's not lighting too well –' He and Melissa were looking at each other, both caught off-balance. Then he sighed, sat down on the only other chair in the room and looked at Cathleen. 'She has told you?'

Cathleen nodded. 'I'm her big sister – for today, anyway. It's a bit of a shock for you, I gather? It always is. For you men, I mean.'

'Have you been caught, too?' said Melissa.

'You mean caught pregnant? No. I never trusted the men I went to bed with. Don't look shocked, Helmut. I was never an easy lay, if that's what you're thinking. But I've fallen in and out of love half a dozen times. I just was never sure if the guys were in love with me. So I took precautions. Are you upset that Melissa didn't?'

'I just took it for granted –'

There was another knock on the door: this time it was the waitress from the commissary. She gave everyone a big smile, wished them *bon appetit* and went. '*Bon appetit*?' said Cathleen.

'She's from Alsace,' said Helmut.

'Another outsider?'

'Not really.'

'Would you be happier if Melissa were not an outsider? If she were German?'

Melissa looked shocked at the question and Helmut stiffened. 'You really are her big sister today, aren't you?'

'Someone has to be. She's a long way from home. Have you eaten? You have? Okay, Melissa, tuck in. You have two to feed now.'

She knew she was being blunt and heavy-handed, but she felt like hitting Helmut over the head. Women alone have patience and are inclined to forgive; together they are as belligerent as any man. Melissa, the silent one in the two-women army, tucked in, feeding two, though so far she was not aware of the baby, only of its future.

'In ordinary circumstances –' Helmut said.

'There are no ordinary circumstances, not when you're pregnant and you aren't married. Don't beat about the bush, Helmut. Eat your dessert, too, Melissa.'

Melissa was only halfway through her schnitzel. 'Cathleen – please. Don't badger him so –' She moved her chair; suddenly Cathleen was facing both of them, big sister or big mother or big teacher. 'He has his problems. With his father –'

'What's the matter with your father?' But Cathleen had decided she was already out-gunned, the victim had gone back to the other side. So much for the US cavalry coming to the rescue. Shirley Temple had joined the Indians.

'It's – business. I only learned about it a few days ago – just before Melissa told me about the baby . . . My mind's all over the place –' He sounded sorry for himself and didn't mean to. 'Once his problem is out of the way . . .'

Cathleen looked at both of them, knew they really didn't want her help. Melissa was a born loser; she would play the role with dignity, a poor man's Greer Garson. Helmut was an aristocrat, even though in pictures; he was honourable and he would play the role of an honourable man. That, of course, she thought, was the trouble: they would both finish up playing roles. She shrugged, attacked her own schnitzel with sharp knife and fork.

'Call me if you want a godmother.'

Then the phone rang. She picked it up, recognized Inge Lang's voice. 'I have some definite news for you, Fräulein. Can we meet?'

'Of course!' Then she tried to rein in her excitement, one eye on Melissa and Helmut. 'When?'

'This evening. Eight o'clock.'

'Same place?'

'Yes. Till then.' She hung up: Frau Lang was a woman apparently afraid of tapped telephone lines.

Helmut, with unaccustomed spite, getting some of his own back, said, 'The Herr Doctor?'

'No, Helmut.' She felt so excited she forgave him his spite; indeed, she understood it. What right had she to butt into his life? Suddenly his and Melissa's problem meant nothing to her. We are all selfish about our troubles. 'Someone has some news from an old friend. I hope.'


2


It seemed to Carmody that Danzig, despite all the political weather of the past weeks, had not changed since he had last been here. The citizens appeared at ease, intent on enjoying the summer; certainly they were going about their work rather desultorily, but it was the real weather not the political, that was causing that. Thunderstorms hung like purple volcanic explosions out in the Baltic and the air in the city was thick enough to be felt. A summer shower passed over and when it had gone the cobbles in the older streets glistened and gave off steam like thermal rocks.

There were German military vehicles everywhere, some rushing through the streets as if war had broken out just round the corner; they carried their own mocking note (or hint of the future? he wondered) with their Danzig licence plates. The nearby hills of Bischofsberg and Hagelberg had been fortified and, coming in by train, he noticed that the roads leading in from Poland were blocked by tank traps and log barriers. Yet within the city there was an atmosphere of complacency, an air of 'what's all the fuss about?'

Except for the drunks. On his only other visit here he had remarked that there were more drunks in Danzig than he had seen in any other city, including Sydney, Chicago and New York. He had been told that was because the farther east one went, the bigger the schnapps glasses and the stronger the schnapps; he had tasted the local schnapps and it seemed to him that it had burned not only his throat but the soles of his shoes from the inside. There seemed, however, to be more drunks this time, some belligerent, some maudlin, some morose, but all of them seeking some escape.

He went into the old part of the town looking for the address the Tinklers had given him. The sky had cleared and the evening light played on the old Gothic houses with their steep gables and their decorated fronts; there was almost a fairy-tale look to them and he shuddered at the thought that soon they might be bombed. Carrying the Tinklers' basket, the food in it still covered by a cloth, he felt like something out of a fairy tale: the fairy godfather, maybe.

He found the address in a narrow street where it seemed that the houses needed each other for support. They were old but their paint and the geraniums in their flower-boxes were fresh; the cracks in their walls were like the cracks in the make-up of old crones. The woman who opened the door to his knock was no crone, however: grey-haired she was, but she shook and shivered with remnants of her laughing youth. She was even bigger than her daughter, a huge woman; one would have found it easier to paint a panorama of her than a portrait. She had none of Anna Tinkler's timidity.

'Herr – Carmody, did you say? Come in, come in! Oh look at what you have brought! Does Anna think I am starving here? Do I look as if I am? No, tell me, tell me the truth, Herr Carmody – do I look as if I'm starving?'

Carmody grinned, shook his head. He looked around for a place to sit down; he had never been in a room so crowded with furniture. He wondered how Frau Pavel, with her massive bulk, managed to negotiate her way through the crush without bruising herself. He watched, fascinated, as she slid between table and chairs, seeming to draw in, like a huge jellyfish, every time she looked like bumping against something. She pushed a chair at him and he dropped on to it, aware of the looming sideboard right behind him that seemed ready to topple, like a black cliff, and crush him. Frau Pavel whipped the cloth off the basket, exposing sausages, jams, cakes, fruit, and gurgled with excitement. Carmody imagined the sound was that of her gastric juices running riot throughout that great body.

She made him coffee, gave him a slice of cake that threatened to break his wrist as he lifted it to his mouth. Cake forks were not for this house; and all at once Carmody felt at home. This was how his mother would have served her cake, though the slice would not have been so big.

'How are Anna and Luis? Are things good for them in Berlin?' He had told her his German was not the best and she had slowed down her delivery after her initial volleys. She had an East Prussian accent, which he found harsh and unappealing; he had to keep reminding himself that she was Polish, not German. 'They want me to join them. But how can I leave here? My family have lived in this house for God knows how long. A hundred and fifty, two hundred years.'

'They are afraid there is going to be war. Haven't you got their letters?'

'No. They haven't received mine? That damned Gestapo!' She bit into a piece of cake, chewed it as if it were Gestapo bones. 'They hound me as if I were some sort of anarchist who was going to blow them up. All I do is speak my mind –' Carmody could imagine her doing that, a great wind of protest howling through these narrow streets. 'Why do Anna and Luis think there will be war?'

'Most people do. I do.'

She shook her head. 'No, nobody here thinks there will be. The Germans here are all sure Hitler will take them back into

Germany. He won't need to go to war to do that. The English and the French won't fight for Danzig.' She curled her lip, then looked shocked at her gaffe. 'I'm sorry, you're English!'

'No, Australian. Irish-Australian.'

'The same thing,' said Frau Pavel, and on the other side of the world Paddy Carmody spun in his sleep. 'They call Danzig a free city. We Poles who live here joke that anyone is free to do what they want with it. And with us. First the Poles had it, then the Prussians, then Napoleon said it could go its own way, then the Prussians had it again – it just goes on and on. Sometimes I wish I'd been born in the South Seas . . . Tell Anna and Luis not to worry. There won't be any war.'

He felt sad at her optimism. 'I hope not, Frau Pavel. Do you want to write a letter that I can take back to your daughter?'

'I have one written! A moment –' She jumped up, the house seemed to shake and Carmody waited for the sideboard to fall on him, and she went clumping up some narrow stairs to the floor above. A minute, then she came gasping downstairs again. 'Those stairs are getting steeper every day! Here –' She handed him a thick letter. 'Tell her not to worry. I shall come and visit them for Christmas.'

She showed him out of the house, clasping his hand like an old friend. He left her, still sad at her faith in peace, and went up the narrow street. At the top he turned and waved. She stood in the doorway of the narrow old house, filling it; she waved a huge arm, a gesture of defiant hope, and he thought he heard her laugh. Then he turned the corner and walked into the two men in the tightly buttoned suits and the recognizable hats.

'Your identity card,' said the smaller of the two men. He was about Carmody's height and build, but had a thin face in which his black eyes seemed to have some difficulty in remaining apart. He had a Prussian accent and a voice that raised Carmody's hackles.

Carmody produced his passport and press card. 'I am here on legitimate press business, for my wire service.'

'What business did you have with Frau Pavel?' The second man was half a head taller than Carmody and seemed to be all

197

muscle; even his broad face bulged with muscle. When he spoke he sounded muscle-bound, or so it seemed to Carmody. He looked at the press card in his partner's hand. 'Did World Press send you to interview her?'

'A woman in a back street, a nobody?' said the first man.

'I brought her some food, a gift from her daughter and son-in-law in Berlin, that was all.'

'The son-in-law, that is Herr Tinkler? He is a Jew?'

Carmody had to restrain a laugh. 'If he were a Jew, would he have a licence for a restaurant in Berlin?'

The two men did not like being asked such a question. The big one snapped, 'Come with us!'

Carmody was about to protest, but knew it would get him nowhere with these two. He could see people looking out of their windows and on the other side of the street passers-by had slowed, but not stopped, and were casting covert glances in his direction. It would be of no use to ask these citizens for help. He had been told that no one intervened in the Gestapo's business.

The Gestapo men hustled him towards a car, pushed him in. He sat in the back with the big man while the other one drove. There was no conversation and that suited Carmody; it gave him time to sort out his thoughts for the interview ahead. He did not feel afraid for himself, foreign correspondents so far had the protection of the Foreign Press Office, but already he could see ripples spreading out to touch the Tinklers and Frau Pavel. And, the thought that chilled him, to touch Cathleen.

The Gestapo office was in a warehouse near the docks. It was obviously a new post, part of the increase in Gestapo activities since the crisis. It was sparsely furnished and the two men and two girls in the office were sitting around, looking as if they had nothing to do. Brand new typewriters sat on brand new desks; the notices on the walls were not yet flyblown or curled at the edges; the electric globes, still free of grime, shone too brightly. Carmody, still feeling safe, wondered wryly if the rack had yet been taken out of its packing.

He was led into an inner room that, though newly painted, had a stale smell to it. He decided it was due to cigarette smoke and the fact that, even on this warm evening, the window was closed. He was told to sit down. Paper and carbon were produced and his particulars taken down in triplicate. Carmody looked at the men and saw them as bureaucrats with muscle, a formidable combination.

'You are in trouble, Herr Carmody.' The smaller man had lit up a cigarette, was blowing smoke as if signalling someone.

Carmody shook his head, deciding on a little philosophy. 'My father used to tell me as a boy, you're not in trouble till you can't see your way out of it. *Then* you are in trouble.'

Both men digested this and seemed impressed; they were not unintelligent. 'You can see your way out of this?'

'All I have to do is tell the truth. All I am is a messenger boy. Frau Tinkler was worried that her mother was not answering her letters. She thought she might have been ill. Frau Pavel told me she has been writing to her daughter, but for some reason those letters have not been delivered in Berlin.'

Neither man commented on this, but the big man got up from his chair and moved close to Carmody, sitting on the edge of the room's one table. He, too, had lit a cigarette and was blowing smoke. 'You are not telling the truth, Herr Carmody. You came here for another reason.'

Carmody suddenly knew the evening might be dangerous, that he might be hurt before he got out of here. He looked around the room; it did not look like a torture cell. There was the obligatory photograph of the Fuehrer; a brand new poster for an event already past, Reich Party Day for Peace; and a calendar with certain dates, already gone, circled in red. Red letter days when victims had cracked? he wondered.

He looked back at the big man and said mildly, as if puzzled, 'What reason was that?'

'You are a messenger for people who are conspiring against the Reich.'

'You are barking up the wrong tree.' Both men looked blank and he explained patiently, 'You have the wrong idea. As far as I know, the Tinklers are just ordinary innocent citizens. The Gestapo in Berlin has never gone near them.' He was not sure of his facts, but he was taking a newspaperman's licence: facts were only for when you were dealing with an honest audience.

'We have read their letters,' said the smaller man. Both men had taken off their hats, revealing bald heads; they looked like Little Brother and Big Brother. Smoke wreathed around their heads; they were smoke manufacturers. 'And Frau Pavel's.'

*I thought you might have.*

'We are not concerned with what our colleagues in Berlin think about the Tinklers, that is their business. We are concerned with what Frau Pavel is advocating here in Danzig.'

'What's that?'

'Rebellion. A rising against the Fuehrer.'

Carmody shook his mind, if not his head. He could see Frau Pavel's rebellion, a gust of honest exasperation at rules and regulations. 'You're blowing it up out of proportion –'

'Blowing up?'

Carmody couldn't help it: he laughed. Before he could duck the big man had hit him across the side of the head and sent him sprawling off his chair. He scrambled up before the Gestapo man could put the boot into him, but the latter had sat back on the table, was grinning at him, puffing on his cigarette again. 'Sorry, Herr Carmody. You were only joking.' But his tone implied that *he* had not been: the blow had been a warning.

Carmody picked himself up, sat back on his chair. His head was ringing from the blow and when he put his hand up to his ear it came away stained with blood. He got out his handkerchief and held it to his ear. 'The Foreign Press Office is not going to like this when I tell them about it.'

'The Foreign Press Office is part of Dr Goebbels' department – he does not run the State Police.' There was no mistaking the contempt in his voice for Goebbels; Heinrich Himmler had set an example for his minions to follow. 'In Danzig you are answerable to us, Herr Carmody.'

What he was saying was that, as an East Prussian, he did not care what Berlin had to say. It was the old regional quarrel; it happened all over the world. Carmody had read that the East Prussians did not refer to themselves as such; they sub-divided themselves even further into Masurians, Oberlanders, Königsbergers and Samlanders. Out of here had come the Teutonic Knights, the knights of the church militant, the Bible in one hand and the sword in the other. History had run down to this: the knights of the black Maltese cross had been reduced to these Gestapo thugs and their swastika. Berlin had meant nothing to the knights, it meant nothing to these men. Danzig was not part of East Prussia, but it soon would be.

'Does Berlin have a file on you, Herr Carmody?' said the big man.

'I wouldn't know.' Carmody's head was clearing, enough for him to be careful what he said from now on. He wanted to ask why they cared if Berlin had or had not a file on him, since obviously they had no time for Berlin itself. But the next clout on the ear might be more damaging.

'Is World Press owned by Jews?'

'No.'

'America is owned by the Jews, isn't it?'

'Not as far as I know. General Motors and the Ford Motor Company aren't.'

The questioning went on while the two men chain-smoked, and, with his head clear again, Carmody kept his wits about him. A file would be started on him here in Danzig; he just hoped that regional differences would keep it from being relayed to Berlin. It was enough that Lutze and Decker had their eye on him; he did not want constant surveillance by a team of secret police. That would mean, sooner than later, that there would be constant surveillance of Cathleen.

At last, with a reluctant look at the passport and press card, as if disappointed they held no incriminating evidence, the smaller man held them out. 'You may go, Herr Carmody.'

'May I come back to Danzig?'

'When it belongs to the Reich? Of course.'

'When will that be?' He saw the big man's hand turn into a fist and he hastily smiled. 'Never mind, I'll read about it in the newspapers.'

When he stepped out into the street the air was something

201

he could taste; or so it seemed after the fog in which he had sat for the past hour. His eyes were sore and his nostrils dry; he just stood and opened them and his mouth to the evening air, warm and thick though it was. He walked down to the docks, stood there and drew in deep breaths of the sea air. It seemed to him that he was breathing something else: freedom. A fishing boat went out of the harbour, carving its way through the absolutely still water as through thin blue ooze; a fisherman stood in the prow looking out to sea and Carmody wondered what his thoughts were. Was he only looking for tonight's catch or for something more?

The flat light threw the buildings and the boats into relief; there appeared to be no one moving anywhere around the quays. There was absolute quiet, at least for that long moment as he turned and looked about him. Then he heard the police klaxon, then another, and he knew that, no matter what Frau Pavel and the other citizens of Danzig might think, peace for the city was an illusion.

He began to walk back towards his hotel, glad that he would be leaving here tomorrow to go back to Berlin.


3


Cathleen, wearing her dark wig and her pale horn-rimmed glasses, left her apartment and walked up to the Kurfürstendamm. There was a man standing in a doorway on the other side of the street when she came out of her front door; it looked like Decker, but she couldn't be sure. She steeled herself not to take any notice of him but to walk away unconcerned; her act succeeded, because he did not follow her. On the Kurfürstendamm she hailed a taxi and asked to be taken to Mariendorf. She got out of the taxi two blocks from the Green Man beer-garden, made sure once again that she had not been followed, and then went on to meet the Langs. Though she was nervous and excited, there were times, even after nearly five months here in Germany on her

202

mission, when everything felt unreal, artificial, as if she were no more than playing another role in another film. She kept wanting to look back to see if the camera was being tracked after her, kept waiting to hear the director call 'Cut!' Then the thought of her mother would drop into her mind like cold water and she would come back to reality, to the knowledge that nothing in this scenario had been scripted and nobody knew the end.

The Langs were not waiting for her; she guessed they were too shrewd, too experienced for that. They would wait till she was seated at a table, had made sure she had not been followed, and then they would make their appearance. Which was what happened.

At first she thought they had missed her, were going to pass right by her. Then Frau Lang grabbed her husband's arm as if she had just recognized Cathleen, they feigned surprise and after a moment's argument between themselves decided, 'Why not sit here? It's our friend, Fräulein – We've forgotten your name! Do forgive us.'

They sat down, and while Lang ordered drinks Frau Lang leaned forward and said in a low voice, 'Forgive all the play-acting. You must think we are very amateurish, but it is necessary. There are informers everywhere. Where is Herr Carmody?'

'In Danzig. You have some news for me?' She was trembling with anticipation.

'A moment –' Frau Lang paused till the waiter had gone away, then she nudged her husband. 'Tell her, Heinz.'

Lang came straight to the point, but gently; he was a man accustomed to delivering bad news. 'Your grandmother, I'm sorry to say, is dead. She died last March, in Ravensbrueck concentration camp. That's where your mother is now.'

Cathleen had known her grandmother only from photographs; there was no sense of loss, just sadness that the old woman had died in such a place. 'Is my mother all right? Was she with my grandmother when she died?'

'We don't know about that – we can only learn just so much. But yes, your mother is all right. Or as well as can be expected, considering where she is.'

'Where is Ravensbrueck?'

They could talk safely, so long as they kept their voices low. The beer-garden's band was playing, something from a Lilian Harvey musical; two violinists strolled amongst the drinkers, fiddling saccharinely in their ears. Lang said, one eye on the violinists who were coming closer, 'It is north of Berlin – there is a big men's camp called Sachsenhausen just south of it. But don't get any ideas of going up there, please. You would only finish up in there yourself.'

'What do I do then? Now I know she's there – and alive –'

The violinists arrived at their table, had just begun to play *The Shadow Waltz*. They were smiling at Cathleen, telling her the music was for her; she felt chilled, looked around for Lutze or Decker, someone who had told the musicians she was American. She remembered Dick Powell singing the song in – was it *Gold Diggers of 1933*? It could have been *All Quiet on the Western Front* or even the Marx Brothers' *Horsefeathers*; her mind just stopped functioning while the music rubbed against her like a torture. At last it was finished, she fumbled in her handbag, gave the musicians a generous tip and waited till they had passed on to another table and another song.

'How did they know I was American?'

'They didn't,' said Lang. 'They often play the more sentimental American songs. Germans are very sentimental in their beer-gardens. It brings out the best and the worst in them.'

While the violinists had been serenading them they had been the centre of interest for those around them; now, with the violinists having moved on, those at the other tables had turned their interest elsewhere. Lang said casually, as if he were picking up a trivial topic that had been interrupted by the music, 'We have tried before to get people out of the camps. I have to tell you our success rate has not been high.'

'But we were told you have got people out –' She was leaning forward, too tense. He's a better actor than I am in this sort of situation, she thought. But then he had had much more practice.

He shook his head, smiling, still relaxed. 'Sit back, Fräulein. We are supposed to be casual acquaintances – we should not appear as if we are arguing. There, that's better. Yes, we have got people out – out of Germany. We have rescued them before they were sent to the camps. It is much more difficult, much much more, once they are inside the camps.'

Cathleen had sat back, but her body felt as if it were an iron framework. Then the iron began to melt as hopelessness, like an acid, weakened her. 'I can't even visit her?'

'Even if you could, what good would that do?' Frau Lang had been quiet, but now she offered a woman's comfort. Lang had not been unsympathetic, but he did give the impression that Mady Hoolahan's case was only one amongst many; or perhaps he, too, had become dispirited, a commander of lost causes. Inge Lang had a natural sympathy about her, a Traveller's Aid for people on hopeless roads. 'You could try at your embassy – they might be able to do something –'

'Is your mother an American citizen?' said Lang.

'No.' Cathleen felt a sudden unreasonable anger at her mother's failure to protect herself. 'She was stubborn – she was Jewish, but she insisted she was German. Do you understand that?'

'Of course,' said Inge Lang. 'My husband and I would not want to be anything else but German, if it were not for –' She trailed off, put her hand on her husband's. 'He had trouble explaining that to some of our friends, those we got away.'

'I think your mother might have been more sensible to have become an American citizen before coming back here to search for her mother,' said Lang. 'There are times when it pays to be expedient.'

'I don't think Mother would even have thought of it. She could be expedient when she liked –' Like advising her daughter to be Irish to get ahead in movies. 'She was never political-minded, but she used to think the Nazis were only a temporary thing – an aberration?'

'What sort of Germany did she want?'

'I don't know. I don't think she knew. Knows.' She had to keep thinking of her mother in the present; Mady Hoolahan was not yet dead. 'She thought of Germany as its people and the countryside and what Berlin used to be like when she was a young girl. I don't think she could ever have named one of your politicians. I guess she sounds dumb to you.'

'Not at all,' said Inge Lang, but she didn't sound convincing.

'Go to your embassy, if you think it will do any good. But don't make too much of a fuss,' said Lang. 'Just in case there is someone in the embassy spying for the Gestapo. Give us a few more days –'

'A few more days? How many? Herr Carmody thinks war may break out any day –'

'We –' Lang looked with sad affection at his wife. 'We have learned to live from day to day. Try to do the same.'

'I wish I had your strength,' said Cathleen admiringly.

Inge Lang smiled. 'You may be surprised at yourself. One never knows till the test comes.'

# 4

When Carmody got back to Berlin the anti-aircraft guns were already mounted on the roofs of some of the taller buildings. There was one on top of the uncompleted IG Farben building opposite the Adlon and Carmody wondered why the Unter den Linden should be considered a target for bombers. The traffic now seemed to be clogged with military vehicles and it seemed that uniforms had multiplied in the streets, like costumes brought out for some mad *Fasching*. The symptoms of war were not to be denied: in fact they were being advertised. War in Spain had already started when he had joined it, but he guessed it must have begun with these overtures.

He went first to his office, where Fräulein Luxemburg greeted him with relief, as if he had just come back from the Somme; or from Amiens. One army's victory is another army's defeat: Olga Luxemburg remembered the casualties of the Great War. It was Friday, so he brought her flowers.

'Did you have a safe trip?' She was arranging the carnations in the vase that had been waiting for them; it suddenly struck him that her life was like the empty vase, waiting to be filled. 'I kept hoping you wouldn't be trapped there –'

'What's been happening?'

'The British Ambassador has been down to see the Fuehrer at Obersalzberg. Things look very bad, Herr Carmody.'

He was looking through the German newspapers. WARSAW THREATENS BOMBARDMENT OF DANZIG . . . POLISH ARCHMADNESS . . . GERMAN FAMILIES FLEE . . . Who believed all this? he wondered. Then remembered Spanish civil war stories in some of the British conservative newspapers, which he had read long after the event and which had made him wonder if he and the conservative editors were thinking of the same war. Still the bias in those stories had not been as blatant as the lies in these German despatches.

'All the English and French correspondents left for the frontier last night, all except Herr Burberry. He telephoned this morning and said he was leaving today. He said he would be at the Adlon till three o'clock, if you came back.'

Carmody looked at his watch. 'Phone London and tell them I'll ring them at six o'clock with my piece. I'll be back here at four.'

On the way over to the Adlon he wondered if he should phone Cathleen out at Neubabelsberg, but decided against it. If the American correspondents hadn't left, then she, as an American, was safe for the moment. He might get his own marching orders, but that would depend whether the Foreign Press Office looked at his passport or his press card.

Burberry, umbrella hanging on his chair-back, was at a table in the Adlon bar. He looked morose, older, like an early mourner at a funeral alone with the deceased. 'Dear boy, I'm afraid the worst is about to happen.'

'Who's going to cover for *The Times*?'

At the worst of times priorities have to be observed. The world may come to an end, but someone must be there to report it. Preferably someone from *The Times*, of course.

'We'll draw from the pool.' Burberry sipped his large

schnapps; he had once been a gin-and-tonic man, but was no longer. 'What a pity our Foreign Office chaps are such sportsmen.'

'How's that?' Carmody was puzzled; it was unlike Burberry to go off at tangents.

'Haven't I ever told you about McMartin-Innes, used to be military attaché at our embassy? They sent him home in June, said he was too militaristic or something. Splendid chap. Had imagination, something one doesn't find often in military attachés. Thanks, I will – I've developed a taste for schnapps. It is not as civilized as gin, but brings out the primitive in me . . . Where was I?'

Carmody had never seen him like this before: dispirited, almost lost. 'McMartin-Innes, the military man with imagination.'

'Oh yes.' Burberry sat quiet till the waiter had brought their drinks and gone away again. 'You know my flat? Overlooks the Unter den Linden, just across the street. Well, McMartin-Innes was up there one evening having a drink. Had to go to the lavatory, so I showed him the bathroom. It was a hot night, just like the nights we've been having. The bathroom window was open and while he was standing there having his piss, he looked out and down into the street, recognized where he was and suddenly had this idea. There must be some connection between the bladder and the brain – I've had some of my best moments of inspiration standing over a lavatory bowl.'

'What was this pissworthy idea he had? I hope he didn't wet his shoes in his excitement.'

'He looked down into the Unter den Linden, imagined Hitler riding up there in his open car in one of his processions – I told you he had imagination –' He took a sip of his drink, paused a moment, then picked up his story again: 'He saw that a good marksman, using a telescopic sight, could shoot Der Fuehrer –' his fruity voice mocked the title '– and get away without anyone's discovering where the shot had come from. My bathroom window is almost indistinguishable from down in the street – the angle is too acute. The marksman could have been gone from my flat, with his rifle dismantled and in a small suitcase, before the security men could have got a line on where the bullet had come from.'

'What happened?'

'McMartin-Innes asked me would I mind his using the flat? What could I say? I'd never be able to write the full story, of course, but one has to make sacrifices in the greater interest. The assassination itself would be a big enough story, though, of course, one would have preferred to add one's own background material. So I agreed.'

'So why was it never attempted?'

'McMartin-Innes put the idea to the FO and they vetoed it. Said it would be unsportsmanlike. Isn't that priceless? They are so simple-minded at times. It makes one wonder, dear boy, if the FO isn't some sort of tennis club.'

Carmody knew there would be many more wrong gestures, sporting or otherwise, before Hitler was disposed of. 'Are you going back to London?'

'Not yet. I thought I might spend a few days in Warsaw with our chap there.'

'You want your head read, Oliver.' Carmody all at once felt an affection for the tall Englishman. They were opposites in every way, in background, education, politics and style; but a bond had grown between them that Carmody realized might now be broken and in the most tragic way. 'If war starts, the first bombs are going to fall there. Don't be a bloody hero. Go home to London. Or into France or Holland or somewhere. Anybloodywhere but Warsaw.'

But Burberry was not to be dissuaded. It hurt him to have to run away from the news here in Berlin. For all his High Church demeanour, his Old Etonian view of the world, he was a born newspaperman: one did not turn one's back on a story. If he could not cover it from the safe end, he would cover it from the dangerous end.

'No, dear boy. Warsaw it is. Who knows, I may even be back here – Der Fuehrer may have a last-minute attack of sanity. That's one of the reasons I wanted to see you before I go.' He took two keys out of his pocket. 'I'm not giving up my flat, just in case I do return – the rent is paid up for another three months. Drop in there occasionally, there's a good

209

chap. Just check if the landlord or the caretaker has been in there looting my wines. Take a bottle or two, if you wish. If war does break out, that means I shan't be back. So take anything you fancy in the flat. Better you than some Gestapo thug.'

Carmody took the keys. 'I'll do my best.'

Burberry finished his drink, shook his head as if the last draught had been fiercer than those before it, rose and held out his hand. 'Goodbye, dear boy. Do take care of yourself. I'm half-inclined to thumb my nose at our embassy's advice and stay on here, but if the roof does fall in, I suppose one might be interned and that would be a damned nuisance. *The Times* doesn't like running stories about what happens to its own correspondents. The editor thinks it's bad form, like Bradman or Hutton phoning in his own cricket score.'

Carmody squeezed the hand in his. 'Good luck, Oliver. Keep your head down in Warsaw.'

Burberry went across to the bar, left a large tip for all the waiters, said goodbye to the room at large and went out swinging his umbrella, to the soft applause of the white-gloved waiters. Some people have a natural talent for exiting in style: actors, the more worldly bishops, confidence men: Oliver Burberry was all of those in a way. Carmody thought: let me go out the same way, Lord. Just don't let me slink out.

He finished his beer, then went out into the Unter den Linden. As he stepped out on to the broad pavement he saw everyone in the street stop and look up. Then he heard the roar, that double-beat of bomber engines that he had first heard in Spain; he looked up and saw the bombers, nine of them, going overhead like winged sharks, heading east. He looked around for Burberry, wanted to run after him to pull him back from Warsaw; but there was no sign of him, and in a moment the bombers had gone. Everyone lowered their faces, looked sheepishly at each other, seeing their own expressions reflected in the faces they looked at: they were all tense and, yes, afraid. Then they moved on, jerkily, out of synchronization, like figures in a newsreel that had been stopped as they were in mid-stride.

Carmody walked back to his office, aware now of the

tension in the city. The weather was warm and sultry; just the atmosphere in which a storm might break. At the office Olga Luxemburg was as tense-looking as those out in the streets. 'We can't get through to London. They have cut off all telephone, telegraph and radio communication to anywhere outside Germany. I bumped into the girl at Associated Press – she said they'd just heard that the German embassies in London, Paris and Warsaw had told all German nationals to leave for home at once. It's going to happen, Herr Carmody!'

He tried to calm her, touching her for the first time since he had met her: he put a hand on her bony shoulder. 'Don't let's panic till it does happen.'

The news that he could not get through to London or anywhere else outside Germany made him feel that, more than anything else, he was being encircled by the jaws of a vice. The questioning by the Gestapo had annoyed him, even frightened him, but he had never been afraid that he could not escape it. The telephone to London and New York had, however, been more than just miles of cable: it had been a lifeline. It had been a conduit to some sort of sanity, a channel down which he could express an opinion without fear of reprisal, a line on which he could call for help if it were needed. Now he was left to his own devices and resources. For one weak moment he thought of following the English and French correspondents to the nearest frontier; not into Poland with Oliver Burberry, but to France or Holland or Denmark. Then the moment passed and he felt a disgust with himself that he should even have contemplated running away. Till the Foreign Press Office withdrew his accreditation, he was safe.

He stayed at the office another ten minutes, reassuring Fräulein Luxemburg. She was not a weak woman, had just shown more emotion than he had seen from her before; she soon recovered and said she would stay on at the office all through the night. He promised he would be back at eight o'clock in the hope that by then the ban on outside communication had been lifted.

Before he left the office he called the Tinklers, assured them Frau Pavel was alive and kicking.

'Kicking?' said Luis Tinkler. 'That would be her. God protect her.'

'I'm sure he will.' But Carmody heard another flight of bombers pass over and he wondered if God was listening.

He went over to the Wilhelmstrasse, made the rounds of the government offices where he had contacts. The tension there was most noticeable, more tangible than that out in the streets: here, people were privy to secrets. A senior secretary in the Foreign Ministry, thin and hollow-eyed, one-armed from the last war, took him aside, said in a whisper hoarse with doom, 'The Fuehrer has ordered the troops to move into Poland at dawn tomorrow.'

'What's happening with the English?'

'The Fuehrer has offered to guarantee he will not attempt to touch the British Empire.'

'That's big of him.'

The secretary did not nod agreement, just looked warily at him. 'Herr Carmody, you must appreciate how the Fuehrer feels about Danzig and the Poles. If England and France leave that matter to him, he will honour his promises to them.'

Here in this marbled corridor, with messengers coming and going (calling Germans home from everywhere in the world?), with whispers rising and falling like a surf, was no place to debate the Fuehrer's sense of honour.

'Let's hope reason prevails,' said the secretary and lifted his stump as if in supplication.

'Whose reason?' said Carmody and left.

Tired and sweaty, in need of a reviving bath, Carmody went home. As he got out of the taxi on Ludwigstrasse, Kreisler, the hurdy-gurdy man, came round the corner. When he saw Carmody he smiled and began to play a mournful song. Carmody wasn't sure, but it sounded like the *Dead March*. 'You should be playing something livelier, Herr Kreisler.'

'*Deutschland über Alles*? A joke, Herr Carmody, no offence.' He looked up as more planes went over, heading east; Carmody recognized them as Stukas, the new dive-bombers.

The monkey on Kreisler's shoulder put its hands over its ears. 'It looks as if the circus is about to start.'

'Will you be conscripted?'

'I'm too old for the first call-up. The war won't last long enough for them to need me.'

'You think Germany will win it that quickly?'

'Of course. The English and the French don't have the will to fight. More's the pity.' He changed the cylinder in the organ. 'I'll have to play patriotic songs from now on. You won't like them, Herr Carmody, but a man has to live.'

'Why not go back to forgery? A joke, Herr Kreisler, no offence.'

Kreisler laughed, his lined face looking as if it were about to crack apart. 'If only I could! Wartime is always a good time for forgers. There are so many opportunities.'

He went on along the street, playing a patriotic song; the monkey, now on its lead on the pavement, danced a jig and clapped its hands. Faces appeared at the open windows, hands fluttered like pigeons and coins came spinning down. Then the bells of St Ludwig's began to ring, drowning out the hurdy-gurdy music; Kreisler made a rude sign at the church, then looked back at Carmody, laughed and shrugged. The monkey, a capitalist, was busy picking up the coins.

Carmody went up to his apartment. The phone was ringing as he entered the front door: it was Cathleen calling from the studio. 'Sean, can I see you? . . . *Now*. I'm leaving the studio this minute. When did you get back?'

'This afternoon – I've just come in. I can't come to your place, darl – I have to stick by the phone.' He explained about the blocked phone lines to London. 'I'll have to be here or at the office.'

'I'll come to your place,' she said and hung up.

Carmody had his bath, put on fresh clothes and had a beer. The previous World Press man had put in an ice-chest; the iceman came twice a week with blocks of ice. Carmody had become accustomed to the lukewarm beer served in the local bars and beer-gardens, but he still looked forward to the refreshing glass from his own cooler. As he took the cold bottle out of the chest he thought of the 'Cobar cooler', the box or tin, wrapped in wet hessian, that was hung in the breeze outside Australian farms and in which was kept the butter, milk and other perishable food. His mother, he guessed, was still using one.

Cathleen arrived hot and breathless. He ran a bath for her, waited till she had got into it, then took in a drink for her and sat on the stool beside the bath. *If Mum could only see me now* . . . 'I tried to call you from Danzig, but all the lines were jammed.'

'I was worried about you.' She half-lifted herself out of the bath and gave him another kiss. He was surprised that he was able to keep his hands off her shining body. *Is this how married couples are with each other? Or do we both have so much else on our minds that all the urge has gone?*

'I know where my mother is –' She had managed to contain her news till now, but he could see the excitement in her. With him absent in Danzig and with no one else to confide in, the knowledge of her mother's whereabouts had been like a fever in her. 'She's in Ravensbrueck!'

'Oh Christ!' He had just taken a sip of beer; it went flat in his mouth. 'The Langs are sure?'

She nodded. 'Absolutely. I trust them, Sean. My grandmother is dead – she died there last March. But mother is okay, they said.'

'But Ravensbrueck! How are you going to get her out of there? I hate to say it, darl, but it's not like an ordinary prison, not from what I hear. You don't go in there for a given sentence . . . Have you been back to your embassy?'

She was deflated, seemed to sink lower in the water. She abstractedly began to sponge herself as she told him what she had told the Langs, that the embassy would not, could not, help her if her mother was still a German citizen. 'But there must be something we can do – I'll ask Goebbels –'

'You won't. Christ Almighty, darl, do you want to finish up in there with her? Your mother's Jewish – he's not going to shove his neck out and get her released just for a piece of nooky –'

She threw the wet bath sponge at him, hit him in the face. She went to stand up, slipped and crashed back into the bath, sending a wave of water splashing all over him as he tried to catch her. She was swearing at him incoherently, suddenly losing control; she slipped under the water and he grabbed at her head, lifting it up. She turned her dripping face, her eyes still shut against the water pouring off her, and bit his wrist. He let out a curse, but didn't let her go.

'Calm down – I'm sorry – listen to me –'

She was quivering, as if in a fit; he had never had to deal with a hysterical woman or one in such a temper, and he was scared. But he held on to her, wrapping his arms round her slippery body; he was on his knees beside the bath and he was wet through. Slowly the quivering subsided, then she was quiet.

'Let me get out,' she said without looking at him.

He got to his feet, handed her a towel. He was about to apologize further, but thought better of it; she was still not looking at him, was in no mood to listen to him. He took one of the other towels, went out of the bathroom and into his bedroom. He dried himself, changed into dry clothes, then sat down in front of the dressing-table and looked at himself. It was his first serious fight with her or any other woman and it had left him drained.

Then, in the mirror, he saw her standing in the doorway, the towel wrapped round her. Without turning round he said quietly, 'I'm sorry, darl. It was a bloody awful thing to say –'

'I never thought you'd be the jealous sort. I'll never go to bed with him.'

'It wasn't just that I'm jealous. I'm afraid of what might happen to you. I don't want to lose you –'

She came and stood behind him, put her arms round his neck. The towel fell from her and he could feel her breasts against the back of his neck. There was a different sort of intimacy, almost motherly, though that image did not strike him: he would not have been able to remember ever having seen his mother's breasts.

'I'm afraid of losing my mother.'

'I know that – and I'd hate it to happen.' He was still looking at her in the mirror. 'I've got more bad news for you.

215

They expect Hitler to send his troops into Poland at dawn tomorrow.'

Her arms tightened round his neck. 'War?'

He nodded. She stared at him a moment, then her face squeezed up in pain, her arms tightened still further without her realizing it. Gently he took her arms away, turned round and took her in *his* arms. Naked, she sat on his lap and began to weep quietly.

They sat like that for several minutes. Protective of her, he felt a contentment in the role; his mind stopped working and there was just the physical pleasure of holding her and comforting her. When the phone rang in the bedroom he started as if he had been woken from a doze.

'I'd better answer that.' But when he stood up he found his legs had gone to sleep under her weight, his knees buckled and he had to grab her for support. It was enough to make them laugh, to bring them both back to facing matters that could not be avoided. Telephones were invented for such reminders.

Fräulein Luxemburg was on the phone. 'Herr Carmody, I have just heard on the grapevine –' The secretaries in all the newspaper and wire services bureaux had their own sources of news. 'They are calling off all the restrictions on phoning to England and France. We should be able to get through to London in a couple of hours.'

'What's happening?'

'That's all I know. Obviously, *something* has happened.'

Carmody told her he would be at the office within half an hour, hung up and stood pondering where to go for his best contact. He was aware of Cathleen getting dressed, but for the moment all his attention was on trying to get a starting point for his story, whatever the story might prove to be. Had the invasion of Poland been called off or had it already started?

'What's the matter?' There was a tense note of worry in Cathleen's voice.

'I don't know – yet.' He dialled the phone, firing a prospecting arrow into his list of numbers. 'Meg? This is Sean . . . Sean Carmody . . .' He looked across at Cathleen. 'She sounds as if she's drunk.'

216

On the other end of the line Lady Arrowsmith, no lady at all this evening, was at least half-drunk. 'That greasy little dago Mussolini –' She had all the English contempt for Latins; it ran right down through the classes and the ages. Julius Caesar, the first dago, would have met it from the Celts of Kent on his way inland from the Dover Straits. 'He has reneged, funked it. He says he's not ready to support the Fuehrer if England fights for Poland.'

'You should be grateful to Musso. He has more sense than the Fuehrer. What else do you know?'

She was a gin-barrel of information: 'They say the English and the Poles are on the point of signing a treaty. Nothing is going right for the Fuehrer –' She sounded maudlin, as if she were about to weep over one of her pet dogs.

He wanted to be angry with her, but he couldn't be; she was too pathetic. 'Where did you get all this?'

'From Nicky. Nicky Klatt – he knows. Darling –' She sounded as if she had taken a deep breath, was trying to sober up. 'You wouldn't like to come over and keep me company?'

'I can't, Meg. I'm working – I'm probably not going to get to bed tonight. Try Nicky.'

'He's home with his wife. See you Sunday.' She hung up abruptly.

He had forgotten all about Sunday; he could not see himself playing tennis out at Schwanenwerder while bombs were falling on Warsaw or wherever. But . . . *Nicky Klatt – he knows.* Maybe, if war had not begun by Sunday . . .

Cathleen was dressed, was putting on her make-up. 'I'll come with you.'

'Where?'

'I don't know. Wherever you're going. I can't go home and spend the night alone. Not tonight. If you're going to your office, I'll come there and just sit in a corner. Or talk to Fräulein Luxemburg or whatever her name is. But I'm not going home.' Though she looked composed again, she was still struggling with her nerves and emotions. She was ashamed at how she had lost control in the bathroom; Sean's remark had been insulting, even if he hadn't meant it, but it had only been the trigger to let fly all the feelings that had

217

been building up for the past week. She wanted someone to hold on to and, she was coming to appreciate more and more, he was as steady and dependable as anyone she had ever known. More so than anyone she had known. 'I want to be with you.'

Perhaps the best part of being loved is being needed; love is a mutual selfishness and men, usually, give less than women. But Carmody, who had never been in love before, was not analytical about it: he just felt warm and touched. He took both her hands and kissed them, a European gesture.

'I like that,' she said, smiling lovingly at him. 'You're becoming Continental.'

He grinned, embarrassed by compliments. 'I didn't want to spoil your make-up.'

I love him, she thought. *Please, God, let us survive.*

## 5

Admiral Canaris was feeding his dachshunds, talking to them as he talked to no one else, not even his family. His wife Erika had phoned him to ask if she and Brigitte should leave Berlin; he had done his poor best to sound like a good husband and father, but he didn't really care; in the end he had said he would leave the decision to Erika's 'good judgement'. All their married life she had prided herself on her good judgement, except in marrying him. Sometimes he felt sorry for her. She had married him, something she regretted; she had had two daughters, one of whom, Eva, was in a mental home and the other, Brigitte, at thirteen was already thought to be slightly eccentric. Whose genes were to blame, his or Erika's? He asked the question now of the dachshunds, but though they were faithful dogs they were not comforting philosophers. They were too German for that.

There was a knock at the door and Colonel von Gaffrin came in. Though he did not like Gaffrin, he envied him: the aristocratic officer seemed to have *his* life perfectly organized. A beautiful wife whom he loved and who loved him, three perfectly healthy children, a beautiful mistress whom he didn't love and who didn't love him . . . There was a file on Gaffrin locked away in Canaris' private drawers along with other files.

'The word has just come through from our embassy in Warsaw – the English and the Poles have just ratified a treaty. The order has gone out for all our troop movements to be stopped.'

'You look pleased, Gaffrin. Almost jubilant.' Canaris put the dachshunds in their baskets, went back to his desk.

'I think you look pleased yourself,' said Gaffrin, though there had been no change of expression at all on the Abwehr chief's face.

'Really? I suppose I am. I wonder how the Fuehrer feels at having to call off the invasion.'

'My information from the Chancellery is that he is quite put out.'

'Well, perhaps peace has been saved. Lift the ban on outside communications – perhaps the English at home would like to know there isn't going to be war.'

Gaffrin looked at him with that sardonic smile that always made Canaris feel inferior to his insubordinate. 'There will be a lot of Germans who will feel relieved, too.'

The file on Hans von Gaffrin showed that over the past 18 months he had been in touch with several influential people in England. He was a frequent visitor to functions at the British embassy here in Berlin. Canaris knew he was bitterly anti-Nazi, that he belonged to a cabal of senior officers who would gladly see Hitler fall; but only Canaris knew it and, anti-Nazi himself, he had no intention of exposing Gaffrin. He was not, however, going to expose himself by identifying himself too much with Gaffrin. He opened one of his pill-boxes, took a pill: he could feel something coming on, though he was not sure whether it was the ague or apprehension.

'What is to happen to all the troops in East Prussia and on the border?' he said.

'Who knows?' Gaffrin was enough of a professional soldier to know that one can't leave standing armies sitting around.

'It will be interesting tomorrow to see what Reichsminister Goebbels says in his newspapers about the backdown.'

There had been another backdown, by the plotters. Events had moved too fast for them; by the time they themselves were ready to move, their troops had already gone. The local commanders sympathetic to the plot were to have taken over the strategic barracks and the entire chain of Gestapo stations this morning; yesterday at noon three of the commanders were on their way to East Prussia. The plot suddenly was no more than cobwebs, the plotters harmless spiders. Gaffrin had spoken to General von Albern last night: the old man had sounded heartbroken.

'Ah yes, Goebbels. The little man will be so busy –'

Gaffrin kept his smile to himself. At six feet four he was surrounded by little men: from that height he often knew the colour of a man's dandruff more than the colour of his eyes. From a foot above Canaris he nodded. 'He is always busy, one way or another. Did you know he has been seeing the American actress Cathleen O'Dea?'

A good espionage man can't admit ignorance, not to another officer. 'I'd heard of it. It's harmless, isn't it?'

'At a time like this? Still, better an American trollop than an English or French one.'

Possibly; but not an American Jewish one. Sooner or later he would show the file on Fräulein O'Dea to Goebbels, but the moment had to be right: he did not want a hollow victory over the arrogant little Rhinelander. 'What has been happening to the English one, Lady Arrowsmith?'

'The Fuehrer considers her a nuisance now. But he can't send her back to England – that would be bad propaganda.'

'Women are always bad propaganda,' said Canaris, who knew.

'Should we keep a closer watch on her? Women spurned can be dangerous,' said Gaffrin, who knew.

Canaris shook his head; dandruff fell on his shoulders. 'I'm sure the Gestapo have their eye on her. We have more than enough to do. Would you like to go to East Prussia?'

'No,' said Gaffrin.

'I thought not.' He knew enough not to push his subordinate, but he wished he could conjure up more authority. 'Well, find out what you can from the English and French, those who are still here. Go to tea with someone.' He smiled to show he had made a joke: no one ever knew, otherwise.

Gaffrin wanted to pat the little man on the head: he was so pathetic at times. Often he had been tempted to take the admiral into his confidence, recruit him into their plot; but one could never be sure what the Abwehr chief was thinking, he blew hot and cold in his attitude towards the Nazi hierarchy. He was a monarchist looking for a monarch to serve, but all the kings were gone.

'I was going riding tomorrow. Damn, why do crises always happen at the weekend?'

He left: no salute, no *Heil Hitler*, just turning on his heel and going. He would salute the generals, Canaris thought; and looked at his dogs, who dutifully barked. Then the phone rang.

It was the Chancellery. 'The Fuehrer has called an urgent meeting, Herr Admiral. He would like you here within an hour.'

Well, thought Canaris, what madness is he contemplating now?

# CHAPTER NINE

## 1

That Friday night was the busiest night Carmody had spent since arriving in Germany. All the major government departments kept staff working all night; twice he went over to the Wilhelmstrasse in efforts to get information when he could not get through on the busy phones. London rang him four times and New York was twice on the line; he began to feel that both offices were disappointed that he could not send them copy on the declaration of war. Cathleen stayed in his office all night, once falling asleep in her chair while he was over on the Wilhelmstrasse. Fräulein Luxemburg fussed over her, giving her all the attention that her maidenly reticence would never allow her to give Carmody. If there was any jealousy or envy of Cathleen's possession of Carmody, it did not show.

At six in the morning the story was cold. The invasion of Poland was off; all troop movements in the East had been stopped. It seemed to Carmody, walking back from the Wilhelmstrasse for the second time, that he could hear a collective sigh of relief coming out of the open windows of the ministries. They were not so much afraid of being killed in war as having their world killed: bureaucracies survive wars better than armies, but war does upset the system, especially of promotions.

He took Cathleen and Olga Luxemburg to breakfast at the Adlon Bar. Fräulein Luxemburg demurred. 'Oh, I can't, Herr Carmody! I should be intruding –'

'Nonsense, honey,' said Cathleen. Fräulein Luxemburg had never been called *honey* before; she looked demurely flattered. 'World Press owes you a slap-up breakfast. We'll have champagne with our bacon and eggs. Don't groan,' she said as she saw Carmody roll his eyes. 'I'll pay if you're too stingy.'

222

'Loot the petty cash, Fräulein Luxemburg,' said Carmody resignedly. 'We'll do what she says. I heard a rumour last night that they're going to announce rationing in the next day or so.'

They walked over to the Adlon. Before they went into the hotel Carmody stood on the pavement and looked up at the sky. It was going to be another warm day; the sun had come up like a red ball out of the east; he wondered if it would have been redder had it risen through the dust and smoke of bombs and shells. He looked across at the IG Farben building, saw the anti-aircraft gun on its roof, barrel pointing to the sky like an obscene gesture.

'What sort of day is it going to be?' Cathleen, despite her tiredness, smiled at him.

'Warm, with the possibility of storms in the east. I'd wear your tin hat and your galoshes.'

'Don't joke like that,' she said and took his hand.

He smiled wanly at Olga Luxemburg. 'She's desperate about being an optimist.'

'All women are. It's the only way to survive in a man's world.' Fräulein Luxemburg herself looked surprised at her statement: it was something she had read and now it had popped out, like a woman's unmentionable from a handbag.

Cathleen laughed, took her arm and whisked her into the hotel. Carmody, shaking his head at the unpredictability of women, followed them. Joe Begley was in the bar and with him was Fred Doe, cornet-case parked beside his chair.

'The help is not supposed to be in here,' said Doe, 'but at this hour and after all the hullabaloo last night, the manager and under-managers have gone home to bed. Do you mind eating with the hotel help, ladies?'

'We're all help at this table, aren't we?' said Cathleen. 'We're all working for someone. Right now I wish I was working for someone else,' she added ruefully.

'Fräulein Luxemburg –' Begley was in his trenchcoat, ready for any storm. 'I've spoken to you on the phone. I know your reputation.'

She looked ready to faint. 'My reputation?'

'The best girl in any news office in town. If you don't know it, no one knows it, that's what they say. I don't know why you go on working for Mr Carmody here.'

'Because he gives her champagne for breakfast,' said Cathleen and ordered Krug '34 to be served.

Carmody looked at her. 'Where did you learn what champagne to order?'

'You learn a lot in the movies.'

Everyone, even Fräulein Luxemburg, seemed determined to put the events of the night behind them; the conversation, for breakfast talk, was animated and at times merry. Cathleen told them of some of the classic Hollywood lines ('Here comes Anytime Annie – the only time she said no, she didn't hear the question'); Fred Doe told them of a film, *Victor-Viktoria*, in which Renate Müller played a woman masquerading as a man and the whole homosexual population of Berlin, male and female, went to see it and shrieked at all the wrong notes; and Carmody and Joe Begley told their best newspaper stories, though they had trouble remembering which was best, since there were so many of them. Olga Luxemburg just sat and laughed and got tipsy on the Krug '34 and Carmody, sneaking glances at her, wondered what she would tell her mother, Goering's admirer, when she went home. Don't ever feel sorry for yourself, he told himself, not while there are people as lonely and trapped as she is.

At last Fred Doe rose, picked up his cornet-case. 'Could I see you a moment, pal? I want to give you a bit more on that story you're doing on me.'

Carmody followed him out into the lobby. He had done no more on the story about Berlin's musicians and he knew that Doe wanted him for something else. The lobby was busy with guests checking out, though there was no impression that they were fleeing the city; he heard some American voices saying why shouldn't they stop off in Cologne before going on to Paris. Go home, Yanks, he told them silently, and he saw Doe looking at them resentfully.

'Rich bastards,' the jazzman said. 'No war's ever gonna catch them.'

Carmody looked at the three couples, all of them expensively clothed, the Vuitton luggage stacked beside them, the air of confidence that comes with old wealth exuding from them like a perfume: they would survive everything, even the next American Revolution. One of the women, about his own age, looked at him; or rather, she looked *through* him. Bitch, he thought, and wondered why he should be so annoyed by a stranger.

'Why did you want to see me?'

'I saw our friends last night –'

'The Langs?'

'No names, no pack drill – ain't that what the Limeys say?' Doe had had too much to drink; he looked as if he were having to hold himself together. 'They told me they didn't give you much good news.'

'It could have been better. Ravensbrueck,' he said cryptically.

Doe nodded. 'I'm sorry, pal. The Gestapo raided the apartments where I live last night – they took away three of my neighbours. The bastards,' he added bitterly.

'Did they question you?'

'Two hours of it. That's where I'd been before I came back here for breakfast. I've had enough, pal. I'm going home.'

'Home? The States?' Had he at last laid the ghost of Bix Beiderbecke?

'All the way, pal. Right home to Charleston, South Carolina. Nobody there will remember me –' He shrugged. 'Pity I hadn't blown a few phrases they'd heard back there.'

'When are you leaving?'

'Soon's I get everything together – there ain't much.'

'Will you be sorry to go?'

Doe shook his head. 'Only that nobody here will remember me, either. Mebbe I was the best trumpet man in Berlin, but what does that mean? Bix would have laughed . . . No, he wouldn't. He was too nice a guy for that. Jesus Christ, I wish I'd done something to be remembered by! Well, so long, pal. I hope things work out for you and your friend in that place.' He didn't say Ravensbrueck; the lobby was becoming crowded, you didn't know which ears were listening to you.

'You do a piece on me, send me a clipping. Josh Wagner, General Delivery, Charleston.'

'Josh *Wagner*? You?'

'A joke, eh? Adolf's favourite composer –' Then abruptly he was gone, seemingly borne out by the group of Americans, the rich bastards, who chose that moment to sweep out to the car waiting to take them to the station. Carmody caught a glimpse of him in their midst, a sad half-drunk man who wanted to be remembered and never would be.

Carmody went back into the bar, where the other three were getting ready to go home to their respective beds. 'I don't have a call till noon,' said Cathleen. 'I'm going to look like hell if there are any close-ups. I'll have to get Helmut to shoot me through thick gauze. Or through a gunny-sack, as Marie Dressler used to say when they got in close on her.'

Carmody paid the bill, wincing as he did so: World Press would think he had gone haywire. Cathleen grinned, but said nothing. Joe Begley did up his trenchcoat, Fräulein Luxemburg straightened her hat with unsteady fingers and all four of them went out into the Unter den Linden. Carmody called a taxi and put his secretary, protesting at such extravagance, into it.

'It's been the most wonderful night of my life,' she said tipsily and rode away in the taxi.

'*That* was the most wonderful night of her life?' said Cathleen.

'A wonderful woman,' said Begley. 'You don't appreciate her, Sean.'

'You're wrong there,' said Carmody. 'I do appreciate her. I just wish to hell she didn't have to stay on in this madhouse.'

He looked up at the sky. It was still cloudless, but the air was already sultry. There were no bombers flying, none coming back from the east.

He took Cathleen home, reminded her to set her alarm clock in time to get her out to Neubabelsberg for her noon call, went home to his own apartment and fell asleep as soon as his head hit the pillow. It was six in the evening before he

226

woke. He got up, had a bath, then sat down to ring around the offices in the Wilhelmstrasse. Though it was Saturday there were full staffs at all the ministries; some of those who answered his calls sounded peeved but they were all polite. No, there had been no further developments; yes, the Fuehrer was still hopeful of peace. But the rally at Tannenberg scheduled for tomorrow had been called off, as had the annual Nazi Party convention at Nuremberg next week: no, they could give no reason except that the Fuehrer had ordered the cancellations. Carmody hung up, convinced that the Fuehrer was no more interested in peace than he was in the welfare of Jews.

He went out and bought the principal newspapers. The lies were as big as ever: POLISH SOLDIERS PUSH TO EDGE OF GERMAN BORDER . . . THREE GERMAN PASSENGER PLANES SHOT AT BY POLES . . . It made him ashamed to belong to the same profession as the men who wrote those headlines.

He walked on over to the Potsdamerplatz. The Saturday night crowds were beginning to appear, intent on a night's enjoyment (their last? he wondered); did they seem a little more feverish than on previous Saturday nights? There was more military traffic, as much as he had seen during the week; he could only guess that on the peripheral roads the convoys were also moving. He looked up at the sky, but there was no air traffic: the bombers and fighters, he supposed, were still there on the border, ready to battle the Polish invaders.

Fräulein Luxemburg was at the office, as he thought she would be. He didn't chide her for her devotion to duty; that would have been cruel. She said she had been at the office since four o'clock, but hadn't called him because she thought he needed all the sleep he could get.

'Don't come in tomorrow,' he said. 'That's an order.'

'But I must, Herr Carmody. Anything might happen –'

'I'll come over first thing in the morning, just in case. If anything is going to happen, it won't be till afternoon. War is never declared on a Sunday morning, not while church is in.' He would go to Mass tomorrow and pray for peace, though he had little faith in the Lord to guarantee it.

At nine o'clock Cathleen rang. 'I'm pooped. I don't think I've ever had a worse day on the set – everyone was so jittery. Thank God we have tomorrow free. Are we still going to Herr Klatt's?'

'Do you want to?'

There was a slight hesitation, then: 'Yes.'

'What about What's-her-name?'

'Meg Arrowsmith?'

'No, you know who I mean.' He couldn't be sure that his phone was not tapped, so, as Fred Doe had said, no names, no pack drill.

She caught on at once, despite her weariness. 'Oh. Yes. I still don't know what to do. All I can think of is going up there –'

'You can't do that!'

'No, I know. Do you think Herr Klatt could help?'

He didn't trust anyone who had influence in Party circles; but he could not continue throwing cold water on everything she suggested. 'We'll go carefully. I'll pick you up tomorrow at noon.' He lowered his voice so that Olga Luxemburg in the outer office wouldn't hear him: 'I love you.'

'I love you.' It was the first time she had said it in so many words and he thought it should have been set to music. But, in the land of Beethoven and Brahms, the only composer he could think of offhand was Hoagy Carmichael.

He did a piece on the general situation, ending with 'your correspondent holds his breath, as does Europe' and phoned it through to London. London, as usual, came back with a demand for hard news. 'All the papers here are full of speculation. Can't you come up with something concrete?'

'I have a concrete brick here I'd like to throw at your head,' said Carmody and hung up. Journalists, he knew, are rarely sacked during a crisis, especially if they are the only ones on the spot.

He rang round the government offices once more, was assured the Fuehrer was still intent on peace. He said goodnight to Fräulein Luxemburg, told her to go home and not come in till Monday morning, then went up to the British embassy, next door to the Adlon. Each time he had come here during the past weeks he had been amazed and amused at the almost languid atmosphere in the big, dignified building. Secretaries seemed to stroll from room to room with pieces of paper that might have been no more important than laundry lists; phones rang and went unanswered till someone, almost as if bored by the interruption, bothered to pick them up; tea and Fortnum and Mason biscuits were always being served, even now at 10.30 at night. Diplomacy, they were saying, was not something to get worked up about.

Wilmington, the assistant press attaché, was in the office he shared with two typists. He was a slim, pop-eyed young man who had been to one of the minor public schools and seemed continually surprised that he should have landed such a plum post as Berlin. A pair of cricket pads and a bat stood in one corner of the office and he was staring at them when Carmody tapped on his door.

'We were going to play the English community tomorrow.' He offered Carmody tea and a biscuit. 'It's taken me all summer to arrange the bally game, and now it's called off.'

'Bad luck, sport.' When it came to cricket, Carmody became very Australian. 'I'll do a piece on it. Other than that, what else is not happening?'

Wilmington, a true Foreign Office product, had been taught that Australians had no subtlety, so he did not look for any joke in Carmody's remark. 'Very little. Happening, I mean. HE flew off to London this morning with another offer from Hitler.'

HE was His Excellency Sir Nevile Henderson, the ambassador, who had been possibly the busiest man in Germany over the past couple of weeks. He was a sincere man, Carmody privately thought but never stated in his despatches, but misguided in his approaches to Hitler: it was almost as if he had faith in the Fuehrer's promises. Cynics, perhaps, are the better diplomats.

'So nothing will happen tomorrow? You could play cricket.'

'It wouldn't be cricket, old chap. Besides, half the other side has gone home. We advised all British citizens to pack up and go. I'm surprised you're still here.'

'I'll go when Dr Goebbels kicks me out.'

Carmody left the embassy, walked up the street, crossed the Pariser Platz and went into the French embassy set back on the square north of the Brandenburg Gate. There the press attaché, a portly man with dark bags under his eyes and a contempt for all journalists except the correspondent for *Le Matin*, offered him Vichy water and no information at all. All in French, too, which left Carmody none the wiser. Carmody thanked him and went home to bed. If the embassies were not worried about Sunday, why should a press bureau be?

He slept without dreaming or tossing, got up at eight, went to nine o'clock Mass. He sat in St Ludwig's in a back pew and looked at all the bent heads in front of him and wondered what they were praying for: peace or the realization of the Fuehrer's dreams? He hadn't been to confession in over a year and his soul, according to the teaching of the parish schools he had gone to, was black with sin, particularly, over the past week, with that of fornication. So he didn't go up to the altar for communion, but watched the priest putting the Host on the tongues and wondered if he, the priest, would offer the wafer to a lapsed Catholic like Goebbels if the Reichsminister presented himself at the altar. So far the Catholic Church in Germany had produced few heroes.

Feeling mean and sour at how the populace was allowing itself to be led into war, he went over to his office, wrote a mean and sour piece and phoned it through to London. 'Christ Almighty,' said London, an atheist, 'what about some *hard* news?'

'I'm going over to the Chancellery now and ask Hitler to declare war tomorrow. Okay?' Anyone who had grown up amongst a team of shearers was never lost for an answer, at least to another man. There were no women shearers, so he was still feeling his way with women.

A train of thought he was pursuing when he picked up Cathleen: 'Are you seriously going to ask Klatt if he can help with your mother?'

She had slept the sleep of the truly exhausted last night and looked better for it. She was wearing a white skirt and green silk blouse and her red hair, freshly washed, was alive with lights. Only he, acutely aware of every expression and mood in her now, saw the hint of pain still in the bright eyes. She had sparkling eyes, which the camera, as well as men, fell for: they were only quiet after she had finished making love.

Reckless now that he was in love, or at least reckless with World Press' expenses, he had hired another car for the day. They drove out to Schwanenwerder through the Sunday traffic; everyone, it seemed, was heading for the Grunewald. Everyone, that is, but the troops. Convoys were moving east again, for a picnic on the Polish border.

The Klatt villa had been designed by someone from the Bauhaus who had lost his nerve: stark angles abruptly melted into curves, glass walls turned into brick halfway down, a portico had been added like a pillared postscript. It had been built for an owner who had made and lost a fortune in the Weimar republic, a man who would always be *nouveau* but had been *riche* for only a short time. Klatt, just as *nouveau* and even more *riche*, had bought it.

As they drove up to it Cathleen glanced through the trees and saw the English-style country house on the rise next door. But before she could orient herself they were drawing up under the Klatt portico and a butler was greeting them and then escorting them through the richly furnished house and out onto a terrace that looked down sloping lawns and out on to the Wannsee. Klatt, immaculate in cream flannels, cream silk shirt and tennis shoes, came booming towards them.

'You brought your tennis kit, Herr Carmody? Wonderful! We shall play before luncheon. Fräulein O'Dea – how delightful you look! Doesn't she, my love?' He introduced his wife, a good-looking blonde woman wrapped up in both her husband and a tight corset; she had a slightly dazed look, as if shell-shocked from years of her husband's booming voice. 'And you know Lady Arrowsmith? And oh, our good neighbours, Herr Reichsminister and Frau Goebbels –'

The Reichsminister and his wife had come through the trees and up the path on to the terrace. Shadowy figures remained amongst the trees; even for Sunday luncheon at the neighbours', the bodyguards had to be present. Goebbels was in a cream flannel suit, as was his wife: Cathleen thought they looked like a vaudeville act who might break into a soft-shoe shuffle at any moment. Goebbels took off a cream doeskin glove to raise Cathleen's hand and kiss it.

'Fräulein O'Dea, what a pleasure. You haven't met my wife. Magda darling, this is Fräulein Cathleen O'Dea, who is playing in our film out at Babelsberg.'

Magda Goebbels was a handsome blonde, taller than her husband and obviously not under his thumb, gloved or otherwise. She was a wife experienced in her husband's liking for mistresses; she looked Cathleen up and down without seemingly moving her eyes. She must have decided that Cathleen was not yet a mistress, because her smile was sudden and charming.

'You must tell me about Hollywood –'

Carmody was shaking hands with Goebbels. 'Herr Carmody – not working today?'

'I checked with all the ministries, Herr Reichsminister. They told me today would be a no-news day. I can see how relaxed you are, yourself.'

'I am always relaxed, Herr Carmody, in this best of all possible worlds.' The Minister could lie to himself on occasions.

Carmody went off with Klatt to change into his tennis kit. Some other guests, three couples in expensive dress and expensive cars, had arrived and were being greeted by Heidi Klatt and Magda Goebbels. Cathleen moved over to sit beside Meg Arrowsmith, who was lolling in a cane chair, and Goebbels joined them. He sat down, arranging the crease in his trouser-legs, took off both gloves and looked at the women with a smile that told them they were his favourites for the day.

'Isn't it wonderful to be able to relax on a day like this?'

'I wonder how the poor are relaxing?' Cathleen said in a light tone, though both Goebbels and Meg looked at her as if she were about to start a debate. She saw their looks and retreated smilingly: 'A rhetorical question. You must be used to those, Herr Reichsminister.'

He nodded, returning her smile, his eyes having difficulty

in focusing above her legs. Meg said, 'I thought there might be a meeting of Ministers today, Joseph.'

'Perhaps later,' said Goebbels airily and looked out at the lake, closing that line of questioning. 'We should all be out boating. The summer is almost over.'

'Is that your boat down there?' Cathleen had now got herself oriented. She could see, through the trees bordering both estates, the small house, his 'fort', where Goebbels had entertained her. Down at the dock there were two boats, the one in which he had taken her cruising and a much larger one.

'Yes, the *Baldur*. The big one. You must come for an outing on it one evening before you go home to America.'

'You've never asked me, Joseph,' said Meg, who had been on his bed with him but never on his boat.

'We must remedy that,' said Goebbels and abruptly got up and moved away to talk to one of the newly arrived men.

Meg looked after him. 'The little cad. He really is an awful swine. I saw him eyeing your legs. I hope he hasn't tried to put his hand up them.'

Cathleen stretched out her legs. 'He'd get a kick in the crotch if he tried.'

Meg laughed hoarsely; she looked wan and listless, as if she were suffering from a hangover. Which she was, though it was a hangover brought on by more than just liquor. 'I never thought of doing that. The trouble I could have saved myself! Unfortunately, men have always been one of my weaknesses. I let them hurt me because I could never bring myself to hurt them. Do you think that's an English thing?'

'I haven't met many Englishwomen, except the ones out in Hollywood and someone once told me, David Niven, I think, that they were always trying to be more English than they ever would have been at home. But Boadicea and Queen Elizabeth were pretty hard on men, weren't they?'

'Ah, but that was a long time ago. Before the Victorians thinned our blood.' She sipped her white wine, looked directly at Cathleen. 'I think, after all, that I like you. Do you mind?'

'Of course not.' Cathleen was surprised at her directness. 'I think I like you, too. Sean likes you.'

'All except my politics.' She held her wine glass up in front of her face, looked over the top of it out at the lake. Small yachts floated on it like gulls with frozen wings; motor-boats cruised amongst them like gross sharks. The far shore shimmered like a dark wave ready to break and the sky was a darker blue than usual, as if the darkness of outer space was pressing down on it. 'He's a sweet man, but he's so innocent.'

'Not quite,' said Cathleen, and Meg, all at once on the same wavelength as her, knew she didn't mean it in a sexual sense. 'I think maybe he sees everything much clearer than us. Than me, anyway.'

Then the clear-sighted innocent came back, dressed in white shirt and shorts, looking much more athletic than the long-trousered Klatt beside him. The muscles in his shoulders and upper arms showed under the tight shirt and Cathleen suddenly showed a possessive pride in him. She smiled at him, like Charles Atlas' mother, whose son had metamorphosed from a 97-pound weakling into a small mountain of muscle.

'You must all come and watch!' shouted Klatt and led the way towards the lawn court at one side of the house.

'How do you think you'll go?' Cathleen said to Carmody as she walked beside him.

'He'll probably wipe the court with me. He has a coach come out three mornings a week to practise with him. He says he often played with von Cramm.'

'Played tennis, I hope. Didn't he get into trouble for playing with boys?'

'I don't think Klatt is that sort. You watch how he's going to impress you ladies.'

The guests seated themselves in the small pavilion beside the court. Goebbels, who had no interest in tennis or any other sport, who felt that any energetic exercise only drew attention, no matter how indirectly, to his club foot, sat down beside Cathleen and looked bored and irritated. He would have gone home, even though it would have been rude to do so, had he not welcomed this opportunity to see Cathleen again. He felt lovesick, a feeling that made him queasy and irritated him even more. Sometimes, he thought, it is much easier to be in love only with oneself. He had tried that and succeeded, but women would keep intruding.

Klatt's service was like his voice, booming. He took the first game to love and Carmody could only console himself that his ignominy would soon be over. Unless the bastard wanted to play half a dozen sets, as he had threatened. Carmody, on his own service, lost the second game after he had managed to get to deuce. Klatt took the third game, but it went to deuce. Carmody began to find some form; he also began to realize that Klatt was a wound-up toy, a totally manufactured player, the product of some coach's patience and persistence. Carmody was a natural athlete, born with a ball sense, but he played only for the exercise and the enjoyment of tennis; if anyone had suggested that he should be coached, he would have given up and taken up some other game. Klatt was flat-footed and badly co-ordinated; all his shots were correctly performed, but they looked like the actions of a mechanical man. Carmody began to run him around the court and took the next four games.

As they crossed over he saw the look on Klatt's face. The look told him he was being a poor guest and he would never be invited again. Heidi Klatt offered her husband a towel to wipe his streaming face, but he angrily brushed it aside and stalked down to his end of the court. Carmody stopped to take a sip from the glass of lemonade Magda Goebbels offered him. He looked at her and she was smiling approvingly at him; evidently she was no admirer of Nicky Klatt. Then Carmody looked at Cathleen and Meg and they were both discreetly shaking their heads. So much for being a show-off bastard, he thought; and went out on to the court to do his best to be a good guest.

He lost the next three games to deuce, making a good job of covering up the fact that he allowed Klatt to win them. When the set ended Klatt came bounding to the net, hand out-thrust to his defeated opponent, all booming grace in victory.

'Well played, old chap! It's too hot to play another set, don't you think? Let's go up and shower and have luncheon.'

Everyone looked pleased that the match was over; even

235

Goebbels clapped politely. 'I think we should give them three cheers,' said Meg. 'Or would that be enough?'

Klatt, who would have given six cheers if the figure of three had not already been set by the too-moderate English, laughed modestly, though his look told Meg this would be her last visit to the house. The group moved up into the house, with Carmody and Cathleen bringing up the rear.

'I thought you were going to foul Herr Klatt's nest,' she said softly.

'He'd have broken my leg or something if I had. Crumbs, how can winning a game of tennis mean so much?'

'You're not his age, darling. When you're forty-five, you'll be busting your balls to lick the young men.'

'You're not only so wise about men, you have a ladylike way of putting things.'

She put her cool arm in his sweaty one and they went into the house. Out of the corner of her eye she saw Goebbels staring at her, his face dark with – what? He was in his early forties and a cripple to boot: she shuddered at the unintended pun in her mind. She took her arm out of Carmody's, told him to go and have his shower and crossed, almost a little hurriedly, to the Minister. She recognized the jealousy in his bony face and felt afraid.

'You seem very close to Herr Carmody.' His voice was soft but harsh.

'He's just a friend. I'm very affectionate. Most actresses are, aren't they?'

'Not all. You haven't been very affectionate towards me.'

'It's our positions, Herr Reichsminister. I was never very affectionate towards Mr Mayer, either, at MGM.'

'A Jew? You showed good taste.' His tongue was threatening to run away from him. He had never felt as jealous as this, at least not since the days with Lida Baarova. He felt frustrated, too, because he knew this affair would be over before it could even begin.

The word *Jew* tripped her own tongue into saying, 'Have you been able to find out anything about Frau Hoolahan?'

He was sharp: 'What made you say that? Is she Jewish?'

236

'Hoolahan?' She laughed, an effort that almost stuck in her throat. 'That's as Irish as my own name.'

He laughed, too, though it took him a moment or two. 'Of course it is. No, I have no information yet, but one of my secretaries is looking into it.'

That, she guessed, meant nothing was being done. 'Well, I'll be grateful –'

'I hope so.' There was no mistaking his meaning. He could no longer waste time being subtle: another week at the most and there would be no time for love affairs.

Cathleen gave him an encouraging smile, just in case. Then Magda Goebbels, recognizing from experience an old symptom, came across to have a second look at her husband's new actress. All three smiled at each other, a white circle of hypocrisy.

'Talking films? My husband is absolutely besotted with films, Fräulein O'Dea. But perhaps he has told you that?'

'He knows as much about American movies as I do.'

Cathleen looked at the wife, a good-looking, intelligent woman who had given her husband six good-looking healthy children, and wondered what it was that drove the ugly, little Minister into so many other women's beds. Was it revenge of some sort on women; or an attempt to prove he had as much sexual appeal as handsomer, less physically handicapped men; or was it just plain horniness, the animal urge that needed no explanation? Or, the saddest prospect of all, had they, after so many years of marriage and all those children, just grown tired of each other?'

'He knows so much,' said Magda Goebbels and made it sound less than a compliment.

But her husband, a deft catcher of compliments, even badly-thrown ones, accepted it. 'I have a good memory for everything I've read. And I've read everything.'

'Of course you have, my darling.' She looked at Cathleen. 'He comes to bed so late every night – he is always staying up to read. Still, I always know where he is.'

*Was it a warning?* 'I'm sure that's a comfort.'

Both women wiped their smiles across Goebbels' throat. He had read everything, so he knew: man to woman can be a

237

fair contest, sometimes; but man to two women is, as they would say out at the Hoppegarten, a two-mare race. He gave them a smile in return, but it was a poor defence.

At lunch Cathleen sat on Klatt's left at one end of the table; Goebbels sat on Frau Klatt's right at the other end. Carmody found himself between Meg Arrowsmith and Magda Goebbels: stone the crows, he thought, if Mum and Dad could only see me now! The other couples had split themselves up and it was obvious they were regular diners at this table. Carmody recognized the names if not the faces of the three men: a banker and two industrialists. He looked along the table at Goebbels and decided the Minister was bored and was growing tired of hiding it. He knew that Goebbels rarely spent any social time with the rest of the Nazi hierarchy, whom he considered below his intellectual level; most of his social round was in the company of people from the arts, mostly from films and the theatre. Bankers and industrialists, it seemed, were, in Goebbels' estimation, on a par with the dullards and buffoons of the Party. The Minister was here, Carmody decided, only because his wife had decreed it. Then he saw Goebbels looking down the table at Cathleen and he knew otherwise. And felt suddenly angry and jealous.

'Steady on, darling,' whispered Meg, leaning forward into her vichyssoise. She pressed her knee against his. 'I can feel you trembling.'

He grinned, tried to relax. 'I didn't think it was so obvious. You know what's upset me?'

'Of course. I'm all eyes and ears, darling.' She looked past him at Magda. 'My dear Australian friend says he feels out of place here. I'm telling him he's foolish to feel that way.'

'Why do you feel out of place, Herr Carmody?'

Out of the corner of his eye Carmody could see the amused glint in Meg's eyes: you bitch, he thought. But he had learned how to think on his feet: 'I'm a newspaperman, a foreign one. At a time like this most Germans are suspicious of us.'

'Only those who write lies about us.' She was a good Propaganda Minister's wife.

'Oh, I'd never do that.' He was learning to be diplomatic. The shearing sheds and the country newspaper office had

238

taught him nothing of diplomacy; nor, for that matter, had Australia as a whole. Diplomacy was for smarmy bastards like the Poms. But the civilizing process will out, since only the unintelligent know the honest joys of being uncivilized. 'I write nothing but the truth.'

'I'm sure you do,' said Magda, who hadn't read anything he had written nor, indeed, heard of him till today. 'You *look* truthful.'

'Exactly!' said Meg and turned her head to scrutinize him, as if looking at him for the first time. 'It's just the word to describe him.'

Carmody felt like kicking her.

'I hope you won't write anything untruthful about our food situation,' said Magda, leaning back so that the maid could take away her vichyssoise plate and replace it with the cold salmon plate.

'What situation is that?' He must have missed something.

'It was announced on the wireless news at midday,' said Meg. 'Before you arrived. I don't know how we'll survive. Five hundred grams of meat a week –'

'*Seven* hundred grams,' said Magda. 'Don't exaggerate, Lady Arrowsmith. I'm sure we'll all get by without too much discomfort.'

'Soap's been rationed. And sugar and coffee. Another month and we'll all be filthy as well as hungry.'

'Nonsense,' said Magda. 'We'll survive.'

Carmody watched both women attacking their salmon, survivors both.

At the end of the table Klatt was complimenting Cathleen, fawning over her with all the grace of a flat-footed bull. He had never met an American film star before; was Garbo really as beautiful as she appeared on the screen? 'Garbo isn't American,' said Cathleen.

'Of course – how stupid of me!' But one knew he really didn't think he was stupid. 'And you are Irish?'

'Half.'

'What is the other half?'

*Jewish.* 'American.'

'What a wonderful combination! The poets and the

businessmen. We don't have that mixture here in Germany. Poets and businessmen don't mix.'

Denis Hoolahan's talent for poetry hadn't got past dirty limericks. He had known nothing of Yeats, who had never written *There was a young man from Byzantium* . . . But then she, too, had never read Yeats or any of the other Irish poets. She did, however, know businessmen. 'You're too flattering, Nicky. You have a way with women.' She wanted to throw up, but, for the glory of Hollywood and America, kept her stomach under control. 'But I suppose you've been told that before.'

'Once or twice,' he said, exaggerating. 'If there is anything I can do for you –' Then he looked down the table, saw the dark eye of the Reichsminister glaring at him. He did no business with the Ministry of Propaganda, but Joseph Goebbels, and particularly Magda, could always put in a good word with the Fuehrer. He backed off, putting business before pleasure: 'But then I noticed that the Minister has also fallen for your charms. I should not like to be his rival.'

Her stomach was rising. 'He has too much else on his mind to concern himself with me.'

'True. Something is happening now.'

The butler had come in, bent over Goebbels and whispered something to him. The Minister rose and went out of the dining room. Silence dropped for a moment on the table, but then Heidi Klatt, an experienced hostess who knew silence could spoil a luncheon party more than rotten strawberries and sour cream, picked up the ball of conversation and threw it down the table at her husband.

'Tell them about your trip to Rome, Nicky. How you arm-wrestled Il Duce . . .'

'And won, too,' said her husband, giving his wife a loving smile for putting the spotlight on him.

'He's so modest,' Meg whispered to Carmody, leaning into his left ear, 'though it gives him a hernia.'

'What did she say?' whispered Magda, leaning into his right ear.

Carmody was saved from the truth, since he couldn't have thought up a good enough lie, by the return of Goebbels. The little man came in, drawing on his gloves, looking self-important and at the same time relieved that he was being called away from the party.

'I'm afraid I must go. There is a meeting of the Reichstag at the Chancellery. Please don't let my going spoil your luncheon. No, stay, Magda.'

He turned on his heel and went out, almost rudely; but then, of course, he was a Reichsminister and he had to be about his country's business. It seemed to Carmody that the little man had grown several inches while pulling on his gloves and stepping out of the role of guest into that of a Minister whose presence at the Chancellery was urgently required.

Carmody pushed back his chair. 'Would you also excuse me, Herr Klatt? If there is to be a meeting, I should be there in case a statement is released.'

Klatt looked annoyed, especially when Cathleen, too, stood up. 'Must you really go? Can't you telephone for any news? Surely you don't have to go, Cathleen?'

'Sean likes me to hold his hand when there's a crisis. It's been a marvellous day –'

'Crisis, crisis – day after day!' Heidi Klatt had lost her good-tempered, resigned look. 'Who wants the damned war, anyway?'

Nobody said anything: she had spoiled her own luncheon party by silencing it. Carmody and Cathleen made their apologies and their exit; the Klatts let them go as if they no longer interested them. Only the butler saw them out to the rented car and as they drove away they both knew they would never be invited back.

'Perhaps we should have stayed,' Cathleen said. 'You might have got a story out of Frau Goebbels.'

'Nobody is interested in Frau Goebbels any more. All London and New York want is hard news on whether there's going to be war.'

'Is there? Going to be war?'

But he didn't answer. He had looked in his driving mirror, seen the car pull out from the side of the road and begin to follow them as they drove out the gates of the Klatts' estate.

He couldn't be sure, but the two men in the car looked like Lutze and Decker.


## 2


The lions were roaring. Not the British lion, which, in the person of its ambassador, was still running backwards and forwards trying to keep the peace; but the Berlin zoo's lions, which sensed that feeding time was near. The zoo's visitors crowded around the big cats' enclosure, eager to show their children how another species besides themselves had no table manners. Babies were held up to see a lioness chewing on half a horse's leg; older children shouted with delight as two lions fought over the butchered horse's rump. It was all good clean fun, a nice diversion from the gloom that lay on their parents' minds.

'Everyone is worried,' said General Kurt von Albern. 'Nobody wants war.'

'Of course they don't,' said Helmut. 'But there won't be any revolution if he declares war.'

The two women, Melissa and Romy von Sonntag, said nothing; men never include women in their discussions on war. The four of them were sitting at an outdoor table in one of the zoo's cafés; their hunger and their manners were less spectacular than the lions' and no children were being held up to inspect them. The atmosphere amongst the four of them was awkward, mainly caused by Melissa's unease at her first introduction to Helmut's father. It is not a comfortable situation when one meets an austere general for the first time and tells him that he is to be presented with his first grandchild and a bastard at that. So far Melissa herself had not broached the subject, but she knew Helmut had told Romy and Romy had told the General.

She liked the appearance of the two older people. Romy had the sort of beauty she aspired to but doubted she would ever achieve, and Helmut's father was slim and handsome

242

and arrogant-looking, the sort of aristocrat she had never seen in Bradford nor in the repertory theatre, where the aristocrats of one week were the Alfred Doolittles of the next. Romy had a warmth to her that reassured her, but she doubted that she would ever find any warmth in the General. Yet, from the occasional glance that Romy gave him, there must be *something* there under Kurt von Albern's cool exterior. Romy, she decided, was too intelligent and experienced to fall in love with a man who did not reciprocate. Yet she knew in her heart that intelligence had nothing to do with love.

'You two go for a walk,' said Romy, patting the general's hand. 'Melissa and I have something to discuss. We'll meet you over in the aquarium in half an hour. Now run along.'

'*Now run along* . . . What a way to dismiss a soldier.' Kurt von Albern smiled at her, and suddenly Melissa saw the warmth in him. And wished that she could evoke the same smile in Helmut.

Helmut looked affectionately at his father. Why can't he love me like that? Melissa thought. Then he looked at her and for a moment she saw (or thought she saw) something in his eyes that gave her hope. He pressed her hand, stood up and walked off with his father into the crowd.

'They are a handsome pair,' said Romy, looking after the two tall, upright men. 'We are very lucky, you and I.'

'You, perhaps. I'm not so sure about me.'

'Why not? Helmut loves you.'

'Does he? I'm not sure.' She was surprised that almost at once she was confiding in this stranger; but Romy von Sonntag, for all her cool elegance that, at a distance, might have been mistaken for hauteur, had a sympathy about her. 'He doesn't want to marry me.'

'Has he said so?'

'No-o.'

Romy gazed at the young girl. She had no daughter, but two sons, both of them Nazi faithfuls like their father. They had been called up into service and were both already on the Eastern Front, one in the Luftwaffe and the other in the Wehrmacht. She wondered what sort of daughter she might have had, but knew she would not have been like this passive, resigned-to-suffering young English girl.

She called for the bill, paid for it and led the way out into the crowd strolling along the pathways between the cages and enclosures. They were a striking pair in their beauty and strangers would have been forgiven for taking them for mother and daughter: the mother, even young men would have admitted, was more striking-looking than the daughter. Melissa had worn her best summer dress, a soft pink linen cut in the simplest line, but alongside Romy's pale beige silk suit she felt as if she were wearing clogs and a shawl. She did herself an injustice: she looked better than all the other young girls they passed: she just did not yet have Romy's sense of style. It is a shock to a young girl, especially a pregnant one, to discover that a woman in the menopause, whatever that might be, can make men pause and turn their heads.

'I love your suit.'

'It's a Chanel. I go to Paris for all my wardrobe. Paris is just that much closer to Stuttgart than Berlin is. But if war comes . . . If Helmut does marry you, what will you do?'

'Stay here, of course. I shouldn't want to be separated from him.'

'What if he is called up into the army? You would be safer in England.'

'Probably.' But Bradford had always been safe: safe, stolid and dull. That was why she had run away from it. 'I'd still rather be here. At least I should see him when he came home on leave.'

They walked past the bird sanctuary. Flamingos moved like slow pink music above soft echoes of themselves in a pond; herons stood still, pale ghosts in the sunlight. In the huge aviaries parrots shrieked like children; from a high perch an eagle looked down with a baleful eye. Melissa looked twice at it, half-expecting to see it sitting on a swastika, as she had seen it so often in posters. Romy glanced at it, looking for the second head it should have, the eagle of the Hohenzollerns, in whom she still believed.

Farther away, Helmut and his father were passing the yards where the zoo's nine elephants were stabled. The huge pachyderms stood close together in a line, a grey mud wall, their wrinkled skin looking as if the mud was beginning to flake in the heat. One of them raised its trunk and let out a trumpeted scream; to Helmut it sounded an oddly thin blast coming from such huge lungs. His father, the soldier, stopped to look at the big beasts.

'To think that armies once used them . . . Perhaps we've come too far. We've made killing the enemy so much easier.'

'Not always, not all the enemy. Only the soldiers, never their leaders. Generals died on the battlefield in the old days.'

The General stiffened; but he had never denied the truth. 'It's the nature of war as it is nowadays. Armies are too big now for a commander to lead them into battle.'

'So he leads from the rear . . . I'm sorry, Father. I don't mean to insult you. As you say, that's the nature of war these days.'

They passed the cage where Pongo, the insultingly-named gorilla, stared at the crowd with his gangster's eye. 'We have decided to kill him,' said the General.

'Who?' said Helmut, looking at the gorilla.

'*Him.*' The General walked on and Helmut, who had paused for a moment, had to quicken his pace to catch up with him. 'The other plan failed. It would have been better if we had been able to carry it out – everything was worked out –' He felt bitter that the army command, the system he had believed in all his life, should have unwittingly betrayed his plan to save it from destruction.

'Father, you *can't*!' Their voices were low; neither of them looked passionate about what they were saying. They were just two very tall men, father and son, discussing the effect of the new rationing on the family housekeeping. 'To have taken him into custody, that was one thing – you might have got away with it. But to murder him! . . . He's a hero to millions.'

'You think so? Do you think all these people –' The General took in the crowd around them with his eyes . . .

. . . *Two couples passed them, elderly and reckless with the opinions of the elderly: 'It's criminal! Who cares about the Danzigers? Would they come and fight for us Berliners?'*

. . . 'Do you think they want to fight for his mad ambitions?'

Helmut saw a vacant bench under a tree, sat down on it, suddenly weary of fighting his father's attempt at suicide. His father dusted the seat with a silk handkerchief, sat down beside him. Their bodies hid the sign: *Juden Verboten*; they had sat down without noticing it. It was a direction not meant for them. Helmut, who had had Jewish friends, had consciously but shamefully turned a blind eye to it over the years: there was nothing one could do about it. His father, who had had no Jewish friends, saw it as nothing more than a sign like *Herren* or *Damen*. Kurt von Albern was not anti-Semitic: he just did not think about the Jews.

'Father, Berlin is not Germany. How many times have you told me that yourself? Berliners don't fall over themselves to *Heil Hitler!* What about the rest of the country? And Austria? He's a god to the young. If you assassinated him, the SS would go berserk. Himmler would take over and he'd be far worse.'

'If necessary, he will be killed, too.' The General had his own blind eye: he would start a war to stop a war.

'How do you plan to kill him? *Him*, I mean.'

'On Wednesday he is to drive up the Unter den Linden, through the Brandenburg Gate and on up to the Victory Column. It is to be a symbolic gesture, saluting the victory before the war has even begun.'

'He hasn't appeared so publicly in weeks –'

'We understand that is why he is doing it. Evidently there has been criticism that he has been isolating himself down in the Obersalzberg. Goering has persuaded him to show himself. The opportunity for us could not be better –'

'Father, you're –' He was about to say *insane*, but was saved from such an insult by the arrival of a young couple who wanted to share the bench. The girl was shy, a pretty mouse; the young man was an SS corporal clad in ill-fitting arrogance. The two civilians stood up, towering over him.

'You may have the seat, corporal,' said General von Albern. 'Do they teach you to salute in the *Schutzstaffel*?'

'Why should I salute a civilian?'

'I am General Kurt von Albern, that's why.'

The young man hesitated, then clicked his heels together and raised his arm. 'Heil Hitler!'

Passers-by turned their heads; two or three stopped, distracted from the animals' antics by this human ritual dance. The General flushed, nodded, spun on his heel and walked away. Helmut hurried after him.

'You asked for that, Father. Trying to start an argument with a corporal –'

'Scum! That uniform!'

They walked in silence towards the aquarium, went in out of the bright hot sunlight to the cool dimness where the fish swam like creatures in a dream through illuminated water. Romy and Melissa were waiting for them by a large tank where tropical fish floated amongst coral, their brilliant colours a sweet pain against the eyes.

'What's the matter?' Even in the gloom Romy felt the General's anger. 'Have you two been quarrelling?'

'No,' snapped the General; then relented. 'I'm sorry, my dear. Helmut was right about a small matter – I let my feelings run away with me.'

Romy looked at Helmut for explanation, but he just shook his head. She said, 'Well, sometimes that is not a bad thing. Melissa and I have been talking about feelings. About love, to be precise.'

'Women do talk about such things,' said the General, trying to be diplomatic and failing.

'Of course we do. We should teach men to do the same thing.'

Helmut looked at Melissa, who appeared to be much more at ease now than when he had left her half an hour ago. 'I hope you feel better for your talk.'

'Oh yes, much better.' A Moorish Idol floated past the back of her head, remained poised for a moment like an exotic comb in her hair. Was it his imagination or had she grown older in half an hour, become much more confident? Could Romy have had so much influence on her in such a short time?

247

'Fish are so calming,' said the General, taking Romy's hand; what he meant was that *she* had that effect on him. 'Perhaps we should buy a tankful for the Fuehrer. What is *that* fish?'

'A Butterfly fish,' said Romy.

'Must be a female,' said the General, trying for a joke, and the others all laughed, not wanting to spoil his effort to regain his good humour.

They went out into the zoo gardens again, moved towards the exit. Helmut held Melissa's hand as they walked behind his father and Romy. 'What have you decided after your talk?'

'I'm going to have a baby, Helmut.' Melissa felt as if she were two persons: one the composed girl giving a blunt but soft-voiced ultimatum, the other marvelling at the composure of this new Melissa Hayes. It was as if she were acting a part, though she knew that was not the case. 'No abortion or anything like that. I'll marry you if you ask me, but I'm not going to hold a gun at your head.'

'Hold a gun at my head?' Did lovers assassinate each other? 'Where did you get that expression?'

'I don't know – it just slipped out. From some film, I suppose. But you know what I mean. If you marry me, I'll stay here in Germany. If not, I'll go home to England and you won't ever hear from me again.'

'You can't stay here! We'll be married –' Out of the corner of his eye he saw a monkey hurl itself off a ring; he caught his breath, waiting for it to crash to its doom; it caught another ring and sailed on across the cage. 'But you'll have to go back to England.'

'No.' She shook her head determinedly but without fuss. She wanted to tell him how she could not bear to be parted from him, but she was learning restraint. *Let him make all the concessions*, Romy had advised.

He took a deep breath, swung off another ring, just like the monkey: 'We'll be married, then. You can go and live with my father outside Hamburg. It will be safe there.' He could only hope that his father, too, would be safe after Wednesday. Perhaps the assassin, whoever he was, would be shot

248

dead before he could be tortured to name the others in the plot. 'War is going to be declared –'

'How can you be so sure?' For a moment she lost her composure.

But he had no answer: the feeling in one's bones is no evidence. They came out into the street. Romy had not brought her Horch; she and the General had come by taxi. Helmut offered to drive them back to their hotel, said he would go and bring the Opel back from where he had parked it.

'I'll come with you,' said his father and the two of them walked off.

'What did he say?' said Romy.

'He will marry me.'

'You don't look ecstatic.'

'I'm still not sure if he loves me. But I'll take the chance. He wants me to go and stay with his father outside Hamburg. Would that be wise?'

'Why not? It's a beautiful estate. If war comes, I'll be there, too. I shall leave my husband –'

'Aren't you afraid of the scandal?' She had come to realize that Romy and the General had positions that she could never hold in German society. Not even if she became Helmut's wife.

'If war comes there will be too much else to talk about.'

Three hundred yards away, in a side street, Helmut and his father got into the Opel. It was warm in the car and Helmut wound down the windows, sat for a moment waiting for the hot air to escape. He looked at his father who, despite his stiff collar and dark jacket, looked as cool as he always did.

'Tell me, Father – how are you going to kill Hitler? With a bomb or with a bullet?'

'With a bullet. A high-velocity rifle with a telescopic sight.'

'Who's the marksman?'

'I am,' said Kurt von Albern.

# 3

*Extracts from the diaries of Dr Paul Joseph Goebbels:*

28 August 1939:

Yesterday (Sunday) the Fuehrer called a secret meeting of the Reichstag in the Chancellery. Secret up to a point, that is; everyone in Berlin must have known about it within half an hour of its finishing. All the Reichstag hacks were there; how galling it is that they are necessary. The so-called democracies are failing because governments have to go through the motions of paying heed to dunderheads; we must not allow it to happen to the Fatherland.

They appeared as much impressed by their surroundings as by the Fuehrer's message to them. The Chancellery was designed by Speer, on the Fuehrer's orders, to show off the grandeur and power of the Reich. It was meant to impress visiting heads of state (Mussolini has nothing to equal it) and diplomats, but nothing is ever lost by impressing one's own underlings.

. . . I must confess I do not like the approach to the reception hall, through that seemingly interminable gallery. One hundred and fifty metres long! Speer should be designing autobahn tunnels.

The Fuehrer's message was an uplifting one that spurred the Reichstag to the task that lies ahead. But he looked grey and tired; he carries such a tremendous burden for us all. He has been bitterly disappointed by the cowardly reluctance of Il Duce to back Germany when we go to war; the Italian leader (*leader?*) says that only in the case of Poland starting hostilities will he bring Italy into war. He has sent the Fuehrer a shopping list that makes us wonder why we ever considered him a partner. Seven million tons of petroleum, six million tons of coal, two million tons of steel, one million tons of timber – the list goes on and on. He must believe in the fable of loaves and fishes . . .

Unless there is a last-minute change of mind by the Poles, war is set to begin at dawn on Friday, 1 September. The Fuehrer, however, did not include this information in his speech. The messenger boys do not have to know the content of the message.

. . . Before going to the meeting Magda and I had lunch at the Klatt villa. I should not have gone, except that Heidi Klatt told us that Cathleen O'Dea had been invited. Against my better judgement, I went; I could not resist the temptation to see her again. Why does she attract me so? Is it because she teases me so?

I had to endure watching a tennis match between two oafs, Nicky Klatt and the Australian journalist Carmody. The Australian allowed Klatt to win and did it with more subtlety than one expected from such a nation of clodhoppers. If it comes to war with England, will the Australians, foolishly believing in the ties of Empire, join up? The Kaiser once had territorial aims in the Pacific, but would we need to bother now?

Watching the tennis match, my foot ached again, as it always does when I have to witness any physical sport. Is it any wonder that I am interested only in intellectual sports? Did Byron and Talleyrand, with their crippled feet, feel as I do?

. . . A busy day today (Monday). I have to get Germany into the right frame of mind for what lies ahead. There has been grumbling at the introduction of rationing; this subversion, even if innocently meant, must be stopped. One wonders why the grumblers did not plan ahead and put stocks away while they were available. One can be sure that the Jews who are still here have done so . . .

Which brings me to this late note, written after I had closed the diary for the night. I took it out of my desk again to enter this item: The missing American woman, Mady Hoolahan, has been traced. She is in Ravensbrueck, a proper place for her. She is a Jew . . .

Has the O'Dea woman been trying to make a fool of me? . . .

## 4

*Extracts from the memoirs of General Kurt von Albern:*

. . . Had the meeting been under different circumstances I may have had a different reaction to Helmut's predicament with Miss Hayes. As it was, her being pregnant and his seeming concern at my feelings towards the situation hardly mattered against the other, more important problems filling my every thought. Domestic matters assume their proper proportion when weighed against the crises of one's country.

Miss Hayes was a pleasant young thing, one I doubt I should have noticed in the ordinary course of events; though Romy told me the girl had more strength and courage than was apparent on the surface. Perhaps she was intimidated by me; as I have grown older I have tended to be less attentive to women. Except, of course, to Romy . . . I suppose there had always been in the back of my mind the thought that Helmut would some day bring home a girl like Miss Hayes; an actress. I, and his mother, had naturally hoped he would marry into his own class; perhaps I was living in the past, though, with Romy, I had fallen in love with a woman from my own class. Helmut, however, had chosen Miss Hayes; or she had chosen him; or perhaps Fate, or whatever it is that makes women fall pregnant, had chosen them both. I doubted that they were made for each other, but disparate elements occasionally produce an amalgam that is effective. One sees it in the army . . .

Miss Hayes had one thing in her favour; she was English. I had, and still have, an affinity for the English, despite all their faults and prejudices. We fought a bitter war against them only a generation ago, yet we are linked in strange ways, as if history were having a joke at our mutual expense. The patron saint of Germany, St Boniface, was an Englishman; the present royal family of England came from German stock. A throne for a throne, though religion and royalty nowadays are not, as the financiers say, blue chip stocks . . . Helmut might have chosen an Italian or a French girl to have an affair with; *then* the situation would have been intolerable. As it was, I think now that my behaviour was intolerable. I gave no thought or help to Helmut and his young lady. I should have been, at least, more sympathetic to both of them. Instead, I left that to Romy . . .

. . . I had prepared myself mentally for the assassination of Hitler. Young assassins, generally, are fanatics; no mental preparation is necessary, just an emotional one. I have always tried to control my emotions; an emotional soldier is a walking wounded before any shot is fired. The assassination plan was a military one and I approached it with that frame of mind. Casualties (or rather, a casualty) were allowed for; but if Hitler's death meant my death, then it would have been worth the victory. There is more than one battlefield on which one can die for one's country . . .

. . . I am well aware of the contradictions in the German character. Christianity, as Heine said, is the moderating factor in the German psyche; we like to think we are the most Christian of European nations. Yet the wildness of the warriors of the pagan gods lies there beneath our surface and we take pride in it; Wagner knew it. What I was planning I saw as a Christian act; a sinful one but not a pagan one . . .

Hans von Gaffrin had been in contact for some time with men in London sympathetic to our hatred of Hitler and Nazism. I should never have accepted them as accomplices in our planned action; that would have been traitorous. Am I splitting hairs? Perhaps; but conscience, too often, is composed of split hairs . . .

The English had told Hans of a suggestion put to them by their military attaché in Berlin. They had rejected the suggestion, though they gave Hans no reason for the rejection; the English mind can be so devious that it was impossible to guess at the complex reasons for not carrying out the idea. It was simple enough: to shoot Hitler from a virtually undetectable ambush, in the flat of the London *Times* correspondent. The flat was now empty . . .

## Meanwhile elsewhere:

# WEST INDIES LEAD IN CRICKET

. . . Following on England's first innings' score of 352 in the 3rd Test at the Oval, the West Indies yesterday took their first innings' score to 6 wickets for 395 . . .

. . . Pressure on the pound sterling continued yesterday. The demand in London for gold for hoarding was active . . .

. . . A Brooklyn blinds manufacturer was yesterday indicted on charges of paying female employees 3 cents an hour instead of the legal minimum of 25 cents . . .

Letter to *The Times*:

Sir, – May I appeal to cartoonists to suspend during the present crisis the practice of making dachshunds the symbol of Nazism and Germany? This idea has produced the risk of thoughtless acts of cruelty against harmless little animals which are English by birth and often by generations of breeding . . .

NOTICE IS HEREBY GIVEN that Elisabeth Latzi is applying for naturalization as a British subject . . .

NOTICE IS HEREBY GIVEN that Otto van Pulsa is applying for naturalization as a British subject . . .

*There'll always be an England*

# ACTORS' AND STAGEHANDS' UNIONS AT WAR

## Broadway Theatres to Close

. . . Fighting between Soviet–Mongolian and Japanese Manchukuo troops on the frontiers of Outer Mongolia has now come to an end. Both sides have said they are interested only in peace . . .

# WHY GIRLS PREFER FACTORY LIFE

**'Training College for Matrimony' says Committee Report**

. . . In Event of War – To be let furnished, Kent cottage . . . Excellent ex-naval manservant, total exemption, remaining as part of rental . . .

. . . Germany beat Great Britain in the athletics contest at Cologne today before 60,000 spectators. Great Britain did not win a single event, but were cheered on by a contingent of 150 of their compatriots . . .

. . . MR JOHN COBB this week travelled in his Red Lion motor car on Bonneville Salt Flats, Utah, faster than any human being has done before on land. He drove one mile at 369.23 miles per hour.

# 42nd Street Trolleys Nearing Last Run

. . . The last trolley cars are scheduled to disappear soon from Manhattan and the Bronx . . .

# CHAPTER TEN

## 1

Monday had been a busy day for Carmody, as it had been for all the other correspondents; a continual round of the government offices and the principal embassies. Coming out of the American embassy opposite the Chancellery, Carmody paused to look at the queue waiting to get into the consular office. There was no mistaking who most of them were: they were the Jews, marked by the yellow star on their clothing, who had somehow managed to survive by remaining in Germany. He had heard that they were arriving from all over the country, desperate at last to obtain American visas and be gone from the persecution they had endured and which they knew would become worse if war broke out. They stood there in the long queue that stretched down the street and round the corner, quiet and fearful, their eyes alight with a frantic hope that made some of them look as if they were drugged. Some had even brought their luggage with them, as if they expected instant freedom. He wondered how many of them had exit permits, but decided not to ask: he did not want to discourage them by raising another hurdle.

On the other side of the street half a dozen uniformed police watched the queue; four men in civilian suits, Gestapo written all over them, strolled up and down in a parody of government clerks out for a breath of fresh air. One of the Gestapo men suddenly broke away from his companions and crossed the road; the queue shivered like a long kite's tail caught in a breeze and pressed in against the wall of the embassy. The Gestapo man said something to one of the Jews in the queue, a tall man with a pronounced stoop; the man seemed to stoop even lower as he was approached, as if his height had always been a handicap to him. The Gestapo officer said something to him, the man replied politely, then the secret policeman went back to rejoin his companions. The queue straightened up, seemed to stiffen, as if wire had been threaded into the kite's tail.

Carmody was about to turn away when he saw Fred Doe on the inside of the queue, leaning up against the embassy wall. He had pushed through the queue before he thought of the possible consequences: he was exposing Doe to the watchful eyes on the other side of the road. 'Fred – what are you doing here?'

Doe did not seem to mind that Carmody had found him. He smelled of drink and looked as if he had not slept for days; he had a grey stubble of beard and his eyes were red-rimmed. He was carrying his cornet-case. 'Hi, pal. You heading for the old USA, too? Join the line, pal. *Give me your tired, your poor* . . . I oughta blow a few notes on that one.'

'But why are you out here in this queue? You're an American citizen aren't you?'

'Sure.' Those near them in the queue were listening, but in the politest way: ears pinned back, but eyes studiedly looking elsewhere. 'But I've lost my passport – some sonofabitch stole it. Well, maybe he wasn't a sonofabitch. Who could blame him? You think I could blame any of these people here if they took it?'

'But you could walk straight into the embassy. There's a desk in there for American citizens – I just passed it.'

'I know, pal. I was here yesterday. But I gotta get in the front door first – once I'm in there I'm okay. You dunno what officialdom can be like, pal. Some of those jerks in the embassy have been in this country too long – they gotta do things the German way.' The listening ears seemed to twitch; some eyes swung round to look at this American who was endangering them all by being so outspoken. Doe gave them a polite but wan smile. 'I'll be okay, pal. I'll play *The Stars and Stripes Forever* –' He patted the cornet-case. 'It's the bullies I gotta worry about.'

He looked past Carmody and the latter turned his head. 'You mean those blokes over there? The Gestapo?'

'They picked me up yesterday morning, kept me all day. They know I've been refused an exit permit.'

'Why?'

'Something about I been living here for eight years, they gotta check I ain't been a communist or a Jew-lover –' Heads turned this time and he gave them the same wan smile. 'Once I got my passport, they'll be glad to be rid of me.'

'If there's anything I can do to help –' There was nothing he could possibly do: the words had a sourer taste than usual when he uttered such hypocrisies.

'There's nothing, pal. Thanks all the same. How's it going with you?'

He meant with Cathleen. 'Okay, but there's still a long way to go.'

'There always is, pal. Ask any of these people.' He looked up and down the long queue; his eyes filled with pain. 'Jesus, what's gonna happen to them if –'

*If they don't get American visas:* don't say it, thought Carmody. But some of those in the queue understood English; what was worse, they understood unspoken thoughts. They looked at Doe as if he had condemned them, had torn their hopes out of them and crushed them beneath his heel.

Carmody shook Doe's hand, wished him luck and turned away quickly. As he walked down past the queue he saw, out of the corner of his eye, the Gestapo man crossing the road towards him. His first instinct was to quicken his pace; somehow he held himself back. The secret policeman caught up with him, put his hand on his arm.

'May I see your papers?'

Carmody took out his passport and press card, said nothing. He was aware of the queue contracting, moving away from him, squeezing in on itself, disowning him. Maybe *I* should be wearing the yellow star, he thought. Or even carrying a leper's clapper-bell.

'Why were you talking to Herr Doe, the American?'

'I was saying goodbye to him. He has often entertained me at the Hotel Adlon. He is a very good musician.'

The Gestapo officer, young and muscular and eager, built

for climbing mountains or promotion ladders, hesitated: so far he had not arrested any foreigners whose papers were in order. 'All right, you may go. But be careful, Herr Carmody.'

'Naturally,' said Carmody, took back his papers and went on his way. The freedom-seekers in the queue looked at him without sympathy: he had raised the temperature of the watchers on the other side of the street.

He went back to his office, wrote a despatch and phoned it through to London. 'Henderson is still talking to Chamberlain and Halifax,' said London. 'They say he's flying back to Berlin tonight. You'd better stay awake.'

'I never sleep,' said Carmody, wondering why ambassadors couldn't keep office hours.

At seven o'clock he rang Cathleen at her flat. 'I'm pooped,' she said. 'Karl Braun is rushing to finish the picture. We put ten minutes of film in the can today, including a musical number. It's like working for Monogram or Republic. How's it with you?'

'I'm buggered, darl. I feel as if I could sleep for a week. But I've got to go over to the British embassy, hang around there. The ambassador is on his way back from London – he's seeing Hitler some time tonight. I'll ring you tomorrow.'

'No, I'll call you at your office. I've got a seven o'clock call in the morning. Goodnight, honey. I love you.'

He would apply for an American visa first thing tomorrow, go back to America with her . . . 'Have you heard anything from our friends?'

'Nothing. I'm getting desperate.'

'Don't,' he said gently. He did not want her going back to Goebbels. 'Leave it in their hands.'

It was one o'clock in the morning before he got to bed. Sir Nevile Henderson had been to see Hitler, had been received by an SS guard of honour and a roll of drums; diplomats have to be honoured, even possible enemy ones, because one never knows when they will be required again as friends. When the ambassador returned to the embassy, looking exhausted and, at last, disillusioned, it was announced there would be no press announcement. The correspondents went home to bed wondering why they bothered to try to save the world. Didn't the diplomats know the power of the press?

Carmody was back at the office at nine on Tuesday morning. Fräulein Luxemburg had taken to scratching off the dates on the calendar with big red crosses; up till two weeks ago she had marked the passing days with just thin blue lines. Today was 29 August: he wondered what sort of mark she would make on the day war was declared.

Cathleen rang at 9.30. 'I've heard from our friends!' Her excitement trembled down the line. 'They want to see us tonight.'

'Where? The usual place?' Then he said hastily, conscious that his line might be tapped: 'No, don't tell me. Meet me at the Adlon at seven.'

The rest of the day was another round of walking and waiting in government departments and embassies. The correspondents knew that they were waiting to write more than news stories, that what they sent over the wires and the phones might be history: they would be instant Gibbons, Trevelyans, Bryces, and de Joinvilles. But news can be chased or whipped up; history makes its own pace. The principal figures in the drama kept their counsel, pushing the world to the brink in secret.

At seven o'clock Carmody walked into the bar of the Adlon to find Cathleen waiting for him. They kissed, walked out of the bar, through the lobby and into the street. Carmody did not look up at the sky this time; instead he looked right, left and across the street. He could see no sign of Lutze, Decker or anyone else who might have been sent to follow him.

'Where do we go?'

'To the Tiergarten. They'll be by the big goldfish pond.' He could feel the excitement in her, like a fever. 'Oh God, I hope they've got good news!'

He wanted to tell her not to raise her hopes too high: instead, he just pressed her hand. 'Let's say a couple of Hail Marys on the way over.'

The Langs were waiting for them by the big pond. The gardens were not crowded, though there were strollers on all the paths and most of the benches were occupied. A few people were in a hurry, office or shop workers taking a short cut home; a pair of policemen walked sedately with a curiously similar flatfooted step, like uniformed ducks. Real ducks floated on the pond and overhead a wedge-shaped flight of them headed somewhere for their night's lodgings. The Langs were feeding some mallards as Carmody and Cathleen approached them.

'Perhaps you would like to throw some crumbs?' Inge Lang handed a paper bag to Cathleen.

Cathleen began to toss bread upon the waters. 'I hope you have good news?'

'I think so,' said Lang. He looked relaxed, but Carmody noticed that, without moving his head, his eyes were constantly on the alert. Carmody at once began to scout the paths, but he could see no one who appeared to be watching them. 'We can get your mother out of Ravensbrueck.'

'Oh . . .' Cathleen's hand quivered; the ducks were showered with manna. 'How? When?'

'It will cost money – certain people have to be paid.'

'How much? It doesn't matter – I'll pay whatever they ask –'

'Five thousand dollars in American currency.'

'Mightn't that be hard to get?' said Carmody.

Lang shrugged. 'I don't know. It would be difficult, almost impossible for a German, I should think. But Fräulein O'Dea is an American . . . Did you bring in American money when you came here?'

'Yes. But not five thousand dollars . . . It doesn't matter. I'll get it. I have a large account at the bank – all my salary has gone in there –'

'Why do they want American currency?' said Carmody.

'They are people old enough to remember what happened to the mark after the last war. If Germany goes into another war, who knows what will happen to the mark? One can't blame them for being so demanding, Herr Carmody. I can remember when the dollar was worth four billion marks – it didn't buy enough food to feed a family. Inge's father shot himself for the sake of a few dollars.'

261

Inge Lang nodded. 'We are fortunate, Herr Carmody, to find someone who does have that sort of memory. One wouldn't be able to bribe any of the young officials.'

'I guess so,' said Carmody resignedly, but it went against the grain. Not against the grain of his thriftiness but against having to pay any sort of bribe for a person's life. I'm still naïve and innocent, he thought; this would never happen in the bush back home. But, of course, there were no concentration camps in the bush back home . . . 'We'll get the money somehow. When do you want it?'

'As soon as possible. Tomorrow, at the latest. If your mother can't be got out by Thursday, Fräulein, it will be at least another month before we can try again. By then it may be too late.'

'That's sudden,' said Cathleen; she was tossing crumbs at the ducks as if they were starving. 'What if the bank wants more time? Why must it be so quick?'

'We don't know how the system works,' said Lang. 'Our contacts gave us the day and the price. If the terms can be met, your mother will be here in Berlin on Thursday.'

'I'll get the money!' Cathleen hurled the last of the bread at the ducks, who ducked as if they had been sprayed with shrapnel. 'I'll be here tomorrow at lunch-time, twelve o'clock.'

A thought struck Carmody, the devil's advocate. 'What about papers?'

'I'm afraid they will be your responsibility, yours and Fräulein O'Dea's. Normally we would have supplied those, but our man was picked up by the Gestapo on Sunday – we haven't heard from him since –'

Inge Lang screwed up her empty paper bag, put it in her handbag. With a detached part of his mind Carmody watched her: she may be Jewish, he thought, but she's a German, neat and tidy, no matter what. 'He has left his wife and four children behind. Now we have to get them out somehow, find papers for them.'

'How did he get the papers for you?'

'They were forged,' said Lang. 'Passports were stolen, usually from dead persons, and altered.'

'And exit permits?'

'He had a stock of government paper – Why do you ask?' Lang suddenly was suspicious. 'You are not going to write a story about this?'

'Of course not,' said Carmody angrily. His mind had never worked so fast: 'If I could find a forger, just for this one case, could you get us a passport and some of the paper?'

Lang hesitated; but his wife said, 'Yes. We'll give them to Fräulein O'Dea when she brings the money. Here, at noon.'

She put her arm in her husband's and off they went, married life-savers.

Cathleen screwed up her paper bag, dropped it at her feet: an American, thought Carmody. He took her arm and they began to walk back through the Tiergarten. He chose a different route from the one by which he had come; if the Gestapo were trailing him and Cathleen, he wanted to make it as difficult as possible for them. He chose one of the narrow paths that wound through the trees and shrubs; there was a certain peace here in the sun-dappled shade. They passed a monument to four composers: Beethoven glared at them stonily. They came to a bend in the path; a man stood there before them, mouth open in a tremendous shout. Cathleen clutched Carmody's arm; he tensed, waiting for other Gestapo thugs to burst out of the bushes in answer to their colleague's shouted warning. Then the shout turned into a strangled note of music, died away.

The man, young and plump, smiled apologetically. 'I am sorry I startled you. I am practising. I have an audition at the Opera this afternoon.'

Cathleen recovered. 'Good luck. What are you auditioning for?'

'Anything they offer me.'

He raised his hat as they walked on. When they had gone round the next bend in the path they heard him start up again. Neither of them knew much about opera. So they did not recognize the song: it was Parsifal telling the knights of the Holy grail that he is their King. The young tenor was playing safe: one could not go wrong with Wagner, not this week.

'He's an optimist,' said Carmody. 'He should be auditioning for the army.'

He heard a sound and looked up at the yellow sky. Three planes went over, coming from the east and disappearing towards the west.

Cathleen noted the direction of their flight. 'Is that a good sign? Are they bringing them back?'

'Maybe they're just decoys. Or maybe they're getting a head-start on bombing Paris or London.' He was heavy with despondency.

'Don't talk like that!'

'Sorry.' He changed the subject, to one about which he felt little more hope: 'Can you get the money?'

'I'll get it,' she said fiercely. 'It's the papers that worry me –'

'I'll get those,' he said and realized there was no time to be lost. 'I have to go looking for someone.'

'Who?'

'An organ-grinder. I'll put you in a taxi.'

'I was hoping you'd come with me, stay the night. I don't want to be alone tonight – I won't be able to sleep.'

He was tempted; but there were things to do. 'I'll try and get there. It may be late –'

'I'll be awake.'

They came out opposite the Brandenburg Gate and an empty taxi, as if waiting for them to appear, cruised by. Carmody hailed it, put Cathleen into it, and sent her on her way. Then he stood looking across at the tall symbolic gateway with its twelve Doric columns. Did Kreisler, the hurdy-gurdy man, ever come here to play his tunes? Where did you go looking for an organ-grinder at eight o'clock at night in a city of almost three million people? He had never seen Kreisler anywhere but in the Ludwigstrasse and then only about once or twice a month; he had no idea where else he might grind out his tunes. In the quiet back streets where children played, outside the Opera House, along the Friedrichstrasse or the Kurfürstendamm?

Profligate to the point of pain, he hailed a taxi and went cruising. Yes, the taxi driver knew the *Leierkastenmann*, but

264

he had no regular pitch; he played all over the city. They drove all over the city centres, up and down the Friedrich-strasse, the Unter den Linden, round the Potsdamerplatz and Alexanderplatz, up and down the Kurfürstendamm. It was there, on that garishly lit street, on their second trip up and down, that Carmody saw the hurdy-gurdy man come out of a side street. Carmody got out of the taxi, paid the fare, which seemed to him a down payment on the taxi, and walked back to Kreisler.

He had set up his organ outside the Café Kranzler, was playing *The Sidewalks of New York* to the crowd at the tables on the café terrace. The monkey was dancing, lethargically and with a tired, abstracted look on its tiny face, like the look Carmody had seen in photos of marathon dancers in the Depression.

'Good evening, Herr Carmody. Do you like my happier tune? A neutral one, nothing about Warsaw or Paris or London.'

'It's better than the ones you've been playing over on Ludwigstrasse.'

'Ah, but that's a different audience there. These people are what Berliners like to think they really are – carefree, cynical, not interested in the Fatherland. See how approving they look?' The drinkers and diners at the tables did, indeed, look as if they approved his choice of music; they were smiling, nodding their heads to the melody, some even looking as if they wished they were walking the sidewalks of New York. 'You have to know your audience, Herr Carmody.'

'Could I talk business with you?'

'You want to hire me for a party? A moment, please, while I collect their appreciation . . .' The tune came to an end. He left his hurdy-gurdy and, with the monkey resting on his arm with a cup held in its paw, he moved along the railing of the terrace, raising his hat politely as his audience dropped coins and notes into the tin cup. He came back to Carmody, stuffing the money into his pocket. 'They are giving more than pfennigs this last week. They are throwing their money away, as if it doesn't have any value any more. What did you want to see me about?'

'Let's get out of this traffic.' The pavement was crowded, but Carmody was not afraid of being overheard by any of the passers-by; he was more afraid of the exposure from the illuminations of the thoroughfare itself. The Kurfürstendamm was said to have the brightest lights in Europe: it was like standing on a brilliantly-lit stage. He had no way of knowing that Lutze or Decker was not in the audience. 'Let's go down here.'

He led the way down the side street, paused in the doorway of a shoe store closed for the night. Kreisler parked his hurdy-gurdy by the kerb, put the monkey back on his chain, and came across to join Carmody in the doorway. He did not seem surprised or puzzled that their meeting was taking on a clandestine air.

'You don't want me for a party, Herr Carmody,' he said flatly.

'No. I want you to do some forging for me.'

Kreisler laughed softly, took out a cigarette and lit it. He coughed after the first puff hit his chest. 'They'll kill me eventually . . . I'm out of practice, Herr Carmody. I haven't done anything like that in years.'

'I'll pay you well, whatever you ask.' It was Cathleen's money he was throwing around, but he would pay it out of his own pocket if needs be. 'I want a passport and an exit permit. I can get you the necessary paper forms for the permit – we may have a bit of trouble getting a passport for you to fix.'

'We?' He coughed again, hit his chest again. Over by the hurdy-gurdy the monkey also coughed, a tiny echo, and Kreisler smiled at it and made a clicking noise with his tongue.

'The only name I'm going to give you will be the one on the passport and on the permit. Will you do the job?'

Kreisler drew on his cigarette, then blew out smoke; there was no cough this time. 'How soon?'

'Thursday evening at the latest. I have to get photographs – I can't get those till the person we're helping arrives in Berlin.'

'Someone from one of the camps, eh?' He knew the

system, didn't query it; he had been in Sachsenhausen. 'How much will you pay?'

'Do you want marks or American dollars?'

Kreisler smiled, his thin face masked by a net of lines. 'Someone has talked to you about inflation? I remember it, too. Dollars, Herr Carmody. One thousand dollars.' He looked at Carmody craftily; over by the kerb the monkey turned its head to look at them, as if it understood they were talking big money. 'It's a big risk.'

'It's a big price,' said Carmody, shocked at it. But he wasn't going to bargain, not with someone else's life at stake: 'Righto, a thousand dollars. You'll get half when I bring you the passport and paper and the photographs, the other half when you deliver. We can trust each other?'

Kreisler dropped his cigarette, ground it out with his shoe. 'I think it's only people at our low level, Herr Carmody, who *can* trust each other.'

That was good enough for Carmody; they shook hands. 'Come to my office Thursday evening, six o'clock.' He gave the address on the Potsdamerplatz. 'Can you leave your organ and the monkey at home?'

Kreisler smiled again. 'I know how to be inconspicuous, Herr Carmody. One never forgets that, when you've had the Gestapo chasing you '

## 2

Helmut was chasing the future, trying to catch sight of its face. 'If we only knew what was going to happen –'

'I'm going to have our baby,' said Melissa. 'That's what's going to happen.'

She was neither worried nor complacent: just common-sensible. Motherhood matures a woman, so they say, forgetting all the mothers who abandon their children because the last thing they want is to be thought *mature*. She was planning the immediate future, mapping out the months ahead;

267

perhaps that she was to bear a general's grandson had given her a sense of strategy. She had decided to accept Helmut's proposal of marriage, even at a discount. Half a love was better than none, especially when you were pregnant.

'I'm a Catholic,' said Helmut, not wishing to put obstacles in the way, just hoping to put things off.

'I'm Church of England, but it doesn't matter. I never went to church, anyway.'

He didn't go, either; but he decided now was not the time for confession. 'We'll be married as soon as you like –'

'Tomorrow?'

No, not tomorrow. 'I can't – Father has some business to attend to – I want him and Romy at the wedding –'

'So do I. Well –' She sat with her hands in her lap, composed, patient. Dammit, he thought, she already looks *motherly*.

'We'll arrange it as soon as possible. I have to find a priest who will marry us without all the business about the banns – that takes time –'

He had come here to her flat on his way home from the studio. He had thought of her during the day, but only in odd moments; to be fair to himself, he told himself, he had thought of his father, too, only in odd moments. Karl Braun, almost hysterical in his haste to finish the film, had demanded more camera set-ups than Helmut had ever done even in two days' shooting; the crew had griped, but, well-trained and responsive to Helmut if not to Braun, they had done their job. At the end of the day Helmut felt he had been shooting half a dozen episodes of an old-time serial.

'Take your time,' said Melissa; then leaned forward, took his face in her hands and kissed him. 'Don't *worry*, Helmut. We'll work it out.'

'I hope so,' he said, and was a little surprised that he meant it.

When he had gone Melissa got up and went to the window and looked out across the drab rooftops. Her flat faced east, towards England, Bradford and home; but she felt no homesickness. She wondered what her parents would think of her situation; it would probably be beyond her mother's comprehension. Pregnant to a *German*, determined to stay on in *Germany* even if war came ... She could imagine her mother's shame, trying to explain *that* to her friends. Her father would say nothing, other than to write her one of his usual short letters in which he would say that he would try to understand, but in which it would be obvious that he was utterly bewildered. He would end by saying he was about to go over to Leeds to see Hutton bat, *Love, Dad*. It was a pity parents were so necessary, though she did love them. Then she thought that soon, in another seven months, she, too, would be a parent and necessary. Then she began to weep, not with joy but with fear.

Helmut drove into Berlin to the Hotel London in Wilmersdorf. It was a modest establishment, solid, neat, well-run; but a hotel more for captains and majors than for generals. It did not run to suites, just to large airy rooms furnished to stand the test of time and the conservative tastes of regular guests from out of town. It was not a hotel for assignations, or if it was, it was, in hunting terms, a well-camouflaged hide.

General von Albern and Romy von Sonntag had adjoining rooms with a connecting door. Helmut went up to his father's room because the hotel's small lobby was no place for the discussion he wanted to have with his father. Romy came into the room through the connecting door, sat down on the bed already turned down for the night. Helmut, looking at the bed where his father and Romy probably made love, was suddenly embarrassed and wished he had suggested to his father that they should go for a walk.

'Everything is ready,' said the General. 'We are just waiting on word from Hans.'

'Father, are you sure you're the one for the job? It's something for a professional sniper –'

'Where does one hire a professional sniper for such a task?'

'Your father can do it,' said Romy. 'We drove out into the country today – your father wanted to test the gun. His shooting was marvellous, on target all the time.'

'The telescopic sight makes it easy,' said the General modestly. 'Don't *worry*, Helmut . . .'

Don't *worry*: he heard an echo of Melissa's voice. 'What sort of gun is it?'

His father produced a small case, opened it. A rifle, broken down into two pieces, and a telescopic sight were fitted into slots in the felt-lined case. 'A Mannlicher – I used one like this on safari in Africa ten years ago. This particular gun is a beautiful model, a pleasure to shoot. It will give me double pleasure tomorrow.' For a moment he sounded almost sadistic, which he was not.

He stood admiring the rifle, remembering happier times for hunting. He had been a noted shot, always welcome in hunting parties; Goering had twice invited him to go shooting boar with him, but he had coldly but politely declined. In his mind's eye now he could see himself, after killing Hitler, bringing this gun to bear on Goering, a prize boar. It was a Mannlicher-Schoénauer $7 \times 57$ mm fitted with a detachable 4-power Zeiss telescope. The Mannlicher had been a prized gun with hunters for years; he remembered that President Theodore Roosevelt had used a $6.5 \times 54$ mm, a favourite he used to call 'my meat rifle'. Tomorrow the Mannlicher would be used in the cause of justice: an Austrian gun to execute an Austrian upstart.

'Are you going alone to this Englishman's flat?'

'Yes.'

Helmut sighed, like a parent deciding that his son had to be protected from himself. 'I'm coming with you.'

'No!' The objection came from Romy; her hand twisted the neat sheets of the bed. 'You must let your father do this himself –'

'It doesn't matter, darling,' said the General. 'I'll be delighted to have him with me. More than that – *proud*.'

Helmut felt he had just been recruited into his father's regiment. He had always, to his father's great disappointment and sometimes anger, shied away from the militarism that had been the family tradition. The big house on the estate outside Hamburg was full of military memorabilia, of portraits of his father and grandfather and great-grandfather in dress uniform; anniversaries of battle victories had been toasted as if they were family birthdays. Sometimes he had felt he was living in a war museum, a museum dedicated to a past that, he suspected, even his father knew had gone forever. Now he had volunteered for a future place in the museum.

The phone rang and Romy, still sitting on the bed, picked up the bedside phone. She had to lean over to reach it and the action drew up her skirt, exposing the inside of a still firm and beautiful thigh. The mildly erotic sight made Helmut turn away as, once again, he saw her and his father in this bed.

'Yes?' Romy turned to Kurt von Albern. 'It's Hans.'

The General took the phone from her. 'Yes? . . . Yes, we can come at once. Is something wrong? . . . I'll bring someone – a new recruit. I'm sure you'll be pleased . . .'

Helmut, standing by the bedroom window, winced mentally when he heard the word *recruit*. 'Perhaps Hans won't be pleased –'

'Of course he will.' It was a long time since he had seen his father so bright-eyed. 'He wants us to meet him at Herr Burberry's flat.'

'Shall I come?' asked Romy.

'Of course. You are part of the unit – why shouldn't you see the place where we are going to make history?'

Oh God, thought Helmut, soon he will be waving battle flags. 'What are you going to do with the gun – leave it here in your room? What if one of the maids starts prying?'

'It's not that sort of hotel,' said Romy, as if Helmut was criticizing her own servants. 'I'll get my hat and gloves.'

*Of course, don't go anywhere out of uniform*: Helmut was cynical with despair.

'We'll go in my car. We don't want to advertise ourselves in the Horch.'

'I'll bring the gun,' said the General.

Twilight was deepening into night: it seemed to Helmut, his cameraman's eyes working subconsciously, that it was the ideal light for assassins setting out on a mission. But as they reached the Kurfürstendamm the last light in the sky faded, obliterated by the brilliance of the lights along the wide, busy street. He was glad when they reached the comparative gloom of the Unter den Linden. He parked the Opel in a side street and the three of them went back to the Unter den Linden.

Hans von Gaffrin, dressed in civilian clothes, stepped out from beneath one of the trees and came quickly towards them as they arrived outside the entrance to the building where Oliver Burberry had his flat. He already had the front-door key in his hand; he opened the door and they went into the discreetly lit hallway. Without saying a word he led them up the stairs to the top floor, paused and smiled at Romy while she got her breath, then opened the door to Burberry's flat and ushered them in.

Only then did he look at Helmut. 'I guessed it was you, from your father's voice. Welcome.'

'You don't mind?' Helmut said hesitantly.

'Not at all.' Then he turned to the General, held out the two keys. 'Take these now. The caretaker is usually somewhere at the front of the building during the day, but at night he's in his small flat at the back, on the ground floor. He gives information to the Gestapo and sometimes we have used him for the Abwehr. You will have to be careful.'

'Where did you get the keys?'

'We had them made. At one time Admiral Canaris had Herr Burberry under surveillance.'

The General was looking about the flat. 'Where is the bathroom?' He saw Helmut smile and for a moment looked puzzled; then he, too, smiled. 'It's not what you think – I don't want to use it. Not for that purpose anyway. It will be my sniper's position.'

'A moment, Kurt –' Hans von Gaffrin was reluctant to give his news; the General was keyed up, like a recruit on his first day at the rifle butts. 'Tomorrow is not the day, the ride to the Victory Column has been postponed.'

'Oh no!' said Romy and reached for the General's hand. 'After all our planning –'

'It has been postponed, I said – not cancelled. He is to address the Reichstag at the Opera House at ten o'clock on Friday morning. Then he will drive up the Unter den Linden, through the Gate and on to the Column.'

'Why the postponement?' The General looked angry, as if the Austrian ex-corporal had disobeyed orders.

'Poland is to be invaded at dawn on Friday. He will be celebrating the first victory of the next war.'

'Great God, that's what we're trying to prevent!'

The General stood stiffly for a moment, then all at once he sat down without looking behind him; fortunately, he fell into a chair. Romy held his hand, lifted it to her lips and kissed it. Gaffrin and Helmut stood silent, the one angry and disappointed at the foiling of their plan, the other relieved and yet afraid. Relieved that his father would now not have to go through with the dangerous attempt on Hitler's life, afraid of what the invasion of Poland would bring.

'We must still kill him,' said Romy, as if she were housekeeping. Women, Helmut thought, have a way of keeping their mind on one thing at a time. War could be attended to later. 'Then the army can withdraw from Poland –'

'Goering will take over,' said Gaffrin. 'He won't disappoint his Luftwaffe by withdrawing.'

'Romy is right.' The General had recovered; he stood up, ready to inspect the situation again. 'Let me see the bathroom.'

Gaffrin said nothing, but it seemed to Helmut that he gave the slightest shrug of his shoulders. He led the General down a narrow hall, leaving Helmut and Romy in the big living room.

'You mustn't try to talk him out of it,' Romy said, as if reading Helmut's thoughts. 'We're not callous or bloodthirsty or fanatical. It just has to be done, that's all. We can't allow Hitler and the stupid men around him to destroy Germany. That's what they'll do, you know. Destroy it.'

'I just wish there were some other way,' he said lamely.

'There isn't. How is Melissa?' she said, going on to less important things. 'You had better hurry up if you are going to marry her. We'll want to get her out of Berlin and back to The Pines before they start bombing the city.'

'The city? Berlin?' Somehow it had never occurred to him that bombs might fall here; they always fell on other cities. 'Yes. Yes, I suppose so. We have to find a priest –'

'I can arrange that. I know Cardinal Count Preysing here –' She would, he thought. There were advantages to belonging to his father's and her class, his own class. Things could be arranged that were beyond the reach of other, less well-born people. 'Saturday?'

'Yes. Yes, Saturday.' An assassination disposed of, a wedding to follow. 'I'll tell Melissa.'

His father and Gaffrin came back into the room, his father nodding with pleasure, a commander presented with ideal terrain in which to attack. 'The angle is acute, but it can be done. We are fortunate he will be driven up the far side of the street.'

'You can come back here late Thursday night, you won't be disturbed. The cleaning woman comes in Thursday morning.'

The General looked around him. 'I'll leave the gun here – it will be safest.'

'Put it in here,' said Romy, still housekeeping. She opened the front of a big, heavy sideboard. Inside were a range of crystal glasses and a dozen or more bottles of Scotch, gin and schnapps; Burberry had left a cache in case of his return. Romy moved the bottles and glasses aside. 'It will fit in there, at the back.'

The small case was hidden behind the bottles and glasses, the door of the sideboard closed. Then the four of them stood and looked at each other, suddenly left with nothing to do but wait.

But then Romy thought of something to do. 'Hans, drive Kurt back to the hotel, please. Helmut and I have something to arrange.'

'What?' said the General.

'A wedding. We're going to see the Cardinal.' She looked at her watch. 'He would not have gone to bed yet. It's only the priests, not the bishops, who have to get up early.'

She knew the nature of men. Or, like most women, thought she did.

Cathleen had a convenient headache – 'Shoot around me this morning, Karl, please. I'll be in this afternoon and I'll work through as long as you like. But this morning I just feel dreadful. I've got the curse.'

'All right, darling.' Braun was sympathetic. She had known directors in Hollywood who had thought actresses had no right to biological upsets. 'Can you make it by two o'clock?'

'Thanks, Karl,' she said and felt guilty at having to lie to him.

She was at her bank in the Uhlandstrasse when its doors opened. Carmody had called her late last night to say he would not be able to come and stay the night, that he had to sleep by his own phone: New York had now taken to calling him every couple of hours, disregarding the time difference between New York and Berlin. He had told her he had contacted someone who would do his best to provide them with forged papers, but the man wanted to be paid in American dollars. So now she had to ask for . . .

'Six thousand dollars in American currency, Fräulein? That's impossible.' The bank manager suffered from a surfeit of overhang: his hooked nose overhung his pendulous lips, his jowls overhung his collar, his great belly overhung his spindly legs; he looked like the various stages of a landslide. But he was a ladies' man, especially if the ladies were beautiful film actresses: 'I'd do anything to accommodate you, Fräulein O'Dea, but a branch of this size –' Hands like giant white starfish were spread palms upwards on his desk. 'It's just impossible.'

'What about your head office?'

'Ah yes, they may have it. But it would take time to have them transfer it to us – tomorrow morning, perhaps –'

'Herr Wanger, could you give me a letter? Tell them I am a valued client – I am, aren't I?'

'Oh, of course, of course! Most valued.' He was a jelly of adoration; he shook with worship. 'But they are so formal at head office – they know nothing of the personal relations we have with our clients –'

'Write me the letter, please, Herr Wanger.' She crossed her legs, gave him the view of the sensual instep. She had played the scene several times with Wallace Beery, Frank Morgan, Charles Butterworth: life now imitated art as Herr Wanger succumbed as had those actors. 'Thank you – you're a darling.'

When he gave her the letter five minutes later she wondered if she should kiss him, but decided against it, for fear that he would collapse in a sprawl of adulation on top of her. She hurried out of the office and caught a taxi for the bank's head office in Jägerstrasse in the Gendarmenmarkt. When she got out of the taxi she was instantly aware of the busy pedestrian traffic. Sober-suited men and uniformed messengers hurried by; six men stood in a tight group as if in a football huddle, then suddenly broke up and disappeared individually into the passing crowd. Cathleen had never been in a financial district before: when she had lived in New York, Wall Street had been too far downtown and, as far as she knew, Los Angeles had never had a financial district. So she was unsure whether this frenetic foot traffic was typical of the Gendarmenmarkt on any day or whether the political crisis had brought it on. As she gazed up at the bank's headquarters, a Gothic fortress, she wondered if anyone inside it would be interested in an American actress who wanted a packet of her own currency.

Someone was interested: the youngest of the six assistant managers. He, like Herr Wanger, was a ladies' man. He was handsome, a fact he obviously knew, and he had an eye for an instep and everything above it. When he gave Cathleen the six thousand dollars in American currency he also gave her his card.

'At any time you may wish to call, Fräulein O'Dea. Day or night.'

'I can't thank you enough, Herr Schrieber.' She gave him her hand to kiss, pursed her lips as if she might offer those at a later date. 'If I do need you –'

'Please call,' said the banker, writing off his wife and three children as bad debts.

It was too early to go to the Tiergarten to meet the Langs. Raised in New York and lately a resident of Los Angeles, she was not a natural walker; still, this morning she decided she would walk over to Carmody's office and felt virtuous at the thought of the unaccustomed exercise. The journey to Potsdamerplatz proved to be shorter than she expected, but in getting there she passed Goebbels' town residence. She paused on the opposite side of the street and looked at the attractive building, something she had not been able to do when the Reichsminister's car had delivered her there that first night. Well, she would not be going there again: she no longer needed the Reichsminister.

Carmody was in his office. They kissed, but only after he had closed the door on Fräulein Luxemburg: he wanted to protect her feelings. 'I'm sorry I couldn't come last night –'

'It was all right. I slept better than I expected. I have the money.' She gave him a thousand dollars in twenty-dollar bills. He put it in the office safe. 'Will you come with me to meet the Langs?'

As they went out of the office at a quarter to twelve he said to Fräulein Luxemburg, 'I'll be back at one, Olga. Don't stay if you have a lunch appointment.'

'I'll stay, Herr Carmody. Don't hurry.'

As they went downstairs Cathleen said, '*Olga?*'

'I finally got round to it,' he said almost sheepishly. 'I asked her first if she minded.'

'Did she?'

'It was as if I had proposed to her.' He shook his head. 'Christ, I wish I could do something for her!'

'You can't, darling. I knew women like her at MGM, in Wardrobe and the Story department. Something always stops them from getting a man – I don't know what, but *something*. They're lonely and I'd give up if I had their life, but somehow they keep going. Some of them last longer than us who think we're happy.'

'I hope so.' But he didn't sound hopeful for Olga Luxemburg.

277

They arrived by the goldfish pond in the Tiergarten at the same moment as the Langs. Envelopes were exchanged, money for papers. 'There is a German passport in there,' said Lang. 'We had some luck – a woman we know died yesterday. How old is your mother?'

'Forty-seven, forty-eight, I'm not sure.'

'Frau Dix was sixty-five. You will have to age your mother somehow to have her match the birth date in the passport. Unless –'

'Unless what?'

'Nothing.'

'Unless she's aged while she's been in the camp?' Cathleen could face the truth; though she hoped she would not have to.

Lang hesitated, then nodded. 'Treatment in the camps is very harsh.'

'Let's face that when we have Frau Hoolahan here in Berlin,' said Inge Lang. 'Because of the German passport you will now have to get an American visa besides the exit permit. Papers, papers . . .'

'The world would come to a halt without them,' said Lang with a smile: he worked in a government department.

'Perhaps the world should never have learned to read,' said Carmody.

'But then how would we have appreciated newspapers, Herr Carmody? Or Goethe or Schiller? There is always a price to pay.' He stuffed the envelope with the money in it into his jacket pocket. 'We shall be here with your mother, Fräulein, at noon on Thursday.'

He lifted his hat, his wife put her arm in his and off they went. Carmody looked after them. 'Is that what a hero and a heroine look like? I always thought they looked like Gary Cooper and Claudette Colbert.'

'Or like you and me,' said Cathleen and put her arm in his. 'Now I'd like to go somewhere and say a prayer.'

She and Willy Heffer put seven minutes of film in the can that Wednesday afternoon. None of the scenes was really good, but Karl Braun announced he was happy with them; it was as if he had decided that the film now was never going to be shown outside Germany and the home audiences could take or leave what was offered them. What the Reichsminister for Public Enlightenment and Propaganda might say was something he evidently was prepared to risk. If war broke out, enlightenment might come from something more devastating than a musical comedy film.

At four o'clock a messenger had arrived with a note for Cathleen asking her to have supper with the Reichsminister at ten that evening. Feeling virtuous for the second time that day, but this time to a greater degree, she scrawled a refusal on the bottom of the note, saying she was too busy filming. A little over an hour later the messenger was back with another note; he must have driven like a fury between Neubabelsberg and Berlin and back again. There was certainly fury in Goebbels' note.

'You misunderstand, Fräulein O'Dea. I am your employer and I wish to see you. The car will call for you at the studio at 9.30.' It was signed with his full signature this time, not just initials.

Cathleen debated whether to ring Carmody or not, then decided against it. She did not want to upset him, to make him jealous again. He had enough on his mind; she had already put too much of a burden on him. She would go and see Goebbels, obey his order, for that was what it was, and Sean need know nothing about the visit.

They finished shooting at 8.30. 'Only one more day, darlings,' said Karl Braun, limp all over, 'and that will wrap up our picture. I'm just *exhausted*.'

'The same here,' said Willy Heffer, showing the strains not

only of the strenuous schedule of the last few days but of thirty years of being a matinée idol. Character parts loomed ahead like skeletons in a grave. 'Oh, to play in a nice drawing-room comedy again.'

Cathleen bade them all goodnight, went to her dressing-room, had a bath, sent her dresser to Wardrobe to borrow a gown to wear for the evening. She had come out to the studio this afternoon wearing only slacks and a silk shirt, expecting to go straight back to her apartment again when she had finished work. If the Reichsminister was in the mood that his note suggested, he would not welcome her looking like Marlene Dietrich on her day off.

The dresser, a motherly woman who had once had non-speaking parts in silent movies, brought back a two-piece outfit in grey silk. 'Discreet but sexy, Fräulein.'

'We'll play up the discreet bit, Trudi, and forget about being sexy.'

'Yes, Fräulein,' said Trudi, who had enjoyed and still missed the Berlin of the 1920s and wondered why sex should be forgotten, especially for a Reichsminister.

Driving in through the warm evening Cathleen noticed the increased military traffic. When she was shown into Goebbels' presence in the house on Hermann Goeringstrasse the military traffic looked as if it was going to be a jam: he was in uniform. She knew all at once that the evening was going to be a battle.

He waited till the butler had gone, then he moved forward, took her hand and kissed it. But when he raised his eyes to hers, they were cold and his smile was thin and mocking. 'So you were too busy?'

'That's what you're paying me for, Herr Reichsminister,' she said in her best formal voice. 'To work.'

'Indeed I am, and your work has been very good. Herr Braun tells me you are easily the best part of the film. I am glad my choice was not an ill-chosen one.'

'I'm grateful you chose me.' The conversation sounded as if it were in splints.

They sat down at the small supper table. The menu was the same as last time; the procedure was the same, she eating hungrily, he ignoring his food. But he poured them both some champagne, raised his glass to her.

'Here's to Frau Hoolahan.' He wasted no time, coming straight to the dagger point.

The smoked salmon stuck in her chest as if, remembering something it had done when alive, it had decided to jump upstream. She played for time: 'You aren't playing any music this evening. No Mozart?'

'No. Nor Gershwin or any of those Jewish composers. Did you know Frau Hoolahan was a Jewess?'

'It's a joke!' She managed a disbelieving laugh, a good effort. 'With a name like that?'

'It is no joke.' He put down his glass; his movements were careful, as if he were trying to restrain himself from breaking out in a burst of temper. 'I do not like being made a fool of. She is Jewish, born here in Berlin –'

'But she had lived in America for so long –'

'How do you know how long she lived there? She is still a German citizen. I demand to know – did you know she was Jewish?'

'No.' The word was like scalding salt in her mouth.

He stared at her, then he relaxed, but only a little. 'It is just as well. It would have been a dangerous game for you to play.'

'Where is Frau Hoolahan?'

'In one of our rehabilitation camps. Where she will stay.'

'What had she done, to be sent there?'

'How would I know such a detail? I'm a Reichsminister, not some prosecutor or clerk.' He wondered sometimes at the intelligence of this American actress. Some actresses he had had affairs with were intelligent but, even if they were not, they had at least appreciated his rank and position. Perhaps things were different in the so-called democracies and Cabinet ministers were considered only equal to every Tom, Dick and Harry, whoever they were. 'The subject is closed, if you say you did not know she was a Jew.'

'What am I going to tell my friend when I get back to California?'

'Tell her she should have told you that Frau Hoolahan was a Jewess.'

281

Her mouth had been effectively shut. If she persisted in the subject she would only expose herself as being a Jewish sympathizer, at best; at worst, she might reveal that she knew more about Frau Hoolahan than she had so far confessed. Her mother was halfway to safety and his help, even if it had been forthcoming, was no longer necessary. Better not to wreck what the Langs had put in train.

'I'll do that.' Her throat was dry and her mouth, it seemed, still scalded; lies had been part of her life in Hollywood, part of the survival there, but she had never had to deny her own mother. She drank some of the champagne. 'This is beautiful. What is it?'

He looked at the bottle, noticing it for the first time. 'Krug 1934.'

'My favourite. But isn't it French?'

Ribbentrop, the ex-champagne salesman, had recommended it to his butler. 'Food and drink, I'm told, are international.' His mood was improving; he turned on the charm in his smile. 'Like films.'

'Are you going to show a picture tonight?' She hoped not; she was ready to fall asleep. The butler came in, put schnitzel in front of her and served her some vegetables.

He nodded. 'One I think you'll like.'

'Joseph, I'm very tired – really – we've been working so hard this week trying to finish the picture in time –'

'In time for what?' He knew, but he acted innocent. 'Don't worry yourself, Cathleen. This film will relax you. Now finish your supper.'

*Like a good girl.* She wanted to throw the schnitzel at him, to get up and storm out of the room and the house, telling him to go to hell and shove his films up his can. Instead, she did as she was told, gave her attention to her plate.

After coffee they went downstairs to the small drawing-room-cum-theatre. The lights went down as soon as they were seated and Leo the Lion came up on the screen at once, roaring at her like Louis B. Mayer. The film was *Anna Karenina*, with Garbo.

'My favourite film,' said Goebbels. 'The greatest actress there is on the screen.'

But his attention was not so rapt that he ignored Cathleen. The film had been running no more than twenty minutes when she felt his hand feeling for hers. She moved her hand, but, since a hand is attached to an arm on one side of the body, its area of escape is limited. She would have laughed in other circumstances; his hand chased hers all over her lap like a ferret after a timid rabbit. Finally he nailed her, literally: she felt his nails bite into her palm.

He was breathing heavily, though still watching the screen, like a man in a blue movie fleahouse. Garbo turned a reproachful eye on him; even Basil Rathbone looked down his long English nose at him. God, Cathleen thought, if Garbo does this to him, what would Jean Harlow do? But she knew the woman up on the screen had little to do with his arousal. He tried to draw her hand towards his own lap, but she resisted.

He suddenly relented and she let her arm relax; at once he plunged both their hands into the bottom of her lap, between her thighs. She did laugh then, a little hysterically; she was too tired to be really amused. She stood up, still trying to extricate her hand from his; she was right in the middle of the projector's beam and Fredric March, another lecher, was all over her. She wrenched her hand free, feeling his nails scratch her so that she cried out, and stumbled out of the room. Garbo looked soulfully after her, but offered no comfort.

Outside in the hall she paused, trying to compose herself. She looked at her hand, saw the bloody scratches on it. She turned back to the door to the drawing room, waiting for him to appear; she wanted to scream at him, throw all caution to the winds of her anger and revulsion of him. But he did not appear. She heard the screen voices, then the slamming of a door and music; but heard and saw nothing of him. He was staying with Garbo, whom he could adore at a safe remove, who would never reject him.

She heard a movement behind her and spun round. The butler, short like his employer but more dignified, stood there with her wrap. 'Shall I call the car, Fräulein?'

'No. No, I'll get a taxi.'

The butler nodded, led her towards the door and opened it

283

for her. Then he whispered, 'Do take the car, Fräulein O'Dea. The Reichsminister won't know. It will be back before the film ends.'

'He will stay in there till it ends?'

'He never walks out on Fräulein Garbo. Goodnight, Fräulein.'

'Goodbye,' said Cathleen. If you can't say goodbye to a man, say it to his butler: there is almost as much satisfaction.

## 5

Thursday morning Admiral Canaris stood looking down on Tirpitzufer, but he saw nothing on the street. Keitel, Chief of the High Command, had sent a hand-delivered note to him an hour earlier saying that espionage abroad had to be stepped up with the coming invasion of Poland. *Fall Weiss*, Case White, was to take place at first light tomorrow; it was expected that England and France would respond within hours. Canaris had no time for General Keitel, but he was preferable to Himmler or Heydrich; that was one advantage of the *Abwehr* being directly responsible to the High Command. The situation would have been insufferable if he, as *Abwehr* chief, had had to answer to the SS or the Gestapo.

A convoy, coming from God knows where, had halted in the street below. It was a peculiar procession, a mix of army vehicles, delivery vans and open transport trucks. Only some of the vehicles were carrying troops; the rest were stacked with supplies. If we are already having to draft in such civilian transport, Canaris wondered, how well are we prepared for a long war?

He turned away from the window as Hans von Gaffrin knocked and came in. 'Have you seen that?' He nodded down into the street.

Gaffrin shrugged. 'That comes of having a corporal as commander-in-chief.'

Canaris could never bring himself to accept Gaffrin's

almost reckless criticisms of Hitler. Though he shared the aristocrat's view, he was much more circumspect. 'You should be more careful, Hans. The walls may have ears.'

'The telephones almost certainly do, but I'm always discreet on them.' Gaffrin smiled, but Canaris sensed there was no good humour in the other man this morning. Something had occurred to upset him. 'As I'm sure you are.'

'What have I to be discreet about?'

'You were sympathetic last year when certain generals approached you.'

Gaffrin was sounding him out for something. He walked across to the dachshunds, began to feed them some biscuits. They licked his hand, trusting him. 'That was a year ago, Hans. Time has run out. We'll be at war tomorrow.'

'How does the General Staff feel about it?'

'They've been committed, have had their orders. They are professional soldiers – how else can they feel about it? They will obey orders.'

'If something happened –'

'What?' He wrenched his hand away as one of the dogs bit him accidentally.

But Gaffrin had had second thoughts; he backed away. He had never been certain of his chief and Canaris knew that; but then no one, not even his own family, had ever been certain of him. It made him few friends, gave him no love; but, in his chosen profession, it gave him a certain security. Spy-masters must make themselves the tightest secret of all.

'I have to go out,' Canaris said. 'I have an appointment.'

Gaffrin knew enough not to ask where and with whom: the chief's movements could be as secretive as those of some of their operatives. 'I have a new roster almost finished. I'll show it to you this afternoon.'

'Do that. We have to recruit more agents. We'll talk about that, too.'

He waited till Gaffrin had gone, then he took two pills, certain that he was now developing hay fever on top of his other ailments, put on his cap and went out to his car. Gallmüller, the doorman, saluted him, but the Admiral, mind on the appointment ahead, went past him without seeing him. Gallmüller, a veteran Berliner, shrugged and dropped his arm. It didn't matter to him if the Admiral didn't want to heil Hitler.

The Mercedes, one of those without armour-plating or bullet-proof windows, professional service chiefs being expendable, took him to the Leopold Palace. All during the drive he thought about his decision to tell Reichsminister Goebbels about the Irish–Jewish actress from Hollywood. He had almost consigned the file on the O'Dea woman to the back of his secret drawer; much more important matters were now demanding his attention and he could see no immediate advantage in blackmailing the Reichsminister, though even in his own mind he did not call it that. There were levels of decency below which one did not drop, even mentally.

This morning, however, a report, unsigned, had been delivered to his house. It was from an agent, unknown even to Hans von Gaffrin and other senior officers in the *Abwehr*, whom he had placed on the staff of Heinrich Himmler, Reichsfuehrer of the SS. A 'mole', a word he had found in the English writer Bacon's history of Henry VII: though he would never use such a word in any official paper. The mole had reported that Reichsfuehrer Himmler had, somehow, come into possession of information that Reichsminister Goebbels was having an affair with the American actress Cathleen O'Dea, who was a Jewess.

He did not have the sardonic sense of humour that, for instance, Hans von Gaffrin had; he did not appreciate the irony of his mole having discovered information leaked by a mole in his own organization. The information in his secret drawer was supposed to have been for the eyes of only one other person besides himself in Berlin; that person, he knew, could be trusted. So was the agent in New York, whom he had thought he could trust, also working for Himmler? All at once he felt he should retire, retreat to some remote spot on the Baltic coast where the air would be clean and trust was something as simple as credit at the village grocer's. But intrigue was in his blood, he would be drained without it. He had to be close to power, even if only to spy on it.

He was shown into the Reichsminister's office immediately The two small men met at eye-level, ignoring the huge room that encircled them; the office itself suggested power, but the two tiny men suggested boys who had crept into it in the pursuit of mischief. Neither man had to draw himself up to his full height: there was no advantage in it.

'It must be something important, Herr Admiral, to ask for such an urgent meeting. I hope it is not bad news?' Goebbels was puzzled. He and Canaris had little to do with each other, since propaganda was all lies and espionage was a search for truth.

'I think it may be bad news, Herr Reichsminister, and I hope you will forgive me for my presumption in bringing it to your notice.'

'Of course, Herr Admiral.' Goebbels smiled as if his throat had been cut.

Canaris gave him the information he had received from New York on Fräulein Cathleen O'Dea.

'When did you receive this information?'

'Only yesterday,' said Canaris, who was not a natural liar but a practised one. 'That, though, is only half the bad news. I received information this morning that Reichsfuehrer Himmler has the same information.'

'Sit down, Herr Admiral.' Goebbels, his limp suddenly seeming to have worsened, led the way to two side chairs. 'Does your Berlin informant know I have entertained Fräulein O'Dea to supper? Does Himmler know?'

'Yes,' said Canaris to both questions.

Goebbels tapped his fingers on the arm of his chair, ran his lips up and down his teeth. Then: 'Something puzzles me, Herr Admiral. Why have you come here to tell me this? You and I have never been friends.'

'No,' said Canaris, who knew the value of truth, if used judicially, 'but Himmler and I are enemies. I cannot stand the man.'

'He, of course, cannot stand anyone but himself.'

'True,' said Canaris, knowing now that he was on safe ground. He smoothed down a white eyebrow that had become nervous. 'I know that he and you have had your differences –'

'You may be more explicit than that. I, too, cannot stand the man.'

Canaris nodded. 'He will use the information against you. Perhaps not now, there is too much happening at the moment, but when the time suits him. So –'

'So?'

'Herr Reichsminister, forgive my frankness. If anything should happen to the Fuehrer, God forbid –' he added as self-insurance: he was sitting opposite the man who had virtually created the myth of Der Fuehrer, who had invented the boringly familiar *Heil Hitler!* 'If anything should happen to him, there will be a power struggle. You and I know who, on the basis of intellect, should succeed him –' He was surprised at the facileness of his flattery.

So was Goebbels. 'I'd always heard that you never had a good word for anyone, Herr Admiral. We must meet more often.'

Canaris managed a smile: he could think of only one thing he wanted less and that was regular meetings with Himmler. 'Himmler would use everything he has to destroy rivals. You are more popular with the public than he is. But if he released the information that you had some sort of liaison with this half-Jewess . . .'

Goebbels had had past experience of Himmler's interference. It was the SS chief who had broken up the romance with Lida Baarova, informing the Fuehrer of what was going on and prompting the latter to step in and summarily tell Goebbels he had to turn his back on Lida and go back to Magda. It had then been left to the SS to see that Lida was banished back to her native Czechoslovakia, that all her films were destroyed and that she was never to work in films or the theatre again. And Lida had not been Jewish . . . This time, if Himmler had his way, it would not be the woman who would be banished.

He resorted to the lie, which, if he had not invented, he had refined:

'What would you say, Canaris, if I told you that I knew Fräulein O'Dea was Jewish, or anyway, half-Jewish? No, no, I was not playing with fire,' he said as Canaris, usually adept at hiding his thoughts, had raised the thick eyebrows. 'I had heard a rumour to that effect and I decided I should try and nail it, one way or the other, myself. I discovered it only last night. I confronted her with it and she confessed. Her mother, a Jew, is in Ravensbrueck. Did you know that?'

'No.'

'Fräulein O'Dea will finish filming tomorrow, on my orders, and she will be deported at once. If Himmler tries to make something of it, I shall anticipate him by telling the Fuehrer what I have learned. Perhaps I should have had Fräulein O'Dea more thoroughly checked before we engaged her, but I understand no one in Hollywood knows she is Jewish. They, like ourselves, all think she is Irish.'

'What if Himmler lets out the news to the public?'

'I don't think the Fuehrer will allow that. Not in view of what is going to happen tomorrow. He wants the country, and particularly its Ministers, united, not divided.' He stood up, went back to his desk; his limp was less pronounced. 'Thank you, Herr Admiral. I shall not forget your friendship. If I can do anything for you . . .'

'Only if something happens to the Fuehrer – which God forbid.'

'Of course,' said Goebbels. 'Heil Hitler!'

'Heil Hitler,' said Canaris and somehow got his arm up.

# CHAPTER ELEVEN

## 1

On Wednesday night Carmody had come home from the office at eleven o'clock to find Meg Arrowsmith waiting for him. As he crossed the street he saw the Invicta parked outside his front door. As far as he knew there were no other Invictas in Berlin; it was Meg's challenge to the superiority of the Mercedes. As he reached the low-slung car she got out of it.

'I've been waiting *ages*, darling.'

'I've been at the office. Why didn't you phone me there?'

'I wanted to see you here – privately. Aren't you going to ask me in?'

He was tired and he did not want to spend an hour or even half an hour listening to her. He was worried too: he had called Cathleen, but there had been no answer from her either from the studio or her apartment. 'Meg, can't it wait? I'm absolutely shagged out –'

'It *can't* wait!' Her breath was heavy with gin, but she did not appear to be drunk. 'Please, Sean –'

He opened the front door, ushered her in, then led the way up to his flat. Once inside he said, 'Excuse me for a moment. I have to make a phone call.'

He went into his bedroom, dialled Cathleen's home number. He felt weak with relief when she answered. 'Where have you been? I've been worried stiff –'

'I'm sorry, darling.' There was a moment's hesitation, then she said, 'I went to see Goebbels.'

'Oh Christ! What for?'

'I had no choice – it was a Reichsminister's order. That was what he said.'

'What did he want?'

'To tell me that he knows Frau Hoolahan is a Jew and that she's in Ravensbrueck, where he says she'll stay.'

'Does he know she's your mother?'

'No. But if he sends some sort of order tomorrow – or if he's already sent it –' Her voice broke; then she recovered. 'They won't let her out.'

He tried to sound reassuring, though his own sudden depression equalled hers. 'From what I know, he can't issue orders about the camps – they're under the SS. He'd have to do it through Himmler. I don't think he'd ask any favours of that bastard.'

'He might, just to get back at me.'

'Do you want me to come over and spend the night?'

Again there was a moment's hesitation. Then: 'I'd like you to, but you better not. I have an eight o'clock call. Let's both get a good night's sleep. I don't want to look like death warmed up when we meet Mother tomorrow.'

'Will you be able to get time off from the studio?'

'I've seen Karl Braun. He thinks I'm having trouble with my exit permit –'

'Are you?' He would have to think about getting his own, just in case.

'I haven't applied. But Karl doesn't know that. He's giving me a two-hour break. It'll be a rush, but at least I'll be there to welcome Mother. Will you be there?'

'Of course.' He told her he loved her, said goodnight and hung up.

When he went back to the living room Meg had helped herself to a large gin-and-tonic from the bottles on his sideboard. He poured himself a beer and sat down opposite her.

'Cathleen?' she said and he nodded. 'I wasn't eavesdropping, darling. I just guessed. I wish I had someone to call *me* to wish me goodnight.'

He hoped it was not going to be a maudlin hour or half-hour. 'Meg, why did you want to see me?'

'Darling – can't you *do* something? Who's writing the truth about what is going on here?'

'I think we're all writing the truth. Or trying to. Your

291

friends don't make it easy for us, not the way they use the Big Lie.'

She made a conciliatory gesture. 'I know – it's that little swine Goebbels. But everyone wants peace, don't they? If England goes to war over Poland –' She looked moodily into her drink, as if it were a dark bottomless well into which she would like to plunge. 'Can't you write a story that is a plea for peace? Something all the papers would run. Ask them to give up Poland –'

'Ask who?'

'Us. The English and the French. What does it matter if Danzig or Poland becomes part of the Reich? Has Austria suffered? Or Sudetenland?'

'They were mostly Germanic people. The Poles aren't.'

He was angry at her, but held himself in. He was tired enough, but she looked beyond that, as if she were just the fragile shell of what she had once been, ready to shatter into tiny pieces when she came to the last immovable blockade. He did not want to be the cause of that shattering, but his innate kindness was running out. There is just so much charity of which one is capable; even saints, in the end, run out of it. Or, if they don't, they have drawn on the Divine, and not the human, stock.

'Won't war be worse for them? Germany will take over Poland anyway. If they could be persuaded to give in peacefully –'

'Meg,' he said wearily, standing up and putting his half-drunk glass back on the sideboard, 'whatever I wrote wouldn't have the slightest influence. Not if *any* of the correspondents wrote it. War's going to happen anyway – Hitler is determined on that – and if I wrote something like you suggest, I'd be branded forever as an appeaser, like Chamberlain and his weak-kneed mob at Munich. Whatever I am, Meg, I'm not an appeaser. I wasn't brought up that way and I'm not going to change now. I think it's time you went home.'

'Home?'

'England preferably. But go home to your flat for tonight. You'd better face it, Meg – your mate Hitler has let you down. Everybody's had enough of him, including England. They're going to stand up to him from now on.'

He opened the front door, waited for her to put on her gloves. Which she did, struggling for some style. But she had very little of even that left now; she had even, somehow, lost the effect of being English. 'Shit!' she said in German and left him, her heels clack-clacking down the marble stairs like bones tapping out some message in Morse.

He closed the door, leant back against it, felt burdened by women. He, who had never been a ladies' man: even Ida, his mother, had said that of him. For a while it had been his ambition, but the effort had been too much. He had realized that a ladies' man is, behind the façade, no more than his own man. He, himself, was not selfish enough for that.

He went to the window, drew aside the lace curtain and looked down. Meg had come out into the street, was getting into the Invicta when the two men came across to her from a doorway opposite. There was no mistaking them: they were Lutze and Decker. They spoke to Meg and after a few words all three got into the car. It was Decker, and not Meg, who got in behind the driver's wheel.

Weariness and despair overcame Carmody; he should have let Meg remain for the night. That was probably one of the reasons she had come; she had wanted company on what might be one of the worst nights of her life and he had told her to go home. He went to bed and stumbled all night through dreams just this side of nightmare.

Thursday morning he was at the office by nine. He rang Meg's flat and her maid answered: 'No, Herr Carmody, Lady Arrowsmith has not been home all night. I am worried this time.'

'This time?'

'She has stayed out before –' The maid was hesitant; it was not her place to comment on where her mistress slept and with whom. 'But the past two days she has been behaving strangely – she has been drinking a lot –'

'I'll ring again later. Stay there, just in case she comes home.' He hung up as Fräulein Luxemburg came into his

293

office with the latest teletypes. 'How's the news, Olga? No, don't tell me.'

'I think the worst is going to happen. My mother got out her flag last night.'

'The Nazi flag? The swastika?'

'I'm ashamed to say so – yes. She has hung it in our front window. I wanted to die when I went home last night and saw it.'

'She's an old lady –' But that was no excuse, and they both knew it. 'I have to go out for an hour. If anyone calls, Fräulein O'Dea or Lady Arrowsmith, anyone –' He hoped the Langs would not call, that everything was going smoothly up at Ravensbrueck right now.

'I'll be here,' she said and he knew she would be, even when *here* was falling down around her: Fräulein Horatius at the bridge.

When he got out into the Potsdamerplatz he looked up at the sky, something he had forgotten to do when he had come out of his flat this morning. It was a warm sky already, cloudless and bright, spoiled only from perfection by the squadron of Stukas flying east. Surely, he thought, all the troops and guns and tanks and planes are in position? These flights must be for the benefit of the home crowd, joy-flights in bombers.

He went quickly up to the Unter den Linden, moving much faster than his usual ambling walk. It had occurred to him during one of his fitful, waking moments last night that it would be dangerous to bring Mady Hoolahan to either his flat or Cathleen's. It was a simple point, the matter of somewhere to hide Mady while they got her papers, but he had overlooked it. He was too inexperienced at this game; but what opportunities had he had to learn? He was learning the game while he played it and already the full-time whistle was close. Burberry's flat seemed an ideal hideaway.

He took out Burberry's keys, opened the door from the street into the building. He had gone up four or five of the carpeted stairs when a figure appeared from beneath the staircase. 'Yes?'

'Oh.' The caretaker had startled him. 'I'm a friend of Herr Burberry's. He – he telephoned me to come here and get a book for him. He wants it posted to him.'

'You have a key?' The caretaker, bony and rheumy-eyed, a walrus moustache hanging beneath his long nose, was surprised and suspicious. 'He didn't tell me he was leaving anyone his keys.'

'He probably forgot. I won't be long.'

He went on upstairs, paused on the first landing and looked down. The caretaker was staring up at him from the bottom of the stairwell, like a walrus waiting to be fed. Carmody went on up to Burberry's landing, put the flat key in the door and opened it.

There was a gasp from somewhere inside the flat, then a voice said, 'Rudy?'

'No,' said Carmody, stepping into the entrance hall. 'I'm a friend of Herr Burberry's.'

A woman came to a door that Carmody saw led into the living room. She was young, blonde, wore an apron and carried a handful of dusters. 'Oh, excuse me, sir. I thought it was the caretaker.'

Stone the crows, Carmody thought, how many defenders does an empty flat have to have? 'I've come to get a book for Herr Burberry – he telephoned me. Are you here all the time?'

She stood in the doorway to the living room, looking uncomfortable. Has she got someone else in here with her? he wondered. 'No, sir. I come only Monday and Thursday mornings when Herr Burberry isn't here. Just to dust.'

'Herr Burberry will be pleased to hear you're keeping the flat clean.' He decided he would have to assert himself. Like most Australians he was not accustomed to dealing with servants; Jack usually thought he was a bloody sight better than his master; it was no training for being a master. 'I have to go in here –'

She remained in the doorway. 'Herr Burberry's books are all in his library, along the hall there.'

'This one, he said, was in the living room.' He was getting

better at lying; he was in the right country for it. 'Excuse me, please.'

He pushed past her, went into the living room. He had been here a couple of times to have a drink with Oliver Burberry; the flat had always struck him as being much more luxurious than his own. The furniture was heavy but expensive, antiques, Burberry had told him, that the owner had collected from all over Europe; the carpets were Bokharas, something else Burberry had told him. The pictures on the walls were Burberry's own, English sporting prints and a painting of Eton College from the playing fields – 'where,' Burberry had also told him, 'when I was playing, nothing was ever won.' Against one wall stood a sideboard, its doors open and a cardboard box standing beside it, half-filled with bottles of Scotch, gin and schnapps. Other bottles stood on the floor and beside them a small suitcase.

He looked at the maid. 'You're being very conscientious, aren't you? Dusting the bottles. Were you taking them home to do a thorough job on them?'

The girl hung her head, wrapped the dusters nervously round her hands. 'I didn't think Herr Burberry would be back. I know Rudy, the caretaker, comes up here and takes a nip –'

'What's this?' Carmody picked up the suitcase. 'Were you going to take this, too?'

'No. No.' She shook her head vigorously. 'I'm not a thief, sir. I've never done anything like this before – ask Herr Burberry. I don't know what that is. I've never seen it before – it wasn't there when I looked in the cupboard on Monday –'

Was something being planted on Burberry? He picked up the suitcase. 'Put the drink back where it belongs. I'll say nothing to Herr Burberry. Where's the kitchen?'

'Through there.' She nodded towards an inner door. 'And thank you, sir. I was tempted – I was stupid –'

'We all make mistakes – What's your name?'

'Jenny.' She was pretty in a heavy, bland sort of way; a few pounds off here and there and she wouldn't have been out of place on one of the Reich's *Strength Through Joy* posters.

'All right, Jenny. Just tidy up in here.'

He went into the kitchen, closed the door. It was an old-fashioned door and an old-fashioned kitchen; there was a key in the door with which the cook could keep out an unwelcome and busybody mistress or master. He turned the key in the lock, put the suitcase on the kitchen table and tried to open it. But, as he had suspected, it was locked.

He searched in a drawer of the table, found a screwdriver. He hesitated a moment, wondering if he were going too far to protect Oliver: what if the suitcase had not been planted on him? But who had left it and why? Did it contain incriminating papers or photos? Who else but the caretaker had a key to the flat?

He put the screwdriver under the two locks, wrenched and they broke. He flipped open the lid of the case and knew at once that he had done the right thing in opening it. The gun, in its pieces, and the telescopic sight came together in his mind: he saw it, assembled, being aimed from the bathroom window, wherever that was, down at the familiar figure riding in the armour-plated Mercedes-Benz up the Unter den Linden. Oliver Burberry, knowingly or unknowingly, was implicated in a plot to kill Hitler.

The door handle rattled, then there was a knock. 'Sir? I have to get some furniture polish.'

Carmody hastily closed the case, pushing down the busted locks as best he could. He dropped the screwdriver back into the table drawer, then unlocked the kitchen door. He was about to apologize, then remembered Germans took their servants for granted more than an Australian ever would. 'Get what you want, Jenny.'

He saw her cast a sidelong glance at the case on the table as she went to a cupboard and got out a tin and a bottle and some fresh cloths. She gave him a tentative smile and went back into the living room. Only when she had gone did he feel the sweat on himself.

He stood pondering what to do. Should he take the case with him? If it had been planted here (by the Gestapo, the SD, even the Abwehr?), were they expecting Burberry to return? The odds, when he added them up, were unlikely: Oliver and all the English and French correspondents were gone for good. So the rifle and the telescopic sight belonged to someone who knew of the advantages of the flat's bathroom as a marksman's hide; but who? Had Whitehall, belatedly reversing its rejection of the British military attaché's suggestion, deciding at long last to be unsporting, sent in an assassin? Though, of course, being sportsmen, they would not call him that. If he were here in Berlin, where would he be hiding? The British embassy was still operating, though Carmody knew they had already begun packing. Was the marksman hidden in the embassy?

Stone the crows, he thought, what a story! Excitement raced through him, something that was usually slow to stir. Then it drained out of him; he was hit by that bane of a newspaperman who thinks he has a beat: second thoughts. How could he write the story? Before or after the event? Could he find out who the marksman was and name him? But then, a chilling thought, the assassin might come after him. Then a sense of responsibility, a handicap every newspaperman hopes will never trouble him, settled on him like a raven. If an assassination of Hitler was planned, then it must be allowed to go ahead: the story had to come *after* the event. World peace was worth more than World Press: it was a trite phrase, the sort of subheading the story would have got from the New York desk. He looked at the small suitcase with its deadly contents and made his decision.

He went back into the living room. 'Are you nearly finished, Jenny?'

'Yes, sir. There isn't much to do, now Herr Burberry isn't here.' She had put away the bottles and closed the sideboard door.

'No, I suppose not. I'll be staying here a little while. I have to make some notes for Herr Burberry from one of his books. I'll lock up.' He went to the sideboard, took out a bottle of schnapps. 'Here. I'm sure Herr Burberry won't miss this one.'

'Oh, I couldn't – not after –' She had the true embarrassment of the truly honest. Caught once, she would never try to steal anything again from the flat.

'Go on, it's all right.' She hesitantly took the bottle and he gave her a smile. 'Jenny, if war breaks out, Herr Burberry definitely won't be back. As soon as the first bombs drop, I give you permission to come back and take the lot. I'm sure Herr Burberry would rather that you had it than Rudy, the caretaker.'

She looked at him, not sure that he wasn't joking; decided that he wasn't and gave him a hesitant smile. 'Thank you, Herr –'

'Smith,' said Carmody.

Five minutes later she was gone. As soon as the door closed behind her, Carmody went back into the kitchen. He looked at the suitcase, wishing he had been able to pick the locks instead of breaking them; the owner of it would take one look at it and probably not even touch it but skedaddle as fast as he could go. Yet he might not: the assassination attempt was itself a high risk, one more risk might be taken with a shrug: the prize was worth it. But could Carmody himself take the risk of putting the case back where it had been found in the sideboard? What if the maid came back? Or the caretaker came up looking for a nip of schnapps? The caretaker, if not the girl, would almost certainly inform the police.

He looked about the kitchen. This was a well-furnished one; it had a refrigerator, which had not been unplugged. He went to it, found a bottle of beer and opened it. He sat down at the kitchen table and sipped the beer while looking at the case. Last night's disturbed sleep was not helping him concentrate; fragmented thoughts floated in his mind like broken pieces of a kaleidoscope that would not form a pattern. He had decided he had to help the marksman complete his mission, but how was he to protect him?

He got up and went out into the living room and through to the bathroom. He remembered the details, small though they were, that Burberry had given him. He stood at the toilet, as McMartin-Innes had done, and looked out of the narrow window and down into the Unter den Linden. The angle was acute, but there were about fifty yards of the wide street clearly visible. Unless Hitler's car was moving at breakneck speed, there would be time for the marksman to draw a bead and fire at least twice. He unbuttoned his fly, used the toilet and flushed it: a nervous pee, something that had embarrassed him as a boy on social occasions, was in order, though this was no social occasion.

He looked about the bathroom, noting the width of the window and the floral curtains drawn back on either side of it. Then he went back to the kitchen, took the pieces of the gun out of the case and assembled it. The two pieces, the walnut stock and the shortened barrel, fitted together on a single screw. He fitted the telescopic sight, sighting down it and being surprised at the magnification of it. He bounced the gun lightly on his palms, appreciating the weight and balance of it; he had never handled a gun as expensive and good as this one, neither in the bush back home shooting rabbits and kangaroos nor in Spain shooting Franco's soldiers. His thoughts now were concentrated: he was the soldier he had been for those twelve months in Spain.

He went back to the bathroom, put the rifle into the inner frame of the window; placed diagonally, it just fitted. Then he pulled the curtains across; the gun was effectively hidden. If the maid came back or the caretaker came up to the flat, he could only hope that neither of them came into the bathroom; or, if they did, they did not pull back the curtains to look out of the window. He reasoned that life, in the past couple of weeks, had become so complicated it was time luck turned his way. He had thought he had become philosophical, but now was the time for prayer.

He returned to the kitchen, took out his notebook, pondered a moment then wrote his message in block letters: *My apologies for opening your case. The contents are in the appropriate place.* It was stilted; it would have been even more so had it been in German. He used English because the chances were that, if the maid or caretaker found the note, they could not read it; he also was banking on the marksman's being an Englishman. He put the note in the case, went back into the living room and put the case away in the sideboard. He stood up, drew a deep breath and let out a long sigh.

He looked at his watch: 11.30. He went to the phone, dialled his office. 'Any messages, Olga?'

'Fräulein O'Dea has been trying to get in touch with you.

300

She has telephoned three times. She sounds rather desperate, Herr Carmody. She's at the studio.'

He hung up, dialled UFA and was put through to Cathleen. 'I'm on the set, darling, so I can't say too much.' Her voice was a hoarse whisper. 'I can't get away – God!'

He thought she was going to break down. 'Easy, darl. What's the hold-up?'

'Goebbels sent a personal order to the front office this morning – I'm to finish up today, get every one of my scenes in the can. There's to be no coming back for re-takes, no dubbing, nothing. I have to be off the lot tonight.'

'Can't you just walk out, tell them to go to buggery?' He could feel himself getting angry.

'That was my first reaction. I'd actually got outside as far as the car . . . Then – I didn't think I had the sort of mind that could put things together so quickly. I thought, what if I walk out and he gets really nasty? What if he has me followed everywhere, if he stops my exit permit? I have to go along with the order – I'll get everything done today – Oh Christ, I'll be glad to be out of here!'

So would he, out of Berlin, out of Germany. He wanted to go into the bathroom, take the Mannlicher and go looking for Goebbels; Hitler could wait. 'I'll go and meet your mother. What does she look like, in case the Langs just leave her there on her own?'

'Okay, Karl, I'm coming. I'm coming!' Her voice was turned away from the phone; then it came back, in the hoarse whispers again: 'Karl's going out of his mind . . . What does she look like? She's smaller than me, has dark hair, not red like mine, blue eyes –'

'Blue?' He had never thought of Jews having blue eyes. He had made up his own stereotype of them.

'Yes. Some of them do,' she said, as if she had read his thoughts. 'That's about all. I can't tell you what she'll be wearing . . .' A pity he thought: women were better at describing a woman's dress than her features.

'Don't worry, darl. Get the picture out of the way and good riddance to it. I'll pick up your mother. I'll take her to the office. Come there as soon as you're finished.'

He hung up, looked once more about the flat, then went to the door. He had opened it, when he remembered why he was supposed to have come here. He went back and along a short hall to Burberry's library and study. He took the first book that came to hand on the shelves, went back and let himself out of the flat. He went down the stairs and, as he had expected, the caretaker was waiting for him in the entrance hall. He held up the book.

'Got it. I'll give Herr Burberry your compliments.'

'Yes, please do that,' said the caretaker suspiciously, 'Herr –?'

'Smith.'

He opened the front door and stepped out into the street, paused for a moment on the narrow step. He was tempted to go back in to see if the caretaker was already on his way up to the flat; he resisted the temptation and walked on. The image of a game his father had played came into his mind: two-up, a game in which bets were made on the toss of two coins. The coins were in the air now and all he could do was hope they came down heads.

He looked at the book he had randomly chosen: it was Ernest Hemingway's *Death in the Afternoon*. He had met Hemingway, once in Madrid, hadn't liked him and now the big braggart was jerking his thumb at him, putting the mockers on him. He flung the book into the first waste-bin he passed.

## 2

The woman sat on a bench gazing out at the big goldfish pond. She did not move, not her head, her hands or her body; Carmody was too far away to see if her eyes or her lips moved. He stood watching her; and watching everyone else in sight. He could see no sign of the Langs; their job, the delivery of Mady Hoolahan was done, and they had disappeared, to remain safe for further tasks. There were only a few people round the big pond: some elderly couples shuffling along as if at the end of their long road, two nannies with their baby carriages, some young mothers with older children, a young SS trooper arm-in-arm with his girl: what Carmody guessed to be a normal mid-week crowd in the Tiergarten. All of them appeared to be preoccupied with themselves, none of them had eyes for the still, lonely figure on the bench.

Carmody approached her, coming at her from the front so that he would not startle her. He sat down beside her, raised his hat. 'Mrs Hoolahan?' He said in English. 'I'm Sean Carmody, a friend of Cathleen's. Don't be afraid.'

She had started, her hands suddenly clasping each other. She looked at him warily, fearfully. 'Where is she?'

'You know she's been making a picture here?'

'Frau Schmidt told me.' The Langs, evidently, did not trust their true name even to those they helped.

'She couldn't get away from the studio – I'll explain why later. She is finishing up today. I hope we'll have both of you on a train or plane for Paris by tomorrow.'

She shook her head, blinking back tears. 'I can't believe it –'

She was much older-looking than he had expected; Cathleen had said something about her being in her late forties, but she looked at least ten years older. He could see the resemblance to Cathleen, but only faintly, as through a cracked and dusty glass. She wore a felt hat pulled low down on her head, a dark brown dress and cardigan that were too big for her, black shoes that looked ready to slip off her thin bony feet. Somewhere, hidden in this frightened, drab woman, was the real Mady Hoolahan. He hoped Cathleen could find her and revive her.

'I want to take you back to my office –'

'What are you? What do you do?'

'I'm a newspaperman. No, no, I'm not going to write anything about you –' She had looked at him suspiciously, again fearfully. 'I have to take some photos of you – for a passport and your exit permit.'

'I have no passport. I have – nothing.' She spread her hands: all I have, all I am, is what you see.

'It's all right, it's all fixed,' he said, and hoped so.

He helped her to her feet, feeling the thin bony arm in his hand, and they began to walk away from the pond. Alert to anyone's following them, he took her along the same path he and Cathleen had followed the day before yesterday. They came round a bend and there was the plump young tenor standing right in front of them, arm outflung, mouth open in the lingering last breath of a soft high note. Mady clutched Carmody's arm as Cathleen had done on Tuesday evening.

'It's all right,' he said and smiled at the singer as the latter, embarrassed again, closed his mouth. 'How did your audition go?'

'I have to go again this afternoon.'

'Good luck.'

He and Mady walked on and as soon as they were out of sight the young tenor took up again, bursting full-voiced into an aria. Mady lifted her head, listening.

'*Tannhäuser.* I've missed the opera.' She didn't say whether she had missed it in Ravensbrueck or Los Angeles and he didn't ask. She was regaining some confidence, even seemed to have a little more strength in her thin body. She looked up at him. 'Are you Cathleen's boy friend?'

'Yes.'

'You're different from the other ones she's had.'

'She's never talked about them.'

'And you don't want me to?'

'No,' he said, but smiled gently at her.

'Good. You're sensible.'

'I'll get us a taxi.'

'No, let's walk. You don't know what it's like to be able to walk freely.'

When he took her into World Press he saw just a slight raising of Olga Luxemburg's eyebrows, but the secretary said nothing. He led Mady into his own office, sat her down and asked Olga to bring some coffee.

'Some food, too?' said Olga, looking at Mady, who was now slumped in the chair, feeling the effects of the walk.

'Yes,' said Carmody, then made a decision. It was not fair to keep Olga in the dark; she was an ally and she had to be

304

trusted. 'Olga, this is Frau Hoolahan, Fräulein O'Dea's mother. She has just got out of Ravensbrueck and we're trying to get her and Fräulein O'Dea out of Berlin by tomorrow.'

'Ravensbrueck? Are you Jewish?'

Oh Christ, thought Carmody, she's an anti-Semite! It had never occurred to him that she might be; they had never discussed the Jewish question. He said sharply, 'Yes, she is.'

Olga looked hurt at his tone. 'Herr Carmody, I don't think being a Jew is a crime –'

He saw he had been wrong; he was more on edge than he had realized. 'I'm sorry. It's dangerous having her here – I have to take some photos for a passport and exit permit –'

Mady, watching them both silently, took off her hat. Olga looked at the close-cropped dark head and said, 'You can't take photos of her like *that*. They will know at once where she has been.'

Mady ran a hand over the stubble on her head. 'It will take months to grow.'

There had been no place for vanity in the camp, but now, out here in the real world where vanities counted, she was rapidly becoming a woman again. Just like a bloody woman, thought Carmody.

But he was wrong: 'She's right,' said Mady. 'We can't put a photo of me like this in a passport – I might just as well wear a yellow star. Can you get me a wig?'

'There's a wig shop on the Tauentzienstrasse,' said Olga. 'What colour would you like?'

'Auburn,' said Mady, a little vanity peeping through. 'It would make me look more like Cathleen's mother.'

'A grey one,' said Carmody. 'You're not supposed to be Cathleen's mother.' He went to the safe, took out the passport. The grey-haired woman in the passport photo looked sadly at the three of them. 'That's who you're supposed to be. Sybille Dix, born November 10, 1873.'

'She looks unhappy,' said Mady.

'We'll try and make you look happier,' said Carmody. 'Righto, Olga. Get some coffee and food sent up, then go over and pick out a wig.'

'Something with a fringe, and short,' said Mady, becoming livelier by the moment. 'And not *too* grey.'

Olga nodded and went out, as brisk an ally as one could ask for. Carmody looked at the phone on his desk. 'I'll call Cathleen and tell her you are safe. But I don't know whether you should speak to her, in case you both break down. I think my line is tapped by the Gestapo.'

Mady looked at the phone as if Cathleen were already on the other end of the line. Then she nodded: 'I'll wait. Just tell her I'm all right.'

Carmody dialled UFA, waited till he was connected to Cathleen on the set. Then: 'Everything is okay. There's nothing to worry about.'

'Can I –?'

He cut in: 'Not now. I'll wait for you here. What time will you finish?'

'God knows. Maybe nine o'clock, nine-thirty. Sean –' She sounded as if she wanted to weep.

'See you then,' he said and hung up. He looked at Mady sitting on the edge of her chair. 'She wanted to speak to you, but I chopped her off. I think it's too much of a risk.'

'Do they watch your office?'

He went to the window, looked out on the Potsdamerplatz. A tram, travelling too fast, went round a curve, its wheels screeching on the rails; people seemed to stop and turned their heads, as if the sound were a more threatening one, like the scream of a shell. People were going in and out of the chemist's on the corner in a steady stream (stocking up against future headaches?). The flower-women, their flowers wilting in the early afternoon heat, were gathering up their baskets to move back closer against the railings and under the trees. The square was busy, everyone seemingly on the move: he could see no one standing watching his office window. Maybe Lutze and Decker suddenly had bigger fish to catch.

'They come and go,' he said.

He went to a cupboard, took out an old Graflex camera he had inherited from the previous World Press man, who had fancied himself as a news photographer and had aspired to work for *Life*. He blew the dust out of it, found a plate and loaded it. 'I'm no Cecil Beaton, but I think I can do a good enough job.'

'Passport photos aren't supposed to flatter you.' She had begun to study him; he wondered if his image in her eyes was flattering. 'What are you doing so far from home?'

A boy arrived from the café downstairs with coffee and rolls and pastries. Over the lunch Carmody told her about himself, to fill in time till Olga came back and to put her mind at rest that he was worthy of Cathleen. Slowly he began to discern the real Mady beneath the mentally scarred woman he had brought in here half an hour ago. Given her own secure environment, she would be more vivacious than Cathleen; given another six months and one would see more of the beauty she once must have been. He found it strange sizing up a woman who would, he hoped, be his future mother-in-law. She was so different from Ida, his own mother; after twenty-six years in America, she was still really European. Ida, a fourth generation Australian, would never be anything but Australian: the bushlife had seen to that. Yet he felt the two women might get on well together: they had a sympathy for others.

'I hope Fräulein Luxemburg won't get into trouble on my account . . .'

'I'll see she doesn't,' he said.

Then Olga came back with the wig in a box. Mady put it on, adjusting it in the mirror hanging behind the outer door of the office. Olga had also brought her some powder and lipstick, something Carmody knew he would not have thought of. When Mady turned round from the mirror she was a different woman, a grey-haired beauty, thin-faced and faded but still a beauty.

'I'll do,' she said matter-of-factly and Carmody knew she had already taken the first firm step on the road back.

He cleared a space against one wall, stood her against it and took half a dozen full-face shots. 'I have to take these down to be developed. Olga will take care of you.' He was about to say, *If we have any visitors* . . . Then he decided against it; he did not want to disturb her again. If Lutze and Decker did

307

appear, they would remain here till he returned. 'I'll be as quick as I can.'

He went over to the *Morgenpost* building, went into their darkroom, paid some money to one of the men there and emerged half an hour later with a dozen prints of passport size. If the darkroom hand, a pale, stained man in his sixties, had any suspicions about the subject of the photos he asked no questions. He had developed and printed pictures of murderers, rapists, emperors, dictators and anonymities: they were all the same to him, faces emerging like ghosts out of his solution tanks.

Carmody went out again during the afternoon to cover the government offices and the major embassies. The atmosphere was tense; there was even an air of unreality. Nobody seemed quite able to believe that the inevitable would happen; war was an impossibility, they said, while the convoys rumbled by their open windows. In the streets that mythical creature the man-in-the-street stopped to look at the convoys; if he were young he was wide-eyed, if he were older he had memories and his eyes were glazed. Diplomats galloped from embassy to ministry to Chancellery; phone wires hummed like dynamos; but tea and biscuits were still being served at four in the British embassy. Carmody sipped tea with Wilmington, the assistant press attaché.

'Packed your cricket gear?' He noticed that the bat and pads were gone from the corner of the attaché's office.

'Afraid so. Got everything packed, just in case. That's just between you and me, of course. We're still hoping . . .'

'You're kidding yourselves.'

Wilmington looked at him; all at once the thin, schoolboy's face seemed to age. He nodded and his voice seemed to deepen with despair. 'Of course we are. Have been for weeks. I'll be in uniform within a month.'

'What will you join?'

'The RAF, if they'll have me. Christ –' He shook his head. 'It's our job here to prevent wars. We really have cocked it up.'

'Not you,' said Carmody sympathetically. 'Chamberlain did that in Munich. Thanks for the tea. Good luck.'

'What will you do? Go home to Australia? I shouldn't blame you.'

Carmody knew he wouldn't be going home, not for a long time yet. His father would write to him, abusing him for staying on to become involved in an imperialist war, even if as a war correspondent; his mother would write of dances at the School of Arts hall, the new shearing team his father had joined, the old racehorse Our Place now on his last legs in the pasture paddock. Subtly, but subconsciously, she would be calling him home; his father, stridently and consciously, would be doing the same. But he wouldn't be going. It suddenly struck him, like a physical pain, that neither would he be going with Cathleen when she left for home.

He went back to the office, wrote his piece and phoned it through to London. Mady and Olga had become friends, but he could see that Mady was becoming impatient to be reunited with Cathleen. At six o'clock Kreisler, minus hurdy-gurdy and monkey, arrived.

He bowed to both women, looked at the photos, then at Mady, then at the passport of Sybille Dix. 'It can be done. But you don't look sixty-five.'

'Thank you,' said Mady, smiling. 'I don't feel it.'

'I'm sorry, that was not very gallant of me.'

Carmody was amused at Kreisler's reaction to the women. The communists he had known back home in the shearing teams had never been gallant towards women; indeed, women had been looked upon as a bloody nuisance, necessary kitchen-maids, in the cooking of the revolution. 'How soon can you do the passport and the permit?'

'You will have them first thing tomorrow morning. Eight o'clock here?'

He bowed to the ladies, tipped his hat and went away. It seemed to Carmody that his walk was jaunty, like that of a man who had, unexpectedly, been returned to his old trade and hadn't found his skills had rusted. Or was forgery more than a trade, was it an art?

At ten o'clock Cathleen arrived. She came bursting into the office, enveloped her mother in a hug that threatened to snap Mady's spine. Carmody and Olga retired to the outer office, both of them moved by the reunion of the mother and daughter.

'They truly love each other,' said Olga. 'Frau Hoolahan has been telling me.'

'Yes,' he said and wondered if she and her mother, the Nazi flag-waver, ever embraced each other.

When Cathleen and Mady came out of the inner office they were both red-eyed and sniffling. 'Oh God, isn't it wonderful! Sean, I can't believe we've done it –'

There was still a long way to go, but he couldn't throw cold water on her, not right now. 'We'll have to find somewhere for you to stay tonight. You can't go back to your place –'

'What about yours?'

'Too risky. Olga, where is there a good hotel that the Gestapo wouldn't be watching, one where there'd be no foreign tourists?' Though all the tourists, he guessed, would have gone by now.

'The Hotel Kern, off Landsbergerstrasse. It caters for ladies. My aunt stays there when she comes up from Dresden.'

What a treasure she is, thought Carmody; what use will they make of her when I'm gone and they draft her into some sort of war work? 'Righto, will you take them there?'

'Aren't you coming?' Cathleen was disappointed.

'I can't – I'm still working. I'll sleep here tonight. Have you finished at the studio?'

'Yes, thank God. I finished the last shot, put on my hat and walked out. I may not even get my last pay-check, but I don't care.'

'You'll get it.' The Nazis, he knew, always paid their debts. He kissed her, aware of the approving gaze of Mady; he didn't look at Olga. 'What about your exit permit?'

'Goebbels must be keen to get rid of me. It was delivered to me this afternoon. No note, nothing, just the permit.'

'Righto, be at your embassy at nine o'clock. I'll meet you there. We'll get your mother's visa and you'll be on the eleven o'clock train for Copenhagen. I couldn't get you on a plane – they're all fully booked.'

'What about you?' Her grip tightened on his arm.

'I can't go with you. Not now.'

She looked ready to weep; instead she kissed, said softly, 'Not even our last night together?'

He was acutely aware of Mady and Olga. He turned Cathleen round, pushed her out the door. 'Tomorrow morning, nine o'clock.'

## 3

General Kurt von Albern stared at the note in the case. 'What does that mean? *In the appropriate place?*'

'I think we should leave at once,' said Helmut. 'Someone has given the game away.'

He and his father had come here to the flat at midnight, parking the Opel three blocks away and walking the rest of the distance. There had still been traffic on the streets, even strollers on the Unter den Linden; lights were on in all the government offices in the Wilhelmstrasse and the main doors to the Chancellery were still wide open, as if for last-minute messengers of peace. Fortunately, no one in Burberry's apartment building seemed interested in either peace or war: they were all asleep. Helmut and his father had let themselves into the building, crept up the stairs and quietly let themselves into the flat. And discovered the broken locks on the suitcase and the note.

'No,' said the General. He left the living room, went along the hall to the bathroom and returned with the assembled Mannlicher. 'It was in the window, the appropriate place. I think I shall stay, go ahead as planned.'

'Why, for God's sake? Father, they *know* –'

'Who knows? The note is in English. Why should the Gestapo or the Abwehr or the SS, anyone German, write a note in English? It is someone who is sympathetic to us, who has guessed what we have planned. Perhaps someone from the British embassy.'

'Too much supposition. As a soldier, I thought you were always against that.'

'One has to take chances. We'd have won the last war if we had been more imaginative.' He had not been a general in that war, but he knew in his heart that even if he had been, he would have been no more imaginative than the others. They had not been trained to be that way. This, however, was different: assassination itself was an imaginative act. Or it was for a hidebound general. 'You do not have to stay.'

Helmut shrugged resignedly. 'We are in this together, Father. You'll need company tonight. I can't leave you alone.'

The General put out his hand. 'You're an Albern, a true soldier.'

'Not really, Father. Just your son.'

That was enough for the General, more than enough. He turned quickly and went out of the room before his tears could embarrass him. Helmut himself felt the tears rise in his eyes, certain that some time tomorrow morning they would both be dead. He did not care for himself, but he hated the thought of his father dying an ignominious death at the hand of some Gestapo or SS thug. The General deserved more than that.

4

The broken-nosed soldier in the Polish uniform looked up as a second soldier approached him. He had been half-dozing in the gathering darkness, his mind drifting in erotic memories of his last leave in Berlin; there had been a different girl every night, some of them paid for, some of them free. It surprised him that one girl's face had kept surfacing in his half-dreams, a girl who had spurned him so humiliatingly in front of a mere caretaker. He should have gone ahead and forced her to have him, not taken no for an answer. American women asked to be raped.

'The canned goods have arrived.'

The broken-nosed man got to his feet, glad that at last action was about to happen. *Canned goods* was the code-name for tonight's exercise, but it also described the dozen drugged prisoners from a nearby concentration camp who had been brought here to Gleiwitz on the German–Polish border. They were dressed in Polish uniforms and, whether they knew it or not, they were to die for the Fuehrer.

'All right, lay them out where we'd planned. Put them in different positions, just like men who'd been shot while running towards the radio station. Smear them with blood from those bottles you have. Then when the shooting starts, put some bullets into them.'

'Why are we doing this?' said the young SS corporal; with his question he marked the end of his chances of promotion. 'Isn't it all a bit elaborate?'

Damned intelligent corporals! thought the broken-nosed man, whose name was Naujocks; though he prided himself on his own intelligence and had once aspired to being an intellectual. 'Yours but to do or die, not ask questions.'

'Thank you,' said the corporal, who had read the English poet Tennyson and would from now on watch his back when Naujocks was around. 'I'll spread out the canned goods.'

Naujocks waited till he had gone, then he roused the rest of his detail. He knew what he had to do, but he could only guess at the higher reason behind it. He had been here two weeks waiting for the order to go ahead and then, late yesterday, it had arrived. He walked across to the fence surrounding the radio station, was challenged by the guard on duty and gave the password.

'Call out your sergeant.'

The sergeant, a lean veteran from the Great War, appeared out of the darkness as if he had been waiting to be called. 'It's time?'

'Yes. Five minutes. When I fire the first shot from over there –' he pointed east into the darkness, into Poland – start shooting. But shoot high – I don't want any of my men killed. This is a mock attack.'

'It doesn't look like a mock attack, not with you in that uniform.'

Another intelligent one. 'All you have to do is obey orders and see your men do the same.'

'Will you be shooting high, too?'

'Of course.' But everyone in this exercise except himself would have to be disposed of later; but that would be someone else's task. 'It'll be over in five minutes. We don't want the Poles to think war has broken out and come charging across.'

'We don't want to start the fucking war *here*,' said the sergeant.

'No,' said Naujocks; but that was the whole idea. 'Tell your men to return fire for two minutes, then retire back down the road half a mile. Take the radio staff with you. I'll take over here and send a message when you can come back.'

'I still think it's risky, so much shooting this close to the border. The Poles are as nervy as hell.'

'You sound nervy yourself, sergeant.'

'Wouldn't you be?' said the sergeant and went off into the night.

Naujocks went back to his own detail of ten men. The corporal was with them, having laid out the canned goods. 'All set to go.'

'Good. Put a couple of bullets into each of the bodies you've laid out, then keep your heads down. The radio station detail has orders to shoot high.' He looked at his watch. 'Time to go.'

'I'd still like to know what it's all for,' said the corporal and Naujocks almost shot him on the spot.

Instead he raised his pistol in the air and fired it. For the next two minutes there was a fusillade of shots from both sides of the road that ran past the radio station; then abruptly it stopped. Naujocks ran forward across the road, jumping three of the bodies slumped at the entrance to the radio station. He raced into the low building and, already having had days to learn its lay-out, went straight into the transmitting room. He switched on a microphone and took a typewritten speech out of his pocket.

Then he began to read in Polish, faking an hysterical excitement: 'We soldiers of the Polish Army, our patience exhausted by the arrogant demands of Hitler and his fascist government . . .'

The excuse for the beginning of the next Great War had taken place, its only casualties a dozen nameless criminals who had made the mistake of being sent to a prison camp close to the Polish border.


# 5


*Extracts from the diaries of Dr Paul Joseph Goebbels:*

1 September 1939: 6 a.m.

War began this morning. At daybreak our troops crossed the Polish border . . .

An incident occurred at Gleiwitz, when our soldiers were fired on by Polish troops. It was, I understand, well staged and will be used by the Fuehrer, when he addresses the Reichstag later this morning, as the reason for our declaration of war. His patience with the Poles (and he has been so patient) has finally run out. They have only themselves to blame for what will happen to them. My only worry, which I have kept to myself in all the belligerence of those surrounding the Fuehrer now, is that England and France will commit themselves to war in support of Poland. What business is it of theirs? But what can one expect of colonial powers? They are forever telling other people what to do . . .

I had the Fuehrer's proclamation to the forces broadcast over the radio at 5.40, just twenty minutes ago; those who heard it will be waking others to tell them. The newspapers will have extra editions on the streets within the hour; any laggard editors will be reported to me.

I have sent suggestions to the Fuehrer for his speech

to the Reichstag this morning and he is pleased with them. I have seen a copy of the speech and he has incorporated them . . .

One upsetting item is his nomination of Goering as his successor should anything (God forbid!) happen to him. Hess is next in line. God protect the Fuehrer, if only for the sake of Germany! What must I do to be in line for succession? Should I have been fat or tall?

. . . The O'Dea woman has been given her marching orders. I thought I handled the situation Wednesday morning with Canaris admirably. I am troubled by the thought that Himmler knows she is Jewish; war, perhaps, has come at the right moment. She will be gone from here today and, if Himmler does raise the matter, I can call Canaris as a witness that I suspected all along that she was Jewish. He will side with me against Himmler . . . Too, the Fuehrer is going to need me more than ever from now on. I have to sell the war to the German people. I know I can do it . . .

But the memory of the O'Dea woman will linger. The unattained still has a sweet taste . . .

# CHAPTER TWELVE

## 1

Carmody was woken at six o'clock by the ringing of the phone on his desk. He struggled up from the couch where he had had an uncomfortable night's sleep, ready to curse London or New York for calling him at this hour. But when he picked up the phone it was Meg Arrowsmith.

'Sean? I rang you at your flat . . . Have you heard the news?'

'What news?' But he knew.

'The army went into Poland this morning – it's just come over the wireless. Oh darling!' She sounded as if she were weeping. 'Come over and comfort me, please!'

'Meg, I can't – where are you, anyway?' She couldn't be ringing from a Gestapo station.

'In the bar at the Adlon. Come and have breakfast with me – *please*. I have to talk to someone –'

There was desperation (and despair, he guessed) in her voice; but he had other things to do first. 'Stay there, I'll get there as soon as I can. But I have to get some work off first . . .'

He hung up and tried to call London. 'I am sorry sir, but all lines to London are closed till further notice.'

'New York? Paris?'

'The same, sir.'

He rang the Foreign Press Office and a jerky-voiced clerk told him, yes, German troops had crossed the Polish border and hostilities had begun. More information would be forthcoming later.

He had a quick wash in the office basin, put on his jacket and hat and went over to the cable office. He wrote out a 10-line piece and handed it to the cable clerk, an elderly man with a squint, who shook his head but said nothing.

'You think it's bad news?' said Carmody.

The man shrugged, looked around to see if anyone was observing him, nodded his head and went away. Carmody left him and went over to the Wilhelmstrasse. He paused for a moment as he came out of the cable office and looked up at the morning sky. The marvellous light that he always admired wasn't there this morning; clouds hung low and the air was thick, almost tropical. He heard the sound of planes, but he couldn't see them for the clouds; early workers on their way to work stopped and looked up, poised to run if they heard the air-raid sirens go. But these were German bombers heading east and in a moment their sound had disappeared. Everyone went on their way again, but Carmody noticed they were now walking appreciably faster.

In the ministry offices on the Wilhelmstrasse nobody knew anything other than that hostilities had begun. 'It won't mean real war, of course,' said the man in the Foreign Ministry hopefully. 'It will all be over by Monday.'

'You don't think the Poles will fight?'

'Of course not. Over Danzig? No, no.'

'What about England and France? They've promised to come to Poland's aid.'

'No, I told you – by Monday it will all be over. England and France will not have mobilized by then. Don't write anything sensational, Herr Carmody.'

'Has Warsaw been bombed?'

'Of course not. I told you – hostilities will be limited.'

Frustrated, not believing anything he had been told, Carmody looked at his watch and decided there was time to have a quick breakfast with Meg before he had to meet Cathleen and her mother at the American embassy.

The bar was crowded with foreign correspondents, all of them looking as frustrated as he felt. Joe Begley greeted him, asking him if he knew any more than they did; this was no time for competition. He told Begley he knew nothing and went on to Meg, who was sitting alone at a table in a far corner. She looked as if she had just come from the centre of hostilities.

'You look like hell,' he said as he sat down. 'What happened to you? I saw those bastards pick you up outside my place –'

'You didn't come looking for me?'

'Meg, I can't afford to shove my neck out, not right now. They're ready to kick me out any moment . . . I've been worried about you, if that's any consolation.'

'It is, darling.' She put her claw of a hand on his. 'You're my only friend, the only one I have left.'

Jesus, he thought; and was saved from an answer by the arrival of a waiter. 'Hello, Hans. I'll have sausages, eggs and bacon.'

The waiter, grey-haired and stooped, a relic of the Kaiser's day, produced a small pair of silver scissors on a cord. 'May I have your ration tickets, Herr Carmody?'

Carmody looked at the scissors. 'When did you get those?'

'Just this morning, sir. From now on we have to clip your ration tickets.'

Carmody felt in his pockets. 'I don't have them. I think my secretary got some for me – they're probably back at the office –'

'Here, Hans. Take mine.' Meg handed her ration tickets to the waiter. 'I'm not eating.' She lifted her gin-and-tonic to show she was taking other sustenance. 'Herr Carmody is my guest.'

The waiter went away and Carmody said, 'You'd better lay off the grog. Things are going to get nasty from now on.'

'The more reason to stay on the grog, as you call it. Darling, I don't care any more. The world has fallen in on me. You may use that phrase if you wish.'

'The world has fallen in on itself,' he said, going one better; or trying to. 'When did the bullies let you go?'

'Our friends, the Gestapo? Last night, at midnight. I've been here all night, looking for a friend to drop in. Nobody has, not till you came.'

'Did they knock you around?' She was dishevelled, all her English smartness gone, but he could see no bruises or blood.

'Physically? No. No rack, no torture, nothing like that. Just questioning, questioning. And abuse. That swine Decker is very good at that. He called me everything –' She shook her head, tears glistening in her eyes. 'What he called me may have been true, but one doesn't like to hear it. Not from the likes of him.'

Carmody didn't ask what she had been called; he didn't want her humiliated any further. 'What sort of questions did they ask you?'

'About you, for one thing. They have some bizarre idea that you and I are in some sort of plot.'

His nerve-ends suddenly felt as if they had enlarged. 'Plot? What sort of plot?'

'Something against the Fuehrer – they weren't specific. I don't think they really know – they were just guessing. They are such a suspicious lot of swine.'

Hans, the waiter, came back with Carmody's breakfast; but Carmody had lost his appetite. He toyed with his food in the same way as Meg had here in this bar a week ago. 'Meg, I think you should go home. Today.'

'That's what Inspector Lutze told me. Go home to England, he said, Germany doesn't want your sort any more. That's what he said.' The tears came to her eyes again. 'Oh God, it was all so different a year ago! I *was* wanted – the Fuehrer, Goebbels, I was a friend of Emmy Goering's, it was all so gay and – and *promising!*'

'It's not that way any more, Meg.' He began to eat, suddenly wanting sustenance.

'What happened, darling? What went wrong?'

'Stone the crows, Meg – do I have to spell it out for you? Hitler went wrong!' He had unconsciously raised his voice. Four men at the next table turned to look at him; fortunately, they were all men from foreign newspapers. They nodded approvingly, then went back to their own conversation. 'Meg, go home – please. Get in that car of yours and drive like hell for home.'

'I can't, darling.' She shook her head. She sat silent for a while, then looked up at him. 'Would you like my car? I shan't want it any more.'

'Why not? What are you going to do?' All at once he was afraid for her. Was she contemplating suicide? She looked in the right mood for it.

'It's too conspicuous – it's an English car. They'd stone me.'

He grinned, trying to lighten her mood. 'So you'd let them throw stones at me?'

'No, no!' She was genuinely concerned for him. Ah Meg, he thought, don't you have anyone else to love, to call a friend? He felt burdened again. 'No, I'd hate anything to happen to you . . . Oh Sean, what are we going to do?'

He looked at his watch. 'I have something to do right now. I'm sorry, I'd like to sit here and keep you company, but I can't –' He put his hand on hers, felt the trembling in the thin claw. He looked into her dark eyes, something he had tried to avoid till now. There was nothing there but utter hopelessness and it frightened him. 'Get out of here, go home to your flat, have a bath and get some sleep. If I can, I'll come round and see you this evening – I'll bring you to dinner here –'

She turned her hand over under his, gave him something of the old Lady Margaret Arrowsmith smile, the one the German magazines had once featured so prominently when she had been such good propaganda for the Nazi cause. 'Darling, I could have fallen in love with you.'

*Paddy and Ida, listen to this* . . . 'We would have had to have met a long time ago, Meg. Before you came to Germany. I've got to go. Thanks for breakfast. Go home, like I said, and I'll do my best to see you this evening.'

'*Auf wiedersehen*, darling.'

'Hooroo,' he said in Australian, because in his ears it sounded better than German.

He went over to the Foreign Press Office. No, no foreign correspondents were being allowed to go to the front; not yet, but possibly tomorrow or Sunday. 'We'll let you know, Herr Carmody.'

'But the war – I mean hostilities – could be over by then.'

The press liaison officer smiled. 'Who told you that?' He was the sort of man Carmody had found in so many press liaison offices, the ex-newspaperman who had grown too lazy to go chasing stories, who preferred to hand them out. 'Do you have information that we don't, Herr Carmody?'

'I got it from your Foreign Ministry,' said Carmody, stirring the pot, dropping in an indigestible.

The press liaison officer looked sour, as Carmody had expected him to. 'They know nothing.'

'That's what I thought. They didn't know if Warsaw has been bombed or not.' It was a shot in the dark, a small bomb of his own.

The officer hesitated, then nodded. 'Yes, it has been bombed, and several other cities. But the High Command hasn't yet released the information. For the moment it's classified. You can't send it.'

Carmody thought of Oliver Burberry in Warsaw, opening his umbrella against the hail of bombs. 'I think the rest of the world already knows by now. You can't classify what the Poles are sending out.'

He went back to his office. The streets were busy now, the city's routine apparently undisturbed: products had to be made, goods had to be sold, money had to be banked. As he crossed the Potsdamerplatz he remembered today was Friday. He stopped by the flower-women and bought a bunch of carnations. Then:

'And some roses. A dozen red and a dozen of those cream ones.'

The flower-seller, fat and jolly with cheeks as pink as her carnations, smiled at him. 'Three ladies? You are a lucky man.'

There was a fourth to whom he should take flowers this evening. 'Not all the time. What do you think about the war?'

'It will be good for business,' she said, no longer smiling, abruptly cautious. 'If they still let the flowers grow.'

'If,' he said, remembering how the flowers had died in Spain.

When he got up to the office Olga was there, had been for the past hour. 'As soon as I heard the news, I came in. Oh, thank you.' She took the carnations, looked at the roses. 'I'll put those in water for Fräulein O'Dea and Frau Hoolahan. You're learning, Herr Carmody.'

'To be a European?'

'Yes,' she said, who had never been so frank before. 'But it may be too late.'

He stood at the window and looked down into the square. The day was still overcast, reflecting the mood of the people in the streets. The weather, they say, is fickle, but it sometimes has an unerring instinct for the right temper. Men were painting white lines along the kerbs; people stopped to look curiously at them, as if they did not understand the reason for the white lines. *Blackout, you fools*, Carmody told them silently. He looked for signs of sandbags, but so far there was none. Had the Civil Defence authorities been caught napping by the outbreak of war or did they think that the Poles wouldn't dare bomb Berlin?

Kreisler was late. The clock across the square showed 8.30 before he knocked on the door and Olga showed him into the office. 'My apologies, Herr Carmody. A little difficulty – I'm out of practice. I worked till three o'clock this morning, then overslept.'

'You're heard the news about Poland?'

'Perhaps I should have stayed asleep, forever. But it had to come, once the madman had put Stalin on our side . . . There.' He held out the passport and the exit permit. 'A little difficult, as I said, but now they are perfect. No one will know the difference.'

Carmody looked at the passport, squinted closely at it; it was impossible to see where Mady's photograph had been substituted for that of Sybille Dix. He went to the safe, took out the remaining five hundred dollars, passed them to Kreisler.

'I would suggest that the new owner of the passport practise Frau Dix's signature, in case she is asked to sign something. Fortunately, Frau Dix was an elderly lady and elderly people often have handwriting that looks as if it came out of a mould. Rather scratchy. She signs it: S. Dix. Very easy.' He scrawled the signature on a pad on Carmody's desk, the artist showing off his skill. 'She should have no difficulty. Good luck, Herr Carmody.'

'You, too. What sort of tunes are you going to play now?'

'Not a polonaise.' He grinned.

'Give my regards to your monkey.'

Kreisler gave a wider grin, raised his hat and left. A survivor, thought Carmody: a month, a year, a decade from now, he would be playing his tunes, still there on the street-corners of God knew what sort of world.

Carmody put the passport and exit permit in his pocket, picked up his hat and went out to the outer office. 'I'm going to the American embassy, then I'm putting Cathleen and her mother on the eleven o'clock train for Copenhagen.'

'Say goodbye to them for me.' Olga gave him back the roses and the carnations. 'Tell them they are from me.'

He hesitated, then kissed her on the cheek. 'Thanks, Olga.'

He went out, laden with flowers, afraid to look at her face. When he reached the American embassy, Cathleen and Mady were already there, standing apart from the long queue that stretched down the block and round the corner. 'The queue is so *long*!' said Cathleen. 'They'll hate us for jumping in ahead of them.'

'You're Americans. Be grateful for that, never mind feeling ashamed of it.' He looked at Mady, who looked so much smarter, even healthier, this morning. 'What happened to you?'

'We just had time to do some shopping before we came here,' said Cathleen. 'She couldn't travel in what she was wearing yesterday.'

'Women!' he said.

They went into the embassy, had a little difficulty with the clerk on the desk in the crowded lobby, then were shown into an office where a second secretary looked up in surprise, as if he had been expecting someone else. He glanced at Carmody, who still had his armful of flowers.

'I'm just their escort,' said Carmody, who knew the second secretary slightly. 'I'm putting them on the eleven o'clock train for Copenhagen.'

'Really?' He was a young man from Harvard, with an East Coast disdain for anyone from the West Coast; worse still, Miss O'Dea was from Hollywood. Carmody had never learned his opinion of Australia, though the Harvard man gave the impression that he didn't believe such a place could exist. 'I take it you have all the necessary papers, Miss O'Dea?'

'All but the visa for my mother.'

'Your mother?' He was looking at the German passport. 'It says here that her name is Dix, that she is German.'

Cathleen glanced at Carmody, but he said nothing: this was her battle. 'Mr Everett, I know you people here at the embassy don't think much of me.' She paused, but if she was expecting a polite contradiction she didn't get it. Everett looked at her without expression. 'You think because I came here to play in a German film, I'm a Nazi sympathizer. Or just a money-chaser, ready to take any part so long as it pays well. Isn't that what you think?'

'One or the other,' said Everett, fingers steepled together. Christ Almighty, thought Carmody, how can the bastard be so smug?

'Well, you're wrong, Mr Everett.' Cathleen was somehow keeping control of herself; she wanted to burst out at this cool, smug young man, but she knew that would get her nowhere. It struck her that she was going to have to woo him, but in a different way, as she had wooed Goebbels. 'I came here to try and find my mother –'

'That wasn't what you told us when you first came to us. You never mentioned your mother.'

She hesitated a moment. 'I didn't trust you, Mr Everett. Not you, but the embassy. I didn't know who you had working for you, if the file on my mother might get into the wrong hands.'

'You should trust us more, Miss O'Dea. You have been working too long in Hollywood, too many spy films.'

'I've never been in a spy film,' she said tartly. 'Anyhow, I finally – with the help of some *Germans* – I found my mother. She was in Ravensbrueck.'

'How did you get her out of *there*?' His expression changed; he showed some surprise.

'That would be telling,' she said, then added sweetly, 'not that I don't trust you, Mr Everett.'

Not much, his expression said. 'Go on, Miss O'Dea.'

Carmody and Mady had sat silent throughout all this, he with the flowers laid in his lap, looking like a lost lover, she sitting bolt upright on her chair, looking like a mother disapproving of her daughter trying to woo the superior young man on the other side of the desk. Without consultation they had decided that Cathleen should plead the case: it needed an actress.

But she was not acting. She could feel her voice rising in her, wanting to break out; but this cool young man in front of her was not going to be swayed by emotion. He would only accuse her of trying to 'Hollywood' him. Nor would he respond to the sensual instep or the promise in the artificially husky voice. 'Mr Everett, my mother came here to try and rescue *her* mother. She failed – my grandmother died in Ravensbrueck.' She looked at Mady, who bit her lip and nodded. 'The chances are my mother would have died there, too, eventually . . . She has lived in America for 26 years, Mr Everett. The only thing about her that isn't American is her passport – but she has promised me she will take out citizenship as soon as we are home. *Home*, Mr Everett – that's where we want to go. That passport she has is a forged one, we'll admit that, but it's all we could get – they took away her own passport –'

'The exit permit – that's forged, too?'

'Yes.'

Everett looked at Carmody. 'Did you know about this?'

'I got them for her,' said Carmody.

'For a story?'

Carmody wanted to hit him. 'No, for humanitarian reasons.'

Everett gazed at him, getting the message; then he looked back at Cathleen. 'I'm sorry, Miss O'Dea –'

Her voice broke out of her then: '*Sorry?* God, what does she have to do to be an American? She –'

He held up his hand. 'Please, Miss O'Dea. I was about to say I am sorry for having misjudged your reasons for coming here. We will give your mother her visa. How soon do you want it?'

'Now,' said Carmody, looking at his watch. 'They are

booked out on the eleven o'clock train for Copenhagen.'

Everett smiled for the first time, looking human and humanitarian. 'You were sure of us, weren't you?'

'Of course,' said Carmody.

But Everett wasn't flattered. 'So are all those Jews in the queue outside. Unfortunately, we are going to have to let some of them down. Good luck, Miss O'Dea, Mrs –' he looked at the German passport '– Dix.'

'Hoolahan,' said Mady, smiling, looking as if she might kiss him.

'A good American name,' said Everett, though it sounded like an effort for him to say so.

Ten minutes later they were out of the embassy and hailing a taxi to take them to the Stettiner station. As they drove away Carmody, without looking back, was aware of the waiting, hopeful, patient people in the queue looking after them. There was no need to look back: he could *feel* the envy, even the hatred, of those fortunate enough to be escaping.

'For a moment there I was going to hit him.' Cathleen sat slumped in the corner of the back seat. She was utterly drained, as if she had just played a long emotional scene; which she had. 'God, why do they always have to be so *officious*? Is that the word I want?'

'It'll do,' said Carmody. 'But he has a job to do – maybe it's his only way of coping.'

Cathleen looked at her mother. 'Never has an unkind word to say about anyone. Except women.'

Mady smiled at him and he grinned back. He handed her the cream roses, gave the red roses to Cathleen and split the carnations between them. 'Those are from Olga.'

'Poor Olga,' said Cathleen and he nodded.

The station was packed, as if at peak holiday time. But there were no holiday-makers this morning; everyone was too sober-faced to be mistaken for one of those. A troop train was drawn up at one platform; young men, some with faces drawn with apprehension, others with a sort of stupid cheerfulness, stared out the windows. The other platforms were crowded with a mixture of civilians and men in uniform. The men in uniform, most of them SS, looked more cheerful than the young soldiers in the troop train; but then they were heading west, not towards the fighting. The Copenhagen train looked already full, but the platform beside it was still crowded.

Carmody pushed a way through the crowd, the women following him. He was glad he had not allowed Cathleen to go back to her flat to collect anything; she had suggested it in the taxi, but he had vetoed it in case Lutze or Decker was there watching it. Without luggage she and Mady would have less difficulty in squeezing into their compartment.

'Here it is!' he cried above the noise and halted outside the door of one of the first class carriages.

'Are you going, too?' said a voice behind him in English.

He turned round, suddenly scared, though he didn't know why; but it was only Fred Doe, cornet-case in one hand, suitcase in the other. 'Fred! Thank Christ – are you going to Copenhagen?'

'Copenhagen, New York – all the way, pal.' He put down his suitcase and tipped his hat to Cathleen and Mady. 'Glad to see you made it.'

'I'm glad to see *you* made it,' said Carmody.

'Are you leaving us, Herr Carmody?' said a voice in German.

Carmody turned round, everything abruptly draining out of him, leaving him weak and sick. 'Hello, Lutze. No, I'm not leaving. I'm just saying goodbye to Fräulein O'Dea and her friend Frau Dix.'

Lutze raised his hat to the two women. 'Good morning, ladies. May I see your papers?'

'They're all in order,' said Cathleen, making no effort to open her handbag and produce them.

'I'm sure they are,' said Lutze, hand outstretched.

Cathleen and Mady handed over their papers. Lutze looked at them, nodded, pursed his lips. Then he turned, looked into the crowd and jerked his head. Decker pushed his way through the crowd; with him were two city policemen, *Schupos*. For one wild moment Carmody thought of knocking down Lutze and pushing Cathleen and Mady on to the train; but they could go nowhere if the train did not move. And here in Berlin they were still 250 miles from the frontier.

'What's the trouble, Herr Inspector?'

'You will have to come with us, we have some questions. The station-master has given us a room.'

Carmody looked up at the station clock: ten minutes till train time. 'Will it take long? They'll miss the train –'

'There will be other trains, Herr Carmody. Please?'

Carmody took the flowers from Cathleen and Mady, gave them to Doe. 'Fred, seats 1 and 2 compartment Three. Keep the seats for them with these.'

'Sure, pal. Good luck.'

The crowd fell back as the small group moved down the platform. Give me the clapper-bell again, thought Carmody. *Unclean, unclean!* . . . The policemen pushed open the door to a small office and Lutze and Decker stood back to allow the women and Carmody to enter. When they were inside, Decker closed the door and stood with his back to it, while the two policemen took up their stance outside.

'What's this all about, Herr Inspector?' Carmody could see that Cathleen was on the verge of explosion; Mady, more accustomed to the Gestapo and their methods, was quiet, almost resigned. He decided he would do his best to keep both women quiet. 'The papers are in order –'

'It isn't the papers, Herr Carmody. It's what you and Fräulein O'Dea have been trying to do. Frau Dix is no concern of ours, except that she is a friend of Fräulein O'Dea –'

'What are Fräulein O'Dea and I supposed to have been doing?' He had to hold down his voice.

'Herr Carmody, why do you think we have been following you and the Fräulein for the past two weeks? There is a plot against the Fuehrer –'

Carmody couldn't help his laugh, though it was harsh and humourless. 'Lutze, this is bizarre –' He used Meg's word; it was almost the same in German as in English. 'What gives you the idea we'd be involved in anything so –' His mind went dead for the moment: he couldn't think of a word other than to repeat: 'bizarre.'

Lutze drew him aside into one corner of the room, lowered his voice. 'Herr Carmody, we are working under direct orders from Reichsfuehrer Himmler. I am not convinced you are involved, but you know too many of the suspects – Fräulein O'Dea, Lady Arrowsmith –'

Carmody shook his head in dismay. 'Herr Inspector, why them?'

Lutze lowered his voice even further; the Gestapo officer and the foreign correspondent stood with their heads close together, like conspirators. 'Herr Carmody, you know what goes on amongst the higher-ups in the Party. The rivalries, the jealousies . . . Reichsminister Goebbels is a suspect – the two women I've just named – they have been seeing him –'

Carmody looked up at the clock in the office: four minutes to train time. 'Not Lady Arrowsmith – she hasn't been a friend of his for months. Neither is Fräulein O'Dea. Lutze, it's all a terrible mistake – let her and Frau Dix go –'

Lutze shook his head. 'I can't. What if the plot goes ahead, if they do what they plan?'

'What is their plan?'

Lutze shrugged; he wasn't supposed to know everything. 'Kill the Fuehrer? I'm afraid I have to take the women to headquarters, Herr Carmody –'

Carmody's mind had been slipping out of gear; suddenly it was working again. 'Lutze, there *is* a plot! I don't know who's involved, but I know where it's going to happen.'

Lutze, who had for a moment looked regretful at the way things had turned out, abruptly looked sharp. 'Where? Why didn't you tell –'

'I'm not going to tell you now, not unless we make a deal. Let the women go on that train, and I'll take you where I think there's someone about to kill the Fuehrer.'

'I don't have to make bargains, Herr Carmody –'

'You do if you want to save the Fuehrer in time. Come on, Lutze, for Christ's sake!' The clock was ticking away above his head. 'It's true – I swear it! Let them go and I'll make you a hero!'

His voice had risen; Cathleen, Mady and Decker were

staring at him. Decker, puzzled, stepped forward. 'What's he up to? What's he saying?'

Carmody ignored him; he stared at Lutze, figuratively grabbing him by the lapels. 'Lutze, there's no time to waste! Come on – please! Let them catch that train!'

Lutze looked at Decker, but he didn't seem to see him. He was an intelligent man, but so far all his decisions had been simple ones, based on the authority of the Gestapo. To take people into custody for questioning had never really needed decision; neither was it his decision what happened to those questioned after he had finished with them. But now he had been put out on a limb: he had no desire to be a hero, but he did not want to be a stupid villain, one who might have saved the Fuehrer but let him die for want of some courage. Decker would be no help: his thoughts never extended beyond the length of his arm.

He blinked, glanced up at the clock, then looked back at Carmody. 'They can go. They will have to hurry.'

Carmody grabbed Cathleen and Mady, pushed them ahead of him out the door, yelling at the two policemen to clear a way for them through the crowd. The *Schupos* looked at Lutze, who nodded, then they started pushing their way through the throng, shouting and waving their batons; the crowd fell back in alarm, and Carmody and the two gasping women ran headlong down the platform as they heard the conductor blow his whistle. Carmody flung open the carriage door, pushed Mady in, then almost hurled Cathleen in after her. There was no time for kisses or embraces; the train was moving. He stepped back, watched it go, all at once feeling empty and alone.

He saw Cathleen leaning out of the carriage window, waving and shouting something. It sounded like, *I love you!*, but it was lost in the hubbub of the crowd and the shriek of the train's whistle as it went round the curve out of the station into the sunlight struggling to come through the lifting clouds.

'Now,' said Lutze behind him, 'for your part of the bargain, Herr Carmody.'

# 2

'Don't worry,' said Romy. 'They will both be with us this evening.'

'Aren't you going back to your husband?' said Melissa.

'No. Oh, I shall have to go back to clear up all the messy legal bits, the divorce won't be easy. But go back to live with him? No. He'll be angry and hurt, but it will be his pride that's hurt, nothing else. Oh, and his reputation. So will mine, for that matter. But it will all soon be forgotten, now that war has come. I remember what it was like in the last war. I was younger than you then, just eighteen when it broke out. Mistresses went to live with their lovers – they grabbed what happiness they could. Kurt and I will do the same. The priests won't give me absolution for breaking my marriage vows, but that's a sin I'll have to carry. I love Kurt too much to turn my back on what time we have left.'

They were in the Horch half way along the autobahn to Hamburg. They had said their goodbyes to the General and Helmut last night when the two men had left for the Englishman's flat on the Unter den Linden. There had been no last-minute love-making, no memories of a last night to take with them. Helmut had been working on *Lola und Ludwig* till late; he had not arrived at the Hotel London till almost 11 o'clock. He and Melissa had gone for a walk, leaving his father and Romy some privacy for their farewell. Melissa, still not privy to what would keep the General and Helmut in Berlin till the next morning, had asked no questions; she was content now, satisfied that Helmut did indeed love her, that their marriage would be a success. She was still a little afraid of the General and if he wanted Helmut with him to do some business, she would not dare to ask what it was. Romy, for her part, had sent the General on his way with a silent prayer. He had assured her that he and Helmut would safely carry out their intention and escape without any danger, and she had done her best to take him at his word. What doubts she had she hid from him, from Helmut and from this innocent young English girl beside her in the car. Innocent in politics, if not in other ways.

'The Albern estate is beautiful, you will like it. It will be a good place to spend the war.'

'How long will it last, the war, I mean? A month, two months?'

The Horch overtook a long convoy travelling west; young men, girded for war, waved and whistled at the two women as they swept by. 'It depends what happens this morning,' Romy said without thinking.

'This morning? What's going to happen this morning?'

Romy recovered: 'In Poland, I mean.' Though the news had been inevitable, it had still been a shock when she had heard it at breakfast. 'If the Poles see that Hitler is in earnest, they may sue for peace.'

'If they don't?' She was desperately trying to educate herself in international politics; *Film Weekly* and *Photoplay* had prepared her for none of this. Her baby, after all, would be an Albern: a *von* Albern. One ear listened to her own future name, Melissa von Albern; it beat anything the repertory stage manager had been able to dream up when he had taken Alice Hayfield's virginity. The other ear listened to herself saying, 'Will Helmut and the General have to go into the army?'

'Of course,' said Romy, who had a sense of military, if not marital, duty.

'Oh God,' said Melissa, and looked out at the flat farmlands under the patchy sunlight, trying to imagine what a battlefield would look like. She had always avoided war films.

# 3

*Extracts from the memoirs of General Kurt von Albern:*

. . . This may be the last entry in my journal. I am writing it in the apartment of Herr Oliver Burberry on the Unter den Linden; writing it on *The Times'* notepaper. Perhaps there is some irony there; one rarely appreciates the hands Fate deals us. I have always admired the English (though not their attitude at Munich last year); *The Times* has always been one of my favourite newspapers, though its editor, Dawson, contributed to the appeasement of Hitler. I understand, however, that Herr Burberry had only contempt for the ex-corporal. When our deed is done this morning I hope Herr Burberry will appreciate whence the shot came . . .

Helmut is here with me; pride and pleasure threatened to weaken me last night. I hope that he, if not I, survives this. He deserves happiness with Melissa: there again is irony, that he should be marrying an English girl. I am not sure that she is worthy of the Albern name, but times and customs and people are changing and one can't live forever in the past. Though, like most ageing men, I should like to . . .

I said goodbye to Romy last night, but not in so many words. She must remain convinced that we will meet again back at The Pines. I long so much to spend the rest of my life with her. Yet if we do not succeed in our objective this morning, if war spreads and the English and French come in, I shall have to go back to duty. I cannot remain on the inactive list, not while the Fatherland is being threatened . . .

When we heard the newsboys shouting in the street early this morning, we turned on Herr Burberry's wireless, keeping it as low as possible, and heard the dreaded news. I was stirred by a mixture of anger and despair. Our history is studded with rulers who were unstable or eccentric; this Austrian is plain mad and his madness seems to have spread to those around him. The buffoon Goering, the obsequious Keitel: I speak only of the military ones. One can't stoop to mention the others, the paramilitary thugs and the would-be diplomats . . .

I looked out of the window of this living room a moment ago. The crowds are gathering in the street below waiting for the ride past of Hitler. The crowds are not as large as one would have supposed; that will disappoint the ex-corporal. Nor is there any air of excitement; we have the window open and there is no shouting, no buzz, as one would expect. How different from that first day of war in 1914! The atmosphere on that Saturday, 1 August, was electric. The streets were packed; bands played; people sang. I remember I was in a car with fellow officers; we raced up and down that very street outside, waving our caps and shouting as if we had all just graduated and been released from long years in some dull academy. Perhaps those people down there now have forgotten, under Hitler the Austrian, what it was like to be a true German . . .

Helmut is getting impatient; he is walking about the apartment, unable to sit down for longer than two or three minutes. It is now 11 o'clock and Hitler should be coming soon. He was supposed to address the Reichstag in the Opera House at 10 o'clock; how long will he rant? Why are dictators always so long-winded? Are they trying to convince themselves as well as their captive audience? . . .

4

Lutze and Decker had a car, a small Opel, but they and Carmody did not get far in it. They stayed on the north side of the Spree, then tried to drive south down Friedrichstrasse but were halted by police barriers. They left the car and, with Carmody leading the way, ran west along Dorotheenstrasse, then turned south on Kanonierstrasse. They ran down it, hearing the shouting beginning to rise, though it was not as tumultuous as Carmody had heard at other parades up the Unter den Linden. As he ran, his breath beginning to tear itself out of him, for he was more out of condition than he had suspected, his conscience, the bane of a newspaperman, also began to tear at him. He was sacrificing someone, a stranger, perhaps even someone he knew, for the sake of getting Cathleen and Mady away; in his heart there had been no other choice, but the mind, and not the heart, suffers from conscience. He prayed as he ran that the assassin, whoever he was, would not have turned up at the Burberry flat; or, if he had, he had panicked on finding the unlocked suitcase and the note and had fled. But had left the Mannlicher behind: that was important. It would be Carmody's only piece of evidence that an assassination had been planned. If the assassin, or the gun, were not there, then he would be hauled off to Gestapo headquarters by Lutze and Decker and, worse, word would be sent to the frontier for Cathleen and Mady to be taken off the Copenhagen express. He suddenly developed a stitch in his side, but it was more like a knife of foreboding.

'Please –!' Lutze had pulled up, was leaning against the wall; Decker leaned beside him, elbows holding his sides. 'We must go slower – I can't run any more –'

Carmody tried to drag a breath deep into his lungs. 'We may be too late –' He hoped so: time for Hitler to be shot, time for the assassin to get away.

Lutze pushed himself off the wall. 'Yes – yes. But let us walk – quickly –'

They went on, drawing closer to the Unter den Linden, hearing the shouting. But it was still subdued; it seemed to come in isolated bursts, as if it were being orchestrated but the audience wasn't responding. As they approached the broad Allee he saw some flags being waved above the heads of the crowd, but even they appeared to be waving listlessly, like washing in an apathetic breeze. He, Lutze and Decker came into the Unter den Linden, turned towards the block where Burberry's flat was; they hurried along behind the crowd. The shouting had increased a little; there *were* groups of SS men who were orchestrating it. Carmody stopped for a moment, jumped up on a bench and saw the procession of cars coming up the wide street. There were two lead cars carrying the bodyguard, then Hitler's big Mercedes and three other cars behind it carrying Goering and other officials he couldn't see, and finally three cars with more bodyguard. Hitler was standing up in the Mercedes 770K, the armoured cap low down on his head, his arm going up and down in his limp salute; he looked grey and strained, sick even, his uniform, as always, seeming to hang on him. But he managed the occasional smile and each time he did, the SS groups would shout *Sieg Heil!*

'Come on!' Lutze gasped. 'Where is this place?'

The front door of Burberry's apartment building was open; the caretaker and his wife were on the steps, waving their small swastika flag. As Carmody and the two Gestapo men reached them, there was a sudden commotion in the crowd on this side of the street. There was a shout, a great concerted gasp, then a shot.

5

Helmut, standing at the living room window but hidden from the street by the lace curtains, saw the procession coming up the Unter den Linden, Hitler standing up in his big car and making a splendid target. Suddenly he knew the assassination was going to be successful; another fifty yards and Hitler would be dead and Germany saved! He felt himself tremble with excitement, hoped that his father, the man with the gun, would be more in control than he himself was.

Along the hall in the bathroom General von Albern stood on the toilet seat, the Mannlicher aimed down at the narrow angle of street to be seen from the bathroom window. It was not the most dignified position from which to save one's country; no one, least of all a general, looks comfortable standing on a toilet. But it gave the necessary elevation for the shot and, as Helmut, the Albern with a sense of humour, had said, it was perhaps symbolic.

The General heard the shouting beginning to rise. He steadied the gun, sighted down the telescope; the 4-power Zeiss brought the street up till he felt he could reach out and touch it. He waited for the procession to come into the circle of magnification, for Hitler to appear in the crossed hairlines.

'Two cars leading,' Helmut called from the living room. 'Ten metres apart. Then *him* – standing up!'

The General willed himself to relax, to take the sudden tension out of his trigger finger. He eased off the first trigger, poised his finger round the hair-trigger.

Then he heard the shots down in the street, first the single shot and then the fusillade. His fingers involuntarily tightened on the hair-trigger and the Mannlicher kicked against his shoulder.

6

Carmody, standing on the step beside the caretaker and his wife, about to go into the building, turned as he heard the commotion. Over the heads of the crowd lined along the pavement he saw the woman run into the middle of the road, behind the two lead cars and immediately in front of the car carrying Hitler. He saw her draw the gun and hold it up, then put it to her own head. There was a shot and she started to fall; before she hit the ground there was a fusillade of shots from the bodyguards in the second car in the procession. Her body convulsed, seemed to sidestep, then hit the ground and lay still. Carmody, horror-stricken, took a moment to recognize the woman: it was as if his mind wanted to deny what his eyes told him, that it was Meg Arrowsmith.

The procession suddenly speeded up. The big Mercedes

accelerated as Hitler, without a backward glance at the body in the roadway, abruptly sat down. The other cars roared away up the Unter den Linden behind it and police began running towards the sprawled still figure of Lady Margaret Arrowsmith.

Lutze and Decker were pushing their way through the crowd, forgetting Carmody. He hesitated, wanting to run; but reason prevailed, there was nowhere to run to. He turned, looking back over his shoulder into the empty hallway.

'You were too late, Herr Smith,' said the caretaker.

'Too late?'

'Weren't you coming to Herr Burberry's flat to get a good view of the Fuehrer as he went past?' The caretaker's wife had pushed into the crowd to get a good view of the woman who had tried to shoot the Fuehrer, but he had to stay and guard his doorway.

'Yes,' said Carmody. 'I'll go up there now. Those gentlemen who were with me – tell them where I am.'

Lutze and Decker were out of sight beyond the humming, straining crowd. He went into the hallway and up the stairs as the caretaker's wife came back to report to her husband what she had managed to see. Carmody was halfway up the stairs when he heard the door open on the top floor. He looked up and saw the two men come out of Burberry's flat; both tall me, but unrecognizable against the bright square of the skylight in the roof on the stairwell. Then he looked down as he heard Lutze and Decker come into the lobby.

'Herr Carmody!' Lutze's shout boomed up the funnel of the stairwell.

Carmody looked up. The two men on the top landing had disappeared; he.had no idea where they had gone, but they were no longer there. 'Here, Inspector! Come on up!'

Lutze and Decker came running up the stairs, caught up with him as he reached the top floor. He glanced quickly around; there were three other doors besides Burberry's opening off the landing; the two must have disappeared into one of them. He put the key into Burberry's door, but it wouldn't go in; there was a key already in it, on the inside. He looked at Lutze, who hadn't missed the fact; then he turned the knob and opened the unlocked door and stepped aside, afraid that the two men might even have stepped back into the flat and were waiting for him and the Gestapo men with guns ready to blaze. But the flat was empty.

The gun-case was open on the table in the living room, an opened box of cartridges beside it. Decker found the Mannlicher in the bathroom and brought it out. 'One shot has been fired.'

'We'll probably find it in the woman,' said Lutze.

I doubt it, thought Carmody. Whoever had been here in the flat would not have shot at Meg, not even out of anger or frustration at having had his assassination attempt foiled; he would have been making his escape as soon as possible. Carmody looked around the living room. Some sheets of *The Times* notepaper lay on the table beside the open case and the box of cartridges, but there seemed nothing else to suggest who had been here in the flat.

Lutze picked up the top sheet of notepaper, held it up to the light.

'Does anything show up?' said Carmody, hoping nothing would.

Lutze shook his head. 'Sometimes the indentation from the page above comes through . . . There's nothing. You had better tell us how you knew what was going on here?'

Carmody sighed inwardly: he was betraying everyone to-day: 'Lady Arrowsmith told me. She didn't say who it was, just where it was supposed to take place.'

'She told us nothing yesterday and last night,' said Decker angrily, and bounced the Mannlicher in his hands, as if *he* should have shot Meg.

'We'll never know now, will we?' said Lutze, looking carefully at Carmody.

'No, I suppose not. But I don't think she was trying to kill the Fuehrer. She committed suicide, for God's sake –' His voice unexpectedly rose. All at once he had to defend Meg; whatever her faults, she had not been an assassin. 'Maybe she was trying to warn Hitler –'

'Why should she shoot herself, to do that?'

'Would he have stopped to listen to her? She told me herself – he would have nothing to do with her, he'd kicked her out of his circle –' Suddenly he gave up, overcome by sadness for Meg. Perhaps she had chosen the best way out, suiciding in front of the monster who had let her down, laying her death on him. Though Carmody doubted that Hitler would care . . . 'It's all over, anyway. Hitler's safe and the war will go on.'

'Yes,' said Lutze, and to Carmody's acute ear sounded regretful. 'You will have to come with us. There will be more questions.'

Down in the street the crowds had begun to disperse, but a big group hung about in the middle of the street, watching Meg Arrowsmith's body being loaded into an ambulance. As Carmody and the two Gestapo men got into a taxi, the ambulance went away down the Unter den Linden, under the lime, the plane and the chestnut trees. Carmody looked up at the sky; the clouds had lifted and the sun was shining. Germany, he thought, was mocking the sad, dead Lady Arrowsmith.

*Meanwhile elsewhere:*

# QUICK NAZI VICTORY SEEN IN YORKVILLE

## But German Language New Yorkers Cautious Talking to Strangers

. . . A dinner dance with a Viennese motif has been planned for the Labor Day weekend at the Atlantic Beach Club, Long Island. Members will wear costumes characteristic of the waltz era. There are few, if any, Viennese members of the club . . .

## LONDON IS LIKENED TO BESEIGED CITY

### Lights Out, Guns Pointed to Sky, City Broods in Incredible Calm

. . . In answer to patriotic and other music played from a German ship in the Port of London yesterday, dockers sang while they worked. 'Pack Up Your Troubles in Your Old Kitbag' and hill-billy songs were the most popular. Even foremen stirred themselves to join in . . .

. . . Police investigating the explosion which reduced the centre of Coventry to a shambles on Friday afternoon believe that the IRA placed a time bomb on a trades-man's bicycle which had been left standing in the street. Five people were killed and 60 injured . . .

. . . The London Stock Exchange had a more confident tone this morning. Gilts hardened . . .

*Wishing will make it so . . .*

. . . In the forthcoming 'Abe Lincoln in Illinois' it was announced that Raymond Massey will be made up to resemble the portrait of Lincoln on the five-dollar bill – the only instance on record where the movies have risked an appeal to the upper income group . . .

## COLOMBIA SUGGESTS SOUTH AMERICAN UNION ON NEUTRALITY

### BRAZIL SETS NEW COFFEE RATES

. . . Orson Welles, boy genius, has officially become part of Hollywood. He has been received by Shirley Temple, has ridden on her merry-go-round and has been photographed with her. All this in spite of the fact that he wears a beard . . .

# SARATOGA IS GAY AS SEASON ENDS

## GERMANS' GAY RUSH TO ARMS

. . . Jitterbugs will take the stage again when Tommy Dorsey and his orchestra put on a swing-and-win contest at the NY World's Fair . . . For those who prefer music of a different type there will be concerts at the Temple of Religion . . .

## *GERMAN AND ITALIAN SHIPS HURRY HOME*

## US LEADS AUSTRALIA 2–0 IN DAVIS CUP

*Somewhere over the rainbow
'Way up high
There's a land that I dream of . . .*

# CHAPTER THIRTEEN

## 1

*Extracts from the memoirs of General Kurt von Albern:*

. . . We were fortunate to escape from Herr Burberry's apartment. As soon as the Mannlicher went off – a stupid mistake for a professional soldier – I dropped it in the bath and hurried out to the living room to join Helmut. There was no question of staying for a second attempt to kill Hitler; we had to be gone from the apartment as quickly as possible. Helmut had opened the door and I was about to follow him when I saw the pages for my journal, face down on the table as I had left them. I had left them there, hoping that Helmut might read them; but he is a man of honour, as I should have known an Albern would be, and the pages had been left undisturbed. I grabbed them and Helmut and I went out of the apartment.

To our dismay we saw that we could not go down the way we had come. Some people were standing in the open front doorway; it was impossible to tell who they were. A man came into the vestibule and started to come up the stairs. He looked up, then paused; he looked vaguely familiar, but I don't know who he was. Then two other men came into the vestibule; one of them shouted a name, which I didn't catch. Then the three of them began to hurry up the stairs.

By then we had disappeared. Helmut had been trying the other three doors on the landing; one of them opened as he turned its handle. We slipped inside; we were in another apartment. We could hear two or three excited voices in an inner room; the owners of the voices must have been craning out of the windows to see what was going on below. I felt acute embarrassment at being in someone else's home unin-vited and unsuspected; it is not something a gentle-man does. Helmut put his finger to his lips, stood with his ear against the front door. We heard the three men come up on to the landing; a moment, then they had gone into Herr Burberry's apartment. We waited a few more seconds, then Helmut opened the door and we stepped quietly out on to the landing. It went against my whole breeding to be sneaking out like this; one should retreat with dignity. But I found myself follow-ing Helmut, who was showing the value of common sense over chivalry; perhaps he learned it in the film business. We went down the stairs, trying, as Helmut whispered to me, to look like guests from one of the apartments who had been witnessing the procession.

The tactic succeeded. The caretaker (I assume it was he) and a woman I suppose was his wife looked at us, but did not hinder us; indeed, the man, with a proper sense of his place, touched his forehead to me . . .

. . . We are now back at The Pines, all four of us: Romy, Melissa, Helmut and myself. For the moment there is happiness on a personal level; perhaps a brittle happiness, but in wartime, as I remember from the Great War, happiness is a day-to-day emotion. Hel-mut and Melissa are to be married at the weekend. I do not know how happy they will be; there seems to be a certain doubtfulness about Helmut's outlook towards the marriage. Romy, however, assures me it will work and I suppose one must bow to a woman's opinion in such matters. I should have thought, however, that she, of all women, would wish for more in a marriage than that it should just *work* . . .

A week, two weeks at the most, to see how the war will progress now that England and France have en-tered it, then Helmut and I will volunteer our services. I had never thought that duty would have a sour taste to it . . .

# 2

*Extract from the diaries of Dr Paul Joseph Goebbels:*

3 September 1939:

. . . We shall win this war! I must never allow myself
to believe otherwise . . .

# 3

Cathleen stood at the window of her and Mady's suite in
Brown's Hotel in London and looked out at Albemarle
Street. The narrow thoroughfare was being prepared for war:
dark blinds were being screwed into place inside the shop
windows, sandbags stood like Roman foundations waiting to
be built upon again, a sign was going up pointing to the
nearest air raid shelter. But the passers-by in the street,
despite looking slightly odd with their gas-masks hanging
from one shoulder like natives' dilly-bags, did not appear to
be disturbed. Cathleen had had only two days' acquaintance
with the English but already she was beginning to appreciate
that they were a nation apart. Patient to the point of exasper-
ating someone as impatient as herself, phlegmatic and with a
self-deprecating humour: they really were like Edmund
Gwenn and some of the other English actors she had worked
with. The hotel seemed to be staffed with waiters and maids
who had come from the English branch of Central Casting.

*I must stop thinking in movie terms* . . . The world had
become too serious for such points of reference.

'Did you know Lady Arrowsmith?' said Swenson, the man
from the London office of World Press.

'Only slightly.'

'It was a good piece Sean did on her. Have you spoken to him?'

'He rang me from Copenhagen last night. He's fine, but I'm glad he is coming to London.'

'They're sending me there to replace him.' Swenson, a veteran of ten years in Asia and Africa, a reporter of wars in China and Ethiopia, wrinkled his nose at the assignment. 'Now his press accreditation has been revoked –'

'I'm glad,' said Cathleen, who, sensibly and womanly, had a selfish attitude towards war. 'For his sake. I'm sorry you have to go to Berlin.'

'I guess it could be worse. They could be sending me to Warsaw.' He closed his notebook. 'I'll do a sympathetic piece on you, Cathleen. When Louis B. Mayer reads that you really went to Germany to find your mother, he'll give you absolution. He might even buy your story for a movie.'

'Sure,' said Cathleen. 'But at a bottom price.'

As Swenson left, Mady came in carrying boxes and shopping bags. 'Oh, I've gone mad! The storekeepers in Bond Street are out on the sidewalks waving little American flags in my honour – What's the matter?'

Cathleen had sat down in a chair and begun to weep. Mady dropped everything on the floor and rushed to her, fell to her knees and put her arms round her daughter. 'Honey, please – it's all over now –'

'I know.' Cathleen nodded, dried her eyes, blew her nose. 'It just hit me –' The train journey to the frontier, the heart-shrinking delay there while everyone's papers were checked and double-checked, the two-day stay in Copenhagen while waiting to get on a ship, the voyage to Hull, the last train journey to London, the anxious waiting to get through to Sean . . . 'It's been a nightmare – I didn't realize it at the time –'

'Honey,' said Mady, who had survived her own nightmare and would have nightmares to remember it by, but who would survive them too, 'it's all over.'

Cathleen took off Mady's hat and wig, stroked the growing stubble on her mother's head. 'It isn't really all over. Maybe for you and me, but not for Sean.'

'What will you do? You and him?'

'I hope we can get married. Then –' She shrugged. 'I don't know. He won't give up his job, not even for me. He'll become a war correspondent and God knows where they'll send him.'

She felt sad, which always gives the proper depth to one's happiness. If she couldn't have everything, she would take what came. She was an optimist now, a proper actress. She wondered if Melissa, the other optimist, the other actress, was still trying for happiness in Germany.

'Things could be worse.'

'Yes, I suppose so,' said Mady, who had never told herself such a thing in Ravensbrueck.


# 4


Lutze and Decker had kept Carmody for three hours, but Lutze, if not Decker, knew when a man was telling the truth. They let him go, but told him his press card would be withdrawn on their recommendation by the Foreign Press Office. 'Will they take any notice of the Gestapo?' Carmody had said.

'They will now war has started,' said Lutze. 'Will you write something about Lady Arrowsmith?'

'Yes,' said Carmody, who would rather have not written anything; he did not want to be an apologist for her, yet she deserved some sort of sympathetic obituary. 'But you have ruined my story. Everyone else has got at least a three-hour beat on me.'

Lutze smiled. 'You will have had time to compose your thoughts, Herr Carmody. Good luck.'

For a moment Carmody was almost tempted to shake the hand of the Gestapo officer; but there were limits to tolerance. 'Do you think you'll track down whoever was going to kill Hitler?'

'Who knows?' Lutze shrugged. 'Somewhere, in some gun

shop, there must be a record of who bought that Mannlicher. It's only a matter of time, Herr Carmody.'

Unless the war escalates, thought Carmody, and failed assassination plots become unimportant. He went home to Ludwigstrasse, pausing to go into St Ludwig's and say a prayer for himself and Cathleen, for the soul of Meg Arrowsmith and for the escape of the unknown would-be assassins.

When he came out of the church he looked automatically for Kreisler; but the *Leierkastenmann* was absent this morning. If he is wise, Carmody thought, he has taken his thousand dollars, his monkey and his hurdy-gurdy and gone to the country; anywhere but here in Berlin, where the bombs would soon be falling. Carmody looked up at the sky and wondered where the Polish bombers were. Was the war in Poland already over?

He wrote a piece on Meg Arrowsmith, a thousand words that seemed to take him an age. Then he rang the central phone exchange and asked to be put through to London; to his surprise he was connected immediately. London, as he had expected, blasted him for being so late with the story; they seemed to think that his excuse of being held by the Gestapo a poor reason for being beaten by the other wire services. They were equally unsympathetic when he told them his press card had been revoked and he would be on his way back to London as soon as he got his exit permit – 'Sunday, probably. In the meantime, will you send Bill Swenson or someone to check on Cathleen O'Dea and her mother – they'll be at Brown's Hotel, I think –'

'Is there a story in her and her mother?' London wasn't going to waste the time of one of its most experienced correspondents on just a social call.

'You can make up your own mind on that, sport,' he said, abruptly, belligerently Australian.

For the moment he was tired of this side of the world; he suddenly felt the weight of Europe's history, its intrigues and betrayals, its wars that drew in other, more innocent people. Even more, he felt the inability of any man to halt the course of manifestly destined events. He had seen, if never in the final image, the impending tragedy of Meg Arrowsmith and he had been able to do nothing to prevent it. He had stumbled on the attempt to assassinate Hitler and had been able to do nothing to stop its failing and had almost betrayed its plotters, whoever they were. He had fought for and written about a cause in Spain that had failed: democracy was dead there for God knew how many years to come. He had covered the spread of Nazism, had written warningly against it, and now all his despatches were just scraps of paper on the wind. Selfishly, forgetting Cathleen for one jaundiced, utterly depressed moment, he all at once longed for what he had tried to escape, the landscape of home. Yet he knew in his heart that even there men failed when destiny prevailed.

'Now I'm going to bed,' he said. 'Don't bloody ring me till I ring you.'

He hung up and went to bed. It was dark when he woke. He got up and went over to the Wilhelmstrasse, did the rounds of the ministries, all of which were now working behind blackout blinds. Saturday he did the rounds again; but now everyone knew he was no longer accredited and no one would talk to him. It was a long day and a long night; all he wanted now was to be gone. Sunday morning he went to Mass, sat at the back of the church and saw all the German heads bent in prayer and wondered whether they were praying for peace or victory. His own prayers were selfish: that he would soon be with Cathleen.

Just after midday he was walking from his apartment over to his office, ambling down the Kurfürstendamm under the shining sun, when he saw the people on the terrace of the Café Kranzler suddenly all stand up. A waiter had come out of the café itself and said something in a loud voice; the noise of the traffic drowned it from Carmody's ears. He moved quickly towards the terrace, reached over the railing and grabbed a man by the arm.

'What did he say?'

'England has just declared war on us! Can you believe it?' Then the man, stout, well-dressed, too old to be needed in the war, recognized that he was speaking to a foreigner. 'Are you English? How could you do this to us? What sort of men are in your government?'

'I guess they're different from yours,' said Carmody and walked on.

People in the street looked stunned; suddenly the war was serious. A bus was halted at a cross-street by a traffic policeman; the passengers in their glass cage stared out at Carmody with the dull hopeless look of the trapped. Somewhere a clock struck: it had no resonance, no music to it, just the sound of iron on iron.

Olga was in the office, standing at the window when Carmody walked in. She turned and looked at him, then burst into tears. He went to her and put his arms round her, without embarrassment to either of them.

'They've just delivered your exit permit,' she snuffled. 'They really want to be rid of you.'

'Maybe it's best,' he said, still holding her, surprised at how solid she was beneath her plain blue dress. 'You should try and get out of Berlin, too.'

'My mother would never leave. Neither would I. This is our city – we were both born here. My mother was born here in the year Chancellor Bismarck made Berlin the capital of Germany.' She drew herself out of his arms, wiped her eyes. Now there was some embarrassment in her face, as if she had flung herself at him. Carmody, comforter of lonely women, he thought; but felt no pride, only sadness. 'I'm sorry, Herr Carmody –'

'Will you come to the station to see me off?' He would be on the evening train for Copenhagen.

'Of course. Perhaps you'll come back here – they say the war won't last long –'

'Perhaps,' he said.

He looked out of the window. It was the most marvellous summer's day, a day for family picnics, for lovers' strolls; the beaches along the Wannsee would be crowded, the Grunewald occupied by children and their parents. The air seemed to glitter, to lift up the skyline of domes and steeples till it was suspended like some child's cut-out silhouette. The leaves sparkled like tossed emeralds in the simmering bowls of the trees in the square; the banks of blooms of the flower-sellers blazed like the bushfires he had fought back home. He lifted his eyes, gazed at the sky, at the brilliant light that had captured the imagination of painters and poets and even hacks like himself, the light that, tinged by the soon-to-come smoke and dust of the bombing raids, would soon begin to fade.

'Perhaps,' he said again, but his voice held no hope: for her, for Berlin, for Europe.

*   *   *

This book was written from background provided by sources too many to mention all by name. Individuals who lived or are still living in Berlin, contemporary newspapers and magazines, the Berlin Library and other archives: I have drawn on all of them. But my constant guide was that excellent chronicle of Berlin in Hitler's time: William L. Shirer's *The Rise and Fall of the Third Reich*. It was invaluable.

Briggsy

# Briggsy

## Isla Dewar

Översättning Helena Olsson

Argasso

Till Bob, Nick och Adam

Isla Dewar: Briggsy
Argasso bokförlag   www.argasso.se
Copyright © Isla Dewar 2003
Svensk utgåva copyright © Argasso bokförlag 2010
Översättning: Helena Olsson
Omslagets originaldesign: Brilliant White Design
Omslagsfoto: Izabela Habur
Tryck: Alma Pluss, Riga, Lettland 2010
ISBN 978-91-85071-80-7

Originalets titel: Briggsy
Första utgåva publicerad under titeln
Walking with Rainbows
Barrington Stoke, Edinburgh 2003, 2008

# Några ord från författaren

När jag gick i skolan hade vi två olika sorters stjärnor – de som lyckades inne i klassrummet och de som lyckades ute på skolgården. De som var duktiga inne i klassrummet var mycket sällan samma personer som styrde lekarna och skvallret ute på skolgården.

Inte för att stjärnorna i klassrummet fjäskade för lärarna. De var helt enkelt bara den sortens människor som gjorde bra ifrån sig inom det systemet. De skötte sina studier och lämnade alltid in hemläxan i tid. Stjärnorna på skolgården gjorde också sina läxor – men bara ibland. De var sällan några översittare och för det mesta rätt populära bland de andra eleverna. Däremot var de inte populära bland lärarna.

En gång gjorde en kille som var duktig i klassrummet något rätt idiotiskt under en av våra lektioner. Läraren sa: "Simon, du är den av pojkarna som vi lärare tror kommer att gå riktigt långt när du lämnar skolan. Hur kunde du vara så dum?"

Hela klassen var mållös. Simon? Vi lade knappt märke till honom. Vi hade alla tagit för givet att Stephen, som spelade fotboll och alla tjejer gillade, var den som skulle lyckas bäst ute i vuxenvärlden. Han var en smart och sorglös typ som visste allt möjligt man inte lärde sig i klassrummen. Och det var det som fick mig att börja tänka på Briggsy. Någon som glänser utanför systemet.

# Innehåll

1. Briggsy 9

2. Idiotklass 18

3. Laga mat 27

4. Stjärnskådning 33

5. Miljonär 39

6. Loppmarknad 43

7. Saker jag älskar 48

8. Stjärnfall 55

9. Den sista loppmarknaden 64

10. Drömmar 70

11. Vad Briggsy hade gjort 74

12. Mer stjärnor 80

13. Fler listor 87

# 1. Briggsy

Jag kommer aldrig att glömma Briggsy. Han var min vän och den mest speciella person jag någonsin har träffat.

Först ignorerade jag honom eftersom jag trodde att han var lite dum, men sedan insåg jag att det inte alls stämde. Han visste allt möjligt som jag inte hade en aning om.

Det var Briggsy som visade mig hur man hittar olika stjärnbilder och planeter på stjärnhimlen, som Stora björnen och Mars och Venus. Han lärde mig hur man gör pannkakor. Jo, faktiskt! Hur man spelar poker. Dansar. Jag dansade nästan aldrig innan jag träffade Briggsy. Men han sa åt mig att strunta i detaljerna och bara köra på känsla. Höra musiken och låta den bli en del av mig. *Vara* musiken.

Han klädde sig alltid i starka färger. Hans t-tröjor var röda eller gröna eller brandgula. Han hade sitt eget sätt att gå, och ibland var det nästan som om han dansade fram. Andra gånger kunde han plötsligt skynda i förväg, vända sig om och gå baklänges framför mig. Eller fånga min blick och börja sjunga på en låt han hade hört på radion.

Briggsy kunde göra sådant – låtsas spela gitarr eller knäppa med fingrarna medan han svajade i takt med musiken han hörde i huvudet. Om jag försökte göra samma sak såg jag bara fånig och klumpig ut. Han berättade vitsar som fick mig att skratta.

Men allra mest är det färger jag tänker på när jag minns honom. Klarröda gympaskor utan strumpor. Svarta jeans och de där färgglada t-tröjorna.

Att vara Briggsys vän var som att umgås med regnbågen.

Året då jag träffade Briggsy kom tivolit till stan tidigare än vanligt. Oftast dök det upp i mitten av juni, strax innan turist-bussarna anlände. Horder av turister sökte sig hit för att promenera längs hamnen, bygga sandslott på stranden, paddla i havet och göra allt det där som folk gör när de har semester.

Inte en enda gång hade jag lyckats se när tivolit anlände. Jag bara klev upp en morgon – och där stod det längst bort vid hamnen, högljutt och färgsprakande och fullt av glatt blinkande lampor. Det var som om det bara dök upp ur tomma intet.

Där fanns en berg-och-dal-bana och flera olika stånd där man kunde köpa varmkorv, hamburgare och sockervadd. Där fanns en karusell med stora, målade trähästar, enhörningar och lejon som snurrade runt,

11

runt till ljudet av muntert klingande karusellmusik. Där fanns ett bingobås, en liten spelhall och radiobilar. Radiobilarna var mina favoriter.

I slutet av augusti brukade tivolifolket packa ihop igen. De jobbade antagligen hela natten, för en morgon kunde jag vakna och upptäcka att allt bara var borta. Utan förvarning. Hamnen verkade plötsligt grå och tyst igen, och bortanför den sträckte havet ut sig så långt man kunde se. Om man kom till vår stad samma morgon som tivolit hade gett sig av skulle man aldrig ha kunnat ana att det ens varit där.

Den första måndagen i april dök Briggsy upp i mitt klassrum på skolan. Han var två år äldre än vi andra men hade placerats i vår årskurs eftersom han låg efter i alla ämnen. Jag minns att han var klädd i en mörkröd t-shirt. Rektorn hade sagt att han inte behövde skaffa någon skoluniform eftersom han bara skulle gå på vår skola i några månader medan tivolit var i stan.

Så där satt vi allihop i våra svarta skol-
jackor medan han glänste som en påfågel
mitt ibland oss. På morgonsamlingen stod
han inte bara ut. Det lyste om honom.

Hans familj skötte radiobilarna på tivolit
och flyttade runt med dem över hela landet.
Briggsy hade aldrig stannat tillräckligt
länge någonstans för att kunna gå i skolan
på riktigt.

Han hade en hel del att "ta igen", sa
vår lärare mrs Jackson till honom, och
han skulle bli tvungen att arbeta hårt.
Jag minns hur han nickade och sa att han
skulle anstränga sig – men han sa det på
ett sådant sätt att alla, även mrs Jackson,
förstod att han inte menade det.

Jag är bortskämd. Alla säger det. Till och
med Briggsy sa det till mig en gång. "Minnie
Grant, du är bortskämd", sa han. "Du tror
att världen är skyldig dig något bara för

13

att du existerar." Sedan hade han skakat
på huvudet och fortsatt: "Men det är inte så
det funkar."

Stött hade jag stormat iväg. Jag hade
blivit så arg på honom. Eftersom jag visste
att han hade rätt.

Jag föddes med ett hål i hjärtat. Det är
bra nu – jag mår bra – men när jag var
alldeles nyfödd trodde mina föräldrar att
jag skulle dö. Det finns bilder av mig från
den tiden i fotoalbumet. Jag är mycket liten
och ligger i någon sorts kuvös av plast.
Slangar kopplade till flera olika maskiner
sticker ut ur mig. Och mitt i alltihop
ligger jag och viftar ilsket med mina små,
pinnsmala armar.

Min mamma säger att det var så typiskt
mig. Hur jag låg där och skrek allt vad jag
orkade och viftade med armarna, medan
alla omkring mig var helt knäckta och
trodde att jag skulle dö.

14

Hur som helst, jag är fortfarande kvar.
Jag opererades några gånger men minns
ingenting av det. Jag blev bättre. Ändå tror
mina föräldrar fortfarande att jag är skör
och ömtålig. De ser alltid till att jag är
varm och trygg. När jag var liten fick jag
aldrig gå ut och leka med de andra barnen.
Vid första tecken på att vintern var på väg
packades jag in i halsdukar, handskar och
en förfärlig grön mössa. Ingen annan hade
mössa.

Jag fick allt jag pekade på, och så är det
fortfarande. Kläder, skor, cd-skivor, mobiltelefoner – rubbet. Briggsy sa att jag helt
enkelt inte fattade att de flesta måste jobba
för att få de där sakerna, att de måste
*förtjäna* dem.

Min mamma pjoskar alltid med mig
och oroar sig för att jag ska bli sjuk. På
kvällarna när mina kompisar får gå på
bio eller fester måste jag vara hemma
senast klockan nio. Jag hatar det. När jag

15

var liten brukade mamma gå med mig till skolan. Långt efter att alla andra hade börjat gå själva brukade hon ge mig en puss och lämna mig där vid skolgrinden i min hemska gröna mössa. Mammor kan vara så fruktansvärt pinsamma.

Jag har en känsla av att mammor kan fortsätta att genera en i resten av ens liv. Min syster är tio år äldre än jag och gift. Men när hon tog med sig sin pojkvän Robbie hem för första gången sa mamma till honom: "Sue var en sån hemsk liten flicka. Hon sög på tummen tills hon var tio och brukade alltid peta sig i näsan."

"Mamma!" tjöt Sue. "Han behöver inte höra det där!"

Men mamma bara fortsatte att berätta om alla fåniga hyss som Sue hade haft för sig när hon var liten. Som den gången då hon klippte av sig håret med en sax hon tagit ur kökslådan. Eller den gången då hon sa att hon skulle rymma. Lite senare, när ingen kunde hitta henne, trodde mamma verkligen att hon hade rymt och blev så orolig att hon nästan ringde polisen. Men innan dess hann pappa komma hem, och han hittade Sue i skåpet i hallen där hon satt och åt ett paket chokladkex.

Sue gömde ansiktet i händerna medan mamma berättade, men Robbie lutade sig bara fram och lade armen om henne. "Det är så roligt att höra vad du gjorde när du var liten", sa han. "Berätta mer."

Och så tittade han på Sue med varma, tillgivna ögon. Det syntes att han älskade henne. Det spelade ingen roll vad hon hade hittat på, han älskade henne ändå. *Det där vill jag också ha en dag,* tänkte jag. *Någon som tittar på mig så där.*

## 2. Idiotklass

I vår skola kallar vi dem idiotklasser. Andra skolor har säkert andra namn för samma sak, men hos oss kallas de så. Idiotklasserna är till för dem som inte hänger med i den vanliga undervisningen. Jag hänger till exempel inte med på matten, vare sig det handlar om addition, subtraktion eller något annat. Briggsy hade hamnat i idiot-klassen i alla sina ämnen, men det spelade ingen roll för honom. Min pojkvän Marc gick inte i en enda idiotklass. Han var bra på allt, och ibland kunde jag verkligen avsky honom för det.

Jag lärde känna Briggsy på riktigt under kvarsittningen. Jag, Marc och Briggsy fick ofta sitta kvar. Jag för att jag sa saker som

jag egentligen inte menade. Som när jag
frågade läraren varför jag måste räkna
matte när jag var så dålig på det och ändå
inte tänkte jobba med något som hade med
matte att göra i framtiden. Sedan brukade
jag sitta där vid mitt bord med armarna i
kors och vägra räkna talen.

Briggsy fick sitta kvar för att han inte
gjorde något under lektionerna utom
att rita i sina skolböcker. Och Marc fick
kvarsittning för att han var butter och
aldrig gjorde som lärarna sa.

Marc och jag hade varit tillsammans i
flera månader. Han gick i årskursen över
mig. Han var lång, hade mörkt hår och såg
bra ut på ett surmulet sätt. Hans familj
hade varit rik en gång i tiden, men så var
det inte längre. Hans pappa hade placerat
pengar i ett företag som gått omkull eller
något liknande. De hade haft swimmingpool
och allt möjligt, men numera bodde Marc
i samma sorts hus som jag. Helt vanligt.

19

Bara ett litet hus med en liten gräsplätt på framsidan och en lite större gräsplätt på baksidan.

Marc brukade inte säga så mycket, och först trodde jag att det var för att han var den tysta, starka typen. Men nu har jag förstått att han helt enkelt bara saknade sitt gamla liv. Han hade gått i en fin privatskola, bott i ett stort hus, klätt sig i snygga märkeskläder, och nu var han inte märkvärdigare än någon annan. Han promenerade omkring på vanliga gator, i vanliga skor. Som jag. Jag antar att det kändes hårt.

Kvarsittningen klarades av under lunchrasten mellan klockan ett och halv två, så vi var tvungna att kasta i oss vår lunch på tio minuter för att inte komma för sent. Marc, som var bra på allt, använde den tiden till att göra sin hemläxa. Jag räknade matte. Hopplöst dåligt.

Briggsy gjorde ingenting. Han satt bara och gungade på stolen medan han trummade med fingrarna mot bänken i takt med melodin som spelade inne i hans huvud.

"Har du ingenting att göra, unge herr Briggs?" sa vår naturkunskapslärare miss Brown. Hon övervakade kvarsittningen den här dagen.

"Jag har massor att göra", sa Briggsy. "Och det är det jag håller på med. Just nu."

"Du verkar mest trumma på bänken och gunga på stolen", sa miss Brown.

"Det kanske ser ut så från ditt perspektiv", nickade Briggsy. "Men jag tänker på saker som jag ska göra framöver. Jag planerar. Reder ut allt i tankarna först."

Miss Brown blängde på honom över kanten på sina glasögon. Briggsy fortsatte oberört att trumma med fingrarna och gunga på stolen. Jag fnissade – ett frustande litet ljud som slapp ur min näsa. Jag önskar att jag kunde sluta med den ovanan.

"Vad är det som är så roligt, Minnie?" frågade miss Brown.

"Inget", svarade jag och försökte se oskyldig ut. Sedan frågade hon varför jag hade fått kvarsittning.

"Jag var näsvis", sa jag.

"Det verkar inte som om dagens kvarsittning har gjort någon nytta", sa hon. "Du får sitta kvar resten av veckan också, tills du har lärt dig att uppföra dig lite bättre."

"Men det är inte rättvist!" utropade jag. "Jag skrattade ju bara."

"Vill du sitta kvar nästa vecka också?" undrade hon.

Jag skakade på huvudet och stängde munnen. Från sin bänk en bit bort log

Briggsy mot mig och höjde på axlarna. Jag tror att han ville säga att han var ledsen.

När det var dags att gå till våra lektioner kom han ifatt mig ute i korridoren. "Vill du ta en fika med mig efter skolan?" frågade han.

"Bara om Marc också får följa med", sa jag.

"Visst", sa han. "Inga problem."

Det var så vi tre lärde känna varandra och började hänga på High Street varje dag efter skolan.

Först brukade vi gå in på Boots, som sålde skönhetsprodukter, eftersom jag ville kolla in schampoflaskorna. Jag är tokig i schampo och måste ha helt rätt typ. Det finns schampo för fett hår, schampo som ger volym, schampo som gör håret glansigt.

Jag tycker inte att man kan ha för mycket schampo.

Om man använder samma typ av schampo hela tiden slutar det snart att fungera. Det är i alla fall vad jag tycker. Alltså måste jag alltid ha flera olika sorter hemma.

Sedan brukade vi titta på läppstift och nagellack. När jag hade testat alla färger jag kunde på mina egna naglar brukade Briggsy låta mig använda hans. Marc hatade det där. Han brukade sucka och rulla med ögonen. Han tyckte att vi var hopplöst tjejiga.

Efter det gick vi till Woolworths. Vi tittade igenom cd-skivorna och valde ut vilka vi skulle vilja köpa. Vi bläddrade i alla tidningar och letade i kortstället efter de fräckaste vykort vi kunde hitta.

Sedan fortsatte vi till Bobs kafé och beställde cappuccino med massor av riven choklad strödd ovanpå.

Vi brukade sitta vid fönstret och titta på

folk som gick förbi, och jag lyckades alltid få en mustasch av skum på överläppen.

Briggsy var bra på att läsa av folk. Han studerade deras rörelser och hur de gick längs trottoaren. Han tittade på deras ansiktsuttryck.

Jag däremot, jag såg bara deras kläder. Och jag hade bara två ord för att beskriva dem. Snygga eller töntiga.

Men vi kom överens om två saker:

1. Gamla tanter med mobiltelefoner ser väldigt roliga ut.

2. Gamla gubbar har ofta ingen bak.

Jag vet inte vart gamla gubbars bakar tar vägen när de blir äldre. Men de verkar liksom bara försvinna.

Fast mest av allt satt vi där och fnittrade. Jag har nog aldrig haft lika kul med någon som jag hade med Briggsy.

Och sedan, precis klockan kvart i fem, brukade Briggsy ställa sig upp, ta sin väska och säga: "Måste sticka."

"Vart ska du?" frågade jag första gången det hände.

"Hem", sa han. "Måste laga mat till föräldrarna."

# 3. Laga mat

Saker som jag hatar. Fast nödvändigtvis inte i den här ordningen:

1. Getingar

2. Folk som pratar med varandra om mig fastän jag står alldeles bredvid. Som när jag gick till affären med mamma och vi stötte ihop med mrs Stolle. Hon heter mrs Stoll, men jag kallar henne mrs Stolle eftersom jag inte gillar henne. Hur som helst, mrs Stolle sa till mamma: "Oj, är det där din Minnie? Jag kände knappt igen henne. Vad hon har vuxit!"

Hon pratade om mig som om jag inte var där. Och självklart hade jag vuxit. Jag är en tonåring. Det är vad jag ska göra. Bli vuxen.

3. Höra mina egna hjärtslag.

Jag avskyr att vakna mitt i natten när hela huset är dödstyst. När allt är svart. Att huset knäpper och knarrar skrämmer mig inte. Det är naturligt att gamla hus låter så när ingen rör sig i dem.

Men mitt huvud ligger på kudden, och i örat som är pressat mot örngottet kan jag höra mina hjärtslag. Det är ett mjukt, vispande ljud. *Da-dunk, da-dunk, da-dunk.* Och jag hatar det eftersom jag är så rädd för att det ska upphöra.

Jag berättade för Briggsy hur mycket jag avskyr att höra mina egna hjärtslag.

"Var inte dum", sa han. "Du skulle aldrig hinna höra att hjärtat stannade. Du skulle redan vara död."

"Men", sa jag, "jag kanske skulle få ett ögonblick. Ett superkort ögonblick då mitt hjärta har stannat men jag inte har hunnit tuppa av än. Och då skulle jag veta att det hade stannat och att jag skulle dö."

"Det kommer aldrig att hända", sa han och tittade på mig. "Oroa dig inte. Alla är rädda för såna där saker."

"Är de?" sa jag. "Jag trodde att det bara var jag."

Ibland kommer jag på att jag är jag. Jag kan hejda mig och tänka: *Jag är verkligen jag.*

Det är som att sjunga. Inte för att jag kan sjunga. Men när jag gör det låter det underbart i mina egna öron. Det jag hör inne i huvudet är inte samma sak som andra hör. I världen utanför låter min sång hemsk.

"Snälla Minnie", kunde mamma säga. "Jag försöker tänka."

"Lägg av, Min", brukade Marc säga med ett stön. "Du tar livet av mig."

Så jag slutade sjunga, trots att jag inte tyckte att det lät så illa.

Jag har samma problem när jag bara är mig själv. Som den gången då jag gick genom korridoren i skolan och inte tänkte på något särskilt. Inte glad, inte ledsen. Någonstans mitt emellan. Och just då passerade mrs Jackson förbi mig och sa: "Gaska upp dig, Minnie. Det kanske aldrig händer."

Vad kanske aldrig händer? Jag hade inte oroat mig för någonting. Jag hade bara gått genom korridoren.

Det måste vara mitt ansikte, tänkte jag då. Jag har den sortens ansikte som ser ledset och buttert ut när jag inte gör något särskilt med det.

Sedan kommer stunderna. Jag kallar dem mina *verklighetsstunder*. När jag helt och hållet är mig själv. Jag går längs gatan eller sitter i ett klassrum eller står

ute på skolgården, och plötsligt tänker jag:
*Jösses, jag är jag. Det här är jag. Jag finns i
verkligheten.*

Och allt omkring mig verkar plötsligt
så *verkligt*. Mer än verkligt. Liksom extra
verkligt. Ljuden är starkare. Och jag hör
inte vad någon säger till mig eftersom jag
tittar på dem och tänker att de också är
verkliga. Jag betraktar dem och ser hur
deras läppar rör sig. Det verkar så fånigt
alltihop.

Jag berättade för Briggsy om de här
verklighetsstunderna.

"Visst", sa han. "Alla har såna stunder."

"Har de?" sa jag. "Jag trodde att det bara
var jag."

"Nä", sa han. "Det är inte bara du. Men
det är inte dina verklighetsstunder som gör
dig speciell. Alla är speciella på ett eller
annat sätt. Du är speciell för att du är du.

31

Kom hem till mig på lördag så lagar jag mat
åt dig. Eftersom du är speciell."

Det här att han lagade mat hade både
Marc och jag lite svårt att släppa. Marc
tyckte att Briggsy var en idiot som lät mig
måla hans naglar och gick vartenda ämne i
idiotklassen. Och som lagade mat.

"Briggsy, män lagar inte mat", sa han.

"Det är klart att de gör", sa Briggsy.
"Massor av män lagar mat. Jamie Oliver och
alla möjliga. De bästa kockarna i världen är
män." Och så slog han sig för bröstet som
Tarzan och fick mig att skratta.

Briggsy kunde alltid få mig att skratta.

# 4. Stjärnskådning

Den lördagen gick jag hem till Briggsy för att äta middag. Marc kunde inte följa med eftersom han var bjuden till sin kusins bröllop.

Vi var tvungna att äta tidigt eftersom Briggsy hade två småsystrar som snabbt blev hungriga. Alltså gick jag ner till nöjesfältet strax före klockan fem.

Briggsy och hans familj bodde i en stor husvagn som stod parkerad bakom tivolit. Den var fantastisk. Prydlig och välstädad, och alla saker verkade så lätta att komma åt. Det fanns tre rum. Ett sovrum för hans systrar och ett för hans föräldrar, och så vardagsrummet där Briggsy sov på bäddsoffan, mittemot den största teve jag någonsin hade sett.

När jag såg mig om i vardagsrummet insåg jag att Briggsy kunde ligga i sin säng varje kväll och titta på teve. Coolt.

Det var *så* coolt att jag nästa dag sa till mamma att vi borde sälja huset, köpa en stor husbil och bara åka iväg vart vi ville.

Hon tittade på mig utan att säga något. Det var den där sortens blick som enbart mammor kan ge en och som får en att känna sig väldigt dum och obetydlig.

"Gå och tvätta händerna", sa hon. "Maten är snart klar."

"Jag antar", sa jag, "att vi inte kommer att skaffa en husvagn, då?"

Mamma, som hade börjat mosa potatisen, hejdade sig och tittade upp på mig. "Nej, det kommer vi inte att göra."

Så jag tog aldrig upp det igen.

Briggsy hade lagat en kryddig kyckling-rätt. Tunna, friterade kycklingstrimlor och starkt kryddat ris som blandats med ärtor. Han hade till och med gjort en sallad. Det var det godaste jag någonsin hade ätit.

"Var har du lärt dig att laga mat?" frågade jag.

Briggsy gjorde en gest mot teven. "Jag kollade på ett matprogram och tänkte att det där såg ju inte särskilt svårt ut – det skulle jag också kunna göra. Och så satte jag igång och testade."

I början hade han stökat till det ordent-ligt för sig och lämnat grytor och pannor i en enda röra över hela köket. Dessutom brände maten vid och blev kolsvart. Men till slut hade han lärt sig hur man skulle göra.

Det slog mig att Briggsy visste en massa

saker som han inte hade lärt sig i skolan. Han var smartare än folk trodde.

När vi hade ätit färdigt gick vi över till nöjesfältet. Det första jag ville göra var att spela på de enarmade banditerna. Jag brukar alltid få mina fickpengar på lördagen och tänkte att jag skulle kunna använda dem till att skaffa ännu mer pengar. Jag är lite besatt av pengar och vill ha massor. Det jag önskar mig mest av allt är att bli rik så att jag alltid ska kunna köpa vad jag vill.

Sitter jag till exempel och bläddrar i en tidning kan jag få syn på de mest fantastiska kläder och tänka att det vore toppen att bara kunna gå och köpa dem. Eller om jag ser ett rum med underbara soffor tänker jag att *de där* skulle passa mig perfekt. Hade jag pengar skulle jag bara kunna knäppa med fingrarna och sofforna skulle vara mina. Dessutom måste jag ju bli rik för att kunna köpa en lika stor husvagn som Briggsys.

Jag förlorade alla mina fickpengar på de enarmade banditerna.

"De där dumma apparaterna tuggade i sig alla mina mynt", klagade jag.

"Det är klart att de gjorde", sa Briggsy till mig. "Vad skulle de vara bra för om de inte tog dina pengar?"

"Vad menar du?"

"Folk flyttar runt med dem över hela landet och ställer upp dem på såna här ställen. Det är så de försörjer sig. Om du tjänade pengar på dem skulle deras ägare inte kunna göra det, eller hur?"

Jag insåg att det han sa lät vettigt. Och det var sista gången jag spelade i hela mitt liv.

Resten av kvällen fick jag åka både berg-och-dal-bana och radiobilar gratis eftersom Briggsy tillhörde tivolit. Det var fantastiskt.

Efteråt följde han mig hem. Jag gick långsamt med huvudet tillbakalutat och stirrade upp mot himlen. Jag brukar alltid titta upp mot himlen på kvällen eftersom jag vill se en stjärna falla.

"Du kanske har tur", sa Briggsy. "Men den bästa tiden för stjärnfall är i augusti. Det är då man har chansen att få se massor av stjärnskott."

"Hur vet du det?" sa jag.

"Teve", sa han. "*Natthimlen* med Patrick Moore. Han är en väldigt cool typ."

Sedan pekade han ut Polstjärnan och Vintergatan och Stora björnen för mig. Han visste så mycket. Man skulle aldrig kunna tro att han gick i alla de där idiotklasserna.

# 5. Miljonär

Mamma och pappa hade gått till puben, så huset var tomt när vi kom tillbaka. Briggsy följde med in, och jag bjöd på kaffe. Vi satte oss i soffan och slog på teven.

*Vem vill bli miljonär?* gick på en av kanalerna och Briggsy kunde svara på nästan varenda fråga. Det var helt otroligt.

"Hur vet du allt det där?" undrade jag. Det var så mycket han kände till som jag aldrig hade hört talas om, och ibland kunde jag inte låta bli att störa mig på det.

Han ryckte på axlarna. "Teve. Frågesporter. Jeopardy och sånt. Och så snappar jag upp saker när jag ligger och kollar på dokumentärer på kvällarna."

"Du är grym", suckade jag. Och sedan sa jag till honom att han borde försöka komma med i programmet. Han skulle kunna bli miljonär – och ge mig några tusen pund för att jag lät honom använda min mobil.

Genast började vi slå numret de visade i teverutan. Vi ringde över tjugo gånger den kvällen, och sedan fortsatte vi på samma vis i flera veckor, säkra på att vi till slut skulle lyckas komma med i programmet.

Vi slutade först när min mobilräkning kom. Pappa brukade alltid betala åt mig, men den här gången gick han i taket. Han klampade runt i hela huset och viftade med räkningen medan han skrek att den var på över 300 pund, inte omkring 20 pund som den vanligtvis brukade landa på.

Sedan tittade han på listan över utgående samtal och ringde upp numret vi hade slagit om och om igen. När han upptäckte att det gick till *Vem vill bli miljonär?* drog han och

mamma in mina fickpengar i en hel månad
som avbetalning på räkningen. Och sedan
förbjöd de mig att ringa till programmet
igen.

Jag försökte förklara att Briggsy berg-
säkert skulle vinna eftersom han visste
så mycket, och då skulle jag få en andel
i vinsten och på så vis kunna betala hela
telefonräkningen på en gång.

Jag sa till dem att om Briggsy fick en
fråga om tevesåpor, som han aldrig tittade
på, skulle han i och för sig bli tvungen att
fråga publiken. Men han var väldigt bra på
djur eftersom han hade tittat på så många
naturprogram.

"Även om han bara skulle vinna 250 000
pund kommer han att ge mig typ 50 000.
Det skulle betala telefonräkningen i flera
månader framöver."

Jag tänkte på hur mycket skor och
cd-skivor jag skulle kunna köpa för de

pengarna. "Och jag skulle kunna skaffa en jättestor husvagn åt oss", tillade jag.

Mamma beordrade mig att inte säga ett ord till om frågesportprogram eller husvagnar igen. Någonsin.

Jag stormade ut. De fattade ingenting.

Just som jag lämnade rummet hörde jag pappa säga: "Hon är bortskämd."

Mamma sa ingenting. Men jag visste att hon nickade och höll med.

# 6. Loppmarknad

Cross Lantgård ligger precis i utkanten av stan. På somrarna brukar mr Jack, som äger gården, låna ut ett av sina fält till en stor loppmarknad. Varannan söndag kommer folk från milsvida omkring för att sätta upp stånd och sälja saker som de inte längre behöver. Och ännu fler kommer dit för att söka igenom stånden på jakt efter fynd.

Briggsy ville gå, men det ville inte Marc och jag. Vi tyckte att loppmarknader var töntiga.

"Man vet aldrig vad man kommer att hitta", invände Briggsy. "Kanske något som är värt en hacka."

"Sällan", sa Marc.

"Jodå", sa Briggsy. "Folk vet inte vad de har. Det kan vara en gammal vas eller en samling koppar som de ärvde när deras gamla farmor dog. De tycker att grejerna är fula och vill bara bli av med dem. Men de kan vara värda en förmögenhet." Han slängde upp näven och hoppade högt upp i luften, som om han just hade gjort mål i en VM-final. "En hel förmögenhet!" utropade han.

Marc och jag tittade på honom som om han hade tappat förståndet. Men nästa söndag följde vi ändå med honom till loppmarknaden. Det var svårt att säga nej till Briggsy. Han fick allt att låta så roligt att man liksom bara sveptes med. Dessutom ville ju jag också försöka göra mig en förmögenhet.

Loppmarknaden var helt värdelös, precis som väntat. Det var i alla fall vad jag och Marc tyckte.

44

"Kolla, det här är toppen", sa Briggsy och började ivrigt snoka runt bland stånden på jakt efter fynd.

Såvitt jag kunde se var det mest bara skräp. Folk stod i rader med sina prylar utlagda på bord. En del sålde gamla skivor, andra högvis med avlagda saker som skedar och gafflar och utslitna skor. Och de sålde kläder som ingen vettig människa borde vilja ta på sig. Det var helt enkelt ett överflöd av grejer som de flesta bara skulle ha slängt i soporna.

Ändå köpte jag en röd t-shirt som senare skulle färga av sig på flera andra plagg när jag försökte tvätta den. Och två cd-skivor, varav den ena inte gick att spela ordentligt. Marc köpte några serietidningar.

Briggsy köpte tre tallrikar.

"Tallrikar?" sa jag.

"Ja, tallrikar", svarade Briggsy.

De såg gamla och skamfilade ut.

"Vad ska du med dem till?" undrade jag.

"Jag ska sälja dem", flinade han.

Alltså återvände vi till stan och fortsatte bort till en antikaffär på High Street. Briggsy tog med sig tallrikarna in medan Marc och jag stod kvar utanför och väntade. Tio minuter senare kom Briggsy ut igen och viftade med en tiopundssedel i luften. Han hade köpt tallrikarna för bara 50 pence. Vilken förtjänst!

"Hur visste du att tallrikarna var värda något?" frågade jag Briggsy.

Han ryckte på axlarna. "Antikrundan. Kollar varje vecka."

Jag stod där och höll i min nyinköpta, röda t-shirt som redan hade börjat färga av sig på mina händer. Jag tittade ner på cd-skivorna. Den som varit i lite sämre skick verkade heltrasig nu när jag kollade

närmare på den. Jag tänkte på hur livet var
en enda lång verklighetsstund för Briggsy.
Hans lärare trodde att han var efter i
alla ämnen eftersom han aldrig stannade
tillräckligt länge på ett ställe för att hinna
lära sig sådant som de tyckte var viktigt
i skolan. Men utanför skolan var Briggsy
redan långt före alla andra. Han visste
massor.

Han var bra på *livet*. Och i det ämnet var
det jag och Marc som gick i idiotklassen
med våra serietidningar och vårt billiga
skräp.

# 7. Saker jag älskar

Jag gjorde en lista på saker som jag älskar mest i hela världen och skrev ner den i en bok som Marc hade gett mig i julklapp.

Det är en underbar anteckningsbok. Den har ett tjockt, glansigt blått omslag som det står *Anteckningar* på i guldbokstäver, och i den skriver jag ner alla mina hemligheter. Som mina önskningar till exempel.

Jag önskar att jag bodde i en stor husvagn, precis som Briggsy, och jag önskar att Marc inte var så butter jämt. Jag önskar att jag hade långa ben och tjocka ögonfransar. Sådana saker.

**Min lista på saker som jag tycker bäst om:**

1. Maltesers-godis

2. Att promenera med Briggsy. Och när han får mig att skratta.

3. Min mammas hemmagjorda choklad-kaka.

4. Stjärnfall

Min lista fortsatte i den stilen. Jag ville skriva att jag innerst inne älskade Marc, men jag var rädd att någon skulle hitta boken och läsa det. Dessutom tänkte jag att allt kanske skulle gå i kras om jag skrev ner vad jag verkligen kände. Då kanske Marc inte skulle vilja vara ihop med mig längre. Alltså höll jag det hemligt.

Fredagen efter loppmarknaden var vår sista skoldag innan sommarlovet började. I flera veckor framöver skulle vi inte behöva göra någonting alls. Jag såg fram emot det. Ligga och dra mig i sängen på morgnarna. Titta på eftermiddagsfilmer på teve. Sitta och hänga på kaféet och dricka cappuccino eller läsk. Eller bara ligga i trädgården bakom huset och försöka bli brun. Jag hade planerat alltihop.

Och det blev faktiskt den bästa sommar jag någonsin hade haft. Jag träffade Marc varje dag. Vi gick ner till nöjesfältet, och om det var någorlunda lugnt på banan brukade Briggsy låta oss åka gratis i radiobilarna. Han stod bakom oss på bilens kofångare medan vi körde omkring och försökte dunsa in i så många andra bilar vi kunde. Hela tiden spelade musik i bakgrunden och ljusen omkring oss glittrade. Jag var så lycklig.

På eftermiddagarna låg vi och solade på stranden nära klipporna. Vi simmade trots att vattnet var kallt, dök ner under vågorna och skvätte så mycket vatten på varandra vi kunde.

På kvällarna när jag hade gått och lagt

mig brukade Marc ringa. En gång när jag sa att jag låg med huvudet på kudden medan jag pratade med honom sa han: "Lyckliga kudde." *Coolt*, tänkte jag.

Dagarna flög förbi. Det var som om jag ständigt gick omkring med huvudet fullt av musik. Mamma och pappa började ge mig fickpengar igen. De slutade tjata om den enorma telefonräkningen. Jag ringde aldrig till *Vem vill bli miljonär?* igen för att få med Briggsy i programmet. Jag hade upptäckt ett nytt sätt att bli rik på: köpa och sälja antikviteter.

Min plan gick ut på att vi skulle hitta saker på loppmarknaden, sälja dem till antikaffären och på så vis göra oss en förmögenhet. Jag, Marc och Briggsy skulle köpa en egen husvagn, och sedan skulle vi ge oss iväg och bara åka vart vi ville. Vi skulle vara lyckliga.

Varje gång det var loppmarknad gick

vi dit. Jag hittade förstås aldrig något
värdefullt, och det gjorde inte Marc heller.

Men Briggsy hittade saker – en skiva
som han tog till en skivhandlare och sålde
för fem pund fast han bara hade betalat
50 pence för den, en stol som han bar hela
vägen tillbaka till stan och fick 25 pund för.
Han visste vad han höll på med. Det gjorde
inte jag, och långsamt började min dröm
blekna bort.

Trots det var sommaren magisk.

I början av augusti åkte Marc med
sin familj till Cornwall för att hälsa på
en faster. Briggsy jobbade varje dag på
tivolit, medan jag vandrade omkring på
stan, tittade på läppstift och gick igenom
cd-skivor alldeles ensam. Ibland efter
middagen gick jag ner till tivolit för att
lyssna på musiken, titta på folk och känna
glädjen och energin som strömmade
emot mig därinne. Ibland gick jag bort till

järnvägsbron och tittade på tågen som rullade förbi. Jag älskade att drömma om alla de ställen tågen hade varit på och snart skulle åka till igen.

Det är så det är att bo i en liten stad. Allt ungdomarna pratar om är att åka därifrån. Man drömmer om resten av världen, om allt som pågår någon annanstans. Gula taxibilar i New York, klubbar i London. Allt man skulle kunna göra. Och samtidigt händer ingenting alls i den lilla staden där man bor. Den enda ljuspunkten är ett litet kafé som serverar cappuccino.

En dag, ungefär en vecka innan skolan skulle börja igen, drog Briggsy mig åt sidan för att fråga mig något. Tivolimusiken spelade, lukten av hamburgare hängde i luften och folk skrattade högt omkring oss. Jag kunde knappt höra vad han sa.

"Vill du fortfarande se ett stjärnfall?"

"Ja!" sa jag genast.

"I morgon natt kommer en stor meteor-skur att dra förbi."

"Underbart", sa jag.

"Vill du se den med mig? Jag möter dig här vid tvåtiden och så går vi ut på klipporna. Du kommer att få se tusentals stjärnfall på en gång."

"Två?" sa jag. "Inte på eftermiddagen, antar jag?"

"Nej, Min. Två på natten. Vi träffas här vid radiobilarna."

# 8. Stjärnfall

Jag hade aldrig varit ute så sent förut. Inte ensam i alla fall. Men jag ville verkligen se stjärnfallet, så den natten låg jag i sängen och ansträngde mig för att inte somna. Strax före klockan två klev jag upp och drog på mig ett par jeans och en t-shirt. Jag smög bort till mammas och pappas sovrumsdörr för att kolla att de sov. Det gjorde de – jag kunde höra hur de snarkade. Sedan klättrade jag ut genom mitt sovrumsfönster och gick för att möta Briggsy.

Det var inte ett dugg kallt ute. Luften var varm och mild. Det var så tyst, och inte en levande själ verkade vara ute. Jag kunde höra mina fotsteg mot trottoaren medan jag gick. Det är lustigt, men allt det där man tycker att man känner väl – gator, hus man passerar varje dag – ser helt annorlunda ut på natten. Jag var lite rädd och såg mig om över axeln hela tiden för att vara säker på att ingen följde efter mig. Ibland smög jag till och med så att vem det än var som kanske följde efter inte skulle kunna höra mina fotsteg. Fånigt.

Briggsy väntade på mig vid utkanten av nöjesfältet. Det var helt tyst vid den här tiden på dygnet, och i mörkret verkade radiobilarna och berg-och-dal-banan ha fått en helt annan form. På något sätt såg de stora och otäcka ut. Jag tänkte att om jag var ett spöke skulle jag gärna spöka på ett tomt nöjesfält om nätterna.

Vi gick förbi husen som vette mot stranden, och när vi passerade det gamla skepparvärdshuset kunde vi höra ljudet av svaga röster och skratt därinifrån.

"En inlåsning", sa Briggsy.

"Va?" sa jag.

"Men tjejen, du vet ju ingenting. Efter stängningsdags drar de för gardinerna och låser dörren så att man ska tro att puben har stängt. Men på insidan är ljusen tända och alla fortsätter att dricka och ha kul. En inlåsning."

"Jaha. Så det du och jag har här ute är en utlåsning, då? Egentligen borde jag ligga hemma i sängen och sova, men i stället är jag här ute och har kul med dig."

"Perfekt, eller hur?" sa han.

Vi gick vidare. Efter att ha passerat det sista huset slog vi in på en liten stig som ledde fram till foten av klipporna. Där tog en trappstege av trä vid och fortsatte hela vägen upp till toppen. Två hundra steg. Det är en lång klättring, men det finns en rostig ledstång av järn som man kan hålla sig fast i. Briggsy sprang uppför trappan, två steg i taget. Jag följde långsamt efter medan jag andades tungt. Då och då stannade jag till och tittade upp mot himlen för att vara säker på att stjärnfallet inte redan hade börjat.

När jag nådde toppen var Briggsy redan där, och han var så ivrig att han hade svårt att stå stilla. Det var inte särskilt mörkt den här natten. En enorm måne lyste alldeles ovanför horisonten.

"Det är en potatismåne", sa jag till Briggsy. "Den är inte helt full så den ser lite knölig ut, precis som en potatis."

"Vi skulle kunna göra månchips", sa han. "Månchips med dill- och gräslöksmak."

"Månmos och korv", fnissade jag.

Jag började darra. Kylan här uppe gav mig gåshud och jag gnuggade armarna för att värma dem. Luften hade kanske varit ljum nere på min gata, men här uppe på toppen av klippan var det blåsigt. Och kallt. Den långa klättringen uppför trappan hade gjort mig alldeles varm och svettig, och jag visste att det här antagligen skulle sluta med att jag blev förkyld. Och senare, när mamma skulle fråga hur det hade gått till, skulle jag svara att jag inte visste.

Och sedan såg jag den. En fallande stjärna som blixtrade tvärs över himlen med en lång svans efter sig. *Svisch.* Jag hoppade upp och ner och pekade på den. "Där är en!"

Briggsy hade också sett den. Vi stod där båda två med tillbakalutade huvuden och bara stirrade. Sedan sköt en till över himlavalvet.

Vi såg på medan den bleknade bort. Sedan – ingenting.

Jag kände hur vinden skar i mig. Återigen började jag huttra.

"Då så", sa jag. "Vi borde kanske gå hem igen."

"Aldrig i livet att det där var allt", sa Briggsy. "Det var bara början. Det kommer tusentals till alldeles strax."

Det kunde jag förstås inte missa, så jag stannade kvar trots att mina tänder skallrade. Jag var redan iskall.

Då och då svischade det förbi ytterligare en fallande stjärna som vi förundrat följde med blicken från vår utkiksplats. Men vid fyratiden var jag så genomfrusen att jag började önska att jag var tillbaka i min säng. Gryningen närmade sig och den svarta himlen hade börjat blekna.

Då kom de. Hundratals stjärnor som störtade ut ur mörkret och blixtrade förbi över himlavalvet. Ett enormt regn av stjärnor med långa ljussvansar. Jag hade aldrig sett något liknande. Jag glömde helt hur kall jag var och började ivrigt studsa upp och ner medan jag tjöt: "Fantastiskt, fantastiskt!"

"Som fyrverkerier!" utropade Briggsy.

60

Det *var* som fyrverkerier. Fast bättre eftersom det var på riktigt. Jag stod under ett enormt regn av flygande gnistor. "Åh! Otroligt!"

"Som raketer", sa Briggsy. "Riktiga raketer."

"Raketer som åker i raketfart över himlen."

Sedan var det plötsligt över, och allt som återstod var vanliga stjärnor på en vanlig himmel. Jag blev ledsen. Riktigt ledsen. Det sägs att man får önska sig något om man ser en stjärna falla. Ovanför mig hade hundratals önskningar just dragit förbi och jag hade inte önskat mig en enda sak.

"Jag glömde att önska något", sa jag.

"Äsch", sa Briggsy. "Kan du inte bara tycka att det var fantastiskt att det hände? Det här är inte en önskegrej. Det är om att få se dem och vara glad bara för det."

Jag antar att han hade rätt. Ändå ångrade jag att jag inte hade kommit mig för att åtminstone önska mig en husvagn. Ibland när jag ska önska mig något önskar jag bara att något underbart ska hända. Men den här gången hade jag inte ens gjort det.

Vi återvände hemåt. De första fåglarna hade börjat sjunga. Klockan var nästan fem på morgonen och allt var fortfarande lugnt och stilla. Gatorna var tomma och gardinerna i husen fördragna.

Jag tänkte på människorna som bodde därinne, på hur de snarkade och sov under sina varma täcken medan tusentals fallande stjärnor susade förbi över deras tak. De hade missat alltihop.

Det gladde mig att jag hade fått se det i alla fall. Jag var plötsligt så lycklig, och när vi nådde min gata slog jag armarna om Briggsys hals och kysste honom.

"Tack. Tack för allt."

"Det var inget", sa han.

Han vände och gick. Jag skakade fortfarande av köld men tittade ändå efter honom tills han var borta. Det såg nästan ut som om han bleknade bort tillsammans med natten.

# 9. Den sista loppmarknaden

Jag klättrade tillbaka in genom mitt sovrumsfönster och kröp ner i sängen så fort jag kunde. Det var först då jag upptäckte att mina fötter var blöta. Jag hade aldrig varit så kall i hela mitt liv. Kölden verkade ha nått ända in i märgen på mig, och länge låg jag under täcket och skakade medan jag tänkte på fallande stjärnor.

Nästa dag kände jag mig konstig. Jag kunde inte äta och när jag inte skakade av köld fick jag hemska svettattacker. Jag låg kvar i sängen mycket längre än vanligt, och först när klockan var runt ett klev jag upp.

Jag ville gå till loppmarknaden. Det var årets sista marknad och min sista chans att hitta något riktigt värdefullt som kunde göra mig rik.

Jag mötte Briggsy och Marc på nöjesfältet, där vi alltid brukade träffas innan vi gick vidare till loppmarknaden. Marc hade kommit tillbaka från sin semester och jag var jätteglad att se honom igen. Men när han fick höra att jag hade varit ute hela natten med Briggsy fick han ett konstigt uttryck i ansiktet. Jag misstänkte att han var avundsjuk på oss för att han hade missat meteorskuren. En ganska överdriven reaktion i så fall, tyckte jag.

Jag klarade knappt av promenaden bort till fältet. Det är lustigt, men ofta fattar man inte att man är sjuk när man blir yr och knäna börjar skaka. *Jag känner mig lite konstig,* tänker man bara. Jag kunde knappt andas och hade ont i bröstet. Jag svettades floder.

Marc gjorde ingen stor sak av hur lång tid

det tog för mig att gå till loppmarknaden. Men Briggsy, som alltid sa att man måste vara på plats tidigt för att hitta de bra grejerna, blev snabbt otålig. Till slut sa han att vi fick ses där och sprang i förväg.

Han måste ha varit på marknaden i ungefär en kvart när Marc och jag dök upp. Jag kände mig så ostadig att jag hade svårt att hålla mig upprätt. Jag var blöt av svett och mådde förfärligt.

Snart fick vi syn på Briggsy vid ett bord som ett ungt par hade ställt upp. Han stod och tittade på medan någon köpte en liten prydnadssak av dem. Jag kunde inte se den ordentligt, men det såg ut som en gris. Den var inte särskilt fin. Jag skulle aldrig ha köpt den.

Mannen som höll på att köpa den gräsliga lilla grisen försökte pruta. "Nej, det är en förfalskning", sa han. "Du får en femma för den."

Paret som sålde den tittade på varandra och nickade. "Okej, då."

Briggsy låtsades att han var helt ointresserad av affären. Han lyfte på tallrikar och koppar, vände och vred på dem och ställde sedan tillbaka dem igen.

Jag kunde knappt tro mina ögon när jag såg vad som hände därnäst.

Mannen som skulle köpa grisen ställde ner den på bordet för att plocka fram sin plånbok. Sekunden efter slöt Briggsy handen om den, lyfte upp den och gick därifrån. Det hela gick så fort och smidigt att det nästan var svårt att tro att det överhuvudtaget hade hänt.

Briggsy tryckte ner den lilla porslinsgrisen i fickan och smälte in i folkmassan. Några sekunder senare såg jag en skymt av honom vid ett annat bord. Sedan försvann han ur sikte igen.

Vid det här laget stod Marc och jag så nära mannen som velat köpa grisen att vi kunde höra vad han sa.

"Hallå där!" utropade han. "Den där grabben tog min porslinsfigur."

"Jag såg inget", sa den unge mannen som försökt sälja grisen.

"Jaha, men den har i alla fall blivit stulen", sa grisköparen. "Vi måste ringa polisen."

"Knappast någon mening att blanda in polisen för en förfalskning värd fem pund", sa grisförsäljaren.

"Fast det där var ingen förfalskning", sa grisköparen. "Den var från Kina och förmodligen runt sex hundra år gammal. Den är värd hur mycket som helst."

Grisförsäljaren fick en lustig färg i ansiktet. Det var svårt att avgöra vem han var mest arg på – mannen som hade försökt

68

köpa den för en femma eller Briggsy som stulit den.

Jag fick själv en lustig färg i ansiktet just då, även om min var mer grönvit. Svetten rann nedför min rygg och jag kände mig matt och svimfärdig. Jag kunde inte stå upp längre och förstod att jag måste sätta mig ner så fort som möjligt. Jag sjönk ner på marken.

Medan jag satt där i leran och fick ta emot undrande blickar från folk som gick förbi, upptäckte jag Briggsy vid ingången till marknaden. Det var så mycket människor där borta att han utan problem kunde smälta in i klungan. Sedan var han försvunnen. Det var som om han plötsligt bara hade gått upp i rök.

# 10. Drömmar

Jag vet inte hur jag tog mig hem. Jag minns bara att jag gick längs trottoaren tillsammans med Marc och att han fick stödja mig hela vägen. Jag hade ett otäckt tryck över bröstet och det gjorde ont att andas. Jag räknade stegen. Ett steg närmare mitt hus. Två steg närmare. Och hela tiden tänkte jag att Briggsy var en tjuv.

När vi kom fram till min ytterdörr ringde Marc på. Mamma öppnade, och jag tror att jag föll rakt in i hennes armar.

På något sätt lyckades hon få mig uppför trappan och ner i sängen. Efter det minns jag bara drömmarna.

Jag var nästan medvetslös. Det kändes

som om jag flöt omkring någonstans långt borta. Jag vet att doktorn kom förbi eftersom mamma berättade om det efteråt. Jag fick en spruta och flera piller, och ett tag trodde mamma, pappa och doktorn att de skulle bli tvungna att ta mig till sjukhuset.

Fast jag visste ingenting om det där. Jag var för sjuk. Jag låg i sängen och drömde om stjärnor och lera. Jag drömde att jag vaknade en morgon och upptäckte att mitt rum var helt tomt. Alla mina saker – min cd-spelare, mina skivor, mina kläder – hade blivit stulna. Jag hatade den drömmen.

Det värsta med mardrömmar är att man inte kan få stopp på dem. Man kan bara ligga där i sängen medan de attackerar en. Jag önskar att mardrömmar var som skräckfilmer på teve, för då skulle man åtminstone kunna plocka upp fjärr-kontrollen och slå av dem.

Senare sa mamma att jag hade ropat högt i sömnen. "Men jag vet inte vad du pratade om. Det var någonting om månchips och dill, tror jag. Och stjärnskott."

Det visade sig att förkylningen jag hade fått när jag var ute på klipporna med Briggsy hade spridit sig mer än väntat. Allt inombords hade påverkats, till och med njurarna som hade slutat att fungera ett tag. Och det är inte bra när man redan har ett risigt hjärta.

Jag var helt borta i tre dagar. Efter det kunde jag sitta upp i sängen igen och var frisk nog att äta lite soppa. Men trots det vägrade mamma att låta någon komma och hälsa på mig.

Alltså dröjde det över en vecka innan jag fick veta vad som hade hänt.

Marc kom förbi flera gånger, och till slut sa mamma: "Okej, du får gå upp och säga hej, men bara en kort stund."

Han satte sig på min sängkant och började berätta om allt som hade hänt medan jag varit upptagen med att drömma och svettas.

# 11. Vad Briggsy hade gjort

Briggsy *hade* stulit den där gräsliga porslinsgrisen. Han hade stått vid bordet och tittat på sakerna som var till salu när han plötsligt fått syn på den. Och just som han tänkt sträcka sig efter den hade en man lyft upp den och vänt på den i handen för att studera den lite närmare.

Briggsy visste att grisen var värd mycket pengar och hade hoppats att mannen skulle ställa ner den igen. Men det gjorde han inte. I stället erbjöd han paret en femma för den.

Briggsy såg vad som höll på att hända. Han visste att mannen som försökte köpa grisen var en handlare som skulle tjäna en ordentlig hacka på att sälja den vidare. Och han visste att paret som sålde grisen inte hade några pengar.

Briggsy förstod sig på människor. Bara genom att titta på hur de stod eller höll axlarna eller böjde på huvudet visste han om de mådde bra eller dåligt. Han kunde titta på ett par i kaféet där vi drack vårt kaffe och säga om de var på sin första träff eller om de hade varit tillsammans i evigheter. Det hade att göra med hur de såg på varandra, sa han, eller talade eller fingrade på sina skedar.

Jag tyckte att han var helt fantastisk.

Jag antar att Briggsy tyckte synd om mannen och kvinnan som sålde porslins-grisen. Det var därför han stal den innan handlaren skulle hinna betala för den. Eftersom inga pengar hade lämnats över tillhörde den fortfarande paret.

Efter det hade han smitit iväg från loppmarknaden och sprungit hela vägen tillbaka till stan. Han gick till antikaffären och sålde porslinsgrisen där för femhundra pund.

"Femhundra pund?" sa jag. "Oj. Det är massor med pengar. Det kunde ha varit början på min förmögenhet."

"Knip igen om din förmögenhet, Minnie", sa Marc.

"Var Briggsy glad?" frågade jag. "Köpte han något för pengarna?" Jag ville veta.

Marc skakade på huvudet. "Nä."

Marc hade följt mig hem den där söndagen då jag blev sjuk. Men sedan hade han gått för att söka upp Briggsy. Det hade inte varit särskilt svårt att räkna ut vart han tagit vägen. Marc hade gått till antikaffären och ganska snart fått syn på Briggsy, som kommit ut därifrån med ett förnöjt uttryck i ansiktet.

"Är du rik nu?" frågade Marc.

"Det kan man kanske säga", sa Briggsy och skyndade sedan iväg över gatan.

Marc fick springa för att hinna ifatt honom. "Vart är du på väg?"

"Tillbaka till loppmarknaden", sa Briggsy.

"Har du inte redan tjänat tillräckligt med pengar i dag?"

Briggsy vände sig om mot honom. "De är inte till mig. Den där handlaren försökte blåsa dom som sålde grisen. Jag snodde den så att han inte skulle lyckas. Nu måste jag tillbaka dit och ge dem pengarna innan de hinner åka därifrån."

Tillsammans rusade de tillbaka till fältet. När de kom fram hade alla börjat packa ihop för att åka hem.

Briggsy hittade paret vid deras stånd, och innan de hann säga något räckte han fram pengarna till dem. "Här, varsågod", sa han. "Ni borde kolla värdet på era grejer innan ni säljer dem alldeles för billigt på en loppmarknad."

Jag ville veta vad de hade sagt. Hur hade de reagerat? Var de mållösa?

Marc visste inte, för precis då hade handlaren som velat köpa grisen för en femma dykt upp. Och han hade inte sett särskilt glad ut. Dessutom hade han haft med sig ett par kompisar. "Stora kompisar", sa Marc. "Stora, biffiga kompisar."

Briggsy hade genast fattat att han var illa ute och störtat iväg i full fart. En hel del besökare hade just varit på väg därifrån, så en stor klunga människor trängdes vid entrén till fältet.

"Briggsy liksom bara försvann i den där klungan", fortsatte Marc. "Jag såg honom aldrig igen."

Marc hade letat överallt. Men Briggsy var borta.

Nästa dag startade skolan igen med en ny termin. Briggsy dök aldrig upp.

Alla turister hade åkt hem. Och tivolit hade plockats ner över natten. Det var också borta.

Så Marc visste inte hur paret hade reagerat när Briggsy gett dem pengarna.

Men jag brukar fantisera om det ögonblicket. Jag brukar föreställa mig att de hoppade upp och ner och kramade varandra. Jag brukar föreställa mig att de grät.

Sedan var det dags för Marc att gå. Han lutade sig fram och kysste mig, mjukt och försiktigt. "Ta hand om dig, Minnie", sa han. "Vi ses sen."

Det var lika underbart som att se ett regn av fallande stjärnor.

# 12. Mer stjärnor

Nästa dag fick jag kliva upp. Mina ben kändes som gelé och var så darriga att jag inte trodde att de skulle bära mig först. Men på något sätt lyckades jag ändå ta mig fram till fönstret och titta ut. Hamnen var grå igen. Några små båtar guppade upp och ner i vattnet. Tivolit var borta. Inga ljus, ingen klingande musik. Det var som om det aldrig hade funnits där.

Innerst inne visste jag att jag aldrig skulle få se Briggsy igen. Och så blev det också. Tivolit kom visserligen tillbaka sommaren därpå, men Briggsy och hans familj var inte med.

Däremot hörde jag ifrån honom en

gång till. Han skickade ett brev som kom
en vecka efter att Marc hade hälsat på
mig. Marc hälsade förresten ofta på efter
det. Han dök upp varje eftermiddag efter
skolan och hade alltid med sig vindruvor
eller choklad. Vi satt i soffan och tittade
på filmer på teve. Vi pratade och hånglade.
Han berättade att han hade blivit helt
vansinnig när han fått reda på att jag hade
gått och tittat på stjärnor med Briggsy.

"Det kommer fler stjärnfall", sa jag. "Du
behöver inte vara avundsjuk för det."

"Jag var inte avundsjuk för att ni såg en
massa stjärnor! Jag var *svartsjuk* för att du
och Briggsy gick ut på klipporna på natten,
bara ni två."

"Åh", sa jag. Det hade inte ens slagit mig
att han kunde känna så. Ibland kan jag vara
så korkad.

Marc berättade om allt som hände i skolan
eftersom jag fortfarande inte var frisk nog

81

att gå dit. Jag fick höra allt skvaller. Och vi pratade om Briggsy. Vi mindes allt han hade sagt och gjort, och vi undrade var han höll hus nu. Jag saknade honom.

Sedan kom brevet. Det var skrivet med den där typiska, kantiga handstilen han hade.

Hej Minnie!

Hur mår du? Saknar du mig? Vid det här laget antar jag att du har hört om hur jag sålde den där grisen och tog pengarna till människorna som försökte sälja den på loppmarknaden.

Festligt, va?

Jag har skickat med något som ett minne av mig. Jag hoppas att du ska tycka om det.

Hör här, Min. Den här idén du har om att bli rik är bara dum. Du har massor av saker att vara glad för. Du har ett fint hem. Du är rolig och ser bra ut på ett uppkäftigt vis. Och Marc är tokig i dig. Det sa han till mig.

Jag tycker inte att du behöver bli rik också om du har allt det där.

Jag hoppas att du går och dricker en kopp cappuccino varje dag och att du tänker på mig när du gör det. Jag ska tänka på dig också.

Kram,

Briggsy

Inuti kuvertet fanns ett litet paket, och när jag öppnade det föll en silverkedja ut på bordet framför mig. På kedjan hängde en knippe silverstjärnor som satt ihop i varandra. Den var underbar.

Jag visade den för mamma. "Titta vad Briggsy skickade till mig."

"Åh, Minnie. Så vackert." Hon hjälpte mig att fästa kedjan runt min hals.

Jag läste brevet om och om igen. Och mamma såg säkert hur jag torkade bort en tår med baksidan av handen.

"Jag saknar Briggsy", sa jag.

"Det är klart att du gör", svarade hon.

Jag berättade för henne vad han hade gjort. Hur han hade stulit porslinsgrisen och sedan sålt den och gett pengarna till det unga paret.

"Det var modigt gjort av honom."

"Jag trodde att han var en tjuv", sa jag.

"Det var kanske därför du drömde att alla dina favoritsaker blev stulna", sa mamma. "Kanske tänkte du att om du förlorade en person som var så viktig för dig skulle alla dina saker också försvinna."

Jag blev förvånad. Mamma hade antagligen

rätt. Ibland kan mammor överraska en. Man tror att de bara sitter och tänker på vad de ska laga till middag, men så säger de något som visar att de förstår exakt hur man känner.

"Briggsy var så levande", sa jag. "Han hade alltid på sig färgglada kläder.
Han kunde sjunga och dansa och spela luftgitarr, och det verkade helt okej. Om jag gjorde samma sak skulle jag bara se fånig ut. Och han visste allt möjligt, om matlagning och antikviteter och sånt. Och om stjärnorna."

Jag berättade aldrig för henne hur jag hade blivit sjuk. Jag sa aldrig att jag hade gått ut mitt i natten för att titta på fallande stjärnor och blivit nedkyld. Hon skulle ha blivit hemskt arg på mig. Så jag höll det hemligt.

"Briggsy visste allt om stjärnhimlen", sa jag. "Han hade så många färger i sig. När jag var med honom kändes det som att promenera omkring med regnbågen. Och nu är han borta. Han bara försvann."

Mamma rörde vid min kind. "Ja, det är vad den gör – försvinner. Det är regnbågens natur. Men man glömmer den aldrig."

# 13. Fler listor

Jag gjorde två listor till för att försöka reda ut saker och ting.

**Saker som gör mig ledsen:**

1. Jag kommer aldrig att få se Briggsy igen.

2. Jag har fortfarande ingen förmögenhet.

Fast jag hade bestämt mig för att glömma den andra punkten tills vidare. Jag skulle inte bry mig om den förrän jag var färdig med skolan och hade tid att ta itu med den på riktigt.

**Saker som gör mig glad:**

1. Marc och jag trivs jättebra tillsammans.

2. När jag var sjuk gick jag ner i vikt –
över två kilo. Men jag håller på att lägga på
mig dem igen nu när jag äter som vanligt.

3. Jag har sett en meteorskur.

4. Jag fick åtminstone lära känna Briggsy.
Han fick mig att skratta. Han lärde mig allt
möjligt som jag inte hade en aning om. Jag
var hans vän, och att vara hans vän var som
att umgås med regnbågen.

När jag tänker på saken förstår jag hur
tur jag har som är jag och ingen annan.

ISBN 978-91-85071-79-1

## Ficktjuvens spöke
### av Catherine Fisher

Något övernaturligt försöker få kontakt med Sarah. En död pojke som vill att hon ska öppna ett litet skrin som plötsligt dykt upp i hennes rum. Har hon fått chansen att rädda en förlorad själ eller är det en livsfarlig fälla?

## Mitt nya jag av Rosie Rushton

Jemma blir rasande när hon får reda på att familjen ska lämna stan och flytta ut på landet. Eftersom hon just har stött ihop med sin absoluta drömkille kunde det inte ha kommit vid en sämre tidpunkt. Nu gäller det bara att få honom att lägga märke till henne innan det är för sent. Kanske är det dags att ta till en del drastiska metoder ...

ISBN 978-91-85071-65-4

**Blindträff** av Chloë Rayban

Det är lördag kväll och Marie
sitter ensam hemma framför
teven. Hon har precis gjort slut
med pojkvännen och är osams
med sin bästa kompis. Allt är
botten. Men så ringer plötsligt
telefonen, och det visar sig
vara en kille på andra sidan. En
charmig kille som har ringt fel ...
Kan Maries tur äntligen ha vänt?

ISBN 978-91-85071-62-3

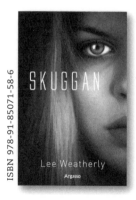

ISBN 978-91-85071-58-6

**Skuggan** av Lee Weatherly

Sarah blev övergiven av sin
mamma för sju år sedan. Nu
bor de bara några kilometer
ifrån varandra – ändå vill
Sarahs mamma inte träffa
henne. Men Sarah kan se
henne. Sarah bevakar henne.
Och hon tänker hämnas ...